Lisa St Aubin de Terán's first novel, *Keepers of the House*, won the Somerset Maugham Award and was followed by *The Slow Train to Milan*, which won the John Llewelyn Rhys Prize. She has written six other novels, poetry, short stories and three volumes of memoirs, including the bestselling *The Hacienda* and her autobiography *Memory Maps*. She currently lives in Amsterdam.

OTTO

Lisa St Aubin de Terán

Virago

VIRAGO

First published in Great Britain by Virago Press in January 2005
This paperback edition published in February 2006

A CIP catalogue record for this book
is available from the British Library.

ISBN 1 86049 837 X

Typeset in Janson by M Rules
Printed and bound in Great Britain by
Clays Ltd, St Ives plc

Virago Press
An imprint of
Time Warner Book Group UK
Brettenham House
Lancaster Place
London WC2E 7EN

www.virago.co.uk

To the real and elusive Otto

This book takes diabolical liberties with the real life of the Venezuelan revolutionary, scholar and sociologist Oswaldo Barreto Miliani, codename Otto. It does so with his full permission and it is dedicated to him and his extraordinary life.

OTTO

PART 1

CHAPTER I

Cancer is a wonderful thing. It is like the bogeyman, el Coco: the one your mother threatened you with when you were a baby. It's the one who lay under your bed waiting to get you if you went for a pee, the one you wet your bed for and got told off for over and over again, because el Coco was so unspeakably frightening you had to do anything and everything to keep out of his clutches.

El Coco is the one you never see. You've caught glimpses of his shadow, felt him hiding in the bushes, heard his breathing and his stealthy steps. But you never see him. Then you grow up and you realise there is no Coco, except to scare your younger brothers and sisters with. You laugh about it. And el Coco fades at about the same time that you begin to be aware of cancer. It does what el Coco never actually did: it steals friends and neighbours, kidnaps aunts, and sends them back thinner, silent and scared. Even after the victims return, it sneaks back and takes them away. El Coco was named to you in your cradle, but cancer is a word that is rarely said. It is identified by a nod and a knowing look. It dusts its victims with ash. You begin to recognise its hallmark in the open coffins as you grow up and stop seeing wakes and funerals merely as chances to play with your cousins and drink oily hot chocolate and eat ginger nuts. You grow into your awkward age and you begin to fear cancer, to dread its facelessness and that sallow grey. You distinguish its smell: a smothering, lingering smell. It is no respecter of age or state. In the arc of a year, it swept away Don Alfonso Linares and the boy who mucked out his stables.

When someone has it, it becomes nameless. It is skirted around in euphemisms. It plays tag round the town and every time someone is 'it', a few of your more tactful relations censor all mention of death from their gossip. Mostly, though, such tact is too exacting. Without death, what can be said of life in a place where people die like flies? So dying gets carved into little pieces of swapped talk, and the listener with cancer, and the one who will miss him most, wince and shudder. Cancer is coming for them in the night, at breakfast, in the shower or at the market. It will come, any time, anywhere: nothing is more ready and willing. No Grim Reaper was ever better prepared. So cancer becomes synonymous with dread – more so than anything else, more than death itself.

At least, that's how it was for me: the ultimate fear. And I tell you, very few kids can have been quite as pathologically afraid as me. I have a Ph.D. in infant terror, but it was nothing by comparison.

Of course, there were other, later things that used fear as a trademark. And I'd be lying if I didn't add torture to that list. Torture is a good one. It stays with you. It's not like a 'will I get it up?' That is more fleeting. A limp dick is a gutter fear reserved for those moments when you forget to look at the stars, and you start chucking up your tripe. Impotence is an occasional worry; torture is a more lasting threat. You'd think pain would be the main factor. The funny thing about it, though, is that it isn't: it's shame. Because if you haven't had it yet, you cannot conceive of such pain; and if you've been through it, you have to forget it to survive. You have to. The fear of torture is the fear of breaking, of cowardice perceived; of a lack of manliness, of letting others down. It is a fear of shame.

Later, of course, you realise that under torture you have to talk. Wire enough electrodes up to enough parts of the human body for long enough, and every man in the world will sing like a canary. After the first time, you know that; you know it's *what* you say that counts, not *if* you say it. Keeping back a name or two takes you to beyond the call of duty. Familiarity with torture doesn't breed contempt, but it does take the edge off it. Once you've been tortured and survived, healed, and learnt how to live with the nightmares, it gets so you don't even fear it much. You get almost blasé. Then, out on the Fear Front, there's just the Big C.

Despite what the papers say, I am far from demonic. Against all the odds, I have survived. I've had the luck of the devil. I think that's fair to say. I survived birth, infancy, illness, boyhood, war and peace. As to revolution: I'm a goddamned hamster! I've turned on that wheel for over fifty years: Venezuela, Hungary, Uruguay, Paraguay, Peru, Cuba, El Salvador, Algeria, Chile, Paris, Italy, Iran and China. I've been in more revolutions than it is really seemly to have taken part in, and, as I say, against all the odds survived.

Allegations that the millions from my bank robberies are stashed away in offshore banks are nonsense. I live in a rented room, and apart from a couple of trunks of books, I have nothing: not a bean. When they called me to Paris in '92 to join a think tank of strategy for the French Ministry of Defence, I couldn't believe my luck. For a few heady months, I became a top civil servant with all the kowtowing and the perks that that entailed. I was in Paris and not clandestine any more: not hiding, not even on false papers for Christ's sake! I had a top government pass and my own driver. It was all hush-hush, but doormen who had always despised me were giving me sidelong glances of respect, despite my looking like an Arab. It isn't such a good thing to look like an Arab in France. But it's OK when you have a hush-hush government pass and (for the first time in my life) a big salary.

I rented a little apartment in the Latin Quarter and I frequented the same cafés and bistros that I'd used before. I bought a token new jacket and a decent pair of shoes, and a tie for really fancy occasions, and I bought dozens and dozens of books and also some good wine and truffles for my breakfasts. Other than that, there were no signs that my sudden fortune had gone to my head, until, that is, I began to feel an annoying tickle at the back of my throat. Were I the silent type, months might have gone by without my doing more than upgrading the strength of the honey and glycerine lozenges to which I have long been addicted. But I am an inveterate talker, and Paris is a city conducive to chatter. You sit in bars for hours on end in the grip of heated discussions about everything and nothing. And the more I talked, the more I felt the tickle.

Under normal circumstances, I wouldn't see a doctor for a tickle. Illness is something we dislike in Venezuela. You don't get any sympathy for being ill. Doctors are an expensive drain, and a funeral (with all its trappings and the catering costs of the wake) has driven many a family to ruin. Then there is the more basic fear of contagion. Standard procedure back home when someone feels ill is for him or her to get a grip and shut up about it. But I wasn't at home: I was the cosseted guest of the French government, and had not only a driver, but a fully comprehensive medical insurance. I decided to indulge myself like my rich aunts in Valera who wallowed in their minor ailments, lavishing care on in-grown toenails, warts and miniscule scars, sharing the gory details of their lavish treatments with their friends and neighbours as they turned pinpricks into major surgery. For some of these aunts, hypochondria was a hobby. And it was a game their husbands and servants played: it kept potential busybodies busy in an innocuous, if expensive, way. But it was always a game of trivia. The rules were very clear: so long as the drama was about blemishes and spots, scratches and little, containable things, everyone played along. That meanwhile real tropical diseases cut their swathe through the town was beside the point: you didn't talk about that.

In Paris, given my new cosseted state, my wealth and elevated position, I decided to act like my spoilt aunts and indulge myself. So I sneaked off to a private hospital and saw an ear, nose and throat consultant in what looked like a five-star hotel. He took a look and a swab and told me to come back later.

I did as he told me, and when I went back for the results, he suggested I sit down.

Why?, I thought. What an absurd suggestion that was, and how charged with irony! Sit down? I was just playing a spoilt-game. I wasn't actually one of my aunts. For the first time in my life, I was looking after the little things on my body, but, man to man, I didn't need them to be turned into a drama. There had been times when for want of any medical attention I had spent nights in agony; and yet now, for a mere tickle, a top Parisian doctor was inviting me to waste his (and my) time. I smiled to let him know that I saw through his ploy: I was no wealthy hypochondriac needing to be guided through a sea of imaginary ailments. I resisted sitting down: I was due to attend a meeting at the Ministry of Defence and the traffic was, as ever, dreadful in the city.

In the curt way of the Parisian upper crust, the doctor gestured to me to sit down. Having peremptorily flashed his command, he then stared at a diploma on the wall beside his desk. I followed his eyes: he was a graduate of the Sorbonne with a second medical diploma from Bologna. A cluster of other certificates held his gaze. He dismissed my initiative to lighten the session, and continued to point to a maroon leather chair, ordering me to sit in it. His manner exuded power, and much of it was the innate authority that doctors have: they are tyrants of knowledge. He spoke again, even more curtly now, implying that I stop wasting his precious time and insisting that I sit. He seemed to have ordered time into suspension until I obeyed his command. His manner was a curious mixture of doctor-knows-best, veiled military authority and a barely restrained jollity. His suppressed smile had stretched into a grimace and made him resemble a predatory reptile. More than a smiling crocodile, though, he reminded me of Maurice Chevalier. And like the 1940s star, he gave the impression that he was about to burst into song.

The potentially sinister, jagged jaw, fused into his urbane manner, helped bridge the enormous distance between his firm but jovial manner and the words that actually came out of his mouth. Although, when he spoke, it was as if what he had to say was of less interest than his minor victory of having subjugated me into sitting down. It was as though the interesting part of my visit ended once he had flexed his power muscle and tamed whatever lingering lion there was in me into a lamb. After I sat down, he did not wait for me to get comfortable. He was brisk: I was not sitting for comfort but through medical precaution. He stopped perusing his Bolognese diploma and focused his gaze on something just beyond and behind me. Then he said,

'You're going to die.'

Was he joking? Was he singing? Was he serious? I looked up at him and saw from his refusal to meet my eye that he was serious. His announcement had come without frills, but so what? I'm not afraid to die and I wasn't then. I found his manner a little pompous for someone who was reinventing the wheel. I had never thought myself immortal: we were all going to die. Even the doctor himself would have to go one day to that big clinic in the sky. He repeated his sentence, adding my name. Then I stared at him and he stared at something beyond my head. His silence was smothering. I prepared to stand up, and as I did so, my mind raced on to the ministry meeting ahead – another heated debate about the pros and cons of supersonic planes – and my throat registered its tickle.

I felt embarrassed for the doctor. He had got stuck in a conversation he could not end. He needed help. I stood up, feeling a bit cheated on details but just wanting to leave. This doctor would not have done for my aunts, I thought. They demanded long medical explanations. I would ask him to send me a report, I would make some pleasantry about Bologna and then I would leave him to stare at whatever it was that had rendered him speechless. I was half out of the chair when he hit me with it.

'You've got cancer.'

For the first and only time in my life, I had nothing to say. I made a supreme effort, one of the biggest yet, not to shit in my pants. Cancer makes el Coco look like Mickey Mouse. It had got me, like a Nazi hunting a Jew. It had come, shown its face and marked my throat with a cross. With one word my entire life was rendered pointless and it would end summarily.

Or not ...

Once the word was out, the secret was spoken, and the unnameable had been named, the doctor became my saviour. He brought the full force of the French medical system to bear on my tickle/tumour.

Needless to say, the private hospital in Paris was a tad more effective than the old 'Guillotine' back in Valera.

I had cancer. I have had cancer – but now it has gone. My throat is my own. I am cured. I am thin and sallow and weak and my hair is very thin, but the grey wash and the smother have left me.

I am cured, and the wonderful thing about it is that my life – that endless and absurd muddle behind me – demands I make some sense of it. Without the cancer, I would never have looked at my life as a whole and tried to understand it, nor would I have bothered to try to put the record straight.

I think I've been afraid all my life. I'm not afraid any more.

I have never done anything I set out to do. Everything has been by chance. For once, I'm choosing. I shall put together the way it was. I have to, and not through vanity, as it will emerge. In all things, I am far less remarkable than the myth has made me. What I know, and will now make clear, is that all my life has been a comedy of errors. I need to see what they all mean, if they mean anything. Or maybe someone born long after me will find some purpose in my life.

Since this is an exercise in truth, I must tell and deny. I must relate what actually happened against a backdrop of what is said to have happened. It is my word against that of many others. But it is my life. I may not be qualified to know what other people's lives are about. My understanding there is something for others to decide and for time to judge. The one thing I am sure I can do better than anyone else is to tell my own story and separate the truth from the miasma of lies. That is my objective and this is my story.

My mother was not a common prostitute on Vargas Street in Valera, and I am not the fruit of a failed back-street abortion. I was not found in a corn sack in a pile of dung, nor am I the illegitimate son of the village idiot of Jajó; nor do I have hoof marks anywhere on my body. It is true that I was born exceptionally hairy, but not that Zara the Madwoman was paid two bolivars to have sex with an orang-utang in San Cristobal de Torondoy and that I am the result of the experiment. Some stories are so firmly rooted by the government and press, be it my origins, my armies, my campaigns and designs, that it will be hard for many to believe my version.

So before I begin, let me say once again: the following is the way it was. It is who I am. I have seen the light, the light of day, each day that I wake up alive, cured of cancer. My throat and tongue have been cleansed by chemotherapy. My secrets didn't die. All my life has been a mixture of chance and need, where I could have made more of chance. Whatever else I do, I now need to tell my story.

CHAPTER II

I am seventy years old. My children have all had the generosity to forgive my absences, my lapses and neglect, and to accept the love I feel for them. They see me as an old man. I refuse to see myself as that. I refuse to be old at seventy, or eighty, or ninety for that matter! If old age is equated by our proximity to death, then I was old at fifteen and I have been old all my life. Death and I have a very domestic relationship. We have stuck with each other through thick and thin. We have never chosen prolonged absences, nor have we ever neglected each other. My body may look old and wasted on the outside now, but it has been old and wasted on the inside since I was in my twenties. Thanks to the high-tech methods taught by CIA instructors worldwide, every inch of my flesh has been tampered with and prematurely aged.

I have accepted so many things, so many indignities, and put up with so many worse names and labels than 'old', but I shy away from age. In part, it is vanity: I want to look my best and continue to be a seducer of women. God knows I was never the most successful lover in my prime! But that doesn't matter. I learnt how to manage, how to chase and pull; and I want to believe I can keep doing that until the day I fall off my perch like an ancient parrot. In part, though, I shy away from old age through fear. I cannot bear the idea of losing my memory and my ability to think logically and clearly.

When we were boys, we used to laugh behind old people's

backs – woe betide to their faces! – about how they repeated themselves and lived swamped in a morass of half-saved memories, and how they moved their mouths unconsciously as though they were chewing water. Well, I am getting there! My hair is a white shock. I like to think of it as leonine-cum-mad-professor-ish. On a good day (when drink has not beaten me half to death the night before) I look a bit like a dwarf Einstein; and I like that! And I have the wrinkles: lots of wrinkles, which no amount of Johnson's Baby Cream can disguise. But the worst trait so far is that chewing water thing, which I catch myself doing while I am shaving. While I am assessing my cellular deterioration, I may as well say that my sexual desire is unabated. Alas (and also in direct relationship to the amount of alcohol I consume), my performance is no longer what it was.

Perhaps, though, the most noticeable change that I perceive as my years increase is an absolute horror of anyone wasting my time. That is my greatest intolerance. I am brutal about it. My children tell me that I overreact; and maybe I do. All I know is that every moment of my life has been precious and every moment that I have left is precious too. I have to make a mark before I go: I have to leave my cut in a baobab or my scratch on a stone. I have spent so many years trying to understand and now I have to make myself understood. Or, at least, I have to try to, and I have not a moment's patience left either to waste or be wasted.

In short, my fabled ferocity, that invented entity, now exists for real. Ticket vendors and traffic wardens, telephone-switchboard personnel and airport staff, menopausal shopkeepers and embittered newspaper vendors, sloppy thinkers and pretentious intellectuals bear the brunt of it. But it is an especially potent response that rears up and snarls out as suddenly as, although less violently than, one of my old friend Rusián's fabled blips of rage. Each time, after a time-waste snap, I ask myself: how come such a small thing can enrage me, when months of being systematically baited under interrogation could never enrage me before?

Such random thoughts come in the small hours. I forgot to add onto my geriatric list the fact that I cannot sleep well any more. I lie awake from before dawn every day and churn my memories.

*

To begin at the beginning: I wasn't born in a gutter, and my mother wasn't a whore. I was born in 1934, in the little lost village of San Cristobal, near Mérida, south of Lake Maracaibo, where my father arrived, fleeing from a persecution that was part political and part personal. He had had to break away from Jajó, from where his parents, grandparents and great-grandparents came. My mother, Camila Araujo Miliani, also came from Jajó.

I was born on 18 September, but the precise moment *when* I was born is not important, which is why I'm going to talk about my origins or, rather, who my family were, and *how* I was born. This is what I've always heard; everyone close to it has always told me the same story, even the people of San Cristobal who were neighbours from that time.

My mother lived in the big house of a hacienda that my father administered. They had two daughters in rapid succession, and then there was a gap in the production line. My father very much wanted a son. Then, in 1933, a son was born and he satisfied my father's greatest desire. My father came from a much humbler family than my mother. Camila came from grandeur: she was an Araujo Miliani and she never forgot it; nor did my father. The Araujos were grandees of pure Spanish descent; they were landowners with an illustrious past. But my father came from a mestizo family with a marked mix of Mayan Indian blood, which, particularly in the Andes, is a social stigma. It was my father's dream to have a white-skinned, blue-eyed son. The dream came true when my older brother was born with an alabaster skin and cornflower-blue eyes.

My father had an obsessive nature, which manifested itself in strange ways. He invented minor laws and then clung to them for dear life, never deigning to explain what they were about. For instance, he decided that all his sons had to bear the initials O.A. or O.O. So he named his first-born son Ostilio Alfonso. And Ostilio was the pride of my father. His two daughters had already linked his own bloodline to that of the Spanish elite, but Ostilio, with his Aryan looks, was visible proof of this link.

It wasn't so long before that people fought duels and killed each other at the mere hint of racial mixture. White was good, Indian wasn't. Beauty was perceived in shades of cream. It didn't matter if a girl was fat and ugly and had volcanic acne: if she was white, she was a beauty. Light-coloured eyes were the top of the chart. Daughters were nice, and they helped run the house, but really they were just fancy chattels. In a macho world, sons were what counted: so a boy with blue eyes was practically a god.

For Camila's family, marriage to my father was a tremendous misalliance. Socially, that may have remained the case, but racially, my beautiful blue-eyed brother made my father worthy in his own eyes and in the eyes of the world.

I was born eleven months after my brother Ostilio: not three months or four months later, as so many gossips make out. I was born eleven months later, and my birth was registered in the archives of San Cristobal de Torondoy. My father, following his own mysterious O.A. design, named me Oswaldo Antonio.

The rest is true – the rest of the gossip about my birth, that is. Unlike my older brother, who was astonishingly handsome, I was astonishingly ugly. I was covered in black hair from head to foot like some kind of monkey. For reasons no one seems to know (but my father did not try to kill me in my cradle) my eardrums burst within days of my birth.

The local doctor, Doctor Cesare, told my mother, 'This little boy is not going to live, and if he does, he's going to be deformed or half-witted with those ears of his. But anyway, he's going to die, which is a blessing really.'

My mother had a streak of defiance in her. She had defied her parents by marrying my father. She defied the malice of her neighbours, the growing indifference of her husband and the paltry yield of our little farms. Her second son (me) might have looked like a hairy spider in a crib, but I was *her* hairy spider and she didn't like being told what to do or made to believe what would happen. When Doctor Cesare pronounced my callous death sentence, my mother determined to defy both him and it.

It was no easy task. To make matters worse, immediately after my birth, my elder brother got ill, really ill. Each day that my own infant condition worsened, my beautiful brother, still a baby himself, also grew more and more sick; until my mother (not yet risen from her forty days of quarantine from child bed) was about to lose both of her sons. Against all the hopes of everyone else in the family, and against all the odds (because Ostilio was older and stronger), it was my brother who died, and I who survived.

I began to grow, and during my early years I gave every sign of fulfilling our family doctor's prophecy by becoming both deformed and half-witted. My mother coaxed me through my infancy, more through maternal reflex, habit and her innate stubbornness than anything else. She protected me, as though to say: Since this runt is all that is left to me, I may as well protect him. But she grieved for the loss of the fair Ostilio. She grieved long and hard. She would go on to bring up nine children, but her real love was the one who died, the one she lost. Later, some of my other brothers and sisters would go some way towards easing that pain.

My own role was clear: I was the living reminder of her favourite's death, the sand in her cut. I was Nature's joke. For Camila, left mostly alone, I must have been a distillation of all that was low and wrong in her marriage. I think it is to her great credit that she never once voiced in front of me what she must have sometimes wondered alone. Having fought so hard to save my infant life, to the best of my knowledge, she never once voiced the question why.

Despite that, neither I nor any of her subsequent babies ever wore the dead Ostilio's clothes or played with his things. They were kept like offerings at a shrine, together with his photographs (most of which were taken after death and almost scared the life out of me). I grew up with more photographs of the dead Ostilio around me than of anyone else.

Despite such a bad start, I began to give signs not only of staying alive and growing into a reasonably normal shape, but also of actually being quite bright. By the age of three, I had the vocabulary of an adult. What was not normal was the way I clung to my mother. She moved around with a scrawny tarantula clinging to her skirts. That was me. I couldn't let her out of my sight. It was generally assumed (outside of our immediate family) that I was backward and deaf. I didn't want anyone to touch me: which was fine, because nobody wanted to. My mother and her female friends talked as though I wasn't there. They dissected the town verbally. They tore into sex and scandal, love and death. They sifted each

other's exaggerations and untruths in front of me. I learnt about
disasters and disappointments, about feuds and lovers' quarrels,
about domestic wars of attrition, and about the aches and pains of
a woman's body. I absorbed all the long words around me, like a
hairy sponge, and gradually I began to lisp them back, talking to
myself, to my mother, and very occasionally to someone else who
might take the trouble to stoop to my height and listen for long
enough to decipher my eccentric speech. I swallowed certain letters in the middle of words, particularly 'd' and 'r', and I couldn't
pronounce them until I was ten years old, at least.

My early years were consciously made up of two things: words
and fear. I was afraid: terribly, massively afraid of everything. I was
afraid of my own shadow, of whatever there was. I was afraid of
rain, of citrus fruits, of geckos, of grass tassels waving in a breeze.
I was afraid of the print on my mother's dress. She thought it was
because I was undersized and weak, but my fear was more than
cowardice. It was not that I flinched at certain challenges, great or
small. I flinched at life itself.

When it rained in San Cristobal de Torondoy, the downpours
were torrential: almost biblical. It seemed as though they would
never stop. It rained for six months of every year, day after day
until the whole world was mouldy. The mud in the streets was
ankle-deep and every stream was a torrent. I look back, and it
seems that it rained continually, but there must have been times
when it didn't. There is the background and there are the details.
I am trying to balance both. So, in those early years, among the
sepulchral remains of my perfect brother and my own blatant
inadequacy, there were flashes of something else.

My eldest sister, Graciela, says that a lady came to our house
one day when I was still a little boy. Finding me alone on the
porch, she paused and talked to me, and for some reason I didn't
run away screaming, as was my wont, but felt safe and at my ease
enough with her to talk. After we'd stopped, joined by my family,
the lady is said to have said, 'What an exciting mind this child
has!'

I have to cling to the raft of that 'exciting mind', praised by a
stranger, to sustain me through the torrents of memories of my
early childhood. It may sound fairly insignificant to you – a mere

sentence spoken in passing – but for me it was a flicker of hope, and hope is a weed that can take root anywhere. Someone saw something worthwhile in me, and I often tried to push aside the morass of my faults and see myself through that stranger's lens.

As a toddler, clutching at Camila's skirts, I learnt how I had disappointed my parents: grieved and shamed them by being born at all, then doubled the offence by surviving, tripled and quadrupled it by my loathsome appearance. Hearing all this as a kid made me yet more afraid and insecure. The story went on and on: it still does. I can't tell you how many times I have heard, and how many times I've been told, what a pathetic, cowering, stunted thing I was.

'Do you remember how scared you were of this, or that? How you cried?'

How could I forget? Or my blue-eyed brother, how could I forget him? The beautiful Ostilio, the big bonny boy whose place I stole. The Andean version of the Aryan dream come true was taken away so unfairly, and as though to add insult to injury, fate played a joke and snubbed my father's pride. It rubbed his face in his low origins. Ostilio was replaced by a shrivelled, hairy, puny thing, born to heap shame on his family. In the racially competitive hierarchy of Andean society, fate did not spare them. From birth, I was fuel to the gossips. Nor were feelings spared in my family. My mother grew to love me, of that I have no doubt; yet she never tired of reminding me of my brother who died. At every turn, she brought up the dead Ostilio who, she had no doubt, would never have feared the night, the moon, cats, dogs, insects, birds, hot and cold water, visitors or, indeed, anything at all. Camila was certain my brother would not have wet his bed or cried like a girl or clung to her skirts as I did. And Ostilio wouldn't have been the one thing my father most despised: a coward. As Camila brushed my coarse black hair into some kind of order, ignoring my protestations and screams of fear (a comb, with all those teeth, often came for me in the night), she would recall Ostilio's blond, silken curls, weeping at the injustice of motherhood.

Out in the Sierra once, many years later on one of those

interminable nights during the armed struggle when our combat group was lost in the jungle with nothing to eat or drink and nothing to do but keep our weapons clean and at the ready, and to talk, this whole business about my dead brother resurfaced as the group exchanged first memories in the dark. A woman in my group had been a psychiatrist before joining the revolution. She grabbed hold of my story as though I had thrown her a hot dog and fries with all the trimmings on that hungry night.

For days afterwards, every time we entered a zone where it was safe to speak, she came hammering after me, whispering about my having an inferiority complex and about my secretly feeling second best, and having the need to compete. I tried to tell her there, but it didn't get through. No woman is at her most receptive to ideas when she is struggling through the jungle with a full-sized army pack on her back, being chewed by mosquitoes and burrowing grubs, battling with the heat, fatigue, hunger and the frustration of not knowing where she is going, and with the added anxiety of maybe being shot by a sniper from one moment to the next. In our particular group, there was also the anxiety of being shot by one of the guys behind us. These were our own guys, but alas they were trigger-happy loons who'd joined the movement for some action, and if they didn't get it soon in the shape of a confrontation with the National Guard or the army were probably going to settle for the less challenging option of picking off their comrades on our long march to glory. It was a tricky moment for Comrade Psychiatrist to lose any more points. So there was no way she was going to give an inch on the interpretation of her textbooks. She was a hardliner; a great girl, and a great marksman, and also, for the record, she had a great arse.

Walking behind her, day after day, fighting intense fatigue and boredom myself, I was able to study her arse in great detail. The cheeks were like two grapefruits: round, firm, pointed and pitted. The cheeks of her bum even had a pinky-red flush to them like grapefruits can. Under her khaki twill trousers, I used to picture those cheeks, pitted with what must have been very severe cellulite. The dimples were so regular, so uniform, as to be curiously attractive. I used to spy on her while she was bathing (we all did). There's a big gap between the idea of saving the world and the blisters and bickering of the everyday reality while you trudge through thick undergrowth to do it. You have to have something to do, something to take your mind off your feet and the mental instability of the guy behind you with a grenade in his pocket and a Kalashnikov pointing very near the small of your back.

I'm not saying I wanted a therapeutic rapport with Comrade Psychiatrist, or that I hoped for a professional doctor–patient relationship. I just wanted her to understand that there was never any question of 'second place' or 'second best' about Ostilio and me. My blue-eyed brother had been born so beautiful, and I was born so ugly. He was so strong, and I so weak. He was so fair, and I so dark. I was a non-starter. I was such a non-starter there was never any question of my trying to compete. Those were the rules, and they were drummed into me so young, I must have been the least competitive boy in the state of Trujillo. What would have been the point? You can't compete in a race you can't enter. I was different, so noticeably different that I was allowed to excel in it. I couldn't be like other boys, and, for years, no other boys wanted to be like me.

I learnt to read when I was three. When I was four, my mother tried to send me to school. I couldn't bear school. Just being there terrified me. And getting there was a nightmare. Sometimes my mother and sometimes my older sister used to literally drag me there. The road to school was the road to hell. I only felt safe on one path away from home. It was the short garden path from our house to our next-door neighbour's, an old lady called Genti. The long path to school was another matter. The threat of el Coco, which had been working for generations to keep little kids toeing the line, had worked too well with me. The country lane, which led into the urban street and the schoolhouse, was far too fraught with hiding places for the cunning and ubiquitous bogey-man for me to ever willingly walk along it.

Genti's house was a different matter. Her garden spilt into our own. The little path between them lay on open ground. After our mango tree, there was nothing flanking where I walked from which even the longest arm could have reached out to grab me. I'd been up and down the path every day, practically from the time I could walk. Hiding behind my mother, gripping her hand, I knew every hummock of grass and every dip of earth. La Genti did most of her chores on her front porch. There were other people in her house, a gaggle of women, but they lurked in the kitchen and didn't bother to come out for a visitor as insignificant as myself. Even when my mother visited la Genti, the gaggle of other women was somehow relegated to the house. They listened to the gossip through the window, but they weren't allowed out. Just the thought of having to say hello to more than one person made me wet my pants. But I was safe at Genti's, it was just her on her porch. I could see our house from there, and see her house from ours.

From the age of four, the one chore I was capable of was to run down to la Genti's and pick chilli peppers. La Genti had a wonderful chilli bush. It was the biggest in the neighbourhood, and my mother often used to send me down to get chillies. La Genti told me I could pick as many chillies as I could count. For two years, I never got past seven, because I could only count up to seven. I must have made dozens of trips to pick chillies like that, when la Genti said to me one day, 'Can you believe it? Camila needs so many chillies, and you come down and all you take are seven, because that's all you can count up to! What is wrong with you?'

I was used to being chided for my ugliness, for my wetness and for my uselessness, but going to Genti's was the one useful thing I did. When she said that, it got to me. I felt so humiliated that I decided to do something about it. So I came up with the first of a lifetime of plans for my self-improvement.

Some local kids came to our house on errands or to play with my sisters, or just to hang around. We had a lot of fruit trees in our yard: mangoes, oranges, pawpaws, soursop and avocados. We always had more fruit than we needed. We also had a patch of plantain palms and a thriving herb garden. So boys used to be sent by their mothers from the village to ask for fruit.

One of these boys was in the third grade. I particularly noticed him because everyone said he was the most intelligent boy in town. I'd seen him lots of times, hovering outside with his frayed sack, sent out for fruit or a handful of feverfew. I could tell that, unlike the other boys, he was a bit shy. He used to stash the sack

in a patch of cannas on the edge of our porch so he could wander
in and appear to be there just to say, 'Hello, can I see your newborn chickens,' or 'Can I play on the swing with Graciela?' I used
to watch him cranking himself up, nervously, to ask for whatever
his mother had sent him to beg. Although I'd watched him often,
we had never spoken. After la Genti belittled my intelligence, I
plucked up the courage to ask this super brain if he could count.

'Of course I can,' he said. 'I can count everything.'

'How do you count everything? Can you teach me?'

He sat me down then and there, with a patience that told me I
was not so much his pupil as a future fruit ally. While he taught
me my numbers, I think he was adding up the chances of getting
me to give him the avocados, lemons and hands of plantains when
Camila was out sometimes. While he guided me through hundreds
and thousands and hundreds of thousands, he was fractioning the
embarrassment he felt at having to wheedle at his mother's behest.

A few days later, my mother called me. I said, 'Coming.'

'Son, can you go to the end of the garden and get me some
chillies from Genti?'

I set off with a small sack, and I picked the miraculous chilli
bush completely clean, counting as I picked. La Genti's house was
full of women as usual, battened away inside. There were never
any men there. Genti must have called the women out while I was
chilli-picking, because by the end they were all watching me: the
seven-chilli runt counting into the hundreds. They were amazed
and began shouting to each other while I left to run back home
with my bag of plunder. Then the women came running and
flapping after me. I was so frightened of those women. They
dressed in black, and with their scraggy necks they looked like
vultures. Black birds were the messengers of the devil. Black birds
spied on you to catch you out in misdemeanours. Then they flew
back with the news to Satan, their master, and he would come in
the night and claim you as a new recruit for his evil army.

They ran after me in a formation of flapping black, croaking
and cawing. They weren't supposed to be let out of their cage.
Genti was the only one I could deal with. I had seen the others
through the window on many occasions: they had cracks around
their mouths and their teeth were full of grey marks and gaps. I

used to watch them from the corner of my eye as I picked chillies, and their greedy raisin eyes filled me with dread. Through the
bars of Genti's window, they used to gawp and grin at me. I had
never greeted them. I was afraid to acknowledge them – to do so,
I thought, might release them from their cage. While they were
locked away, I could just tolerate them. But my habitual fear was
compounded that day when Genti let them out and they came
running after me.

I had a head start, but they were gaining ground. I had never
really run before and it felt as though my lungs were exploding.
When I got back, I hid behind a huge scrubbing board in our
kitchen and pleaded with my mother, 'Don't let the women see
me. Don't let them come in!'

They were right behind me, though, and the fat women in black
came pounding in, panting and shrieking. Given the dozens of
crises I went through every day, I see with hindsight that my
mother could not have known that this was a terror to end all terrors. At the time, it felt like bare-faced treachery as she let them
in. She let them get me; she betrayed me to those hideous women.
They had pursued me to give me kisses because I was so clever.
My panic was such that my mother was forced to sedate me in the
end. For years afterwards, those women hunted me in my dreams,
personifying half my fears. And they marked me for life with a
streak of anxiety about women pursuing me, attracted by my
intelligence. I have a fear of women chasing me.

I have to pause here, because I can visualise too many smirks
over my last remark. At this point in my story, I was five or six
years old, and the incident marked me. I am not trying to deny
that I have been a dog when it comes to the fair sex. I admit that
I have dedicated more time and energy than most intellectuals to
love, lust and sex (not necessarily in that order). I know I'm like
a goat and I have been since I was an adolescent. But I am a goat
on my own terms. So it isn't true that I have as many bastard
children as there are days in the year. I have four children: two
sons and two daughters. And in an inadequate way, I have done
my best to be a good father to them. I have been led astray a few
times, and I have often gone to extraordinary lengths to seduce

(or more often to try to seduce) women whom chance has thrown my way.

However, I did not personally deflower every woman and child in the east of Venezuela. Nor as a guerrilla fighter did I ever liberate villages by extorting the virginity of their pubescent girls. Contrary to the popular press (the most inconsistent source of information imaginable – one minute I am supposedly raping nuns, the next I am a mincing faggot), I am not a homosexual. Within the guerrilla movement, scholarship was despised. So an intellectual like myself was automatically queer. I have never owned, run or worked in a brothel, although some of my friends are, or have been, prostitutes. Also, I don't screw corpses, and I never have. While I am clarifying my sexual feelings, I'd like to say that I've always been a bit squeamish about touching animals at all, and that I have never had sex with one. So that story that went around Caracas in the 1960s, that I was cohabitating with a donkey with full carnal knowledge, is yet another lie.

Back in my childhood, I was afraid of the fat women in black chasing after me. I was afraid of their insistence on kissing me, and of their power to do so. I remember being hauled out screaming from behind the scrubbing board while my mother looked on, laughing. I remember being pulled and hugged and forcibly kissed, and of having brought that onslaught of slobber on myself by counting: by learning. To this day, I am afraid of predatory women. Perhaps because of this episode, I am enchanted by the chase – by me doing the chasing after endlessly unsuitable (and usually, unobtainable) women.

CHAPTER III

Somehow or other, my mother eventually got me to attend school. In the moments when I wasn't crying and I managed to think about myself, I felt like a bug in a jar. I was so frail and afraid of everything. I became aware that other kids weren't like that. I'd only really spent time with my sisters and brothers (there were more babies in our family by then). It had been a lot easier to get away with being so weak and scared at home. If the teacher left me on my own for a moment, I'd run back home to my mother.

By most standards, ours was a tiny school in a tiny village, but everyone called the village a town. To my eyes, this 'town' was a place of no safety, an urban gauntlet I was forced to run. Being so physically and emotionally different from everyone else, I found even the slightest change in my person unbearable. The smallest bruise, splinter or spot caused me days of concern and tears. My mother and I were the only safe areas in my life. My mother's body had already swollen and distorted several times in the most alarming way, which meant that there was really only me, my own hairy skin and bones, left to rely on. In school, on constant alert, I spent a lot of time examining myself for reassurance.

One day, I was looking at my hands in class when I noticed that a bone in my wrist was sticking out in a funny way. I looked around at all the other children's wrists, and they weren't like mine. Faced with this sudden, new deformity, I ran out of the classroom, bawling my head off. As I ran home, the disgust I felt at my mutated hands grew with every step.

I hurled myself onto the porch and told my mother, 'Look, look, I'm deformed! Look at this bone!'

Camila was used to my running home, and more than used to my being a cry-baby, but this time I was convulsed by sobs. So she looked at her own wrists and found they were not like mine. She did her best to reassure me, but I was having none of it. I was deformed. Unable to either quieten or console me, she eventually took me round the town to find a wrist like mine. Nobody had one. The trip, designed to reassure me, was making things worse. Eventually, she exhausted the shops and houses and went into the school to do a wrist survey there. It confirmed what I already knew: none of the children had lumpy wrists like mine. Then she came up with my teacher, Ruben. He had lumps like mine. I felt a huge relief: I was deformed, but so was Ruben. We were two like beings sharing our difference. I was so grateful to him for having bony wrists that I worshipped them and, by association, him, and so felt a lot better at school from then on.

When I was about six, in 1940, my teacher Ruben became intrigued by the contradiction in me. He saw in me a child terrified by so much, but who was also brighter than most of his other pupils. It was also around then that I consciously realised that I was a boy who was different from other boys: an imperfect being who had replaced a perfect one. I had always known it subconsciously, but being able to articulate it to myself had a settling effect on me.

I began to spend less time worrying about myself and more time studying. As I have said, I was not competitive, but I enjoyed learning. It was my teacher who pushed me to stand out. There was a festival in our town and the schoolchildren put on a sort of play. We all had to recite poems and give speeches. The best speech at the festival was mine. Naturally, my teacher, Ruben, had written it, but I delivered it. Then the best poetry recited was also mine. It was a poem about a tree:

The yawning tomb
Asked the basking rose,

Whither your glory
This morning . . .

I have never been able to find out what poem that was. But that
apparently insignificant verse was significant to me. From that
time, I have given my life to poetry, and literature, and to giving
speeches. My first speech was given (lisped) there in San Cristobal
de Torondoy. And yes, the audience was entranced; and no, I
didn't hypnotise the town, causing the death of a woman of eighty
who never came out of the trance.

Over the next four years, I managed, gradually, to adapt, to
become more normal and less afraid. I managed to integrate into
our little town. Until then, I had been a self-made victim invent-
ing my fears. From then on, real problems began to line up on the
outside because my parents decided to move to Valera. I had just
reached the point where I felt safe in my surroundings of San
Cristobal de Torondoy when we moved to a real city. Valera was
the biggest metropolis I could imagine. It was bigger to my eyes
than Paris itself. The jump from our jumped-up village to a city
was a huge shock, but so was the journey there. We travelled to
the port of Bobures. It was a fairly sleepy little port on the edge
of Lake Maracaibo, yet to me it seemed immense and infernally
busy.

Until then, I had never been in a town where there was any
form of transport other than animals. I had never seen a car. Up
until then, there were only beasts of burden, and these could be
good or bad, wild or docile, horses, donkeys, mules or oxen, but
they were always four-legged. When we arrived by boat to
Bobures, I was astonished by the sight of cars, lorries, trucks,
trains, and the hundreds of people. So Bobures counted for more
than any great ports I came to see later in my life. It has always
remained more impressive to my eye than Marseilles, or
Hamburg, Algiers or Rotterdam. As I had never even seen or
heard a car, imagine my reaction to a steam train! In twenty-four
hours, we not only left the safety of our mountain village and the
comforts of our known house, neighbours and friends, we children
were thrown into the twentieth century, confronted with technology, and relocated in what seemed like a completely alien

environment. For any boy, such a move would have been a shock. Given my propensity for fear, the shock was so great it took me some years to recover.

I was amazed by Bobures, but the sheer size of Valera filled me with awe. It was actually quite a big city: the biggest in the state of Trujillo. When we moved there, it must have had about thirty thousand inhabitants. My home town, San Cristobal, had sixteen houses. There were a few scattered shacks as well, but in the 'town', beside the shops, there were sixteen houses and two frayed ribbons of mud shacks and a total population of about a hundred and thirty souls. I knew every one of the families who lived there, and everyone knew me. By the time we left it, I was the most prominent child of San Cristobal. I had grown up a lot and I even fought with the other boys. But more than that, I was their leader. I decided what we did out of school, and in school I was an ace student and renowned for it. I also wrote songs for the little kids, and I gave speeches. I was a big boy there.

Then I arrived in Valera as a nobody: the cousin from the country. My parents had grown up in Valera, so there were family links and memories on both sides. (Jajó, where they were born, is a stone's throw from Valera.) I had loads of cousins on my mother's side. Through her, we were kin to all the Pacheco Araujos. These two patrician clans virtually ruled the town. As their cousin, I should have had allies – but they were all rich, and by comparison we were poor, so they shunned me more, if anything, than a stranger. Being part of the grand and illustrious Araujo tribe worked as a handicap in those early years. The sons of the chiefs resented my clothes being threadbare, and our living in the wrong part of town. If my mother imagined her cousins would help her children, she was wrong. We studied together, and I got by because I was a good student; but I was alone. I had to fight all the boys: the poorer ones for my puny size and snobby heritage, and the richer ones because my shabbiness let their side down. The two bullying factions didn't mix socially either, but they were, at least, united in seeing the need to punish me for being an outsider, a hick, and a bumpkin with the wrong accent and the wrong attitude.

In Venezuela, as in most macho societies, not only do boys take precedence over girls, the male presence defines a household. More than any other time in my life, I missed the father I hardly knew. I missed his presence as a stabilising factor, as a passport to fitting in, and as a guide through that baffling new world. I had to combat my loneliness alone, though, because my father was never home. He didn't live with us because he worked far away in another town. On top of everything else, the unusualness of this situation was thrown in my face as a daily taunt. 'Bastard, bastard, where's your dad?' set to the tune of an old Mexican ranchero, was sung, chanted and sometimes merely hummed. A few bars were enough. I knew the cruel lyrics the town kids had made up. They didn't have to sing them for me to hear them in my head. And it hurt more than any of the other taunts because it was true: my father couldn't bear the sight of me.

My father's disappearance from our family life didn't stem from our move to Valera: he hadn't lived with us in San Cristobal either. Even though he administered the hacienda there, it was a smallholding, and never produced enough for our needs. He had put a foreman in, and then checked the place out from time to time in person. So my father would spend a few days with us, get my mother pregnant and then return to Bobures, where he worked in personnel administration for the great sugar factory. He was a trader, although 'trader' is too pretty a word: he trafficked in people. He'd get people to leave their towns and villages and come to work in the factory. In the latter years in San Cristobal, he worked in the same field for the petrol companies of Guachaquero, displacing peasants. In many ways, it was a dead-end job. I think it must have been almost as much of a disappointment to him as it was for my mother, but he had little choice. The ruling family in San Cristobal, the Schulers, were never going to give him a break with his hacienda, and while its returns diminished, prices rose sharply. There was no other work in or around San Cristobal and he had bills to pay and mouths to feed. As the family grew and coffee prices fell, we began to sink back into the peasant status he had fought so hard to escape.

CHAPTER IV

We moved to Valera because my father decided to start over and work in Trujillo. We had family there and he had high hopes of doing well through the connection. The most reactionary right-wing part of our family was in Trujillo. One of our close relations, Atilio Araujo, was governor of the state of Jaracuy, but other members of my family were also big in Valera. They were powerful people with good jobs in their gift.

We arrived in Valera in April 1946. My father was sure that his family would give him a good job. He had once been the chief bodyguard of Juan Batista Araujo, and as such my father was owed favours. He had practically been Juan Batista Araujo's right-hand man, and Juan Batista Araujo, who was my mother's uncle, had practically been a god. My father never spoke of those years, but later I heard from others that there had been several occasions when Juan Batista owed him his life. That had to be worth a job! It undoubtedly would have been if fate had not rudely intervened.

Just five months after we arrived, Acción Democratica (the Democratic Action Party), the opposition party, carried out a coup d'état. It happened a month after my eleventh birthday. The coup was seen in my house as a super-tragedy. It gave all the people who'd been kept down by the Araujos a chance to get their own back and to rise up. It was the day of the enemies of the Araujos, who were the enemies of my parents by proxy.

Supporters of Acción Democratica are called Adecos, and the Adecos began to rule Venezuela. Venezuelan politics are like a merry-go-round: every time a different government gets in, every-thing changes. Every single job is given to its supporters. The whole fabric of the country, right down to the postal service, changes. The Adecos (who, under a liberal, almost leftist façade, are today about as left-wing as Senator McCarthy) appointed a whole bunch of semi-literate peasants to rule the country. For instance, the guy who sold paraffin from door to door, who'd sold us paraffin for the last five months, was the number one candidate for chief municipal councillor. And Ippolito Peña, a labourer on the hacienda of Cesar Terán, became the governor of Valera. Ippolito Peña had been in charge of a work gang on the hacienda, but he was still an illiterate peasant labourer, a peón. Before they moved him into Government House, he'd lived in a mud shack and shat in the bushes. He had to have his shoes specially made for him because he'd never worn any before he became governor and his feet had splayed, the way bare feet do. Maybe this sounds like snobbery and sour grapes, but that is not the case.

I would be one of the first to admit that some of the finest minds come from the foulest backgrounds. I am no snob, but for such changes to work, power must be placed in the hands of those who are in some way prepared for it. I don't give a toss about ancestry when it comes to who rules whom, but education is important, and ability is crucial: to ignore both is absurd. There were many absurd aspects to the coup. Looking back, I can laugh, but at the time, it wasn't funny.

The coup was a catastrophe for my family. All our relations in power lost that power. My father had to go and work in Bachaquero, in a construction company. Together with our little hacienda in San Cristobal, this allowed him to scrape by to main-tain his family. By 1946, he and my mother had nine children. We lived in Valera in very precarious circumstances, but my father always worked. Compared to our grand cousins, we were really poor. There were thousands of other kids poorer than us, but they weren't Miliani Araujos.

Despite our relative poverty and the fact that there were nine of us, I went to school every day and so did my brothers and sisters. We did not, as one so-called journalist proclaimed, 'spend the months after the Coup of '46 begging for food and small coins in the Plaza Bolivar, desecrating the memory of our glorious Liberator, led by the boy who should have been strangled at birth, whose dubious gift for oratory was dedicated, in his youth, to haranguing the good people of Valera to feed his starving siblings'.

We fell on hard times, and everyone knew it. The gossip redoubled. My sisters had to start thinking about training for work (which was a shameful thing for a girl from a 'good family' to do in those days). Meanwhile, I began to study for my baccalaureate.

In the third year of my baccalaureate, the left-wing Adeco government fell, and the Right took over again. The Araujos celebrated fit to burst as they stepped back into power. Three Valeranos drank themselves to death at the parties they threw. This return to the Right opened up my father's prospects. He returned from Bachaquero and he was appointed administrator of the hacienda Las Cenizas, which was a government-run cooperative of small farmers. It was a model hacienda. The Cenizas project was actually Atilio Araujo's baby, together with another local bigwig. Atilio Araujo was my mother's first cousin twice over and a friend and drinking companion of my father's. He shared his post with my father by putting him there in situ. In effect, he created a job for him to help him out.

I only know about my father by piecing together fragments of what other people knew about him and collating them. He was a reticent man who never, ever talked about himself. He was born in Jajó, and he came from a family of small farmers. His name was Felipe (Felipito). His surnames were Barreto Briceño. He was one of the youngest sons of his parents. At some point, as a child, he moved to Valera. He stood out as a boy for his courage; he was proud and he was a fighter.

I know that while still a boy he had to flee back to Jajó. And when he was twelve he was shot for the first time. I know this because my father tried to send me on an errand, on my own, from Valera all the way back to San Cristobal to collect some money for him. My mother (who hardly ever stood up to him or intervened on our behalf) was horrified by the idea of any twelve-year-old, let alone her own weakling son, making that arduous journey through the hills alone. She said, 'How can you think of such a thing? He's still a child.'

And my father said, 'He's not a child, he's nearly thirteen. When I was twelve, I already had a bullet wound in my leg.'

This information thrilled me but did little to calm her fears. They had one of their rare arguments and, to my relief, she saved me, and I didn't have to go. I never learnt how or why my father was shot in the leg, but for years afterwards, I had nightmares in which I was sent out alone into the hills of Jajó to be riddled with bullets. And even in my dreams I was a coward.

If you saw Jajó, you'd think it was just another sleepy little Andean town with its houses washed in blue and its balconies leaning over empty, cobbled streets. But Jajó was the cradle of the Araujos. It was a place lost to the world in the days before there were roads. Long after my father left it, it was to be the only place in Venezuela that would offer armed resistance to the Adecos when that party carried out its coup. Jajó was home to General Batista Araujo, son of the Lion of the Andes and the supreme commander of all the resistance of all the extreme Right in the state of Trujillo.

This General Araujo was my mother's grandfather. Almost everyone was a general in those days, but Batista Araujo was a famous one. And all three of his children (with Camila Briceño, his wife) each married one of the three children of an Italian family, which was fleeing the liberal Garibaldi's republic. The three Araujos in question were Juan, Victor and Rosa. Imagine that mix: the most reactionary people in the state of Trujillo marry three of the most rabidly reactionary children of Italy! My maternal blood-line is an impeccable pedigree of the extreme Right. The Italians came from the island of Elba. They were the Miliani Balestrini family, and they settled in Jajó as coffee planters. Rosa Araujo married my grandfather, José Miliani. It was from that marriage that my mother was born.

As you can see already from all the names, Andean society is like a less benign version of the Scottish clan system. Family is everything and everyone knows every name within the family. A man exists in places like Valera and Jajó not for who *he* is or what he has done, but by his ancestors and who *they* were. This is a very

Latin thing, common to all Latin countries. It is just that it is accentuated in the Venezuelan Andes to the point where one could say: 'I am related to so-and-so and so-and-so, therefore I am.'

When my father fled back to Jajó (from whatever trouble had lodged that bullet in his leg when he was a twelve-year-old boy), he became one of the bodyguards of Juan Batista Araujo (who was my mother's uncle twice over). A bodyguard then had very little social standing. A bodyguard was just a courageous peasant. Bit by bit, though, my father became his master's man of confidence.

My father began to court my mother in Jajó. He was warned off by her family. Despite the esteem his master held him in, by blood line my father was, and always would be, a peasant; so it would have been too unequal a match. It was unthinkable that a daughter of José and Rosa, a Miliani Araujo (who was also the prettiest girl in town), could marry a man like Felipe, whose only claim to fame was his bravery. People who do not come from tribal societies can never really understand the power of family ties and the taboos that rule them. The Venezuelan Andes are both tribal and feudal. Within the hierarchy, there was only a handful of ruling tribes. Each had its own territory. The Araujos had Jajó. They spread over to Valera and Trujillo and fanned out across the hills, but within their citadel, they owned everything and everyone. To say that my father was ambitious when he decided to marry my mother would be a gross understatement. It was more like a cocktail of ambition, recklessness, courage and a big shot of sheer madness. And yet, that was exactly what he set out to do. To get closer to his future wife, he became very friendly with two of her cousins twice over: Atilio Araujo and Miliano Miliani. This Miliano was the most valiant of all the cousins.

From birth, I may have drawn out and distilled much of my father's racial mix, but that would be one of the few ways in which I would ever resemble him. He was a daredevil; I was a coward. He was a macho man par excellence, while I was a puny wimp. From my adolescence onwards, I constantly walked into trouble, but as I shall explain, it was almost always by chance ('almost' because there are two notable early exceptions). Felipe, on the other hand, walked into trouble over and over again, but he courted it, flirted with it and invited it into his life.

In his early twenties, Felipe started going out with a local girl whom he took to live with him. Unless a girl was a whore or a peasant, you just didn't do that in those days. If a man from Felipe's station in life was prepared to flaunt taboo to the extent of setting his cap at Camila Miliani, he just wasn't going to care about such things. Again, not to care was tantamount to madness. When the girl's father and brother went to remonstrate with him about the dishonour he had done them, they arrived armed. The story goes that my father seriously wounded them both. The girl in question was neither a whore nor a peasant, and the wounded men also had connections. So the matter could not end there. Felipe was Juan Araujo's right hand but, despite all the power the Araujos wielded, my father would have been sent to prison or gunned down. Before the incident, he had been involved in so many others that it just wasn't possible to protect him any more. So Atilio Araujo smuggled Felipe out of Jajó.

He fled to a hidden place in the hills of Mérida, which had the reputation of being the area where people went if they were fleeing justice. The place was San Cristobal. Another family, of Italians, had also been drawn to that distant redoubt, but they were coffee planters, and all the land around San Cristobal was ideal for coffee. Within a few years, some more Italians joined them, coffee planters all. So there were, on the one hand, the planters, and on the other, fugitives from the law. My father was a brave and hard-working fugitive who quickly fell on his feet. He became the sharecropper on the most important hacienda in San Cristobal, Los Limones. With the money he made, he bought two little farms called El Charal and Romero. In San Cristobal, my father was able to alter his social position. He jumped from peasant labourer to landowner, and thus became a man with prospects.

Despite being so tiny, San Cristobal was cosmopolitan. It not only had its Italian enclave, it also attracted some Germans. I don't know exactly when they arrived. I know it was before my father, and I think it was just after the First World War, in 1919. They settled in that lost place and built a coffee-processing factory.

To get to San Cristobal in those days, you had to take a boat to

Bobures, then a train to the Central de Venezuela, then a lorry to Santa Cruz, and then ride into the hills for at least ten hours by mule. It was because it was so inaccessible that it became a haven for outlaws. It just wasn't the sort of place strangers could find. Yet the Germans had heard tell of the fine coffee grown there and they set out to find it. Of course, they not only found it, but within a few years they had taken it over. Before they came, the most that the local farmers had been able to do was find a cylinder to wash their coffee in. Perhaps because the Germans had lost their war in Europe, they were determined not to lose any more battles, including this battle with nature. They took one look at the coffee cylinder and then set about building the most modern factory in the whole of Venezuela. Every single piece of that factory, every nut and bolt, had to complete the arduous journey through the hills.

On a traditional coffee plantation, you've got two choices: either to dry the whole coffee beans (with their two beans inside each small pod) on a dirt floor, or to dry them on a concrete floor. Either way, you have to wait for them to dry. Then you grind them in a mill. Traditionally, this mill has a big grinding stone on top, which is turned either by mules or oxen. Once the coffee is ground, it has to be threshed, picked over and packaged. It always took from one and a half to two months from the time when you picked the coffee to the time you could sell it. You couldn't always count on the sun because its drying power varied from day to day, and the beans were sold all mixed up, with only the rotten ones taken out.

The Germans changed all that. They arrived and built their factory and then, in eight days from their harvest, their coffee was packaged and ready to sell. It was also classified into four categories: first, second, third and shell. All the local coffee planters, big and small, sold their coffee to middlemen. The Germans took one look at that arrangement and then cut it out, taking their coffee themselves to Maracay, whence they shipped it straight to Hamburg. They cannot have been poor when they arrived because the factory couldn't have been cheap. Needless to say, though, they grew very rich with their coffee.

The Germans were called Schuler – Juan and Rodolfo Schuler.

Bit by bit, they took over the entire town. I don't know how or why (I have never been able to find out), but my father was an enemy of Juan Schuler's. In San Cristobal there really wasn't a worse enemy to make, but caution was not a word in my father's lexicon. Thanks to his feud with Juan Schuler, my family could never truly prosper there. Thanks also to the same feud we were never able to have electric light in our house. The Schulers owned the electrical plant and they refused to allow us light. Until we moved to Valera, I lived by paraffin lamps and candlelight.

CHAPTER V

There are flickers of light in the myths that surround me, flickers of truth. Slander cannot work without a grain of truth. Something has to click in the memory of the listener. A man who tries to unravel calumny will often find a grain of truth like a milepost on a road, then he finds another, then the search tends to stop en route, with the searcher shocked but satisfied, converted to the apparent truth of a lie.

Take the Germans of San Cristobal, for instance. They were there, and they did arrive after losing the war in Europe. But they were not 'Nazis so evil that even Hitler baulked at their methods and exiled them to the end of the world'. They arrived long before the Gestapo was invented. They arrived after the First World War, not the Second. Their presence had nothing sinister about it: they were coffee planters. This was not a front. The Schulers grew coffee and their factory was proof of their almost complete dedication to coffee. The handful of locals left from my ten years in San Cristobal may well remember my name linked to the Germans because I am Felipe and Camila's son, and the feud between our two families must have been the source of much speculation and gossip. Those Germans did not 'indoctrinate me with their philosophy of destruction and world domination'. By example, they showed our entire country a philosophy of progress and enlightenment; socially and economically, they dominated our small town as a decent and upstanding family.

Yes, I was the brightest boy in San Cristobal when I left there
at the age of ten. And yes, I knew who the Schulers were; everyone did. But there was a feud with my father. Such things are
taken seriously in the Andes; so I never even spoke to the
Schulers. So I could not have been 'their chosen pupil, coached
from earliest youth in the demonic methods of human torture', nor
was I 'turned against nature to despise and abhor the Venezuelan
race', as a syndicated profile of me gloatingly declared. The mixed
heritage of Spanish and Indian blood coursed through my veins
like almost everyone else's. Where the hell did my dark skin and
hairiness come from, if not from a strange turn in that mix?

Not once was any venture of mine financed with German
money 'thinly disguised under a veneer of coffee dust, but cruelly
plundered (as we all know) from the melted-down gold fillings of
our European forefathers'.

Forget the part about me. It is blatant nonsense, and there's a
limit to how much one man can deny. But take the palpable
idiocy of the 'gold fillings'. Venezuela never gave a shit about the
Second World War. Then 'our European forefathers' – since when
was Venezuela Jewish? There are only about eleven Jews in the
entire Venezuelan Andes. We never let them in! And as to there
being any Jews in San Cristobal, or any pure Europeans other than
the Schulers themselves and the three founding families of
Italians – the idea is absurd. No immigrants could have found it;
it was a miracle that the Schulers had. San Cristobal was a lost
place behind God's back.

The old racial obsessions are skin-deep in Venezuela. The
patrician families pride themselves on the purity of their Spanish
blood. But, state by state, at some time, every family has screwed
every other family. And now we are all Indians somewhere along
the line.

It doesn't matter how far some families will go to defend their
supposedly Aryan pedigrees, it is all bullshit. The pattern of
mixing was set from the start. When Cortés arrived in Mexico, it
was the Indian girl he took to his bed who helped him enslave the
Aztecs. On the one hand, there was Montezuma, who had it all; on
the other, there was Cortés with his concubine and his little band

of desperados. The Spaniards were outnumbered by tens of thousands to one, and yet they won. Chance was on their side the whole way and to such a degree that, with hindsight, it seems absurd. In a book or film, no one would swallow such a piece of luck being added to the plot. Yet, Cortés arrived in the very year that an Aztec prophecy announced a god would return from the sea with a 'chalky face' and reclaim Mexico from Montezuma. Guns, beards and horses (which were all unknown quantities to the Aztecs) lent credence to Cortés being that god. The Indian girl translated his wishes and needs, and the rest is history.

The five strands of that conquest are five elements forever present in Latin American society: greed, lust, cruelty, truth and poetry. The Conquistadores were driven by greed: a greed for gold that was obsessive. They were fuelled by lust, time and again defeating the Indians by seducing their girls and turning them traitor. The cruelty was there at every turn, imported from Spain, and left to rampage in the heat of the tropics. Truth and poetry mingled then, and continue to do so today. They coat the unpalatable with something acceptable, and transform the stuff of every day into something miraculous. Cortés wanted gold; it was really all he wanted. The Aztecs, thinking him probably a god (but not quite sure), played on the safe side and brought him great quantities of it. The sight of gold set off the Conquistadores' insatiable greed: they wanted a lot more of it to ship back to Spain. If Cortés had then displayed that greed, the Aztecs might well have seen through him. Just as if he had withheld the truth they must have seen through him. But Cortés said to Montezuma, 'My men and I suffer from a disease of the heart, which can only be cured by gold.'

With that one sentence, the Aztecs were touched and doomed. Las Casas records how appalled the Spaniards were at the temple of human sacrifice in Mexico City. Catholicism was then forcibly introduced, and, in its name, whole tribes and nations were sacrificed. The Ten Commandments crossed the Atlantic, and were preached throughout the Americas. It seems they got seasick on the voyage, however, and threw up little bits of themselves. 'Thou shalt not kill', for instance, lost its 'not'. The same thing happened to stealing, coveting thy neighbour's wife and blaspheming. The word 'not' just did not travel.

Five hundred years later, our society is still driven by insatiable greed. It is standard procedure, upon obtaining power, for governments to steal hand over fist. It is built into our society to screw (or at least try to screw) every female you meet. Cruelty is so much a part of every day that many Latinos do not even perceive it as such. Ours is a violent, harsh world in which the ability to inflict and to endure pain is seen as an asset. The truth, and its hundred and one versions, is woven into the fabric of every day, made poetic by that process which comes so naturally to every Latino but which is perceived as a literary invention elsewhere. Magic realism isn't about books, it's about life; it's about that disease of the heart that can only be cured by gold and soothed by sex. It has a cultural, racial blend. It is a double-bladed knife: it makes the horrible poignant, and the poignant, horrible.

Even the Conquistadores found the gold scarce in places. There are archives full of complaints about the paucity of gold. I don't recall a sentence anywhere about the lack of sex. The two things almost equate: if you can't get rich, you can always get laid and sow your own seed and thereby harvest a kind of wealth. Look at my father: ten children in thirteen years, and the guy was hardly ever there! Then, draped over everything like an afterthought, an aesthetic touch, is the token Spanish mantilla. It is a veil of 'racial purity'. It's a coy statement, a lacy façade concealing a cauldron of deceit. It would be hard to find anywhere more miscegenated or more racist than Latin America. We are all so full of bullshit. I see it in myself. And that shit has to be taken into account. In Valera, when we talk about really knowing someone, we say, 'You have to weigh them with all the shit inside.'

Growing up in a society as racially confused as ours, you have to sift some of that shit to understand what is going on. I have done a good deal of sifting, helped, no doubt, by my darker self replacing the fair Ostilio. Where others have sifted through my story, the grain of truth and the poetic licence have linked me to the Schulers, who were German, and Germany did invent the Final Solution. And I did visit Nueva Germania in Paraguay, but it was not to find Dr Mengele, the notorious Nazi who supposedly hid there for years after the war. I was looking for Fatty Gomez and the group. God knows I'm no saint, but I'm no Nazi either. Just look at me! If I'd been around in Germany during the war, they'd have pushed a whole bunch of kids back in the queue to shove me into one of their ovens first. With my face, I could have been on one of those propaganda posters about the Untermensch. Mathematics is not everybody's strongpoint, but this is an easy sum. Hitler came to power in '33. I was born in '34. The war ended in 1945 when I was eleven years old. Even in the Andes, surely that makes me too young to be a Nazi!

Since some people make such a meal of this supposed German link, I will add that I have read Nietzsche (who was no Nazi either, but that is another story), and I have also read most of the German philosophers. And my last German connection in Latin America I stumbled on thanks to my complete lack of any sense of direction. I was supposed to rendezvous with a guerrilla unit fifteen kilometres south of a town called Elizabethville in Paraguay on a particular day in the spring of 1966. I was on a special mission for Fidel Castro. Instead, I got completely lost and found myself wandering around a malarial swamp for over a week with very little food and a heavy bag full of Cuban dollars. When I eventually found a way out, thanks to the charity of a half-blind Indian with a donkey, I found myself in a former German colony called Nueva Germania.

I was particularly struck by the irony of this forgotten Fatherland in Paraguay. Three generations after it was founded by the philosopher's sister, Elizabeth Nietzsche, and her Jew-hating husband, the supposedly racially superior colonists had degenerated into a gang of emaciated peasants starving in the jungle.

Brutality has been the trademark of Latin American history, and its despotic leaders have vied to surpass each other in their eccentricity and cruelty. But the history of Paraguay is particularly bizarre and particularly brutal. For instance, by going to war with all three of its neighbours simultaneously, Paraguay's rulers sacrificed almost the entire male population of the country. Meanwhile, Eliza Lynch, a former Irish prostitute who became the president's mistress and then the country's virtual dictator, enslaved the ruined nation's children to build palaces as sumptuous as Versailles.

In 1886, Nietzsche's sister (a female *Führer*) lured some pure Aryan settlers out to a malarial swamp in Paraguay, which she sold to them in lots as both prime farmland and the site of New Germany's racial salvation. Twenty-seven families of rabid anti-Semites bought the barren lots, sight unseen. They followed Elizabeth and her loony husband to what she christened Nueva Germania. Then in a grotesque parody of Eliza Lynch's despotic behaviour half a century earlier, she practically enslaved her colonists, while insisting from the comfort of her own luxurious villa that she 'loved them to death'. True to her word in that only, an early death was what greeted most of her followers.

Towards the end of the nineteenth century, she either ran away, or was chased away, leaving her starving colony in the lurch.

By the time I met the remains of this 'super race', they'd chosen to mix genes with some very stunted Indians. The ones who hadn't were too weak to scratch a crop into the ground. As an experiment, the results were pretty clear. The blue-eyed guys were so weak with tertiary malaria they didn't look as though they could get it up, even with a winch. So the results of the experiment came through too late to help them mend their ways. For all that, when I stumbled into their patch, they made it quite clear that I didn't come up to their incredibly low racial standards. I was not invited to dig in.

As I said, I merely wandered into Nueva Germania. It was not that I wanted to become a malaria-monger with a gaggle of blue-eyed inbreeds. I was lost as hell and looking for the guerrilla unit that Fidel was subsidising. As I have said, we were supposed to rendezvous about fifteen kilometres south of Elizabethville. I arrived ten days late and there wasn't an insurgent in sight. I gave my Paraguayan comrades two weeks, but when the time was up only Fatty Gomez and his sidekick Fernando had shown up. I had a hefty cash delivery to make, but I also had to return to Cuba, so I handed my bag of dollars over to Fatty and then buggered off. To this day, I don't know what happened to the rest of that unit. The jungle has a habit of swallowing people up without a trace.

As a young man, I lived in Germany, because some of the leading philosophers were there, and I needed to learn German so that

I could read everything there was published in that language. It had nothing to do with the Schulers and nothing to do with the Nazis.

And, finally, here's a footnote. Some years ago, in Paris, I bumped into Fatty Gomez on the Champs Elysées. He looked pretty different in a pinstriped suit, and without his red bandanna and his jungle fatigues, and the knife he always insisted on carrying between his teeth. But that scar across his forehead, where he smashed into a girder when we were pissed one night in Montevideo, and his mammoth gut made it unmistakably him. He was with a gorgeous young girl – mistress or daughter, I shall never know, because he took one look at me, staring open-mouthed to greet him, and then he looked right through me, pulled the girl closer (as though to drag her out of reach of my potentially poisonous breath) and marched away without so much as a hello.

Fatty Gomez: my friend, my lieutenant, my fellow dreamer in the forest. He was no Nazi either.

What next?

CHAPTER VI

My father was a landowner, and he could have been a coffee planter and well off. It was what he wanted; but because of his feud with the Schulers, he wasn't able to expand enough to do that. In the end, he made it up with Rodolfo Schuler, but Juan, the other one, was ultimately in command, and my father was never able, or never wanted, to mend the quarrel with him. That was why he always had to go away and work somewhere else to earn his living.

My father had bought two haciendas, but he was left with only one. The other was either sold to or taken by a local landowner, and I think that was at the core of his hatred for Juan Schuler. There must have been some fast manoeuvre, some trickery or something in which my father got the worst of it and never forgave the slight. God knows, Felipe was a proud man, but his rancour at the Schulers was not all pride. The remaining hacienda just did not yield enough to support us. It was something I saw with my own eyes: ends did not meet, and that was why I grew up without a man in the house.

When the Adecos fell from grace and the right-wing junta of Perez Jimenez came to power, my father did well out of it, like I said, because the administration of the Cenizas cooperative fell into his lap. That was from 1948. Those were the years when I became Valeran. I started to live Valera. Something important happened to me then.

*

Until I sat down to remember all these things, I would have said that mine was a life that should have been about words but which has actually been about action. When I piece it together, though, I see that words have played a crucial role in everything I have done. For instance, my early training as a public speaker has probably had a greater effect on the course of my life than any other single factor. I became an orator, but that oratory began with me as a reciter of doggerel. It all began in San Cristobal de Torondoy when I had learnt to recite. I don't mean that I learnt to read poetry aloud, I mean something else altogether: a funny and dramatic way of reciting, which nobody uses now. Once upon a time, the myth and history of the Andes were recited in rhyming couplets, peddled from village to village, altered, learnt by heart, and occasionally updated. This archaic delivery was full of ups and downs, sighs and dramatic pauses. It is a lilting theatrical sing-song long fallen into disuse. It was my first of many ways of dominating a crowd.

In San Cristobal, in school, we learnt verses by Julio Flores, that master of staged atmosphere. Sometimes we were taught better poets, like the Colombian, José Asunción Silva, but they were still built around heavily rhyming line-endings, full of rhythm and drama. Andeans loved them and flocked to the recitals. And I loved the power and fame reciting gave me, and so perfected both my delivery and my repertoire.

When I was twelve, I spent a year away from my mother, in Mendoza Fría, a hill village about twelve miles outside Valera. My mother's eyes were not 'finally opened to the hybrid monster she had reared'. I had a bit of asthma as a boy, and the cooler climate of Mendoza Fría was better for my chest. Valera was suffocatingly hot and dusty. My oldest sister, Graciela, had married (aged sixteen) a schoolmaster (many years her senior) called Guillermo, and they lived up in Mendoza. Reluctantly, on doctor's orders, I went to stay with them. Guillermo was the director of the Padre Rosario school there. Up in Mendoza, I learnt yet another repertoire of awful poems and thus had the most extensive repertoire of anyone in the state of Trujillo. To this day, I could run on for hours in that plodding doggerel.

Under my brother-in-law, Guillermo, I studied with all the

sons of the big landowners: the Valeros and the Briceños as well
as the village kids. My own father's name was Barreto Briceño, but
he wasn't one of *the* Briceños. He got the name the way slaves got
theirs – by working for rather than being one of a grand land-
owning family. But I was the one who knew the most. I found it
surprisingly easy to get along with the local boys, but Guillermo
himself loathed me. He couldn't stand how little effort I made to
study, and yet how far ahead I was of his other pupils. I was
younger than all the boys in my class, a lot younger. Guillermo
saw me for the show-off I undoubtedly was. He saw me as boastful, and he loathed my refusal to fall under his rule, coming into
class with all my exotic knowledge. I am sure he loathed the fact
that I was there at all, disrupting both his house and his school.
Graciela, my sister, was a feisty young woman with a formidable
temper which had simply overruled her husband's over my
extended visit. Then, to add insult to injury, although I lived
with them, I spent my evenings at his neighbour's house, reading
her encyclopedia. So I knew about things that were not on his curriculum and that it niggled him to have me know about at all. I
was supposed to learn by his dictates at his pace. I was not supposed to know about foreign things like the crusades and Richard
the Lionheart, or the life of Federico Barbarossa, or Mad King
Ludwig of Bavaria. What bugged Guillermo most was that I was
such a braggart and know-all when he knew I hardly opened my
schoolbooks, his schoolbooks. It was as though all the facts I knew
were stolen rather than learnt.

The ensuing domestic battle was my first guerrilla campaign.
Played out in the micro-world of Mendoza Fría, it lasted for a
year, during which time I sabotaged my brother-in-law's peace of
mind with my usurped knowledge. Once I realised how much he
hated my learning forays, I did learn things just to spite him, and
I never missed a chance to show off these nuggets in class. To
make matters worse, in his own house his wife saw no harm in her
little brother climbing up the tree of knowledge by an unorthodox
ladder, and rather than turn on me for it, she turned on him and
(as I know from their screaming rows) teased him about his bigotry when they were in bed. By the end of the school year, the
atmosphere chez Guillermo was poisonous.

To get his own back, Guillermo decided to fail me. He persuaded my other teacher to join forces with him and give me fifteen out of twenty as my mark for the year. If Guillermo had had his way, I would have had to leave school and get a job as a shop assistant or an under-clerk.

At breakfast, traditionally a big meal in the Andes but one that passed in stony silence in Guillermo's household, my dour martinet of a brother-in-law would glower at me with venom distilled in his insomniac nights into pure hatred. For a couple of heady days, however, when he thought he could fail me and ruin my life, he gazed at me with a smile, which turned his moustache into a writhing ferret. Ever the man of habit, he could not bring himself to talk to me socially, as it were, so he talked to himself, chuckling as he listed the shops and warehouses where the losers in his class might profitably apply for jobs. He tried hard to draw his wife into his glee, but she was having none of it. (Some years later, she got up one morning and walked out and left him. I like to think his petty spite to me was a contributory factor, but it may have just been that there is only so much a woman can take of a boring, pontificating fart.)

When my game with him backfired into my failing the school year, I was in a state of clinical shock. It had never occurred to me that such a thing could happen and the consequences were too terrible for me to take in. At thirteen, I was no more ready to give up school and embark on a lifetime of menial work than I had been to brave the hills and bullets of San Cristobal at the age of twelve. Everyone in the school and village was talking about me, and I knew that within a few days the news would travel to Valera and the circle of my shame would be complete. I hid in my room or at the neighbour's house and cried while contemplating suicide. At mealtimes (which are unmissable in the Andes) Guillermo rubbed salt into my wounds. His cruelty made the food turn to ashes in my mouth.

Once again, fate played a role in my life. The newly ruling Adecos, by governmental decree, lowered the yearly school pass mark to fifteen. So anyone with fifteen points or over was now eligible to study for the baccalaureate. And I had fifteen points. Guillermo was so pissed off he raged around the house, cursing the Adecos and trying to take it out on my sister. Although thwarted by the government ruling, he did not give up. He managed to persuade my other teacher to lower my points for the year to fourteen. (With hindsight, it would have been better if I hadn't boasted quite so blatantly about my reprieve.) With fourteen points, I was once again mixed in with the chaff, and would have to leave school and get a job.

Guillermo, in his turn, gloated insufferably. On the rare occasions when he got drunk, he used to play a little four-stringed guitar. In the Andes, when a man really gloats, he pretends to strum an imaginary guitar. Well, Guillermo nearly wore his fingers to the bone playing those invisible strings. I hated him so much I thought my veins would burst. The mere sight of him in that week of my shame and failure made my blood pump so alarmingly that my sister packed my things and I prepared to return to Valera. I bade farewell to my school friends with the 'da da da da DA!' of my brother-in-law rattling in my head.

I was still very religious at the time. I remember I went to the church and prayed for Guillermo to be struck down, and I prayed for me to be struck down and for his strumming fingers to drop off, or for some kind of miracle to save me from the humiliation that lay ahead of me. His fat, sweaty fingers remained intact, and neither he nor I was struck down, but a huge stroke of luck did come my way. The timing was such that it really seemed like a miracle.

The Adecos were chucked out of power and Perez Jimenez and his junta took over the country. The junta decided that anyone with a grade of ten points or over was to be promoted. They saved me. Can you imagine my delight now? In church, kneeling on the damp stone floor, I had promised to crawl to the Virgin of Santa Clara on my knees if I ever gloated again in the ridiculous way that I had after my first reprieve. When my second, even more unlikely salvation came along, I should have behaved with grace, but I'm afraid I was incapable of it. Guillermo took to his bed and I took to the cobbled street, whooping like a demented Red Indian brave.

The new low pass mark wasn't as good for the country as a whole as it was for me. You had to be as thick as two planks to get only ten points. The ruling saved my academic career, but it gave away many others into the hands of the inept and the unqualified. Every time I go the dentist, and the dentist is roughly my age, I think about that. The guy with his hand in my mouth, about to switch on a potentially deadly electric drill, must have got his degree under Perez Jimenez, and still might not be able to read. It has made me very wary of dentists: I hardly ever go. So I owe all my own degrees and Ph.D.s to the dictator, Perez Jimenez, but I owe my bad teeth to him too.

Back in Valera, when I registered for my first year of baccalaureate, I was very noticeably poorer than the other kids. Only rich kids went to high school. Poor ones worked. I wasn't a part of any of the gangs, and I still didn't really know the kids in Valera. Mendoza Fría was only twelve miles away, but it was like another continent. When I was there, I was there. The journey between the two was by the old road and all its curves, riding a donkey or being jolted around in a horse-drawn cart. Mendoza is 500 metres higher up. My ears always ached like anything on that road, and I got sick from all the winding. The only straight place in the entire journey was the one people call Jaime's Straight in front of the big house on the hacienda of Don Cesar Terán. The rest was one bend after another for over an hour.

Although I returned to Valera victorious in my battle with Guillermo, and the hero of all his school, I was like an exile in the big town. As I was lonely and broke, the only place in town where I could go to was the library. It was called the Carmen Sanchez de Jelandi library (between the Calle Urdaneta and Avenida Sucre) and it opened at six in the evening. A few high-school kids and I went there from six till nine. What began as an escape for marginalised kids became a brotherhood of curious and serious minds. We knew exactly when the library was going to open by our mothers' radios.

Obviously, there was no television yet in Venezuela. It was 1947, and the radio was like a hydrating drip. Everyone listened to it. You could hear the same programme blaring out of Bakelite wireless sets all along our road. At exactly a quarter to six every evening, we heard Panchita Duarte's music programme come on air. It always began like this: 'We now present Panchita Duarte, "the Trujillan Skylark".'

And she always sang, 'El malvado cardinillo, Que la flor se marchitó ... '

When she finished that song, we knew that the library was about to open and we'd dash out to get there. We'd sit down and read Emilio Salgari, Jules Verne, adventure stories and some lovely encyclopedias called *The Key of Knowledge* and *The Pictorial World*. We hardly ever opened our textbooks. Being there wasn't about school, it was about culture and being together.

There was another section in the library which I only discovered after I'd worked my way through all the adventure books and the reference section. I wanted to read from that other section, but I couldn't because it was permanently locked. I kept hoping that one evening it would be open. The books looked interesting and exotic: Flaubert, France, Freud, Hardy, Hesse and Huidobro were on the shelf at eye-level, but they all had such strange and intriguing names on them. The more I saw those exotic-sounding names, the more I wanted to get at the books behind them. I had no idea what secrets they hid, but because they were locked away, they seemed immensely more interesting than all the other books put together, and I became obsessed with the idea that I had to read them. When I asked the librarian, Señora Dubuc, if I could, she refused and seemed put out by my audacity.

'No, only Nene can borrow them. They are reserved for special people: like writers.'

I tried a second time, but she was adamant.

'They're not for the likes of you. They are for people who really understand poetry.' A dream-like, satisfied smile gave her thin lips a sudden girlish twist and her rigid shoulders relaxed as she said, 'They are for people like Nene: he's the poet here who understands such things.'

That was it and she turned away. But I followed her, and addressed her firmly retreating back, 'Who is this Nene?'

That anybody could not know who Nene was seemed to strike her as so monstrous that she wheeled back round and told me crossly, 'Nene is that boy over there.'

Her long bony index finger with its swollen joint jabbed at the air, pointing out the one boy who struck the fear of God into Valera. I stared at him in astonishment and then turned quickly away.

CHAPTER VII

I had come across Nene before. He was not a boy to stare at, and although I knew I wanted to see the books, I knew with an even greater certainty that I didn't want Nene to see me. He was one year ahead of me in school (but two years older than me) and he was a terrible bully. He was one of those people you sometimes come across who can do everything. He was the best stone-thrower in Valera, and the best fighter. He was the nearest Valera came to having its own Leonardo da Vinci: its very own Renaissance man. Except that, warped somewhere along the genetic spiral, Nene was more of a Renaissance delinquent. He was always the top of his class and he was first base in the base-ball team. He was, quite simply, at the top of everything he touched and first in every sport. He was naturally so good at life he rebelled against it by being bad. And he was good at that too. He was unbelievably pretentious and, what was worse, he was the brains of the most feared gang in Valera: the Silencers. His was a patrician gang made up of all the bad rich kids in Valera. When they hit the town, they were nasty. They stole from all the shops, vandalised, terrorised and bullied. Wherever they went, they per-petrated disasters, all under the protective wand of the wealth and power of their parents. No one stood up to the Silencers. No one dared.

Under different circumstances, my early scholarship would have been drawn to Nene's brilliance, but I had never so much as spoken to him – I wouldn't have dared! Although we hadn't talked, I had been chased and tormented by his gang. I kept as big a distance as possible between them and me. Now, by bad luck, by all the bad luck there is, he was right there in the library. And if Nene had the key to the cupboard, I had about as much chance of ever reading those secret books as I did of becoming my beautiful, blue-eyed brother!

Knowing that Nene was in the library took the edge off my pleasure at being there. Even though it seemed to be the one place where he didn't bully, he had turned it from a safe haven into a potential minefield. I thought about giving up going there just to avoid him, but since he didn't take his gang with him, and since he left me and my friends alone to pore over our encyclopedias, and since I loved that library, I kept going. When he was there, I read with one eye and watched the town terroriser warily out of the corner of my other one. While I read, mentally, silently, I invented Jules Vernesque escape routes for myself lest Nene changed his policy and decided to come and get me. From Monday to Friday, I was safe: Nene was elsewhere. He only came on Saturdays when the library was open all afternoon. Weeks passed and nothing happened, but I never dropped my guard.

Then, one Saturday, from across the reading room, someone pointed me out and told him, 'This kid knows how to recite.'

I watched with dread as Nene came over to me. Despite all my fantasy plans, there was only one way into the library and only one way out, and Nene was blocking it.

He gave me his customary sneer and asked, 'Oh yeah! And what can you recite?'

To our mutual surprise, my voice acted independently of my feelings. While my heart was struck dumb and reduced to palpitating, my mouth recited some things in the old Andean way, which was my way. They were short pieces. By the third one, my voice had grown louder as I saw that Nene wasn't going to hit me. But I also saw that he wanted to laugh. My hands and arms joined my mouth in the recitation while I watched Nene struggling to restrain his mirth. I had never seen him restrain himself before, and I found that restraint almost as frightening as his violence. It so threw me off my balance that something in my confusion gave me a rush of defiance and the courage to defend my performance. I can still remember the look on his face: it was as though he took pity on me for the things I said were poetry.

He said, 'Look, that isn't poetry.'

'What is then?' I asked, surprised that I was daring to speak to him at all, let alone challenge him.

Certain moments in life freeze and stand in isolation. They are so clear that they remain so despite the passage of time. As they happen, they unfold with a halo of awe and they carry indelible labels that announce their significance. We do not always (or even usually) grasp what that significance is, we just know it is there. We feel its presence. Back there in the library, I knew that something momentous was happening because I saw pity in the eyes of Nene, who showed no pity to man nor beast. I sensed that there was something about poetry that mattered intensely and in ways I did not understand. I am the sort of person who needs to understand things. So I was not only ready to learn that afternoon, I was ready for a revelation.

Nene (two years ahead of me translated into a physical bulk that gave him a god-like stature compared to my puny frame) towered over me as he told me to go and ask the librarian to give me Pablo Neruda's poems of love.

I remember thinking, Just like that? What chance did I have of getting her to give me anything? But Nene had told me to go and so, obediently, I went and told her, 'Señora Dubuc, Nene said you should open the cupboard for me.'

And just like that, she said, 'Fine then.'

And then she took down the key to the forbidden shelves. I held my breath and watched as she opened the latticed doors and took down *Twenty Love Poems and a Song of Despair*.

I sat down and read it then and there, expecting to be transformed. But when I saw that stuff, I thought it was awful. Pablo Neruda struck me as absurd, especially in his 'Poem number 20', which 'Nene' had signalled out as the best. 'Nene' – 'Baby'. I had never dared even to think his nickname before, but as I read Neruda, I mentally rolled the silly name across my tongue. For a great big bully like Nene, the diminutive name didn't make any sense, but, I told myself, if he liked this rubbish, perhaps it did suit him after all. The twenty poems didn't make any sense. And the stuff didn't even rhyme! It was flat and weird, and I kept thinking, where the hell is the rhyme? Worse still, it contradicted itself blatantly.

> I don't love her anymore, it is certain,
> But maybe I love her ...

What was that shit? Did he, or didn't he? I completely forgot that Nene was the town bully and I went right back to him and told him what a big mistake he was making – the stuff was crap! I wasn't intimidated any more: he'd tried to do me a favour, so I'd try to return it.

'Listen,' I said, 'that isn't poetry!'

We had a huge discussion about it. I argued pretty well, but I couldn't shift him an inch; and there was no way he was going to win me over. Our discussion grew so loud that the señora Dubuc finally asked me to leave. Señora Dubuc worshipped Nene: he was her wayward genius and her unfulfilled life found a sense of purpose in nurturing what she reverently called 'a true talent'. She lived trapped between dusty shelves battling with bookworms and the woodworm that chewed silently through the rafters of her emporium of knowledge. She would never escape, but Nene would – he would be her ambassador to life. She was brittle and creaking into old age, but Nene flirted with her and made her coquettish. She fluttered girlishly around him, grateful and hungry for any look or word from him. I can see now how it must have cost her to have remonstrated at the noise in her library that afternoon. She would have done anything not to annoy or offend her darling Nene, but the sound of our shouting had carried into the street and a little crowd of gossips (who had never set foot in the library before) had gathered in the reading room to observe our heated contest.

That day, as I swaggered down the street and sat triumphantly with my handful of cronies in the Plaza Bolivar, I was proud to have held my own and I was unconvinced of any of 'Nene's bullshit'.

Only later, and gradually, could I slide through other doors.

Having re-read Neruda, I was able to read other things. The concept of not loving and still loving and maybe loving began to make sense long before the lack of rhyme became acceptable to me. As I read and began to understand T.S. Eliot, Lorca, Hermann Hesse, Borges, Unamuno and Machado, I began to enter that previously unreachable group around Nene. I was able to borrow the special books without anybody else guiding me through them. On my own, I moved from spine to spine until I was a part of something.

That was how Nene became my mentor. For years, he was like a god. He was like a mythical creature. He not only opened the door to poetry and so many other fields of learning and thought, he also opened the door to sex for me. One Saturday when my school friends and I were reading, Nene came into the library. He still only ever came in on Saturdays. He called over to us, 'Come here, all of you, and look at what Freud says.'

Nobody else had even heard of Freud in Valera, let alone read him. I'd seen his name on the special shelves, but I hadn't got round to reading him yet. We hurried over to his table. This was something I had done alone, but my friends had never been included or allowed to approach him. This general invitation was a big thing. Nene, the bogeyboy, was somewhat tamed in their eyes by my budding friendship with the delinquent leader. So they were not afraid to be summoned, just grateful and excited to be noticed. Had he read us a verse from Ecclesiastes, we would have felt pleased and flattered. As it was, he talked about sex. He said the taboo word out loud. He burst it open and amazed us. 'Look what he says about sex.'

We were silent, entranced and waiting for the rafters to crash down and bury us alive. Everyone in the library looked up. Señora Dubuc blushed so hard her face and neck became a uniform vermilion. We all blushed. All except Nene who kept going as though it was quite normal to hold an entire room in thrall, as though the word 'sex' had ever been uttered in a scholarly context in our seething, venal town before.

'Sigmund Freud is the greatest psychiatrist there has ever been. He invented psychoanalysis, which is the only shit that tells the truth about people and sex.'

All the boys at his table were entranced. Then he read out a bit where Freud writes about masturbation being not only normal for boys, but necessary.

'It is a completely normal bodily function. It says so here. So come on! Let's all go to Avenida Las Acacias to masturbate!'

The excitement around our table was huge. Nene was not only talking about sex in a public place, he was saying it was OK to do so. He was exuding energy, and so excited by what he was doing and by the energy he was releasing that he laughed in a sort of gurgle. For me, more exciting than anything he had read out or said was the fact that he was inviting us to go somewhere with him. Neither I, nor we, had ever been invited to join him outside the library. We were being asked to go with his patrician gang, to run with the Silencers, invited by their leader. And we weren't going to go just anywhere: we were going to Las Acacias, the Beverly Hills of Valera.

It was an astonishing social leap. All the boys in the library followed him out, shoving and pushing as we ran through the town to the Avenida Las Acacias with all its fine mansions and manicured lawns. I, Oswaldo the runt, was running with the Silencers! I was not running from them, I was running with them, and with Nene himself. And we were going to masturbate! I was very excited about going to masturbate at Las Acacias, but I didn't know what masturbation was, and I kept asking the boy next to me to tell me.

'You know,' he said, 'wanking.'

But I didn't know. There was very little sex to spy on in our house, what with my father away for months on end. I didn't have an older brother or cousins or friends close enough to take me down to Crazy Carmen's shack. I don't know why the hell I'm apologising for it! Suffice it to say, I'd never wanked before and I had no idea what it was over and above being a mild insult. So on the way to the avenue of mansions, I kept asking, 'But what is wanking?'

The boy next to me refused to answer any more. So I ran on excited but confused until Nene ordered us to stop and pull our cocks out right there in the (admittedly empty) street. I had no idea what was going on and tried one last time, whispering to my neighbour to enlighten me. He hissed at me 'to shut the fuck up'. Then I copied what the other boys were doing, and I found my answer three minutes later.

That was how I started wanking. But I was less impressed by it than by the power Nene had over us. All the time there, I kept thinking, If only I had that kind of power! (Of course, later, when I got it and much more, the idea of power waned and I kept turning back to that moment in my childhood and thinking: if only I'd been less impressed with wanking, my life could have been very different.)

By that stage in my boyhood, Nene's gruesome reputation and indubitable erudition had gone a long way to making me his pupil. The added ingredients of sex and absolute power made me his willing slave. From then on, I did all I could to hang around with him. I became his disciple. Naturally, because of our different ages and our social worlds apart, there was gossip in town about my being his bum boy. I can still hear it now. Why else, according to the town's evil mind, would Nene have any interest in me?

'Felipe's boy is shameless! Would you believe it – he spends hours locked away with Nene!'

'I'd believe anything of him ever since I heard he has had his own key made to shelves of books with pictures of cocks and slits, and books written by the devil's disciples. I've heard there are books not written in Cristiano and they are all down at that library place; and, apparently, Barretico did something weird to the librarian and ...'

'What sort of weird?'

'So weird, the person who told me was ashamed to say.'

'Who told you?'

'La Nena Blanca.'

'Jesus! Pray for us sinners! If la Nena Blanca is ashamed to say it, it must be horrendous. La Nena is so foul-mouthed and shameless, she would fuck a stray dog and then tell children about it over their breakfast. Ai ai ai! Imagine that Barretico up to such disgusting tricks ... I must go and tell my sisters – they have no *idea* how terrible this has become.'

Most people in the Andes didn't realise we spoke Spanish.

They called our language 'Cristiano': Christian. You could argue until you were blue in the face about it, but Spain, and therefore Spanish, was an alien concept. All things foreign were taboo. The social battle to establish the purity of any given family's Spanish blood was seen only as a battle of white against brown. Even the scions of the most Spanish families would have been appalled to realise that their white skin was actually the mark of their being foreigners.

This xenophobia spared nothing and no one, not even the Church. Women, in particular, went to church and were, nominally, Roman Catholics, but the idea that there was a Pope in Rome, a foreign person, telling them what to do, was so inconceivable everyone just ignored it. God himself in all probability was a forebear of one of our patrician families. Life revolved exclusively around our town with its hierarchy and its surrounding sugar and coffee plantations. What happened beyond, in faraway Caracas, Maracaibo or the east of Venezuela, was of minimal interest. What happened abroad was of no interest whatsoever. What happened across the street was what was endlessly fascinating to all and sundry.

My mother, with what were perceived as her airs and graces, and her visible poverty, was the butt of particular malice. No one seemed prepared to forgive her for crossing the class boundary. Everyone was on the look-out for the slightest misdemeanour by one of her children to pick up and throw back in her face as an act of divine justice. Perhaps it was a good thing she got some early training in surviving slander, given the barrage of calumny that was to come. In Valera, my mother had to live with the taunt of, 'Poor Doña Camila! Sex once a year and nothing but rice on her table!'

Thanks to my friendship with Nene, this was compounded with the gleefully relayed addition, 'She'll have to climb down off her high horse when she hears how her runty son is a faggot!'

'Is Barretico really ... one of those?'

'Oh yes! Haven't you seen how he follows Nene around like a stunted catamite.'

'Really! Whatever next! Do my cousins in Carbajal know about it?'

'Everyone knows about it!'

Disappointed. 'Oh!'

There was nothing more disappointing than being the last to know a titbit of gossip and nothing more exciting than being the one to convey fresh scandal. The town had a plethora of scapegoats. It persecuted those who were different in any way, ridiculing every attempt at self-improvement. (That Nene could get away with writing poetry and retain the respect of the town was nothing short of a miracle.) Within the dusty basin of its streets (littered with fruit skins, mangy dogs and human dregs), the townsfolk kept a constant watch on my mother. She had been tried and found guilty by the rich side for her misalliance and the shabbiness of her children. The poor side of town had convicted her for her inveterate snobbery. Her punishment was to be grief. To hasten the process, the town watched her every move and spun it into its sewer. She was known as '*Doña* Camila'. Her title, supposedly a mark of respect for her patrician heritage, was stressed in such a way that it became a sneer.

'*Doña* Camila is buying quantities of pig fat, which she claims is to cook with, but which everyone knows is a balm for a split rectum. Doña Ana has haemorrhoids (and no prizes for guessing how she got them, with that donkey of a husband she's got! Her maid says he's hung like a baboon — and she should know — and has been inside his wife's every orifice except her nostrils). Well, Doña Ana swears by pig fat. And *Doña* Camila bought a ten-pound jar of it on Wednesday. Ten pounds! And you know they haven't got a red cent there to mend the children's shoes.'

'Ten pounds is a lot! Barretico is probably bending over for the whole town.'

'You can see it in his face. I never liked him ... You should hear the stories I've heard about them from San Cristobal! You know Oswaldo killed his own brother when he was a baby and ...'

Despite the malice, my friendship with Nene survived. He taught me to read poetry and understand it. He taught me to read properly and to think for myself. And he taught me a lot about how to behave in life. He told me that I had to fall in love with a girl, and not be fooled by all the macho talk. He told me

I was different because I had spirit, and that I didn't have to do what everyone else did. When they weren't venting their psychotic tendencies, he and his gang spent their time rollerskating and kiting. (Nene was, by the way, a kite-flying star.) I tagged along after them sometimes, but he encouraged me to stay away and take a real interest in poetry and writing. I drank in his words, his advice and his thoughts.

He was a distant hero, even then. Our paths didn't even cross at school: I was at the Federal College, while he studied at the Salisiano. He was also a year ahead of me, but when the two schools merged the following year, we were, at least, on the same campus.

I failed my third year of high school and had to repeat it. More than once, it has been said that I hold my professorship at the University of Caracas under false pretences, that I graduated only through bribery with menace. Proof for this hypothesis is supposed to be my low marks in Mendoza (linked to the suspicious circumstances of the school director being my brother-in-law), and the black-and-white fact of my failing my third year. What more evidence could anyone need that I was, in truth, no better than a halfwit? Hadn't Dr Cesare, the doctor who delivered me, as good as certified me as such at birth? What can I say? Guillermo was my brother-in-law, and yes, I did fail my third year of baccalaureate.

My physics teacher loathed and despised me. That didn't help, but really, I was all over the place inside my own head and pretty much deserved my lot. As I failed, Nene shone. He jumped a year, so when I was restarting my third year, Nene had graduated and left for Caracas. I wrote to him there, but it wasn't the same. When he came back to Valera for a holiday, he had met Juan Sanchez and discovered a whole new world. Suddenly, he was out of my league again, and out of my reach. He was in the swim of new ideas, while I was still swimming for dear life to stay afloat in the swamp of Valera.

When I say my family moved to Valera, or my family this or my family that, I mean my immediate family: my mother and father and my nine brothers and sisters. And when I say in Valera, this or that happened, you have to understand a little bit about

Valera, because it was a strange place. It is probably the most spiteful town in the world, certainly in Venezuela. A lot of towns have an undercurrent of spite, of malice. Valera seethes with it: it specialises in it. Malicious demolition is something they all learn on their mothers' knees. Valeranos celebrate misfortune, wallow in accidents and illnesses, and adore scandal. Over 90 per cent of the population, having left school, will never again open a book. It just wouldn't occur to them to do so. There are no books in their houses, and yet their mouths are full of metaphors and venomous words, all honed and sharpened.

Valera is an isolated city with a lot of money and a history of power. It is by no means unique in Latin America in being a bastion of alcoholic excess and a cauldron of sexual extravagance. But we do relish gossip like nowhere else I've ever seen. We gather it, nurture it, churn and embellish it, and spread it thick when we pass it on. It's like a Roman circus. People die from the poisonous slanders that circulate round the sultry streets. It is as though the standards of cruelty from ancient times had been carefully preserved in Valera. It is a cruel town, even love is expressed through cruelty. The city creed is that people were put on this earth to be laughed at, humiliated and verbally slaughtered. You exist to be put down. No peasant will challenge a patrician, but they'll crucify him with words.

The squeamish can't survive in Valera. You grow a skin like plated armour, knowing that thousands of idle eyes are just waiting for a chink.

That is one side of Valera. Turn it over and it is the same. Turn it again, like a pyramid, and nothing is changed. But like a pyramid, it rises to a peak. The handful of citizens who manage to struggle up there are fully apprenticed in the warfare of words. They come armoured with a natural resilience, wit and subtlety. Valerans have a battery of surprising metaphors, and a genius for observing human behaviour.

I have often thought perhaps that is why so many writers, poets and painters have emerged from Valera. Believe me, the place is a cultural desert! Yet those who rise above the abyss bring all the paraphernalia of gossip with them; and the best of them have forged it into a powerful voice.

You must have read the works of Adriano Gonzalez León, or at least heard of him: he is so famous now. Then there was Mendoza Pimental, Alfonso Battista, Carlos Contramaestros, Rángibel ... I tell you, it was a phenomenon.

CHAPTER VIII

A poet called Ector Vierja Villa Lobo (who was an enemy of the Adecos) was banished to Valera after the Adeco coup. Being sent to live in Valera was the Venezuelan equivalent of throwing Christians to the lions. However, as I have explained, there were a few bubbles of air in the cess, and this Villa Lobo gathered them together and founded a group of intellectuals. He also founded a newspaper called *Brecha*. The government was oblivious to any threat from poets lurking in the provinces, since poetry, to the average macho, was faggot shite. Villa Lobo's group brought out *Brecha* as their mouthpiece. Their great thinker was Filadelfo Linares.

Linares lives in Germany now (he is highly thought of there, and everything he has ever written has been translated and published in German). When I was a boy, though, Filadelfo Linares was in Valera. Together with the others, Pimental and Battista, they all wrote for *Brecha*. It was my dream to get something of mine accepted and published there. I never managed to, but *Brecha* was certainly a guiding light.

Nene, my mentor, returned to Valera shortly after the military coup of '48. The military junta had taken over and was 'cleansing' the capital. I was fourteen and Nene was nearly seventeen when he came home with all the latest literary ideas. In Caracas, he had got in with important intellectuals. In particular, he became friends with Juan Sanchez Pelares (who came from Chile, and had been a member of a surrealist group there called Grupo Mandrágula). When Nene arrived in the capital, Juan Sanchez did for him what Nene had done for me. He told him, 'Neruda isn't the question, that's old hat, you have to see beyond that. You have to read Rimbaud; you have to read Breton and Virginia Woolf. Read *The Waves*.'

And Nene came back to the outback, to Valera, full of these new ideas. He told me, 'Oswaldo, forget everything you know, it's all lies! You have to read Hegel, Rimbaud, Breton and Woolf. You have to read Sartre. Read about existentialism . . .'

I followed my leader. One of the books he suggested was Gomez de la Selva's now famous *Ismos*, where he talks of all the -isms: cubism, surrealism, nihilism, existentialism. I felt inspired. At fifteen, I wrote an essay on Kafka, with an analysis of all his works available in Spanish translation.

Can you imagine what it was like in Valera, surrounded by all my cousins who lived only to cruise cars and get laid? They were playboys then, the same playboys as now. They never changed: they just got older. Among the Araujos and the Teráns there were gangs of predatory peacocks.

A handful of us resisted the atmospheric inanity. There was Carlos Contramaestros, the painter; and another painter, who was my close cousin, Marco Miliani. Then there was Alfonso Montilla, who was erudite to the point where we could not understand how he managed to consume so many books. No matter how many nights I stayed up reading, Alfonso Montilla was always ahead. We were a tiny group: Rómulo Rángibel, a poet (who was to die pretty young), me, and half a dozen other boys.

Villa Lobo, the famous writer who had been banished to live among the Philistines of Valera, left (recalled by the dictator Perez Jimenez himself). Villa Lobo's place was taken by a professor called Geografo something or other. I can't remember his surname – call him Professor X. Under the new government, and without Villa Lobo, the newspaper *Brecha* ceased to exist. The lower ranks of the group, that is, my friends and I, decided to launch a kind of literary manifesto in its stead. We couldn't afford to publish a proper newspaper and, of course, even if we'd had the money, we had no access to a printing press and no experience whatsoever.

For us, it was an in-school affair: something we kids were doing to emulate the 'real intellectuals' who had once given us *Brecha*. We referred to it as our newspaper. We got round the distribution problem by deciding our cultural manifesto would be a series of posters to be pinned to the students' noticeboard. In homage to all the confusion around us at that time (that is, the normal chaos of everyday life in the tropics, multiplied and churned up by the imposition of the new dictatorship), we christened the manifesto *Termidor*. I was chosen to be in charge of it.

I remember rushing to get it done, working nights, racing around the contributors, chasing up articles with the zeal of the editor of a national newspaper.

Time passed so quickly then: days, months, years fled by at the accelerated rate of a bucket of piss rolling off roof tiles. There was never enough time to get everything done or to read all I wanted to read. One of the adolescent pleasures of visiting the great patrician houses in the Avenida Las Acacias was pissing out of an upper window with our host onto the pristine terraces below, splashing his mother's ferns and gardenias.

Now that those years are so far away, thousands of days have merged into a fistful of incidents, and the action replay is in slow motion. Recalling them feels a little like crawling uphill through molasses.

For you to decide what I am, whether that be the 'Red Terror' of the national press, or 'the pompous piece of shit' of the provincial rags, or something else altogether, there is still a way to go. I am only fifteen so far in my story. I have yet to span four continents, and there is half a century more to cover. Bear with me. I have to recreate the preparations for the battle of my life. By the age of sixteen, just one year further on in my narrative, I began to believe that I would be the Saviour of my People. Don't ask me why. I mean, I was a teenage boy whose only rebellious feature was his hair, and my passion was for poetry and philosophy. I was a high-school boy, not a military cadet; a bookworm, not a soldier. Why did I spend almost my entire adult life involved in skirmishes, battles, ambushes and raids? Where the hell did that come from?

The ancient Chinese called warfare 'the Tao to survival or extinction' and turned it into an art form. In Venezuela, we only managed to turn gossip into an art form. Loose lips and military strategy do not naturally walk hand in hand. To show where I was coming from and how I got there, and where I wanted to go, I have to reconstruct the key elements that shaped me. Storytelling, like war, has its strategy: I must place my battalions with care, and ponder the terrain and show where the enemy stood and who they were. I must reveal my network of spies. I must analyse my strengths and weaknesses and know what is true and what is false.

You see, from that school manifesto on, my life was actively part of a battle. I became, against all my preparation and inclination, a soldier.

Unless I show how absurd my entry into the world of politics was, I cannot show how that absurdity compounded. The ridiculous nature of my debut has to be seen because, battle by battle, and country by country, all the enterprises of my adult life began and ended with the ridiculous.

My father's childhood ended when he was twelve, when someone shot him in the leg. Mine ended at fifteen when our in-school poetry manifesto fell foul of the authorities.

My written contribution to this magazine or 'newspaper' (as we insisted on calling it) of which I was editor, was an article, the gist of which I can no longer remember. It was a literary essay entitled 'Evolution or Revolution?'

Portillo, the member of staff who was also the director of cultural activities, intervened. He took my essay, before it could be 'published' on the students' noticeboard, and censored it. With a red pencil, he crossed it out, line by line, until it was all gone. Then he moved on to the rest of the contents of our *Termidor*, and censored out the entire manifesto with the exception of one short article.

Remember this was before the days of the dictatorship-proper in Venezuela. There was a dictator in power, but he was new and we were not used to him. We weren't used to censorship at all, let alone having our thoughts on poetry censored. It seemed outrageous that a man like Portillo (who couldn't even take a piss without soaking his sleeves) should dare to tamper with our sacred literary thoughts. Not many pupils gave a toss about poetry, but our group did, and we knew that most of the school held common cause in disliking Portillo. Counting more on that antipathy than our own sense of injustice, we convened a general assembly of all the students for that same afternoon. Having called the meeting, one of our poetry group had to address it. As editor of the manifesto and also as the only one who actually enjoyed public speaking, I was elected to address the hundreds of students who would almost certainly rally to our call.

For this momentous occasion, I had nothing to wear except the shirt and trousers I'd put on that day for school. I didn't have a jacket with me in which to address the meeting. In those days, in Valera, a guy without a jacket was a peasant: a nobody. The meeting was to be a formal occasion and not only did I see it as the biggest day of my life, but also as the moment when I would pull my hidden light out from under its bushel and let it shine. It was a moment I would embrace as befitted an Araujo Miliani. That couldn't mean dressed like a peasant. I absolutely had to wear a jacket and my time was running out. So I ran all the way home to get one. All the way there, my head was swimming with the fine words that needed to be spoken to protect the fine words of our literary manifesto.

When I was put in charge of the manifesto, I had pretended to be pretty cool about my mini-editorship, but it was a big thing for me. It seemed like the stepping stone to scholarly glory. Apart from the outrage of censoring our manifesto, Portillo was also crossing out my own personal future. I was passionate about protecting my own hard-won dot of power and about protecting our right to the free expression of our literary views. The whole situation made me feel like the champion of truth and a hero in the eyes of my friends. All that stood between me and such glory was a jacket.

I have never been much of an athlete. I was born weedy. But that day, I ran like the wind. I ran past the shops with their faded displays, past the stalls selling fritters, past the cart that sold

ground ice with crimson grenadine, and the cart that sold paraffin.
I ran past the church and beyond to the poorer part of town. I
dodged through the traffic, and the donkeys, and the drunks in the
gutter. I ran past the blind man who stood like a statue on the
corner of our street with his hand outstretched for charity in all
weathers and whose fingernails curved up like carved horn around
the empty leather patch of his palm. I ran past our neighbours'
houses, one by one, past the peeling palette of pinks and blues and
greens, each with its sturdy, bleached shutters protecting the
meagre contents so like our own. And I ran past the fat, prying
women who sat in shifts on rickety wicker chairs half-heartedly
shelling beans while they kept the street under surveillance. I ran
through the entire neighbourhood raising dust and attracting stares
until I reached home.

There were no telephones and I really had run hell for leather,
but news travels fast in Valera, and my mother already knew that
I was the elected speaker. My mother had spoilt me. She had put
up with all my nonsense when I was a little kid, and when I got
older and was a bit wild and headstrong and forever getting into
scrapes, she'd always been my ally. She had humoured me at
every turn, even though she neither understood, nor approved of,
many of the turns I took. I was her eldest son and already set on
becoming a philosopher. In the dire financial straits she and my
younger brothers and sisters were in, the prospect could not have
been comforting. She longed for me to become a lawyer or a
doctor – anything steady that would guarantee an income. By my
choosing to become a scholar instead of a man, she was not only
personally disappointed but also forced to share in the ridicule and
shame such a decision entailed.

For all that, she had never once opposed me, not until that
moment when she stood outside our locked house and told me in
front of all our goggling neighbours, 'Son, you are not coming in!'

I pleaded with her. 'Mama, you've got to let me in! You've got
to let me get a jacket. I have to go to the meeting.'

She knew I couldn't go without one. I would have been booed
off the stage. It was her way of stopping me.

'I will not let you in, and if you try to get past me, I'll give you
a hiding.'

I was so out of breath, I hadn't noticed until then that she was holding my father's riding crop.

I thought she had gone mad. I had no idea why she was so upset. You see, not only did I have no interest in politics, I had no idea they were dangerous. My family were as right wing as it is possible to be. Apart from my having noticed that when the Adecos came to power with their coup, reactionaries like us got spat on in the job market, my interest in or knowledge of politics was non-existent.

Despite that, intuitively, my mother knew that if I went to that meeting, I'd be doomed. It was the 'female intuition' I had heard so much about when I had eavesdropped on my mother gossiping with her friends in San Cristobal. Wrapped in her skirts, as safe from fear as I could be, I had heard all about what women think. She was convinced that if I addressed that meeting, my life would be ruined, and she was prepared to fight me to stop my getting to it. My mother was a gentle, long-suffering woman whose whole life had been bowed to men. With the notable exception of marrying my father, she had spent her entire life trying to avoid confrontations. Yet on that day, she stood outside our house like a harridan, shouting at me at the top of her voice for all the neighbours to see. The scene was a gift to the neighbours, who stood around us gawping and offering their analyses of why and how Doña Camila had turned into a dragon, and also of the nature of this 'meeting' that my mother insisted I would attend only over her dead body.

We stood in the street and screamed at each other: each of us was passionately defending our cause and each of us was deaf to the other's pleas. This huge and potentially violent clash of wills took place in front of a growing public who didn't understand then, and probably don't understand to this day, the significance of my getting or not getting that jacket.

Despite all my mother's tears and threats, I refused to listen. Now, and for many years past, I have put great stock by female intuition. It has saved the day many times and many times saved my life. Then, alas, I was too young and headstrong to attribute any worth to it. She had told me I would go to the meeting 'over her dead body'. I realised that, were she actually to fall down dead, and the last breath already gone from her, I would have jumped over her corpse to get my jacket and get to the meeting if need be. Given her frame of mind, I pretended to give in to her wishes (with a very ill grace) for just long enough for her to drop her guard and let me into the house. Whereupon I grabbed a jacket and bolted out through a back window, across our yard and on back to school.

The podium was my element. I had been reciting since I was knee-high in San Cristobal. It was a power I had and it was one I've always loved. Before the general assembly, the drama (drained out of my early recitations by Nene's leadership) was funnelled into the oratory I had been perfecting for a couple of years.

I knew that most of the students couldn't care less about our poetry manifesto, but I wanted them to. I wanted to make them care. I knew I could. I knew I had the gift. My speech that afternoon was impassioned (even more impassioned than I had made it in my head as I ran home for my jacket because I had defied and humiliated my mother for it). I had a microphone, and all the town could hear me. Well, not all the town, but a lot of it.

I spoke about the vacuum caused by Villa Lobo's leaving, and how everything was dead for us without him; how we suddenly had no hope and no role. I said we had to resist this: we had to fight to preserve our rights and maintain our standards. I was referring, of course, to something concrete: our poetry manifesto, and our right to publish it. I was defending our right to discuss writers and writing, and our need to maintain our own literary standards. I meant by 'fighting' that we had to oppose the censorship of our essays in the school magazine.

However, my speech (which was heard by half the town) came at the delicate time when the dictator was fighting to consolidate his position by cracking down on the rebellious Adecos. My speech was seen as the voice of the Adecos speaking out against Perez Jimenez. I was fifteen years old, it was my moment up there on the podium and in that moment I was referring exclusively to literature. Politics never came into my mind, for the simple reason that they never had. But, if I am honest, my personal motives were not quite as pure as the driven snow as I sometimes make them out to be when telling this tale. The speech was absolutely not about politics. It was about poetry, but the reason I put so much passion into it was vanity.

As I have said, I had never managed to get any work of mine accepted by *Brecha*. Our newspaper was a kids' comic compared to *Brecha*, but it had been the only thing to remotely replace it, and in my mind some of *Brecha*'s literary glory had rubbed off onto ours. And I was the editor. I could choose my own work, and thereby publish work so brilliant that people would come up to me in the street and say, 'I had no idea! Let me shake your hand, Oswaldo! That essay on Sartre was fantastic! Your analysis of Kafka was inspired!'

Far away in Caracas, Nene and Juan Sanchez would be sent cuttings, and then I, too, would be summoned to the capital: an equal among a handful of geniuses. It didn't bother me that there were so many geniuses around, I refused to be hampered by my lack of experience or to question any possible gaps in my talent. I was dreaming at full spate. As a result of that speech and the, so I thought, inevitable revival of my manifesto, I foresaw years of laurels and recognition. I foresaw my bastard of a physics teacher from third grade (the one who failed me) licking my boots in apology. I foresaw my father (who was never there) come hurrying home from Cenizas to slap me on the back, and see in me something to feel good about.

If ever a kid let his father down, that kid was me. Just suppose he could forget my lack of blue eyes and my hairy unpatrician looks; suppose he could accept me as his eldest son (which he couldn't, and wouldn't), I was still a coward. Felipe had been a gunslinger for ten years. Imagine what having a son who is afraid of everything from his own shadow to tepid water does to a man. If the whole town swaddled me in admiration, and even the high and mighty reached out to praise me, maybe Felipe, my disappointed father, would find a way to accept me too.

With a red pencil, Portillo had wiped out my one shot at greatness. My father judged men by their ability to shoot. Let's say I didn't quite make the sixteen out of twenty on a firing range of school exams (sixteen out of twenty was also the decent, old-fashioned pass mark before revolutions and coup d'états started tampering with the school grades). I didn't have a steady hand, so

I was never, even with the most powerful gun, going to make it as a marksman, but I had a shot at making it in my world, and I couldn't take it unless I swayed the audience in that general assembly in our school hall.

So I gave it all I had and more than the subject merited. I said, 'We cannot continue in our submission to the authority of this man' – meaning the slimeball, Portillo – 'who has no mandate of power and no real authority over us.'

I was speaking with passion, the way many since have heard me speak, but in a way that I had never heard myself speak until then. My closing line was: 'Who is he? Who sent him? Where does he come from?'

That was the end.

There was a stunned silence, then stomping applause. And there and then, as I made my way through the hall, the authorities threw me out of the lyceum. My poor father was called to the school. They told him that not only was I expelled, but I had been declared 'an enemy of the government'.

That was the beginning.

CHAPTER IX

The official capital of the state of Trujillo is the town of Trujillo.
It is a fraction of the size of Valera, and dominated by a barracks
and an old stone prison. A cousin of ours lived there. She was an
old woman who kept a kind of boarding house where sons of my
many other cousins from Escuque lived. After my speech, I was
sent to live with them, and to attend the Lyceum Cristobal
Mendoza. All those cousins hated me. They had before, and they
did so even more when I went to stay there, tarred with the revolutionary brush.

They all belonged to the ultra right-wing party, COPEI
(Christian Democrat Party). Their views were clear and simple:
slavery should never have been abolished, Genghis Khan was a
wimp, and Hitler was a moderate. Anyone from the Left, Right or
Centre (but particularly the Left) who was less bigoted than they
were should have his head blown off with a sawn-off shotgun. My
cousins were clamouring to do the shooting. They were all revved
up and as furious as a pack of wolverines in a cage.

I was still in shock when I arrived. I couldn't believe what had
happened, or why.

When I said goodbye to my mother, I felt I was leaving her for
ever (which, in a way, I was). When she held my face in her two
hands to kiss me goodbye, even though my father was looking on,
I cried. I don't suppose he could have thought any worse about me
than he already did. My mother smelt of almond soap, fresh

coriander and the jasmine that trailed from our one window box. The three smells of home. Affection, guilt and safety.

Dirt-diggers often cite this moment as further proof of my falseness. At least a dozen journalists have uncovered documentary evidence that I left school at fifteen, expelled under a cloud, and that my mother threw me out, 'never to darken her door again'. They make me 'the professor who never was', and the ungrateful son.

A far better man than I wrote of himself: 'I did not in the beginning choose to place my people above my family, but in attempting to serve my people, I found that I was prevented from fulfilling my obligations as a son, a brother, a father, and a husband.' Nelson Mandela was a born leader who chose to serve his people. I am not a born leader who served his people by mistake. Either which way, I shat on my mother, who loved me, cock-ups and all.

What with the sudden scandal and the loss of my immediate family and friends, I was dazed when I arrived in Trujillo. Without any time to get my bearings, I was thrown into school. For the first time in a new school, I wasn't bullied. No one even challenged me to a fight. I was amazed and rather worried, wondering what they knew that I didn't. I discovered that my reputation had preceded me, rewoven into a savage cloth. My fellow pupils watched (sometimes with overt fear) the adolescent 'enemy of the government'. Even my cousins who hated me were momentarily restrained.

On the way to my very first class, someone approached me and told me in a whisper to meet him in the afternoon at such and such a place. Usually, it takes weeks, months, and sometimes years to get invited to things at a new school. Now, there was to be a meeting and I'd been invited to it by a complete stranger. Immediately after school, I met the communists. They made me a member of their clandestine group, no questions asked, because they'd been told that I was a communist too.

The irony was that I didn't know what communism was. I hadn't come across it. When the word came up quite early on in that first meeting, it rang no bells. I certainly had no idea that it was a political group. All our groups in Valera were about poetry, literary criticism, reading, or, at the other end of the scale, wanking and pissing on people's gardenias. But I liked being treated as a hero and regarded as 'he who knows more than us'.

As I was pretty well versed on some other -isms (I could, for instance, have lectured on surrealism and I could hold my own on impressionism), I reckoned I could hold my own with this new group and bluff my way into whatever -ism communism was close to. I didn't understand much of what they were saying at that first meeting, but I didn't mind. I was lonely and dazed and they had asked me to join them.

Because I was 'an enemy of the people', I was a hero in their eyes. Key phrases of my speech had been relayed to them, word for word. They loved it! 'We cannot continue in our submission to the authority of this man, who has no mandate, and no real authority over us ... Who is he? Who sent him? Where does he come from?' They repeated these phrases from my speech, nudging me and slapping me on the back for having dared to proclaim them. Out of context, they seemed alarmingly wild to me, but they also made me think about myself: who was I? Who sent me? And where did I come from?

That first evening, I became a communist with a card and everything. Actually, it wasn't a membership card – as in 'a card-holding member of the Communist Party' – it was like a little library card from the Carmen Sanchez library in Valera. I remember thinking how infantile it was to have cards at all, but I went along with it. I joined their youth committee. I didn't know what this youth committee was about, but it seemed to be a thing of passion and debate and they were obviously very keen on it, and I was used to being in a group of like-minded youths debating passionately about writers. These ones seemed dismissive of Hegel, Woolf and Rimbaud, however. 'It's all lies, comrade!'

For them, it was 'Marx says this' and 'Marx says that'. I didn't want to get elitist with these guys, but they were in Trujillo (the sticks) and I had just come from Valera (shelter of Villa Lobo, home of Filadelfo Linares and Adriano Gonzalez León). These Trujillanos might have read a couple of books I hadn't, but I had read hundreds of books that they hadn't. I had written a god-

damned master essay on Kafka, and, for a few heady weeks, I had
been editor of the newspaper that had replaced *Brecha*!

So there was no way I was going to admit that not only had I
not read their Karl Marx, but that I had never even heard of him!

Almost every boy wants to be a secret agent. It was before the
days of James Bond, but not before the desire to be like him. I
arrived in Trujillo a wild card like a dangerous secret agent,
licensed to kill. The comrades were proud of me, and in my
vanity, I grew proud of myself. I puffed up like a mating pigeon
and strutted around, sustained by the aura of menace I brought
with me.

It was my first taste of power and it went straight to my head.

I'll just pause here, and explain that I wasn't used to hanging out
with girls. In Valera, I had spied on them, stalked them, chased
them, teased them and grabbed them. Had I done my damndest to
dazzle them? Yes! And had I wanked over photographs of them?
Yes, yes! But I had never been in a small room, hip-to-hip on a
bench, with girls who were not only sexy, but full of fire for these
foreign writers and for me.

By fifteen, I had long outgrown those days of doubt, when
people stared into my crib and wondered if I really was a cross
between an Araujo and an orang-utan, but I was still no oil painting. I was skinny, dark and hairy. And my hair, even under an inch
of Vaseline, had a will of its own. The attention and back-slapping,
hand-shaking and elbow-grabbing of those pubescent Trujillan
beauties was not unwelcome.

By the time the meeting was over, I had made myself cock of the
roost. I corralled them with Kafka and then not only rested my
case but sat smugly inside his quotation: 'We are sinful not merely
because we have eaten of the Tree of Knowledge, but also because
we have not eaten of the Tree of Life.'

Having shot this maxim into their midst, I lounged back and
basked in their admiration. I remember still what a near-perfect
moment that was. I imagined my photograph on the front page of
the newspaper under the headline 'Valeran celebrity graces small-
town gathering'. And I remember thinking that if only my hair

would stay even halfway slicked down, then I'd be about as cool a customer as they come.

In Valera, if anyone thought anything of Trujillo (which wasn't very often), it was as a dismal fortress town lost in the hills on the old Royal Road through the Andes. It was where people went if they went to prison. It wasn't a place you would ever choose to go to. It had an old cathedral, and honourable mentions in all the history books, but it was a dump and a cultural backwater. My first impression of Trujillo had confirmed all these rumours. All along the bumpy cobbled road I was also dreading having to live with my horrible cousins. Since natural and unnatural death pruned our family tree with the zeal of a topiarist, funerals had given my rabid cousins ample opportunity to show me *their* verbal manifesto.

But my impression of Trujillo, after this meeting, was very different. Some of these Trujillanos were no slouches! It seemed quite natural that such a meeting should be secret: book lovers would obviously be pilloried in a place like Trujillo. Look what happened to me in Valera, the birthplace of poets!

Despite the enthusiasm of my new comrades for their Marx, Engels, Trotsky and Lenin, I never came to share their exclusive championship for these writers. I read them and I took their thoughts on board, threw some of them back into the bush, and continued to read and study the poets and philosophers I had already come to revere in Valera. But, albeit by mistake, I did become the first-ever communist in a vast extended family of extreme right-wingers.

While I was living at the core of that reactionary household, I gradually became a part of the extreme Left. My crossing the floor was completely secret. Had my cousins known, they would have put me down like a dog. Even without that bit of information, we fought day and night.

It was like a madhouse. We had arguments over breakfast, lunch and dinner, arguments that literally screamed into the night. They had obviously been doing it long before I arrived, but my presence was a catalyst for their shrieked abuse. The head of the household, the old woman who ran the boarding house, spent most of her time on her knees in the cathedral. When she wasn't praying, she was playing gin rummy with a widowed sister who lived in the cathedral square. Both sisters wore mantillas of the finest Seville lace when they went to church. My landlady carried a big leather purse like a pouch hung around her waist. This was full of coins in the morning and usually empty by night. The two sisters were known to play gin rummy for money and our one was, so people said, a habitual loser. She kept her boarding house to stay in the game. I think she saw us boys as a wound to her pride and a reminder of her constant bad luck. She had an answer for everything. It was always the same.

'Line them up against a wall and shoot them!'

She had dull, tawny eyes like strips of dried mango. They lit up when she passed these imaginary death sentences and I imagined they lit up, too, whenever a deck of cards was cut. Her house throbbed with shouted insults. We could kill each other for all she cared, so long as our fees were paid on time to subsidise her gambling.

Those arguments were endless and pointless. Not that that stopped me from arguing too: I screamed along, hurling abuse at my cousins. Despite feeling quite sure that it was a waste of my time and energy, their intense bigotry was bait that I rose to day by day.

At heart, I was indifferent both to my fanatical cousins' beliefs, and to those of my own communist friends. I believed, even then, absolutely, in individual thought: in the creative power, in the free spirit. Communism is directly opposed to these tenets of faith.

CHAPTER X

1950 saw the centenary of the birth of Francisco de Miranda. His name, together with that of Simon Bolivar, Venezuela's Liberator from its Spanish colonial rule, is hallowed. Francisco de Miranda is our national hero and the founder of our state. During the time I'd been in Trujillo, sandwiched between my clandestine meetings with the communists and the endless slanging matches with my cousins, I had kept my nose clean. Well, becoming a communist was a snotty move, but since no one outside of the cell knew about it, I seemed like a model schoolboy. My teachers saw me as a little boy who was very well mannered and bright, and also as someone who had done well at school. To celebrate Miranda's centenary, there was to be a recitation in the school hall, at which the governor of the state of Trujillo, Major Santiago Ochoa Briceño, and the bishop of Trujillo were to be present. At school we took it in turns to be the class speaker, and on the day of the famous anniversary of the death of Miranda, it happened to be mine.

The little town was puffed up with adrenaline. The streets were solid sheets of flags. Everyone was excited. The fritter vendors had brought in a convoy of mules with extra cornflour and oil, onions and sweet potatoes; and cows and pigs were being slaughtered with wild abandon. The streets were full of the heavy smell of old blood and entrails mixed with wafting cinnamon and nutmeg. Trujillo was literally buzzing: not least with the swarms of fat, bluish flies that had gathered for the big day and sat like heaving black mats on the rubbish in the gutters.

Back at the family lodging house, my cousin's cook had been making her own culinary preparations for days – muttering loudly about the imposition of having to make such unreasonable quantities of sweetmeats and preserved fruit, but secretly loving the urgency and attention the forthcoming event focused on her dark, primitive kitchen. On the evening after the ceremonies and speeches, there were to be feasts in every household, with guests wandering from house to house, as was the custom, savouring the party fare from all the various cooks. Only on such occasions could a put-upon kitchen servant rise to a moment of limelight. My cousins even eased up on their arguing as they concentrated momentarily on the splendour of their attire for the big day. Of course, there were fights about who had hidden a particular shirt or used up someone's special pomade or left the lid off the bottle of bay rum cologne and thereby wantonly destroyed that fragrant but ephemeral substance.

I was as excited as everyone else. I had grown up venerating Francisco de Miranda: he was the father of Latin American democracy and the greatest statesman in our history. He hovered up there in the stratosphere and on the plinths of statues in every town. He was the only person who was bigger than Simon Bolivar, our Liberator, and our Liberator was worshipped and honoured more than any god. The Liberator was less grand, less European and more human to us. He loved his dog and left it in the Andes; he suffered from paranoia like the rest of us. He had got fevers and the shits and was surrounded by enemies – he was still human in ways that allowed us to get to grips with him. Miranda, on the other hand, was a name in an aura of immortality. So I was fully aware of the honour conferred on me, albeit by chance and the position of my name on the class rota.

Giving the speech was the second most significant public moment in my life. And it was a chance for me to shine as my mother wanted me to shine, and in a way that would reflect well on my father and bring me to his notice in the way I wanted. So, while my cousins prepared their attire, and the town prepared its festivities, I prepared my speech.

*

If I were to leave the following episode out of my story, it would be a lot easier for me (or anyone else) to make some sense of my life. But it is something I did, and to this day, I don't know why. When you study history, and more particularly when you study strategy, you come to realise that there are crucial moments in which the fate of a battle, of a campaign, of entire countries, is decided by someone's inexplicable action. I think we all have those moments when we fuck up knowingly, but don't know why we do it. I climbed up onto the podium and fucked up in front of a double row of dignitaries.

Unlike my speech in Valera, in which I had unconsciously offended the powers-that-be while appealing to my school friends, in Trujillo I deliberately and consciously set out to antagonise and offend all the dignitaries present in the hall. I harangued them with the most malign adjectives I could muster. I looked the governor straight in the eye and said, 'Look what you are reduced to doing! Look how low you have sunk! What we need is a man with the balls to be a man – someone who can give us back our liberty.'

Everyone (myself included) thought I'd be arrested and marched straight off to jail. Nobody moved. The entire audience sat open-mouthed. My form teacher was actually dribbling. After what seemed like a long time, the governor stood up and said, 'Your words have moved me.'

Then he left, smiling, followed by a procession of bewildered officials and ecclesiastics. Since the governor was smiling and didn't seem to be pissed off with me, nobody else dared unleash the storm over my head until he was safely off the premises.

If I had been truly politicised, then OK, I'd think I'd insulted the governor because I cared about what he was doing and I was prepared to risk my freedom and possibly my life to expose him. But not only had I nothing against him, I had no idea what his policies were, and I really didn't care. Was I depressed or suicidal? No, I wasn't. Was I trying to impress the youth committee? I had already impressed them. What was I trying to do? And why did I do it? In Valera, I had put my mother through hell, but at least she knew it was unintentional. What I did in Trujillo put my whole family at risk.

What I did, I did through choice, and yet, looking back now, I also see a similarity between my hurling myself at trouble in those schools, and my father's reckless youthful behaviour. We had both courted disaster and when fate saved us we taunted it, inviting that same disaster back. Unlike my father, early recklessness didn't make me brave. In fact, it made me extra-cautious for the rest of my life. Locally, no one knew why I had done what I did, but they all had a name for it: it was a labastida.

The Labastidas were an aristocratic Spanish family who settled in Venezuela, arriving (via Santo Domingo) on the second voyage of Christopher Columbus. They were so proud of their lineage that they refused to marry anyone who wasn't, like them, a Labastida. For centuries, they did just that, inbreeding to such a degree that they became physically and mentally marred. By the mid-nineteenth century, they were famous for doing inexplicably stupid things. They may not have married outside of their own family, but they shagged like goats up and down the state of Trujillo, spreading their trail of imperfect genes in so many families that absurd and pointless actions became the order of the day.

Not surprisingly, they didn't want me in my school any more after that, but given the governor's own leniency, the authorities didn't prosecute me. I was banished from Trujillo and sent back to Valera in disgrace. In Valera, the risk to me had died down considerably by then – the new dictator's secret police had bigger fish to fry – but it still wasn't entirely safe for me to stay at home. This element of risk shielded me from the full brunt of my mother's grief and my father's wrath. But my mother's joy at our reunion was numbed by fear. I was lucky in that my family's shock at my behaviour was so profound it precluded my being beaten half to death for it. The household of cousins I left behind threw a celebration party that lasted for three days after I set out for Valera.

I had dishonoured Trujillo. In the Andes, you don't mess with honour. At best, those who do risk getting gunned down like dogs; those who survive that initial risk get wrapped in shame and then cocooned in it. They stand out like no others; they are also shunned like no others. Shame is contagious: it spreads both by contact and by family tie. When I returned as the prodigal son to Valera, my shame contaminated my entire family.

My parents really didn't know what to do with me. But the scar on my chest is not the vestige of a bullet wound from that time. And my father did not 'take me behind our house and shoot me like the sick animal I was'. In fact, he didn't even give me a taste of his belt. It was as though he was reluctant to touch me. Several times, I saw him glance at me with bewilderment tinged with what must have been concern for his own manhood. I could see him wondering: since I came from his seed, did my being such an unwholesome monster somehow diminish not just his good name but also his virility? Since it wasn't the sort of question he wanted on his mind, his answer was to leave town and return to the safety of his work. So, as usual, it was mostly up to my mother to decide what I should do. I was still a minor, and yet I had managed to alienate the two biggest towns in the Andes.

There was nowhere left for me locally, so she arranged for me to study my fifth grade in Caracas some 600 kilometres away. School, back then, was a luxury. You couldn't just turn up at a school, enrol and go there: you had to be formally accepted. There were few good schools, and these had a social cachet as formidable as a top English public school. People connived and fought to send their children there. Names were put down at birth on the long waiting lists. There was a veritable traffic in donations at the top three schools. And a cornerstone of that academic triangle was the Fermín Toro Lyceum. Many of the sons of the rich and powerful went to the Fermín Toro. Several of the country's leaders had been there. Socially, it was a powerful calling card. And I too was inscribed on its prestigious register. I shudder to think how many blood ties and strings had to be pulled for my parents to do that.

Once again, I was being given a chance to make good. At the end of the summer, I would be given yet another chance to finish my education. Once again, I had got off lightly and was almost being offered a prize instead of a punishment for what I had done. All through the long summer between one school and the next, my mother kept asking me why I had done it.

'Why have you made yourself a target? Tell me, son.'

I couldn't tell her, because I didn't know. It was just one of those things: a labastida. Inside the gentle, polite, studious me, there was a hothead with a big, foul mouth and the gift of the gab.

I wanted to do something with my life, and I knew what it was. I wanted to be a philosopher. My dream was to go to Germany, to Freiburg University. At sixteen, I tried to get there with almost all my energy. I read criticism and pure logic. I saw myself as an important thinker, as someone who would one day excel in the field of philosophy. I say I did this with *almost* all my energy because with the other bit I was a militant for the communist cause. When I wasn't studying philosophy and grappling with Hegel and Kant, I was distributing illegal leaflets and painting illegal slogans up on our school noticeboard and political graffiti on the playground wall.

My expulsion from the Fermín Toro Lyceum was a foregone conclusion. The dictatorship was tightening its repression, and my political activities were recklessly open. When I look back, I see it as a wonder I ever graduated. I was given break after break, but I was my own worst enemy. I was saved the shame of seeing my mother's grief, because Caracas was too far away for me to get back to the Andes. I stayed in the capital as a hero to a few of my comrades and an embarrassment to all of my family.

As I am telling my entire story, it seems only right to explain my motives where I can. It would be fair to assume that by now I was a true believer in the political cause I was so publicly espousing. But the strangest thing is that I wasn't. I think I was drawn by the risk factor and the show-off factor. I liked being thought brave. I was Felipe's cowardly son risking my neck for all to see.

It hit me only after my third expulsion that I might never get to Freiburg if I didn't get my baccalaureate, and in order to do that, there was only one option left to me in the whole of Venezuela. So when my mother wrote and begged me to finish my studies and leave politics alone, I was actually happy to do just that. Something inside me, which had been goading me to rebel, calmed down and then (I thought) left me. I distanced myself from the Left to fully concentrate on my forthcoming exams and I spent a quiet interlude, which finally equated to my actual age. I was sixteen and I behaved like any sixteen-year-old who aspires to academic heights.

I spent many hours a day in the library and I studied late into the night. I read avidly, literally consuming books. The more I learnt, the more I kept present in my mind the words of Miguel de Unamuno: 'True Science teaches, above all, to doubt, and to be ignorant.' I immersed myself in Hegel and Heidegger, in the Greek philosophers and in Kafka and Sartre. Tracing the philosophy of the Enlightenment and the French Revolution through Hegel to Marx, I began to gain some understanding of the socio-historic context of socialism. I began to yearn to go to Paris, and to imagine that City of Light as a terrestrial paradise in which the Word of God was handed down from Germany through their archangels the philosophers, among whom Martin Heidegger was still alive and well and teaching in Freiburg.

In my teenage imagination, I saw myself picking up the torch of groundbreaking Thought and carrying it into the future. I imagined myself, an Andean boy with Indian blood coursing through my veins and mud under my fingernails, breaking through barriers with the sheer force of my mind. As the brass ventilation fan clicked round and round in the sultry afternoon heat, tired from months of sleep-deprivation I would sometimes doze over my texts and find myself dreaming.

Once, I dreamt I was on a podium in a great vaulted hall at Freiburg University to give an acceptance speech for the honorary doctorate Heidegger had insisted they confer on me. It was an honorary doctorate in philosophy. I was the youngest boy ever to have been awarded this honour, and my parents had sailed with me from Venezuela to witness my moment of glory.

I looked out across the crowded room and was struck by how like a gathering of elderly penguins the audience looked with their gowns and mortarboards and their round, mostly bespectacled eyes. I remember I was very full of myself because some of the penguins were actually the world's great philosophers and they were all waiting for me to speak. I recognised Thomas Hobbes and John Stuart Mill, José Ortega y Gasset and Ludwig Wittgenstein. Karl Marx was standing near the back, leaning against the pleated oak panelling and whispering to Heidegger. The two of them were pointing me out to a Chinaman whom I took to be Lao-tzu. Heidegger's mortar was a leather-bound edition of *Being and Time*.

As I bowed my head to gather my notes, I saw that the crisp black gown I was wearing had been so chewed by cockroaches that it was turning to dust. My mother was sitting in the front row together with Felipito, my father, who was wearing a traditional white liquiliqui suit and a Panama hat, both of which made him stand out like a sore thumb in that assembly of scholars. Camila was picking up flakes of my disintegrating gown and sticking them into our family album with a paste brush and a big pot of glue. I tried to signal to her to stop, but she was studiously ignoring me. As greying flakes fluttered to the floorboards, Felipito followed their trajectory with a disapproving eye.

Adriano Gonzalez León was sitting doubled up on the stone ledge of one of the Gothic windows high above me to my right. He looked like a bat. I winked up at him as if to say, 'Listen to this! This will show them!'

Time slowed and the silence in the hall was broken only by Heidegger as he beat a devil's tattoo on the wooden panelling and the rhythm seemed to tom-tom a general impatience.

Everyone was waiting. Only Felipito was asleep and snoring lightly. Heidegger's finger-drumming got louder and louder. I picked up my notes and looked at the audience and I began to speak with tremendous confidence.

'Erudition tends to mask the fetid sore of moral cowardice that has poisoned our collective soul' — I noticed that several of the eminent were listening attentively — '... others use it to shirk the necessity of thinking for themselves, limiting themselves to expounding what other men have thought. They pick out a book here and there, extracting sentences and doctrines which they put together and stew ...' The last shreds of my gown fell from my shoulders, leaving me standing in a short-sleeved Hawaiian-style shirt. Heidegger and the Chinaman sidled out of the room as I continued in a clear, loud voice, '... or they spend a year or two or twenty rummaging through files and stacks of papers in some archive or other so that they may announce this or that discovery. The object is to avoid looking into one's own heart and plumbing it, to avoid thinking and, even more, feeling.'

I bowed and prepared to leave the podium. As I stepped down, Felipito woke up and asked in that too loud way of people who have been sleeping but who pretend they have not, 'Who said that?'

I said, 'Unamuno.'

He glared at me and shouted, 'Who?'

Everyone turned to stare. Felipito clicked his heels together in the Prussian way Andean men do and turned to my mother.

I said, 'Miguel de Unamuno.'

'I thought you said Oswaldo had written something,' he said accusingly to my mother. Camila shrugged her right shoulder quickly in a way she tended to do when asked anything, regardless of what was being asked of her or what she was called upon to give or bear.

'He's only a boy, Felipe.'

My father rose slowly from his carved-back Gothic chair and turned to face the assembled dignitaries. He gathered everyone's attention almost casually, knowing that he could compel them to both look at and hear him, then his baritone voice crashed into the hall.

'When I was a boy, death and I were the best of friends.'

After that dream I stopped composing Nobel Prize acceptance speeches in the shower, and I curbed my highly developed tendency to show off. I realised that having a good mind meant that I had a duty to use it. The pursuit of praise and glory was like a cheap trick I had been playing on myself. I saw that in some ways I was no better than Trinidad, my parents' parrot. It was I who had been avoiding looking into my own heart and plumbing it, and despite what I thought I had been doing, I had been avoiding thinking and, even more, feeling.

Gradually, I began to see that my role was to observe and think, to see and rationalise. There was no place for vanity.

Another effect of that particular dream was to liberate me from the need-to-please-my-father complex I had carried around with me until then like a wounded albatross.

Often, the media and my enemies made me seem ridiculous. Almost as often, they didn't need to because I did it myself. Voltaire said once that he 'only ever made one prayer to God, a very short one: "O Lord, make my enemies ridiculous." And God granted it.' Sometimes I tried to believe my more devout enemies had to be praying really hard. Well, I'd try anything in those days rather than admit that I often acted like a complete arse.

CHAPTER XI

Meanwhile, the political climate had deteriorated fast. Perez Jimenez was already a fully fledged dictator. The concentration camp of Guacida (the worst in Venezuela) was up and running. People had already been killed. People were being tortured. And the University of Caracas had been shut down. The worse the political situation became in the capital, the calmer I became, and the deeper I entered into the world of academia.

Politics was a foreign country I had visited by mistake, never understood, didn't really like, and didn't ever want to visit again. My life was still full of passion, but it was a passion for nineteenth-century German philosophical thought (and my almost complete failure to fall in love, and my complete failure at getting any kind of sexual experience over and above masturbation). My passion was genuine, so genuine that my teachers completely believed in it (the former part, that is, because I hope they knew nothing of my sexual yearning), and they completely believed in me.

With all the revolutions there have been in Latin America, presidents and governors don't get to keep their jobs for very long. Perhaps that is why we pump more ceremony and protocol into our public occasions than in most other countries. Everything gets steeped in pageant. Public events, however small, are macerated in pomp and then decked out in momentary splendour. Moments are glorified. Little local visits take on the kind of pomp and lavishness of a state visit. Minor dignitaries are treated like royalty, and act as though they were. Such celebrations are fleeting. With the wheel of fortune spinning like a fairground attraction, people in power make the most of their moments. The populace clutches at the symbols of security and order in the whirlpool of chaotic politics with such fervour that even municipal farts are occasions for civic celebration, and every move and gesture from anyone in a uniform is decked with protocol. Our graduation ceremony was no different. It was a great occasion and all the stops were pulled out.

For my part, I was as excited by the graduation; after all, in my case it had seemed unlikely that I would ever have one. Then, for all of my class, it was a big moment. Our school was being singled out to be honoured by important visitors. There was going to be a real event and I was going to play a key part in it.

As I had been blessed with multiple reprieves, it was truly never my intention to give a political speech that day. In fact, I was so determined not to breathe a word of politics that I had even gone over my lines to sift out any double meanings. And, to be on the safe side, I had written out my short literary speech word for word. All I had to do was get up and read it out.

That would have been easy enough, I suppose, if I hadn't spent many of my younger years prey to a wild card: the labastida, which was like a mad dog that had to be kept down. As I grew older, I learnt to pre-empt it, ignore it and even to control it. I learnt to know it was there: that insane and illogical inbred Andean streak. In my teenage years, alas, this was not the case. Like a rabid lap dog, those labastidas had a way of jumping out at the most disastrous moments. And like the vain, decadent family the word came from, they particularly liked occasions of pomp and ceremony.

While I was awaiting my turn to go on stage, I wasn't nervous. I had even managed to keep my unruly hair glued down to my satisfaction with Vaseline. I felt good and I felt calm and confident. I knew I could do the school proud and show my own mettle in the process as a controlled and reasonable speaker. So I wasn't nervous at all. Perhaps I should have been. I had noticed a crippled guy hovering in the wings. I registered that he was from the communist youth movement. I had seen him once before, but never spoken to him. He had very little hair, I remember. And my strong impression of him (then and also the first time I had seen him) was that he was a sinister guy, and that I instinctively didn't like him. He sidled up to me and started talking like a radio announcement, breathlessly fast, but with the volume turned right down.

'We are very proud you're speaking here tonight, and we want you to make three points: one, talk about the closing of the university; two, talk about the concentration camp of Guacida; and three, say that not one Venezuelan will go to the Korean War. The party expects this, this is your moment: one, talk about the closing of the university; two, talk about the concentration camp of Guacida, and three . . .'

You know when you watch those old B-movies, and the hero is dying, shot about six times, but still has the time and the breath to deliver a ten-minute speech? Walking up to the stage was like that. It wasn't far at all, and even as I walked it, I asked myself, how can this creep have time to say all that? I kept walking towards the stage, wondering how this could be happening, but still not really bothered because there was no way I was going to do what he asked. Not wanting to cause a scene, or embarrass any of the organisers, I shook him off easily by saying through my teeth, 'No problem, I can do that.'

I said it to get rid of him. I assure you I had no intention of doing it. I had my speech and I had that puffed-up cockerel feeling, because the speech I had written was an absolute corker, a masterpiece of erudition.

Well, I started my speech, and it was going very well, very naturally. I talked about writers as recorders of society as a pure, untainted force. To clarify my discourse, I took our own professor of literature, Cueste Cuesta, who was Ecuadorian.

'Look,' I said, 'Cueste Cuesta is part of the generation who committed genocide against the Indians of Ecuador. He was part of the elite who ceased to be elite through their actions. That same generation produced a great writer to record this, to denounce the execution of those Indians when they tried to break a statue of Christ.'

I paused and looked out at the sea of faces and was surprised to see that I wasn't quite holding all the audience's attention; I detected a little restlessness at the back of the hall. Maybe, I thought, my microphone wasn't working properly. Maybe they couldn't hear me. Maybe I should throw my voice more. So I spoke louder.

'Consider this ...'

Raising my voice seemed to do the trick. I had reached the point when a mesmeric quality could take over. From there on, reading from my notes, I just had to slide across a fistful of other writers, comparing their styles and their works, drawn from their own background regardless of what that background was. I'd just got the audience where I wanted them: anxious to hear more, ready to be captivated entirely by my voice, delivery and cogent wit, when, out of the blue, I was interrupted.

There was a very feminine voice, high-pitched and excited, really excited, shouting at me. A young woman had jumped up, so she stood out among all the seated audience. Her eyes were excited: they sparkled. And her voice was not asking, it was urging.

'Yes, yes, say it all! Tell them everything!'

She said it the way a woman says things in bed, urging you to shoot your load. No girl had ever said it to me, but I had dreamt one would. I found the way her voice shrieked deeply erotic. It held me in her power. Something about her out there in the auditorium made a connection that managed to give my dick a life of its own inside my new black trousers, and also managed to make me rant like a suicidal fanatic. Egged on by that girl's burning eyes, I skipped my entire pile of notes and asked this instead.

'But who will write about what we are doing in Venezuela? Navarete can't, because he's in the concentration camp of Guacida. And the dictator, Perez Jimenez, won't let anyone else write anything, or tell anything, so who will record our atrocities?'

The director of the school was jumping up and down in her seat in the front row. She was like a cricket on a spring, right down to making a clicking noise between her words. She was almost apoplectic, twittering in her snobby voice, 'That isn't what you were going to say, click, that isn't your speech! Click. You know it isn't! Click.'

I rolled on. The school director was clicking somewhere near my feet, but I was up on the podium. I was in the limelight and I couldn't stop. When you are an orator, and you get to that point when the audience is yours, half-hypnotised by your voice, you can say what you like and it is hard as hell for anyone to interrupt you. The flow has a power of its own. You feel the entire hall in thrall, hanging on your words. And without getting spooky, you see it as an out-of-body experience, you see yourself controlling that sea of faces. So the director was clicking to stop me, and the girl heckler was chanting me on, and I told them, 'None of us wants to go to Korea. We want the university open. We will not be silenced!'

The hall was full of static. I saw only the girl's shining eyes, and was aware only of my own powerful voice drowning out the director, whose semi-hysterical twittering rose to a strangled cry.

'That isn't what you were going to say! That isn't what you were going to say!'

It was her voice I heard as my friends pulled me off the stage and dragged me out of the back door of the theatre.

They chucked me into the back of a lorry and I was driven away into the night and out of the city. How or why there was a lorry there outside the theatre, I don't know. Nor do I know how or why it was driving to the Andes. But it was and it took me, hidden, all the way back to Valera. It was a night and day's drive away from the capital. A friend came with me for the first bit of the journey and filled me in with what I had done and what had happened. It turned out that the theatre had been packed with government agents. While I was being dragged out of the stage door, the front door was barricaded, and no one was allowed out. One more minute, and I would already be in the concentration camp I'd denounced. I'd be there if I was lucky. But, as my friend pointed out, the most likely outcome would have been a bullet in my head.

Just before the first roadblock, my friend got out and left me to make the long journey back to the Andes on my own. Like me, he was still a boy. He was a good friend, but he didn't want to be around me. For one thing, it wasn't safe. But there was something else as well, something about me. He was uneasy around me, the way people are uneasy in the presence of lunatics.

I actually slept for most of the twenty-five-hour journey. I had to stay more or less concealed in the back of the lorry. We stopped for roadblocks, and to eat and drink and pee. I know the lorry wasn't searched, but I can't remember much of the trip: it was as though I were in a trance. I don't know what the deal was with the lorry driver either. I just know he smuggled me back home.

CHAPTER XII

It may seem unbelievable now that I could be the most wanted man in the capital and still be able to have a safe haven in another state, but that was what it was like in Venezuela then. Valera was like a city state. It was another world, governed by my mother's cousin. Some cities were actually mere villages, but they were ruled by their governors, hand-picked for their party politics and then left to get on with it. You could shit in your lunchbox in one state, and still have a place to run to and make a new pack of sandwiches in elsewhere.

I really was in a trance when I left Caracas, and the hours of winding road compounded it. When I arrived, I was still so dazed that I don't remember much of my homecoming except that I didn't actually go home. I had come back from the capital with 'Trouble' tattooed on my head. Some arrangement must have been made because my mother's cousin, the governor, Atilio Araujo, took me directly under his wing and protected me. He sent me to live with my uncle, Don Emiliano Araujo, in a big safe house.

From that moment, everything about my life changed once again. The way that I behaved in that big safe house must be proof enough that I had no ambitions to belong to that class of society to which so many aspire (and into which, it has been claimed, I have forever tried to claw an entrée): that is, the idle rich. Living with my Uncle Emiliano threw me into the lap of luxury (or as near to it as Valera could provide). Had I made even the smallest effort to conform to what society expected of a young patrician, I had there the opportunity to become one. However, as my behaviour under that gracious and hospitable roof will show, to join the idle rich was the last thing on my mind.

The two aspects of my uncle's house that did truly impress me were the following: the toilets and the food. Back home in Valera, you were lucky if you had running water inside your house, and you were virtually a tycoon locally if you had a squalid hole in a concrete slab over which you could squat and drop your business if one of the other fourteen members of your household hadn't got there before you. A lot has been written about potty training and bowel control and its effect on character, and maybe some of it is true. All I can say is that such theories cannot apply to the Third World. Potty training and gastroenteritis are contradictions in terms, as are bowel discipline and amoebiasis. Compound these with the sheer number of people competing for every single toilet and you can see how impressed I was by the five toilets of my Uncle Emiliano's house.

Although I was pretty excited by the quality and quantity of my rich uncle's lavatories, I was, quite simply, overwhelmed by both the quality and quantity of the food on his table. I had, of course, been to wakes and funerals at my uncle's house when I was younger, but I had thought that the food provided was the stuff of special occasions and not the household's daily fare. On the rare occasions when we had to entertain at home, my mother scrimped and saved for months so that she could feed our cousins and neighbours. But chez Don Emiliano Araujo, the dining table groaned with goodies on a daily basis.

I knew that up in the rich part of town, on the Avenida Las Acacias, people ate steaks the size of a Panama hat. Out in the hills and in the poor streets around our house, we ate black beans. The staple diet of Venezuela is a small black bean like a little basalt rock that has to be soaked overnight and boiled for at least four hours to render it edible. Every household had a cottage industry of black beans at their various stages of preparation. Breakfast, for instance, consisted of black beans fried up in pig fat; lunch could be a soup of them, and supper, the staple, drier, beans and rice.

In Venezuela, whoever you happen to meet, wherever that may be, you can be sure that he has black beans rumbling somewhere inside him. So at my uncle Emiliano's there were black beans too, but there were also steaks and chickens, fried white cheese, eggs and quantities of pork. There were plantains and yams and tropical fruits, there were dips and mojos and baked bananas. There were fritters and chillies so hot they made you see stars. Then there were tropical fruits boiled in syrup and various forms of fudge and sweetmeats. We ate like kings. We ate like pigs. And I ate frenetically as though there were no tomorrow.

In fact, back in Valera, enmeshed in its tissue of gossip, surrounded by endemic lethargy, I did everything frenetically. In particular, I threw myself into political activity. My flight from Caracas and the jaws of death had made me desperate to prove that I was alive. I found I couldn't sit in the library and read any more. I had to be out and about doing something – anything – making a mark, stirring up the handful of black-bean eaters who, like me, felt they were different and alive. I became a crusader, determined to convert the infidel. I set out to convert the inert mass of citizens – with their consent, or, if need be, without it.

Taking a leaf out of my Trujillan school's book, I founded the Communist Youth Group of the State of Trujillo. We didn't have very many members, and we didn't have a clue what we would have done if our ranting demands had actually been met and we had been ricocheted to power, but we held clandestine meetings and voted to paint slogans all over Valera. There were usually about four of us at the meetings. I conducted them, of course, as though we four were a vast and dangerous proletarian army. Our business was 99 per cent concerned with painting slogans on walls and choosing walls to paint these slogans on and then discussing the earth-shattering effects, as we perceived them, of having painted these slogans. We treated each word as though it was a lighted stick of dynamite. What we did, had done and would do to walls was a top-secret topic. We went to extraordinary lengths to buy or steal the paint and get it in and out of our meeting place. And we pretended that nobody could possibly know who was doing the painting. In fact, the whole town knew it was me. Even the police knew that it was me who painted the slogans and graf-

fiti on the city's walls, but they let me do it because I was protected by my cousin, the governor, and I lived in the house of my
uncle, Don Emiliano.

My friends and I were playing a game with the police and the
authorities in blissful ignorance of the reality of the hard times our
country was living in. The police (a sleepy and semi-literate handful of unsuccessful soldiers) had been jolted out of their lazy ways
to take part in the violent upheaval of society. Tremors of this
upheaval were beginning to rock the Andes, and the policemen
were thrown into almost constant confusion as one edict after
another hit them from the central administration in that baffling
faraway place: Caracas. Like every good Andean, they resented
being told what to do from over there. Nobody tells an Andean
what to do! A man in the Andes knows instinctively how to be a
man. All of which made the military police's job, prior to the dictatorship, a leisurely and rather enjoyable way to strut about in a
uniform alternately letting off steam and capitalising on the priv-
ileges of power. The playful elements of a policeman's job, like
beating up the odd drunk and hauling in and raping the odd hys-
terical prostitute, were coming to an end. With me playing a
game, the police rose to the bait and played with me, happy (I
think) to find a little fun in their newly organised lives. Most of
them were illiterate and most of them knew as much about politics as Crazy Carmen, and cared even less.

While I raced and crept around pretending to be carrying out
top-secret missions, paintbrush in hand, the local forces of Law
and Order watched me indulgently. I was the governor's naughty
cousin and protected. No matter how many slogans I painted up,
the police never came for me. Don Atilio Araujo, the governor
himself, had given them strict instructions to leave me alone, so
leave me alone they did. I was so full of myself and my daring that
it never occurred to me that I was getting away with it because
my cousin had covered me. I was convinced that I was cleverer
than everyone; cleverer by far than the stupid policemen, none of
whom were quick enough to catch me.

My cousin Atilio saw things more clearly. He'd call me in from
time to time, and lecture me. He used to say things like, 'Oswaldo,
make up your bloody mind! Weigh the consequences of what you

are doing. Get real, boy! You're acting the way you do because we
are here, because I can protect you. But think: you idiot, without
us, what then?'

I never argued with him, I just listened respectfully and then
ignored him. After all, I was the boy wonder! What did he know?
I was the one who had defied death, imprisonment and torture. I
was the one who had berated the governor and thumbed his nose
at the dictator. I felt invulnerable. I could get away with anything.
I knew that in Caracas people got dragged off to jail and shot for
painting leftist slogans: it was a wild and daring thing to do. I
couldn't think of anything else revolutionary to do in Valera, but
I knew I could write inflammatory words on walls. I was quite
blind to the fact that they inflamed no one and irritated many, and
I was both blind and deaf to the fact that I was being allowed to
do it.

Later on, I learnt a lot from my cousin Atilio Araujo's advice.
Back then, though, I kept right on painting slogans and shooting
my mouth off and refused to listen to him. Although, at the time,
I gave up on him, he didn't give up on me. He kept trying to talk
some sense into me. As a man of politics, he could see where I was
heading long before I saw it myself. Despite his lectures, I think
that deep down he was proud of me. Most Andeans like a hothead.

I didn't stay in Valera for very long, but the months I was there
were frenzied. It was as though I was mutating and had to go
through a buzzing stage like a fly in a bottle. It was partly me and
partly Valera. I felt there was something contagious about the
city's lethargy, and I had to fight it or it would smother me.

Whatever else was going on beyond its sprawling suburbs, nothing changed there at the hub. People sold fritters buzzing with
flies; people worked, drank and died. People made sallies out of
the almost overwhelming apathy that lived in our lives like an
endemic parasite. People stole moments and raised them out of the
dust so there would be something new to gossip about. Rich kids
cruised and vandalised and poor kids toiled. And the heat of every
day, year in, year out, sat like a suffocating blanket over everyone.

The Church held a few families in its indolent grip, and kept a
few women at the confessional, whispering sins. But not even the

Church could be bothered with the Indians in the cane fields, or the heretics and heathens who lived in the suburbs. Catholicism had a hard time getting to grip with Venezuela. What use was a religion that forgave sins? Ours was a culture of non-forgiveness. We weren't in the market for turning the other cheek. If someone spent months of their life (years, sometimes) sticking a knife in their neighbour's back and turning the blade, the last thing they wanted was for either side to be absolved. Where was the satisfaction in that?

Like most other things in Valera, it seemed that religion had been invented to have the piss taken out of it. Some of the local families, like the Teráns, had been atheists for generations. They hedged their bets a bit by the women paying lip service to the Church, while the men mocked them. Their sons lost their virginity and their faith at approximately the same time, aged about twelve. Virility, gossip, honour, dominoes and family (in approximately that order) – those were things to take seriously. No self-respecting Andean man took religion seriously. And politics was all right so long as your side won and you beat the shit out of and humiliated the other side. But books and ideas and faggotty stuff like that weren't worth thinking about, let alone discussing.

Since the Left was so averse to religion and was tearing at its fabric in other more pious parts of the country, I should have welcomed its militant atheism. But unlike most of my compatriots, I was a devout Catholic. When I wasn't painting slogans on walls and haranguing apathetic shoppers, I spent some of every day praying. I was racked by doubts. I prayed for guidance and for forgiveness for my many sins, not least of which was the mortification my behaviour was causing my mother. I spent far more time repenting of the grief I gave her than I did with her.

Communism and Catholicism were diametrically opposed, but I didn't mind about that. What wasn't diametrically opposed in my life at that time? My religious streak had been fairly well concealed until I moved into my uncle Emiliano's house. For some reason, though, it became the focal point of my time there and we argued about Christianity and the Bible on a daily basis. It had become a habit with me to eat and argue simultaneously. It was one of the two legacies I brought with me from my year in

Trujillo: I joined a political party I neither understood nor liked, and I learnt to be inexcusably boorish at table.

My uncle Emiliano's family saw all my passion as a hilarious circus act. They never believed a word I said, but they enjoyed watching the frenzy I got into while saying it. They used to switch me on like a nightly soap opera on the television (only, of course, there was no television then in Valera). They could switch me on, but they couldn't switch me off. My uncle Emiliano's family liked to goad me into religious discussions. They always knew they could get me going at suppertime. Eating was a serious business. It was one thing to antagonise the country's dictator, but it was another to miss a meal. Supper, in particular, was a big deal. No matter what I was doing, or how important or rebellious I thought whatever I was doing was, I never dared miss a meal. I was at my place at the table every night. I would have loved to crusade on what I saw as their necessary political conversion to the Left, but no one wanted to talk about politics with me, not wanting to risk their digestion as I launched into one of my interminable speeches. (Oratory, like bagpipe music, is best played at a distance and to a crowd.)

What they enjoyed, like taunting an enraged, caged animal, was winding me up for a few minutes so that they could sit back and enjoy the ensuing spectacle. And I was like a clockwork toy. All they had to do was say something (anything, really) about the Bible and I was off like a hungry dog with a bone. They didn't want to hear anything that might spoil their meal, but since religion was one big joke to them, it was a safe bet.

'God's balls! "Thou shalt not take the name of the Lord thy God in vain." What is a person to do? Wear a gag? Be condemned to silence? Oswaldo, tell me you don't find that one absurd!'

I could have just let it go, but I was seventeen. And seventeen was red-rag year for me and I'd go for it like a fighting bull, to the delight of everyone else. We had the same argument just about every day: they'd run through the ten commandments, trashing them one by one. While the meats and salt fish did the rounds, I would defend the tablets of the covenant to a chorus of jeers and applause from my cousins. Far from being a rebel, I was their favourite clown. They played me and my limited repertoire like a four-stringed guitar (except that they knew that three of my strings were missing and they wanted to see if the fourth and last one would snap). It was a game in which I was the one completely dependable player: one of them threw down a gauntlet and, night after night, I grabbed it in my teeth and shook it half to death.

Once I got started, nothing could stop me until the sonorous announcement by my uncle Emiliano that pudding was about to be served. Whereupon he would deliver his punchlines and the conversation would move on to sex as the topic to accompany the dessert.

I see now all the farcical elements of those family dinners. My uncle's concluding speech was always the same and, at the time, I thought him vain and silly to pander to the assembled crowd. With hindsight, I see that his few lines were an intentional set piece merely designed to call everyone to order; and I, not he, was the fool. He always announced his summarised sexual analysis of the ten commandments as though he had just reinvented the wheel. His pseudo-theological commentary was always met by the rest of the family with approval and guffaws. Only my aunt (the long-suffering victim of his myriad infidelities) would express her own mini-rebellion by exchanging a complicit glance with me.

'"Thou shalt not kill!"' You might as well say, "Thou shalt not breathe!" And as for not coveting your neighbour's wife! What's a man supposed to be, some kind of faggot? Forget it!'

That was always the cue to move on to the sweet things. I couldn't forget my summarily interrupted monologue, but I had no choice but to shut up. Uncle Emiliano's household was patrician, not to say feudal. His word was law. To have continued shouting my defence of Christianity would have probably invoked the non-Christian (but typically Andean) response of one of the many armed men round the table shooting me in a non-fatal way. In the Andes there were social rules and laws far more integral to our society than anything the federal government could ever cook up or enforce. Within our local rules: meals were obligatory, the head of the household's word was law, and all things sweet to eat were virtually sacred.

The huge Indian cook, who hovered over the table with her misshapen bundles of fat trussed into an enormous apron, knew her cue. Beside her, fidgeting silently, were four or five child maids. Not one of them was over twelve, but not one of them retained any flicker of childish hope in her dulled, permanently lowered eyes. Life had taught them all swiftly both to know their place and to accept the constant rain of blows that kept them nailed to it for fourteen hours a day with nothing in return but the scraps from our table. When the girls were old enough – that is, over thirteen – a young patrician would be planted in their bellies, with or without their consent, by any, or sometimes all, of the males in the family as was (and sometimes still is) the custom in many 'decent' Andean households.

At the time that I lived as a guest in that luxurious mansion, I was far too concerned with my intellectual socialist zeal to notice such injustice. I was into texts and slogans, political discussions and major Marxist demands. So, ironically, although I was on a crusade against social injustice, I was so blinkered by my adolescent zeal that I did not recognise its daily enactment there. It happened in the kitchen or the back yard and I did not bother to decipher the muffled cries and sobs until years later.

I did not screw the teenage maids who were fair game to my uncle and cousins. But my abstinence, I regret to say, was not due to any purity of my soul. I had not grown up in a patrician house and so did not know that I too was entitled to shag the servants. I thought it was a perk reserved to the middle-aged. Had I known that I was licensed to screw, I would certainly have abused those Indian girls as carelessly as everyone else there did.

Like all patriarchs, my uncle Emiliano had what Hollywood would call 'presence'. And like all Andean heads of households, he was a consummate actor. Power is something that has to be nurtured and maintained. Timing was all-important. For the dinner ritual, my uncle had obviously honed his lines and their timing and orchestrated the response, because the serving of the dessert was always like a little play. As he began to pronounce 'Thou shalt not covet thy neighbour's wife', the cook and her maids shuffled into action centrestage, heaping the syrupy fruit, the quesillo, the blancmanges, and whatever else she had sweated over that day as a dessert on the table. That done, she and her gaggle of child maids cleared off, backing away like courtiers from a royal banquet. Their leaving the dining room was the cue for the table talk to get filthy and personal.

Most Venezuelans eat things so sweet they have to be washed down with several glasses of water or they cloy in your mouth and set your face like plaster of Paris. At my mother's table, our sporadic desserts were mathematically divided between us children. One tenth of a small cake or one tenth of a doughnut was more of a tease to our palates than a pleasure because, like most Venezuelans, we were addicted to sugar and craved large amounts of it.

In San Cristobal de Torondoy, we had not only been better off financially than we were in Valera, we had also been surrounded by the basic ingredients of puddings. Our own back yard provided endless supplies of delicious tropical fruit, and sugar straight from the factory sat in 24-kilo packs in our storeroom. My mother was a crystalliser of fruit par excellence and would turn out enormous jars of syrupy figs, guavas, mangoes and pawpaw for us children to feast on almost at will. Then, at San Cristobal, we had kept our own goats and chickens, so milk and eggs were readily available. On Saturdays, my mother cooked delicious quesillos and the Andean fudge, dulce de leche, which is so sweet and so concentrated it seems to defy mathematics: litres of milk, kilos of sugar and dozens of eggs are boiled into a mere smear of sticky paste. This dulce de leche was rationed out into no more than a taste per person, but a taste was enough to cause a sort of nuclear fusion in your intestine, which was both so alarming and, subsequently, satisfying that children all over the Andes brainstormed to find ways of stealing that magical sticky substance. Dulce de leche is kept in a sealed jar in a cool place. It looks a bit like the yellowy, Vaseline-based pastes used to rub on sores on goats and cows. Somebody seeing Andean fudge-paste for the first time would not possibly think, Hmm, that looks delicious – I must have some. You have to know, as we did, that the essence of sugar, the elixir of taste satisfaction, is contained in that unappetising-looking blob in a hidden jar.

Within months of my family's move to Valera from San

Cristobal, as the aftermath of the coup d'état emptied out our larder, and without either our orchard or the packs of sugar, we all craved sweets and sweetmeats. In San Cristobal, when there hadn't been any pudding or fudge to get sick on, and on the few occasions when my mother locked the fruits in syrup away, we used to eat chunks of brown sugar. In Valera, most of the time, we just yearned for it and savoured the memory of those good old days on our farm.

'Tell me what you eat and I'll tell you who you are.'

I think there is a correlation between cruelty and sugar. It was as though, in that harsh society, there had to be those sweet moments. They were like a reflection of our lives, all our lives, peppered with inflammatory chillies and softened by honeyed interludes. At every meal, you stopped destroying and dismantling, you stopped bickering and verbally poisoning, and you sweetened your mouth and savoured that sweetness. Of course, once you had swallowed, you could move back to the verbal attack with renewed vigour, but while the sweet things were in your mouth, they enforced a truce. They were like the moments when everyone stopped whatever they were doing because the serenaders under the balcony sang a song that wrapped up hearts. They were like those moments when a tune in a bar full of drunken brawling moved everyone to stop and dance in the street.

It wasn't until I went abroad that I saw that in other countries people didn't take five lumps of sugar in a small coffee and then finish off the sugar in the bowl. If it was there on the table, I would eat half a pound of jam at breakfast, as would any Andean who wasn't actually diabetic.

When my political misdemeanour landed me at my uncle Emiliano's table three times a day, I was in sugar paradise. Part of his kitchen was a constant sweet factory churning out all the old Andean favourites, which I consumed at a rate that made up for my past deprivation. My appetite was one of the few things that the grander part of my family approved of. Real men had huge appetites. A real man's worth and valour was measured in direct proportion to his capacity to eat and drink, shag and fight. I fell short on all the other counts, but I ate like a boy with a giant tapeworm and my rich uncles and cousins were proud of my gluttony.

Looking back, I am not proud of those months in Valera. In fact, it is one of the periods of my life of which I am least proud. I didn't understand the risks I was running and I was too pig-headed and rebellious to listen to anyone's advice. For my family, who did understand the risks I was running, not just for me, but also for them, it must have been a nightmare. It was as though I had lost my mind. I was like a clockwork toy that was permanently overwound. Fifty years later, if a boy did what I'd done, it would be assumed he was on drugs. Our drugs were drink and sugar and adrenaline. No one had even heard of amphetamines in Valera. I buzzed around doing damage and stirring things up until I learnt that lesson any peasant can tell you: trouble comes from the outside.

CHAPTER XIII

In 1952, when I was eighteen, the dictator got it into his head to get himself democratically elected. The days of the city states were about to come to an end, and with them my own days of playing politics.

For all my adolescent delinquency, there were a number of incidents, accidents and crimes that occurred in Valera during my brief visit, but which were in no way connected to me or the little delinquent group I founded. So, the fire in the Pacheco's grain warehouse was nothing to do with us. Nor was I the one to put sugar in the tanks of all the school buses, 'destroying their engines, and thus depriving an entire generation of the opportunity to read and write'. I did not put that pile of dog shit on the cathedral steps, or smear the cushion of the confessional with spunk. And I did not strangle the twin babies who were found dead in their cot at the convent orphanage, and, as far as I know, they did not have my initials branded into their dead cheeks.

I did a lot of silly, juvenile things. Some I did because I wanted to make a point for my group, and some I did because I felt rebellious. So I played into the hands of my detractors and gave a lot of fuel to my enemies. But the things I did were never overtly cruel. So I did not stab a prostitute on the Calle Vargas and bite her left nipple when she refused to join my group. (Years later, in Montmartre, a prostitute bit *me* on the nipple, and the ensuing infection nearly killed me, but that is another story, and can be told later. The grains of truth get muddled and ring the wrong bells.)

And last, but not least, I did proselytise the aims and tenets of communism to a mostly unwilling audience, but I never used physical force when my reluctant audience wanted to leave. So I did not tie up Crazy Carmen (the town bicycle) and hang her by her feet from a mango tree. Nor did I 'thrash the poor demented girl to within an inch of her life, until, through this barbaric torture, she was forced to recite *The Communist Manifesto*'.

That was written by someone who didn't know me, and who didn't know Crazy Carmen either. Crazy Carmen was a deaf mute. For fifteen years she had done nothing but grunt and spread her legs. If Fellini had been around in Valera then, he might have tried to give her a look in on his *Satyricon*: she was a natural, a grotesque nymphomaniac. I didn't ever try to cast her for anything. I never even screwed her (which was another thing that made me different in Valera). She was free and willing, and it was standard procedure for every boy in the town to give her a go. I did go down to her shack a few times. People took her food, and she ate it all covered with dirt and flies. Nene had filled my head with this 'finding a girl and falling in love' thing, and sticking it into Crazy Carmen was so not that, I couldn't do it. I was pretty knotted up with the 'sex equals sin' of the Church, and I was looking for romance and poetry. Well, the Church also said that masturbation was a sin and would bring on hairy hands, blindness and, eventually, insanity. My religious fervour did not stop my hairy hands from stroking the straw many, many times a day. And it would only have taken one look at Crazy Carmen to see she was no Juliet to my Romeo, but despite that, I did go to her squat 'a few times', and it wasn't to read her *The Communist Manifesto*.

I didn't do any of the things the papers said I did to her. But I did keep going to her shack with the intention of screwing her: it was what everyone did. It was free and easy and almost a compulsory rite of passage. I was seventeen and broke and my testosterone was rioting. I had been a few times to the prostitutes on the Calle Vargas and paid for several ten-minute goes. Once, on my seventeenth birthday, my friends had even clubbed together to give me a double turn. But I was of an age when I wanted a lot more than that several times a day and yet I didn't have enough money to go more than once every six weeks. There were several of us in the same boat, hence the popularity of Crazy Carmen, who was both insatiable and free.

My friends said, 'You just have to close your eyes or put a paper bag over her head and she is red hot. Once you are in there,' they insisted, 'it doesn't matter.'

What my friends hadn't mentioned was the smell. Crazy Carmen was into sex, but she wasn't into personal hygiene. Lust took me towards her and disgust and shame turned me back. On each visit, I would slink back to my uncle's house feeling horrible as I picked my way over the slum debris. I was ashamed of my desire, but even more than that, I was ashamed that people had to live in such filth. And mostly, I was ashamed that I could have even thought of having taken advantage of someone reduced to the kind of dire poverty that Crazy Carmen lived in. Worse even than the slum barrio, her squat defined her as an outcast of the outcasts. She was an Andean version of an Indian untouchable without the Indian caste system that would, say, in Calcutta, have made her unscrewable.

Lust makes men blind. I was brought up blind, we all were. I was brought up to feel sorry for my own family's poverty compared to the upper rungs of the Araujo clan. We weren't brought up to see the grinding poverty all around us. It was there, but invisible. I had to go to Trujillo, where there was vastly less destitution, to begin to consider the plight of most of my compatriots: their drudgery and actual hunger. Yet even in Trujillo, the communist theory was just that: it was theory, it was a creed, it was an idea. International communism was about the masses. Individuals never came into it – unless, of course, they were the venerated Marx, Engels, Lenin and Stalin. No one else mattered as an individual. We were all part of a mass, a rising mass like a huge bowl of dough. We talked about entire countries and about governments and political parties and their needs. We never talked about people as individuals. We never talked about helping the likes of the homeless in our streets. We were going to save the world, so we had no time to see what was actually happening in the real world under the rarefied stratosphere of party politics.

Despite that, it was in Trujillo that I first became aware that the world, as such, might require any changing at all. And it was there that my mind widened from considering the fortunes and fate of my family and friends to contemplating the collective fate of the human race and working towards changing it for the better. Socialism alone could not open my eyes. I read about the terrible plight of the workers and their unjust oppression, but it was only when I returned to my home town of Valera that I actually began to see that plight. And again, only when confronted with the stark contrast of the overabundance of my uncle Emiliano's household, and the startling lack of it in the sprawling shanty town, did my eyes begin to see what poverty really meant.

My eyes opened in the dark as I picked my way back and forth across the trash field en route to Crazy Carmen. It was as though I had had cataracts, and they had been surgically removed. I began to see my world: to actually see it. It shocked me. It shocked me so much I didn't know who I was any more. I had to do something. I had to open other people's eyes.

Creeping back from my sordid abortive forays to Crazy Carmen's, I saw families as big as mine huddled under a single sheet of corrugated iron. I saw naked children curled around their mothers like baby rats in a nest, lying in dust and mud. I saw beggars sleeping in ditches as they clutched an almost empty sack, and I realised that in that one torn piece of hessian a man (not unlike my own father to look at) had all he owned. I saw street children living in a disused drainage pipe. Their big eyes stared out of their blackened faces so that from a distance they looked like a cluster of bush babies. In the dark I could not see who they were, but I realised that I must have seen them hundreds of times before on my way to and from school, and on my way to and from the library, and they must have begged from me, as they begged from everyone, and I must have ignored them, as we all did, without ever wondering what their orphaned lives were like, or where they slept or what they ate. If I had noticed them at all, it was to see their dirt and scabs and to avoid them as my mother always told us we should.

As I sneaked over the wasteland to satisfy my own sordid longings, I saw a young couple in love who had sneaked out to sit under a tree and be alone. They held each other protectively and spoke in entranced whispers. They were locked into their own cosmic space and oblivious to everything around them (including me as I eavesdropped on their poetic mutterings). They were dirt-poor and uneducated and yet they described their feelings for each other in a lyrical and deeply moving way. Their future was each other. Among the shit and the carcasses of dead dogs and the scavenging vermin, they had twinned their souls in just the way Nene had told me we had to do as the highest aim of our lives. The destitute couple under the ficus tree had done this when I, with all my learning and yearning, had failed to do so. They had something pure and true. Their clothes were rags and their skins were blotchy with ringworm that glowed fluorescent in the night, in little perfect green circles. Those glowing green circles haunted me and have stayed in my memory as one of my guiding lights: life is about people and people are guided by love.

It wasn't as simple as that. It took me many more years to truly see the light and to focus its beam, but it started there in the wasteland.

What struck me most were the little domestic details. I saw that even the destitute washed their clothes and left them to dry on thorn bushes just as my own mother did. And in a tumbledown, one-room reed shack a family was gathered round a flickering oil lamp listening to a story. As I approached furtively, giving the shack a wide berth, several of that family burst out laughing. That laughter frightened me. What was there to laugh about in their dire straits? People like me, like my family and friends, laughed. If outcasts could laugh too, then I had no understanding at all of who they were. If they could laugh and love, if they could feel things, then they could not be that other species I had heard about (the one that had no feelings and, like plants, felt no pain).

I began to see that those people, the marginalised, the outcasts, were actually very like us: very like me. And, therefore, their suffering was as great as mine would have been.

Once that sense of brotherhood, of shared blood, dawned on me in the shanty town of Valera, it was like a viral infection and it took over my system. Almost everyone I knew was either blind or blinkered to the poverty around us. It had always been there, they shrugged. It was a part of life and I should just thank my lucky stars that I had been born into the patriarchs and not the peasants.

I knew that it would never be enough for me to thank my stars. I also knew that as a contribution, it wasn't enough for me to just forgo shagging some poor mad girl. I had to do something more. I had to change things. It was almost as though some of Carmen's frenzied craziness lodged in my brain like an infestation of head lice. They gave me no peace. And like head lice, my ideas were literally biting and stinging me at that time. By comparison, my boyhood will appear to have been the calmest, easiest time of my life. Since it is all relative, yes, they were the least violent years I have known; but I was crazy and out of control.

Give or take, until I was seventeen, I called the shots. From 1952, everything changed, and the trigger was the electoral campaign in which Perez Jimenez, the dictator of Venezuela, became sensitive to the criticism of the world and decided to get democratically elected and thus continue his repression while looking good in the eyes of the West.

CHAPTER XIV

By 1952, the easy part of my life was over. It hadn't always seemed easy, and I certainly didn't always make it easy, but those years were the slow and simple part. As I say, my life took off from the time of the general election.

There were two clandestine political parties: the Adecos (Democratic Action Party) and the Communist Party. The legal parties included the URD, a left-wing party, which the communists campaigned for and supported, hoping for a coalition.

The central university in Caracas was still shut down, so Nene, my first mentor, was back in town. He could not have been less interested in politics or this forthcoming election. As a wealthy young man of twenty, he had all he wanted: plays and a social life. All his talk about having a different spirit and having to show it seemed to have gone overboard. For the first time since he had converted me to truth through poetry, I disagreed with him. It was he who had fanned my passion and now I felt passionately that I was right and he was wrong. Someone had to make a stand, to campaign, to show their face, and naturally that someone was me.

It was early days, of course, and I saw injustice only where I chose to see it. Like a war correspondent back from his first mission to the Front, I had been to the wasteland beyond the town and seen its destitution and I returned filled with a revolutionary zeal to right wrongs. I could have personally righted many wrongs in small, practical and pragmatic ways on my home front in and around my uncle's household, but I was not ready for that. Nor did I notice, in my sweeping zealotry, the small but sustained flow of good deeds performed by my aunt. While I disdained her as a bastion of capitalism (which she was), I failed to see how she simultaneously sustained not one but dozens of peasant households behind her husband's back with clandestine gifts of food, materials, money and medical supplies. While I threw myself into the big issues, I remained blind to what went on in my immediate surroundings. Only when I had time to reflect – and spending prolonged periods of time in solitary confinement in a prison cell does offer that – did I see my own shortcomings and the faults and merits of those around me.

While I was campaigning in Valera, I still was not ready to see my friends, my allies or my enemies as individuals. I had spent the run-up to the election campaign writing slogans. I was into slogans, and in my head I lumped everyone and everything into slogans. By that reckoning, my aunt was an oligarchic capitalist and I was a socialist militant.

Under the URD, we (my slowly growing group of adolescent leftist followers and me) launched Leonelli as our candidate. Leonelli was a real nitwit, but he was what we had. There were plenty of people in opposition to the dictator. A few of us were communists, most were with the URD, and some were just looking to get Perez Jimenez out of power. Soon, there were whole gangs of us campaigning. I just took the lead.

For me it was entirely political; for my family, it was more about family. I have explained how my family was as reactionary as they come. They were so much on the dictator Perez Jimenez's side that many of them held official positions in his government. The ones who didn't adored his dictatorship and were so far up his arse that all you could see were the soles of their shoes. Don Atilio Araujo, the governor, was at the pinnacle of that power in the Andes. He was the grand señor. And he also behaved like a true gentleman. He didn't intervene to stop my campaigning, even though I was trying like crazy to get him chucked out of office. He didn't even remonstrate. I lived in an Araujo household, surrounded by Perez Jimenez officials and campaigners, and I sat down to eat as a traitor at their table. Like Atilio Araujo, they did not restrain me.

My father, however, was another matter. He was churned up with rage and indignation that his own son was sticking his neck out and biting the hand that fed him. I probably had more contact with my father during that electoral campaign than at any other time in my life. We had screaming rows in which he brought up my ingratitude, madness, delinquency and repulsive ideas. I threw out that our family was a great family. The Araujos didn't have to support a two-bit dictator – they were worth more than that. They had helped shape not only Venezuela's but Latin America's history over two centuries, and they could again. He didn't believe all the calumny that was whizzing around Valera about me. He didn't believe that I desecrated the church and strangled babies; he just thought I was full of bullshit, and ought to be gagged and bound for a few months.

In Venezuela, we don't like being told what to do. On the whole, we won't be told what to do by anyone outside of the family. Because the Adecos had already been in power and given the underdogs their day, there were plenty of voters ready to put them back in power so the underdogs could have their day again. One way or another, the dictator had made himself pretty unpopular with the country as a whole over the previous year: hence his reprisals and the need to whitewash his image by holding this free election.

After the elections were held on 2 December 1952, Perez Jimenez announced that he had won. The polling stations, though, announced that he hadn't. These polling stations insisted that he had lost, and that his party had tampered with the count. Nationwide there were calls for a recount. Since Perez Jimenez wasn't an aspiring politician who wanted to be elected but a ruthless dictator trying to whitewash his image abroad, when a democratic recount was formally requested, he put an end to the election game and ordered a coup d'état. It was an easy enough move. He already had the power – he just had to make sure of it. And he did in time-honoured Latin-American style.

Absolute power has, by its nature, to contain a large element of fear. To ensure that this fear element was properly covered, the Seguridad Nacional came into being. It was the Venezuelan equivalent of the Gestapo. Its formation obviously owed much to the German model, and actively imitated the Gestapo's tactics of cruelty, ruthlessness and arbitrary terror. Unlike its Hitlerian prototype, though, it not only lacked organisational brilliance, thank goodness, it lacked almost any organisation at all.

Despite that, it was autonomous and rampaging; and Atilio Araujo (who was still, nominally, the governor of Valera) told my father he could no longer protect me. He said that the Seguridad Nacional was going to kill me for sure. There was no time to lose. I had to be spirited out of the country. We, the opposition, hadn't reckoned on a coup. I, personally, had been convinced that we, the opposition, would win. I was up to my neck in Venezuela, and I had thoroughly stuck my neck out. After the coup, there was nowhere to go but abroad.

My father made arrangements to send me to Spain. Despite the insularity of Valera and the refusal of most Andeans to heed or even acknowledge the outside world, everyone who was anyone in Valera had cousins abroad. My own family had cousins all over Spain. That may sound like a paradox, but I have already said that, sexually, Venezuelans are like goats. The secondary effect of this is that we all have hundreds of cousins. Although most of these cousins never strayed as far as Caracas, let alone abroad, some of them had drifted across the Atlantic and established mini enclaves in Spain. If Venezuelans travel now, they go all over the world. For several decades before that, they went to either Miami or Madrid (being two places where Spanish is spoken and there is no need to learn so much as a word in a foreign tongue).

But when I was a boy, Miami hadn't become the Hispanic Mecca yet, so the standard foreign destination was Madrid. It was rumoured that from Madrid a few scions fanned out across the whole of Europe, but no one knew for sure. Once any of these cousins left, none of them returned, so very little was known about that country or any other. From what I had heard and read, I didn't want to go to Spain. As far as I was concerned, the only good things to come out of Spain were its writers and painters and the writer-philosopher Miguel de Unamuno, and they had done just that: got out. I didn't want to jump out of the frying pan into the fire by leaving our new dictatorship for General Franco's older one.

I wanted to go to Paris. I had read enormous amounts about Paris, to the point when it had become a sort of dream destination. I told my father in no uncertain terms that I didn't want to go to Spain and that I did want to go to Paris. I could have said 'France', but France was Paris to my still ignorant mind; anything beyond the capital was of so little interest to me I refused to acknowledge that it existed.

Since reason applied to my behaviour was an alien concept at that time of my life, I didn't see my escape as such. I saw it as a continuation of my studies and as a step towards the glorious future (as an admired and respected philosopher) which I was convinced awaited me. So I not only didn't want to go to Spain (which did not figure in that future) but I felt I had to go to Paris (which was a necessary step on my path to academic glory). While my father struggled to save my life, I fought him at every turn. He said Spain, I said Paris. He was beside himself with rage, and accused me of once again failing to see the predicament I was in.

'You've got to go, or they are going to kill you!'

That much was clear to me, too, but he was right: my sense of reality was atrophied. I had to go, but I had to go to Paris! I longed for Paris: to study at the Sorbonne, to walk the boulevards Rimbaud had walked, and to see the Seine. My father accused me, on top of everything else, of being a dilettante who just wanted to lounge around in Paris while my family suffered for my sins back home. I refused to listen to him. I was driven by two impulses, to change the world by haranguing it, and to change the world through philosophical thought. God knows my father hadn't seen a lot in me, but one thing he knew he could count on was for me to be pig-headed. So Paris won.

Just for the record, we shouted at each other a lot on the day after the Coup of '52, but we used words and words only. I didn't 'come at him with a knife'. The scars on his body were the scars from his gunslinging days.

I was a militant, a communist and a reckless hothead. I was a dreamer and thinker who yearned to study philosophy at Freiburg University and at the Sorbonne. I was a braggart and a bigmouth. And I was just eighteen. My birthday came a few weeks before my departure. That year, with so little to celebrate, it came and went without any special attention. We never paid much heed to children's birthdays in the Andes; it isn't part of our tradition. That we do so nowadays is just another sign of the Americanisation of our world. When I was a boy, anniversaries were celebrated for the dead; the living didn't get honoured just for having survived another year. My mother gave me an overcoat she had had made. It was to wear abroad. And my sisters made me a batch of vanilla fudge, which they delivered to my uncle Emiliano's house with the new coat.

My father and Atilio Araujo between them made all the complicated arrangements to have me smuggled out of Venezuela to France. I don't know to this day how they planned that escape. All I knew was that a condition of this escape was that I had to go via Spain. My father was the sort of person who couldn't step down once he got into a fight. He only knew how to shoot his way out of situations. He hadn't been able to win me round to his Spanish suggestion, but he couldn't let me go directly to Paris without losing face.

Before anyone else sees my life laid bare, I am seeing it myself. What comes across to me most clearly is my lack of forethought. It stands out the more for my insistence on that dual strand as a thinker. And I see the jumps, introduced from the outside, that made me become something I was not.

There is a French biochemist, Jacques Monod, who won a Nobel Prize; I don't remember in what year, but it was in the 1970s. Monod (who was once a Marxist himself) wrote a fascinating book, which is conclusive for anyone who has any doubts about the horrors of Marxism, and about its biological and theological errors. In it, he discusses the evolution of the world and its evolutionary problems. The book is called *Chance and Necessity*.

My life has been a balance between chance and necessity, in

which the only thing I have done is accept a kind of gift. For example, I wasn't the son my father wanted; I was the other one. But I was born, and my brother died, so it had to be. And I was never going to be a politician. I was never interested in politics. I was interested in philosophy. But the politics happened, and I have made the best I could of them. I have done it well because it was there, and it was pushed my way.

Later, I was going to become a Sartrean thinker – and I am still fascinated by Jean-Paul Sartre's thinking (which is about choice, and where that liberty lies that we could choose). That is what I would have been and would have done, if chance and necessity had not made things jump.

I have never really chosen any path that I've been down.

For Monod, that extraordinary jump nature makes from inorganic to organic is fundamental. He dwells on those inanimate particles that group and become animate. That jump had no reason to happen. It just happened. And then, once it had happened (by chance), it became a necessity: a must, for that living organism to reproduce itself endlessly.

How the hell did nature orchestrate that?

I don't know. And following that line of thought, I don't know if everything happened to me because I stopped being a child at that precise moment and became an adolescent. And I don't know if the race began as it did because I was just eighteen (just a man) when I left my country. I had no choice; I had to go then. I had to flee Venezuela because of my communism, and I didn't even want to be a communist. Of course, in some ways, I brought it upon myself. But I know I would have chosen the pen and not the sword.

Once my pattern was traced, then I could choose a bit. But it was different: it wasn't a true choice.

For example, once you are in the Communist Party, choosing is difficult. For communists, there is only one real choice: to join. After that, you obey. In other circumstances you can choose. Some of those choices can turn you into a traitor, a coward, a hero, or whatever else.

Like Wittgenstein I can say that 'I sit astride life like a bad rider on a horse'. And I can affirm that 'I only owe it to the horse's good nature that I am not thrown off at this very moment'. It has always been like that: with first this horse, and then that horse, and from time to time a donkey. For me, things just happened. That is a great ambiguity. Sometimes I don't know if that is my particular fate, or if it is that of twentieth-century man in general.

PART 2

CHAPTER XV

I arrived in Spain in the new year of 1953, and I stayed there until the following July. My visit was the compromise I had made with my father: a transition en route to France. Those months in Spain were decisive ones in my life. I have never spoken to anyone about them before now, about what happened there. And yet, every time I think at all seriously about my life and what I have lived, I see the origins of so much of it back there, in Spain.

My exile was not unwelcome to me. In fact, by the time I left for Europe, I was delighted to be going there, and to be nearing, albeit circuitously, Germany and Tübingen, where a friend of mine had been washed up, and where the philosopher Heidegger was currently lecturing. I decided that, if need be, I would bleach my skin and dye my hair blond to creep past any vestigial racial laws to be the great Heidegger's disciple. From Tübingen, I would get to Freiburg. If need be, I would even walk to Freiburg. Europe was a big adventure. Freiburg was my ultimate goal, Paris was my interim one, and Spain was a stopover: a sop to my father.

The journey to Spain was the first time I had ever set foot on a boat and my first close contact with water in any quantity bigger than that which could fit into a bucket. Apart from the odd sulphur tub at the thermal baths of Mototán, I had never even taken a bath (we always had showers at home). I didn't learn to swim until I was a grown man. Nor had I ever been to the seaside. I had read and heard about beaches and waves, yachts and boats, and I had passed through the port of Bobures as a boy and caught a glimpse from afar of the dockside, but I had never actually seen the sea.

I was so cocksure about myself and my very superior knowledge of all things cosmopolitan that I wasn't expecting to be overawed before my journey had begun. It was my intention to arrive in Paris and take it by storm with my erudition and wit, rather in the way the young Rimbaud had done. Yet it was the journey itself which first shrunk my big head to something little more than a pygmy trophy. First, the ship was enormous to my eyes. I took one look at that mass of iron and thought that anything that heavy must surely sink. I knew before embarking that the voyage would take over two weeks, but I had failed to grasp that those two weeks would be spent either sharing a tiny, airless cabin with a fat man who snored like a muzzled hog, or vomiting my guts out over the deck railing. I was dazed and confused by the time we reached Spain.

After an emotional farewell to the Caraqueñan cousins who escorted me to the ship and my semi-clandestine embarkation with the connivance of the ship's purser (who would only put my name on the passenger list after we left Venezuelan territorial waters), I watched the shoreline grow smaller from the deck with a sense of elation mixed equally with foreboding. Between La Guaira and Port of Spain, the shortest leg of the journey, I curled up in my bunk and stirred only to throw up. Being inexperienced at the latter, my aim was poor and I several times managed to splash either the fat man's bunk or the fat man himself, thus making an enemy of my travelling companion from day one.

Upon arrival in Trinidad, I tottered down the gangplank like a drunk, gripping hold of the handrail as I staggered ashore with my day pass. Noticing my sorry state, the friendly purser assured me that I would soon find my sea legs. In that, he was wrong – after another fifty years I am still looking for them.

Port of Spain put me firmly in my place. I could not understand one word of what anyone said, having never come across English before, and I managed to find my glimpse of the island weird but not really wonderful. Even little things like bread were worrying. We did not eat bread in Venezuela. We ate flat corn cakes called arepas. And the 'coffee' in Port of Spain was a curious watery concoction. What perturbed me most, though, was having absolutely no idea of what that island was about. I found that very disconcerting and I crawled back like a snail with my ignorance on my back for what I imagined would be another gruelling twenty hours of wall-to-wall vomit. Twenty hours? It was more like twenty days! At least, it went on without stop for ten interminable days and nights.

When I eventually disembarked on Spanish soil, the confidence I had lost on board did not return and come with me. As a result, I found everything that should have been part of the average young traveller's challenge and joy, a terrible effort. My uncles (probably pre-empting my spineless reaction to the world at large) had arranged for me to be shoe-horned into Iberia via the chaperoning role of one of our many distant cousins. My instructions were to make my way by train to Madrid and then to put myself under that cousin's protection.

It is another curious characteristic of Valera (so claustrophobic, narrow-minded, xenophobic and self-obsessed) that on the rare occasions when its sons and daughters do manage to rise up to the surface for some air, they tend to leap out of the cauldron and fly as far away as they can. Even in the 1950s, I could traipse across Europe from Valerano to Valerano, finding them in the most obscure places. They were like the legendary travelling Chinaman. For me, they were stepping-stones.

The sheer numbers of people and cars intimidated me to the point where I was afraid to cross the street. I had been told to make my way there by train. Well, that sounded fine in Venezuela, where we had no railways. But when you have never seen a train outside of a picture, then the noise and the steam and the size of one is truly alarming.

In Spain, at least everyone spoke Spanish, though no one spoke to *me*. Worse still, no one knew me or even knew who my family was. And, apart from the grudging concierge of my cousin's building, no one seemed to know my cousin either. That was truly shocking to me and brought home more than anything else what an alien place I had come to. How could this distant cousin live here and yet no one know him? How could he be 'gone away' and yet no one know where he had gone? What kind of city was this? And what kind of people lived here? I had never met people who were not driven by intense curiosity about what everyone around them was doing. And I had never been anywhere where strangers existed.

Hanging around in the street outside my elusive contact's apartment, I felt violently homesick.

Numb with a mixture of culture shock and cold, I found that my cousin was 'out'. A small grille in a massive, carved door clanked shut like a prison door, locking me out in the freezing street.

Reading about winter and feeling its sting are two very different matters. When I rang the doorbell only to be told by a sadistically jubilant concierge that my cousin wasn't in, I felt as though the wrinkled old bag who told me this had kicked me in the stomach. I felt completely lost. My suitcase was hideously heavy and my arms were absurdly inadequate to the task of carrying it.

In Valera, when someone isn't in, it makes no real difference: a visitor is ushered in anyway in their absence and made much of by the servants to rest and drink water and coffee and to recover from the trials of travelling. A visiting cousin could not possibly have to wait in the street just because the person they were visiting was out. And I had travelled! I had crossed the Atlantic Ocean! I had spent weeks getting to this cousin's house: what kind of hospitality left family out in the gutter like a dog? Bemused and insulted, surprised and with mounting fear, I sat in a bar and drank coffee. But even bars, it seemed, resented the intrusion of outsiders. The hostile stares of innumerable Spanish workmen made me feel so uncomfortable that I eventually moved back out onto the street.

I had no gloves and my fingers seized up around the handle of my case. I waited in the street, waited in a different bar, returned to the first, returned to the building, and all the while a ball of panic grew in my throat to the point where it literally stole my voice.

The entire day passed in slow motion. I hadn't wanted to come to Spain in the first place and every moment of that first day underlined the hugeness of my mistake in being there at all. As the

cold day ended and the bitter wind increased, my mounting fear
turned to panic. What would I do? Where would I sleep?

Everything and everyone struck me as grey and dour, and filled
with an insidious crawling lethargy. It was not the sensuous
lethargy of the tropics; it was more of an austere shackling of life.
Even the darkness crept and crawled. The sun did not go down as
it does in the tropics with a clean sweep from day to night. There
was a no-man's-land in the sky, a twilight zone that lingered
threateningly. It drained the last vestiges of sunlight in a cruel pro-
traction. I leant against a chill wall across the street from my
would-be resting place and contemplated how to survive a night
in the open in that inhospitable city.

The street was busier than it had been all day. I supposed
people were going home from work. I envied them all – all those
slow, hostile people who had homes to go to. I began to imagine
my first letters home. I began to feel ashamed of my ineptitude:
this was not the triumphant entry into Europe that I had boasted
of to my friends. This huddling against cold stone like a miserable
lizard was not the sort of behaviour to be expected from a dash-
ing young hothead like myself. By lecturing myself, I merely
managed to keep upright instead of giving in to my true inclination, which was to slide down the wall and slump onto the
pavement. My presence was attracting a lot of not-very-friendly
stares. The more pedestrians there were, the more hostile these
stares became. Several people had accosted me and suggested I
move on. By the time night had smothered the street, I knew that
I would have to go somewhere else: but where?

To give myself some much needed courage, I began to whistle.
Tunes have never been my forte, but I think my mounting desperation must have done something dire to the volume of that
whistle because my cousin's concierge came rushing out of her
building across the street and began to threaten to call the police.
A little crowd gathered, as mostly women emerged from doorways
like woodworm from their holes. A big man with a squint stepped
up to me. Despite his vast frame and his intimidatingly rough face,
he asked me not unkindly, 'Where are you going, son?'

Where indeed? I had been whistling the Augostín Lara song
about the Bar Chicote. Not knowing what else to say, I blurted

that out. The man grinned knowingly and laughed, shooing some of the women away from me.

'You're in the wrong part of town,' he told me. Then he pointed out the way to the Bar Chicote and sent me off in its direction, giving me such a violent pat on the back that I almost choked.

Luckily, the Bar Chicote was relatively near by and after a brisk ten-minute walk I reached the only place in Madrid that was familiar to me, albeit from a Mexican song.

At that time, the Chicote was a bar of prostitutes frequented mostly by middle-aged working men. As soon as I walked in (lugging my suitcase), the whores made much of me. What with my youth and my generous offers of whisky, they were so welcoming that I ended up spending the night with one of the girls. Rarely can they have found a client who was happier to be there than I was that night. It was also the first time in my life that I had slept an entire night with a woman. Before, it had always been ten minutes on the Calle Vargas, twenty if you paid double. I woke up with the Madrileña on my first morning in Europe. It was 7 a.m. I left, marvelling at how my life had changed, and went out into the street, thinking to find the sun up, as it had been all my life in Venezuela. But it was dark outside: deathly dark. It frightened me.

CHAPTER XVI

When I finally tracked down someone who knew my cousin, I was told he had left for Salamanca. My entire European plan began with finding this cousin in Spain. Like the first domino in a stack, he would lead me to my other cousins, who would sort out my accommodation, my food and my life until phase two began in Paris. I seemed to have no choice but to go to Salamanca and find the elusive key to my visit.

I never found my cousin in Salamanca, but I found a dark side to myself, and my subsequent conflict with it was so intense that my struggle with religion resolved itself. I went to Salamanca quite by chance. I could have gone anywhere in Spain, but I went there to a society so closed, so repressed, sinister and bitter, that even now I find it hard to describe. Subservience to the Church was total and grim. Everywhere you looked, there were widows in black, nuns in black, and a bleakness of the human soul. The bells tolled for everyone in Salamanca. And the bells tolled day and night. The churches were brimful of chanting, whispering men and women. In Valera, churches only ever filled for funerals. But in Spain, they seemed to be full from dawn till dusk, and life was all about sin. To my young, tropical eyes, the contrast with Valera was so huge it was like Sartre's *Argos*. Everyone who lived in Salamanca seemed to be spying out sin. It was a time when the whole of Spain was spying on each other, with every Spaniard lacerating the next, for varying degrees of guilt.

Spain had lived its moment of liberty, but after the civil war it had been battened back under fascism and the stranglehold of the Church. Salamanca lived and breathed a terror of 'the Reds', of what communism could be. People talked only of God and death, of sin and eternal suffering. I became locked into that vengeful reaction. Although caution had never been something I exercised before, I developed it now to the point of paranoia. Given the climate of Franco's fascism there, it was probably just as well, but in my case, the fear of becoming known compounded with the fear of death.

I had promised my father to stay for six months in Spain. He was, of course, under the impression that I would be in the bosom of our extended family, and not cowering alone in a freezing boarding house in Salamanca. I was there in the days before Valera had a proper postal system or telephones, so my family had no way of knowing what I did or didn't go through. Letters were sent if and when someone was travelling back to Caracas, and that didn't happen very often. Despite my father not being able to know what I got up to, to appease him, and to prove to both him and myself that I was not going 'to lounge around', as he called it, I registered at the university in the faculty of Law. I studied hard, like a monk in a cell, in my dreary hotel room. That winter, which was the first ever winter of my life, was very intense and very cold.

What I know of the city of Salamanca – its architecture, even its skyline – I have read about subsequently in books. While I was there, living in it, it was a city I almost never saw. All I saw was the inside of my books and the inside of my depression.

Three months into my visit, I witnessed Easter in Salamanca. Easter for us, in Valera, was about eating and getting drunk. When I was a boy, there was a visit to the church and a little procession down the dusty street of San Cristobal with the gaudy tin leaves around the crucifix glittering in the sun while a straggle of peasants whooped and cheered, before going off to fly their kites. When I got older, we dropped the procession, and just flew the kites. Easter, though, was a holiday, and holidays were supposed to be fun. Easter in Salamanca shocked me profoundly. It was the first direct point of reference between the religion I had known and grown up with, and the one I was living in Spain. Theirs was an Easter of unleashed fanaticism, of a religious fervour that obliterated everything else. Monks with their backs trickling blood lashed themselves in the streets. Sinister men in hoods wailed in the alleyways. People crawled in the procession, leaving dark trails on the flagstones like brown snails' glair. Old people with torn knees crawled for Christ. The noise in the streets was like an embodied madness, there was crying and wailing, sobbing and screaming.

One of the few people I saw on a daily basis was the chambermaid at the boarding house where I was staying. She had not changed her clothes (or washed them) in all those three months, and she stank like a badger. She worked with a mute subservience such as I had never seen. I had given up trying to say good morning to her, because it threw her into such fear that it meant my room went uncleaned for at least a week afterwards. In three months, we had never exchanged a word, nor had I ever heard her speak even to the dragon who ran the house, but she returned from the Easter procession semi-hysterical and screaming that she had seen the Seven Wonders.

I can't tell you how much Easter in Salamanca depressed me. It was like a big black blanket smothering everything. It blocked out sunlight itself; and it unravelled and forced its threads choking and strangling everyone and everything. It was like the big, hairy, bird-eating tarantulas that had so terrified me as a child, but merged with the deadly sting of the insidious black widow.

Although it took several months for me to come to terms with my religious doubts, that Easter, with its black trappings, was a traumatic experience. I tried to incorporate that Spanish fanaticism with God, Catholicism and the Church as I knew them. I couldn't do it. It just didn't fit.

In the end, I lost my faith and became the anti-Catholic, and anti-clerical, man I am today. My faith had been deeply rooted, and as I lost it, I felt a need to go back to its roots. I read again a number of fundamental philosophical texts, and also Marxist thinking. With communism outlawed, the latter wasn't so easy. There were only two Marxist books in the Law faculty library (there were none in the public one). The ones in the faculty were *Das Kapital* and *The Communist Manifesto*. Re-reading the communist ideology, I found it hollow. It didn't touch me, and I wondered how I could have ever thought it could. If that was communism, then I wasn't a communist, and the realisation made me more depressed than ever. Most of what I read, though, were religious books, none of which was able to ease my dilemma. Occasionally I read other things, but I was on a mission to save my soul and in that darkness I rarely let any lightness in.

Most memorable of those other things were Rilke's *Three Requiems*. In Spain I read and re-read my favourite poem, 'Requiem for a Friend'. I returned to it every afternoon, as a touchstone to life as I made my way through the gloomy streets.

There was an acrid smell of charcoal from every doorway. In the mornings, there were endless funeral processions, as though, day by day, the Inquisitorial populace of Salamanca was whittled away. No place has ever so nearly eclipsed me as Salamanca did. No prison cell, however squalid, small or dark, has ever effaced my spirit as that city had. And it felt as though all around me there were the human dregs of those who had already been effaced. It felt as though it was literally chewing us up. I came from the tropics and was used to seeing cripples. Gangrene was a fact of life in Valera, and the odd missing leg was unremarkable. But Salamanca was so full of people missing bits and pieces (scarred by the civil war), it was as though the Grim Reaper was running a hire-purchase agreement on the entire town. Madrid had probably been full of cripples, too, but somehow I hadn't noticed them. In the freezing gloom of Salamanca, it felt as though winter had frostbitten limbs and faces. With all its windows closed, and its citizens hushed and dulled, it was a city in mourning. It was blackened by soot, draped in black cloths, black shawls, black suits and black looks.

From huddled, half-empty bars, the odour of sour wine and charcoal belched onto the grey pavements. Bars were for men only. I never sought out the other bars, like the Chicote in Madrid, where prostitutes went. I suppose they were there somewhere, but my dick was one of the first parts of me to die in Salamanca. 'Decent' women never raised their eyes except to spy out guilt. I was a foreigner, and foreigners were trouble. And I was a dark, hairy foreigner – a Moor perhaps? – a threat, for sure. In Valera, I had been aware of the surrounding lethargy: that heat-induced, amoebic stupor, which I lived on my guard against. In Spain, there was a sour lethargy, a collective lack of will. It was a mass ecrasia, a cancer of the soul.

The hoof clops, the subdued shouts of delivery boys and vendors, the rattling of traffic over cobbles, the whispered prayers and the relentless clanging of church bells invaded my head. I slept fitfully, if at all, trying to square the Spain I had found with the Spain I had read about. Where were the enlightenment, the life, the liberty, the colour and excitement of Lorca and Machado? In Pio Baroja I had read about half-starved peasants scratching the sun-baked earth to bung in their onions and then trudging for hours to get back to some hovel to suck on a crust of stale bread. I could have dealt with drudgery; what I couldn't deal with was the depression and the overwhelming sense of death. And I wasn't in a barren field full of hungry peasants at the turn of the century. I was in a great university town in 1953. I found the city itself so soul-destroying, I never once set foot outside it for fear of falling straight into an abyss. I rarely even strayed into the suburbs. The grime there and the even more overt hostility were such that I didn't dare to. Where was the brotherhood of Miguel de Unamuno? Where was the wild gypsy music, the spirit and dignity, depth and subtlety, the sensuality – even the cruelty, of this fabled nation? Where was its life? And where was mine?

I didn't parade through the streets flagellating myself for my sins, but for five interminably long months did I torment myself. I can describe my days there, but I cannot justify them with the name of life, because I didn't really live at that time. I just got through it. I drank coffee and more coffee. I ate next to nothing, and slept even less. Twice a day, the clay pot that hung on a chain under my small table was topped up with charcoal and hot ash by the smelly, stunned chambermaid. The cold consumed me as I grappled with religion and with my god. When the fumes from the charcoal became unbearable, I stumbled around the streets.

From January to June, if I surfaced, it was only to torment the people around me. I threw stones at priests on the street. I swore in public and then ran away. These things strike me as infantile now, but I know I did them then to stop myself from going mad. I had to share the burden of my vanishing faith. A shadow of myself slunk out to the Law School, and a shadow studied in my place. A shadow hunched in the faculty library. Every afternoon, the boy I had lost, and the man who had gone missing, read Rainer Maria Rilke's 'Requiem for a Friend' at the little bookshop round the corner from the university library before sinking back into another night of despair.

Tell me who, who are these travellers, more fugitive, even,
than we? Who, from the very beginning, seem driven
and forced by a will — and whose is it? —
which unrelentingly wrings and bends them,
hurls them and swings them; tosses them, catches them
back.

Almost against my will, I felt less anguish as summer came to Salamanca. One day I remember I was waiting for dawn. For hours, I'd been waiting for the sun to come up so I could go and drink a coffee at the little bar on the corner of my street. I'd been re-reading Unamuno without much success, sentence by sentence: it just wasn't happening. 'I am a man and I regard no other man as a stranger ...' I wasn't a man, I was nothing, and every other man was a stranger. I was half-drunk with fatigue. When I finally went out for my coffee, I was particularly distressed by my loneliness. I had grown used to the cold breath of winter, but summer was on its way and the air was a warm balm that reminded me of home. I found the reminder painful as the tepid air tried to swaddle me. I wanted even the warmth to leave me alone: because I didn't belong there.

Some workmen passed the door of the bar. I didn't notice much in those days, but for some reason I noticed them in their worn blue overalls. There were four of them: three were in their early forties, and one was younger. I had been up all night and was slinking into the street like a phantom, but they looked full of energy as though they had set out to embrace the day. They turned into the same bar I was heading for. I was struck by the way they talked to each other with a certain camaraderie and frankness. One of them said something and the others smiled. They were connected by an almost tangible energy. They were at their ease: they were a group and they belonged.

Their smiles released something inside me as I sat huddled up at my end of the bar. I looked at myself in the spotted mirror behind the counter and saw a miserable outsider obsessed with himself. Seeing those workmen, I suddenly felt: That is life! That is what life is about: it's what is going on in them. It's what happens to others.

And I realised I didn't need to be a miserable sod any more. I didn't need to worry so much about myself. I could live through other people. I realised that being human was something going on outside me. With that discovery, I found a new dimension to politics: a face that was acceptable to me, and was not the ideological, intellectual side I kept gagging on. In that dimly lit bar with sawdust on the floor, I felt myself part of the human race, and my torment diminished in direct proportion to the extent to which I took an interest in people in another way.

At the end of June, I passed the first year of my law degree with honourable mentions in all subjects. I was pleased by my teacher's praise. I knew by then that it was easy to glow in a fishbowl, and harder to shine in the sea. As soon as my last exam finished, I was determined to be out of Salamanca. I had served my time, appeased my father and I was finally going to France. To that end, I had already written to a compatriot, a man called Rodolfo Izaguirre, whom I had met briefly in Caracas while I was a Party militant working from school. He was one of the few Venezuelans abroad with whom I couldn't claim any kinship whatsoever (not even by scratching back for several generations) but I had met him a couple of times and he had mentioned that he was en route for Paris and he'd given me an address there, which by some miracle I had kept.

On 11 July 1953, I left Spain for Paris. I travelled by train, third class, with a ragbag of Spaniards, and discovered more about Spain on that journey than I had in the six months I had lived there. Everyone, men and women, took off their shoes as soon as the train pulled out of the station. The combination of that fetid stench, the heat and the rocking motion of the train was almost narcotic. From having ignored even the broadest details for five months, it made the smallest ones seem deeply significant. Dust from the scorched countryside settled over the carriage. The Spaniards had all brought picnics with them which they unwrapped ceremoniously and then shared. The dust gritted into the cold, greasy omelettes and fat salamis and into every mouthful of bread. Despite that, those dusty picnics on the train were the best meals I'd eaten since I left home.

As the hours clacked by, and particularly once we'd crossed the frontier at Hendaye, the combination of the skins of coarse red wine and the leaving of General Franco's domain brought laughter into our squalid compartment.

At the Gare du Nord, the three Salamancans still left from the journey embraced me half to death. They were covert socialists all, who had been forced to live under a pious mask on their rare visits to Spain.

'We're the lucky ones,' they told me. 'We can get out.'

I didn't ask them how or why.

After five months of not drinking, I'd got pretty drunk on the train. I entered Paris full of hope, and full of Spanish omelette, thanks to the generosity of a bunch of travellers who'd treated me like a friend. My new companions hadn't been particularly brilliant or particularly gifted: they were just decent people who deserved better times.

I staggered along the station concourse, struggling with my luggage and a giddy head, while drinking in the exuberance of free France. Although I had never been there before, after the rigours of Salamanca, it felt like coming home. I thought of my father then, and knew that in some ways he had been right. All my earlier messing around had been bullshit. And I had been a dilettante. But all that was going to change. It was by no means the first time that I had decided to change my course. What made it different was identifying my direction. For the first time I could see not just a distant goal, but also a visible path to travel that would lead me to that goal. I felt like a trapped animal in the hands of a healer. I felt able to stop throwing myself pointlessly against the bars of my cage and able instead to start finding a constructive way of prising the bars open. If I really wanted to find myself and save my people, I had to leave my anguish and recklessness behind. I had to recognise my strengths and weaknesses. On the one hand, I was weak, impulsive, poor and alone. On the other hand, I had a gift for rhetoric, I could think fast and clearly, I was capable of being objective, I was ambitious and young. After my moment in the bar in Salamanca, and again on the train, I felt that I had a purpose: if I dedicated my life to other people, to the workers' movement and the revolution, I could make a difference.

Since this is my moment of truth, I had to include my Spanish interlude, complete with my crash course in the blatantly obvious and my five months of religious torment. Until now, they have been closely kept secrets. There hasn't been a torture invented that could have racked this confession out of me when I was younger. Whenever I tell my story, the from-the-horse's-mouth, abridged version always takes me straight from Valera to Paris. The longer version drops me in Spain, pauses at the University of Salamanca, nods to the architecture and the religious bigotry and then bales out again, only weeks later, to the Sorbonne.

Of course, loads of people I know have been through religious crises. It's a very Latin socialist thing. But they had short ones, and you can get away with that. Some guys even talk about theirs. You know, when you are stuck in a bunker somewhere for weeks on end, the talk often turns confessional. A loss of faith is OK, it's like losing your virginity, it had to happen somewhere. Losing your way, too – that can happen. But not being able to laugh at yourself – in fact, not being able to laugh at all – that is something no Venezuelan can forgive.

Before I began, I set out to tell the truth, and yet I have had to stop myself from lying to myself. I was a devoutly Catholic, deeply religious child. In San Cristobal, I was up there in my surplice, swinging incense and croaking in Latin with a priest who marvelled at my vocation. Look at me! I have written out my childhood in San Cristobal and never mentioned that shit, as though it just didn't happen. It's piled in with all the things I haven't bothered to deny, with the lies I've let stand. Reading over this memoir so far, I see I have taken the trouble to lie about it. Why? The habit of concealment is so ingrained that I am like a woman lying to herself about her lovers, mentally eliminating the ones who let her down. If ever people asked me, 'What about you? When did you drop out of church?' I'd shrug it off, and say, 'Venezuela is the only Catholic country in the whole world that is officially recognised as having no vocation. All our priests are Spanish. You know, in Valera, religion wasn't such a big thing. We had other fish to fry.'

I have never been able to admit before that I didn't 'drop out': I fell out from a great height and hit the ground in pieces.

The press has an unerring nose for hounding out grains of truth. They don't know about my Spanish months or my one-time vocation, but they do know there is something about me and churches. As usual, they have got it wrong. The truth is not that I have a shameful past of burning down monasteries and raping nuns. The truth is that 'arch-criminal Barreto' hid in a darkened room like a frightened child, and that he threw stones at priests in the streets of Salamanca.

CHAPTER XVII

I don't want to harp on about the religious thing, but now that I have come clean about my early fervour, I can say that I was someone predisposed to revelations. I was waiting to be amazed. As a kid, I did quite a lot of things like renouncing my share of the fudge pudding at weekends in the hope that God would reward me with a special sign. Or I would stand on one leg for an hour in return for a revelation. For years I had lived on permanent standby for miracles, trying to lure one to me by sacrifices that went unnoticed at all levels. At night, as I contemplated the ravaged rafter over my bed and watched the transparent gecko that used it as a nocturnal hunting perch, I prayed that I would wake up the next day and be astonished. Geckos are supposed to have magic powers and·can, supposedly, impregnate virgins. My fervent prayers were not answered in Valera, which was thin on apparitions and virgins alike.

Then I went to France, and as the words form in my mouth, I feel I have to say more. I can't just say 'then I went to France', without describing the revelation, the vision that France was to me. To a boy in love with poetry and philosophical thought, France was my Mecca. I had dreamt and imagined her, pored over engravings of Notre Dame, the Louvre and the Sacré Coeur. Those were things I'd memorised and yearned for. Revelations are, by their nature, unimaginable.

As the train pulled across the Spanish border at Hendaye and I entered France, I saw women in the street who were half naked! It was a hot summer's day, and the women of France, wearing shorts and T-shirts, were showing almost everything they had. Coming from Spain, where all women wore long sleeves and thick black stockings, I was stupefied. I was astonished by those arms and legs and shoulders. I got hot and cold flushes of amazement at such liberty. That was freedom! Bugger books! They were mere seeds. This flowering of bare flesh was the living proof of France's greatness: the land of free-thinkers, of the French Revolution, of poetry, of everything that was the opposite of dark, priest-ridden Spain.

That was how I saw the waves of flesh as the train made its way along the coast to Marseilles. By the time I discovered that girls wore T-shirts and shorts in most Western countries, I had already attached myself to France so firmly it would have taken a surgical operation to loosen my grip. Meanwhile, along the Riviera I saw bare legs, knees, thighs, necks, elbows, shoulders and, sometimes, as girls waved on platforms, breasts glimpsed through sleeveless apertures. At San Raphael, I swear to God, I saw a nipple. In our compartment, we drank to the freedom. In the squalid toilet along the corridor, I wanked to it. At the Gare du Nord, we travellers embraced it. Hallelujah!

Paris itself was fabulous in all her splendour, blazing with lights after the dim bulbs of Salamanca. Izaguirre (who was really only an acquaintance) greeted me like a long-lost brother. He was full of enthusiasm and glad to see me. Having been invisible for six months, I was moved by that gladness; I arrived on the night of 12 July.

Next day, Izaguirre guided me through that City of Light. I saw bookshops, the likes of which I had never dreamt. The shelves were brimming over with titles and they stretched across floor after floor and overflowed into the street. The city invited everyone to enjoy it, to consume and admire it. I ate hot croissants, and drank cold beer by the Seine. I saw the Sorbonne: it was milling with exuberant students. These students didn't slink as we had in Salamanca, they were laughing and shouting as they effervesced with excitement. I saw the Luxembourg Gardens. I ate Vietnamese food with its bean sprouts (which looked like the kind of worms dogs vomited into the gutter in Valera, but which were crunchy and good to taste), and noodles in soy sauce, which refused to stay on my fork. I drank pastis as Rimbaud had, and I choked on my first Gitanes cigarette. I stared at girls and they stared back at me, eyeball to eyeball, until I looked away.

The entire city was a celebration. It was as seductive as a courtesan displaying a tray of jewels. It blended the senses. The streets were a bouquet of perfumes and a mélange of sensual waves in overlapping invitations that said 'eat me', 'taste me', 'take me'. It was a place that exuded confidence. It had merged all that was aesthetic with the intellectual and the sensual. It was a tourist's paradise and I was a tourist. Every second shop was a temple to food. The fruit was polished and arranged in ways to inspire a host of Arcimboldos. Izaguirre told me that I had to see a cheese shop. In Venezuela we had cheese: queso blanco, and then not every day. With so much to see, I couldn't see why we should go and see a whole shop of it, but Izaguirre insisted.

Marvelling at those smelly shelves with over a hundred types, with names like a new liturgy for me to learn, I felt that I was standing in some kind of temple. When we walked back onto the sunny street and I could feel the surge of life, I was entranced, surfacing for air in that wave of excitement, surrounded by bright colours and novel sensations.

The next day was 14 July, the anniversary of the storming of the Bastille. All Paris was on holiday, celebrating the birth of her present greatness. There were little tricolour flags everywhere and children carried red, white and blue balloons.

Izaguirre took me out to breakfast in his local café. We ate strips of crusty French bread with butter and strawberry jam and drank wonderful coffee while he explained that he was taking me on a demonstration: a march from Bastille to la Nation. In Venezuela we had protests and riots. Izaguirre had tried to fill me in on the background of the march as we made our way to Bastille in that miraculous underworld of the metro. Of course I listened to him as best I could, but what with the rattling of the train and the other conversations around me, and my state of general euphoria, it was not clear to me what the fuss was about. Coming from Valera via Salamanca, it would have been hard to be more ignorant of world politics than I was then. Between stations Izaguirre told me that there had been a trial somewhere in the United States.

'The verdict was an offence to democracy, the victims were Ethel and Julius, and the civilised world is in outrage at a travesty of justice. All of France is up in arms against it.'

The train pulled into Voltaire and yet more people got on. A girl with huge knockers pushed in between Izaguirre and me. I am not tall, she was. My face was virtually pressed into the cleavage above her yellow cotton blouse. My attention was divided in unequal parts between Izaguirre's résumé, the girl's tits and my own rampant body.

'Last year, the French won the right not to join the Korean War. You should have seen it, Oswaldo – the country was full of demonstrations! There's a backlash against the state of submission in which most of Europe lived under the Nazis. This is our moment. It's a time of maximum independence of spirit!'

The girl moved away, and I managed to repress some of the independence of spirit that was happening in my trousers. Izaguirre moved closer.

'We'll be marching beside the Algerians,' he said. 'They are our neighbours and they've invited me to join them.'

Until the day before, I had never heard of Algeria, let alone seen an Algerian. There was a Turk who came through Valera a couple of times a year selling rugs and lamps. So I had seen an Arab, of sorts. But the Algerians, with their Berber mix, looked surprisingly like me (or I like them) and it had struck me, as I wandered through Izaguirre's neighbourhood, that if I dropped my hick clothes and let my hair grow a bit, I wouldn't stand out like a sore thumb there.

At Bastille, we poured out of the train together with just about everyone else. The freedom of spirit was almost tangible. That complete freedom of spirit was what I wanted, and what I felt. I had never seen such a crowd, or such colours or so much flesh. Leaflets were being distributed, written by Jean-Paul Sartre himself. I clutched mine like a prayer sheet, feeling my own career had grown wings by this vicarious proximity to the master. It was a tract against the Americans entitled 'Les Américains Sont Malades de la Rage!' I knew about twenty words of French, but I got the title, and I remember feeling absurdly grateful for picking up on that double entendre (sick with rabies/sick with rage). Imagine, me, a boy from San Cristobal de Torondoy, understanding something written by Sartre himself in French! And he'd written it specially for this march in Paris that I would be on!

I marched with Izaguirre beside the Algerians. They were a big contingent and I slipped in among them. I felt proud just to be alive: this was Bastille Day and I was spending it in France! It was such a fine moment. It felt as though nothing could spoil it. Then only a few minutes into the march, it started to rain. In Venezuela, when it rains, it really rains. That day in Paris, by any standards, it was bucketing down. But we didn't care. It continued to rain hard, and all the demonstrators just pushed on (I have never, before or after, seen so many erect nipples!).

There was a tremendous camaraderie on that march and I was suddenly a part of something. As we walked, I gleaned some more about whom and what we were marching for. Ethel and Julius Rosenberg, two American Jewish intellectuals, had been electrocuted for espionage in the United States a month before. They had been framed by the FBI and the American judiciary. The entire liberal world had tried to prevent their execution. The trial was a scandal.

Izaguirre took me under his wing. He stayed by my side for the first hour of the march, sharing his chewing gum and his knowledge with me.

'The Rosenbergs' only real crime was their communism, for which they have paid with their lives. Look at the crowd here! It is just one of hundreds of marches all over the world. This is a global protest. You arrived at a key moment, Oswaldo! Now you can say you were here.'

And the march went on and on, and the rain kept on and on. At regular distances along the route, policemen formed a gappy human fence between the marchers and the people on the pavements, many of whom were waving little tricolour flags and also waving at us. Despite the rain, there were quite a lot of spectators.

The French police uniforms looked very tame compared to our own paramilitary National Guard. They did not interfere with the marchers in any way and some of the policemen even smiled and returned pleasantries with some of the marchers.

Izaguirre made friends with a girl from Lyons who had travelled in specially for the march. She had short brown hair and speckled grey-brown eyes like a trout's belly; and about halfway through the march they began to hold hands. I overheard them making what sounded like plans for the evening. My French wasn't up to following closely, but their body language spoke for them, besides which Izaguirre kept giving me gloating winks to confirm that there was more in this than just a coffee and that I too should look around me and find myself a girl for the evening.

Izaguirre had been in Paris much longer than I, and he probably wasn't going through the aftermath of a religious crisis, and maybe the march did not have for him the neo-spiritual quality it had for me. I saw the sexual potential of the march but had neither the inclination nor the knowledge to take it further. I was almost orgasmically happy just to be marching. Izaguirre was, I think, both amused and slightly disappointed to discover what a country bumpkin I was, and he and his girl from Lyons fell back and drifted away in the mass of marchers behind me.

Without him to talk to, the rest of my march was mostly silent. Some of the Algerians around me tried to strike up comradely conversations, but they gave up with nods and smiles when they found out that I didn't speak French. For all that, they went out of their way to be friendly, and one of them, a boy not much older than me, kept trying to pass the language barrier. His name was Reski and he worked shovelling something, but despite his charades, I was not able to decipher what.

As we approached Nation, the air of excitement that had abated a little as the marchers trudged on doggedly through the rain began to rise again. The pace quickened and the surge and push of the crowd behind was like a solid wave pressing us on. The word itself, 'Nation', was bandied backwards and forwards like a battle cry, accompanied by little exclamations of achievement and joy. The volume of talk increased and became as deafening as it had in the beginning. When I looked away, lost in my glorious Sartrean reveries, Reski kept trying to make contact; he jumped up in front of me clowning, and then squeezed my arm inviting me to laugh with him, which I did.

Just as we approached Nation itself, several of the Algerian groups began to turn back. I remember thinking, What a bunch of idiots! They've put up with the rain all the way here, and now they're turning back just as we're arriving! In that crowd, it was no easy thing to fall back. It had been noisy as hell since we set out and now, at the end, the noise was at a climax. Between the rain, the talk, the chanting and the laughter, there was a deafening din. Through the noise, I heard something ahead, but not quite clearly. I heard what sounded like muffled fireworks. It added to the excitement and I looked up to see what I thought would be a sky full of coloured sparks. The sky was grey and heavy and almost completely without light.

I looked back down and realised that the bulk of the police were ahead of us. The muffled bangs continued and then suddenly it became clear: they were gunfire and the police were firing guns straight into the crowd.

All around me, people crumpled and fell. Reski doubled over right beside me like a gymnast and hit the ground head first. For several seconds, I stood and watched, astonished, as his folded body lay at my feet. Nobody moved. I stayed glued to the road, not realising what was happening, thinking that it was all part of the spectacle. Whatever else was happening, I felt sure that Reski must be putting on an act. In a moment, he would jump up again.

Time wasn't happening. Everything was wrong. My mind was numb. The puddle at my feet in which Reski was lying was filling with magenta, (the way the sea colours when your boat squashes a starfish as it beaches.) I was drawn out of this colour trance as, gradually, the Algerians around me began to scream and shout. A girl came up to Reski and as she stared down at his inert body, a chilling, curdled sound came out of her. It was a signal for the crowd to react. Other women began to wail. And then everyone began to run. That was when I saw that there were several more bodies strewn on the ground, and scarlet spots bleeding into the rain on the cobblestones.

The adrenaline of the crowd massed and turned sour so

suddenly that it was sickening. The mood went from euphoria to panic as the last of the vanguard fell back in total disorder.

Everywhere I looked, there were Algerians (who looked like me) running for their lives. I didn't run immediately: I just stood in shock. But when another man in front of me keeled over sideways, shot, I was aware of thinking, This is death, but it is for other people, not for me. I was not afraid, I was shocked.

The front ranks surged back over the man's body, trampling his checked green shirt. I didn't know if I too had been shot. I didn't know what being shot felt like. I didn't know what was happening. I just knew that I must not die before I had achieved something: anything.

After the march broke rank and scattered, everyone was running and I ran too. I don't know how the hell I got away. People were stampeding and screaming in all directions. Some were falling down, many were crying.

It was mayhem. And from somewhere in its core, a sound that began in the throat of Reski's mourner rose up and gripped the air. I had never heard it before but I would hear it again, years later, in Algiers. It sounded inhuman: it was a visceral, ancient wail of outrage and mourning.

Fourteen Algerians were killed and dozens more injured on that Bastille march. Fourteen from among the group I was marching with were dead. I didn't know them. I knew the name of one of them, of Reski, who smiled a lot and worked shovelling something, but what he shovelled I would now never know.

It was only my second day in the City of Light, and fourteen young people, armed only with Sartre's words in their hands, were shot dead by the police of that enlightened city.

Somehow I found my way back to Izaguirre's room. Until the day before, I had never seen an Algerian and I couldn't have cared less what was or wasn't happening in North Africa. Nor could I have accurately located Algeria on a map. Whatever might have been happening in that distant territory was, at that time in my life, too far away in every sense to capture my allegiance or even my attention. But I had marched beside them; and a boy called Reski had clowned for me and then died at my feet; and his sister or his

sweetheart had wailed her unearthly wail in my ear, throwing down a gauntlet to injustice and indifference. And I was there. I saw what others hadn't and I felt honour bound to pick that gauntlet up.

So from that day on and for the next six years I was part of the Algerian Movement. I was part of a group of foreigners campaigning for their freedom from the colonial French, from the Pieds Noirs who ruled and abused them.

How different my life would have been if I had arrived in Paris just one day later. I would, almost certainly, have followed a very different, more scholarly course. I would have gone to the Sorbonne as a thinker and graduated as that: someone set to plan and navigate men's lives through the cogency of ideas. The compass that set my course for Algiers was set by chance. It was set by gratuitous violence, which pitted the armed and strong against the unarmed and weak. It was a battle that drew its own lines, challenging anyone who was there to take a stand.

That night, in the Algerian quarter, the wailing and warbling filled the air, imprinting a new and alien culture on my brain. The Paris of my dreams came and went in twenty-four hours. My days of tourism lasted for a day. My childhood ended when I gave my first school speech. My boyhood ended on that march.

If I had sat in a café and read Rilke instead of going on that march, if I hadn't been in the thick of the Algerian marchers, or if I hadn't looked so much like an Algerian myself, things might have been different. If, if, if, and again: things just happened.

CHAPTER XVIII

I wanted to study sociology: to study what was global. As luck would have it, you couldn't take a degree in sociology in Paris in 1953. You could take a diploma in it, and then only with a degree in either law or philosophy. So I registered for law. And I also applied to be a militant within the Communist Party.

Well, the law faculty took me on as a student, but the party turned me down. It had been decreed from above that no foreigners were allowed to be militants in France. And that brings me back to the 'ifs'.

I felt that I could be useful to the party, given my experience in Venezuela. Each neighbourhood in Paris had a communist group, and each group had a small band of militants. My neighbourhood was chock-full of Algerians, Vietnamese, etc., who, being French colonials, were technically French. I was out one day, buying my copy of L'Humanité, when the newspaper vendor asked me where I was from. I told him I was Venezuelan. Being an ignorant guy, he thought Venezuela was part of a French colony, and he asked me why I wasn't a militant for the Communist Party of France like everyone else. He was quite pushy about it.

'So are you going to?'

'Of course I will,' I told him.

The vendor pinched my cheek as though I was five years old and then he organised it for me. He got me my carnet and everything. That was in November 1953. I had been in Paris for five months, and could just about speak French, although with the marked Algerian accent which I still have today.

Within the party, you could transfer from group to group so long as you were entitled to do so. Since I was a legitimate law student, I asked, eight months later, to be transferred to the law faculty branch. To be transferred, as it were, to head office. Of course, the same people who had turned me down before just had to let me in. They had no choice: I was a legitimate neighbourhood militant, a legitimate law student and all my papers were in order. That was how I became the only non-Frenchman to be a militant in the French Communist Party.

I got what I wanted but the arrangement turned out to be good for the law faculty too. Being lawyers, they were a bit low on theoreticians. They liked being active, but they carried on in the party just as they would have done in a trades union or club. For me, it was different. It was an international link. One reason why a lot of communists just do as they are told is that, even at high levels, they can't argue, because they don't actually know what the hell it is all about. The orders are simple, but the theory is complex. Of course, I first became a party member in Trujillo without even knowing what communism was, let alone what underpinned it. But as I grew up with it and within it, I grew some more. From the moment I realised that it was a political and social movement rather than a literary club, I tried to study its complex theory. So although it was a bit like locking the stable door after the horse had bolted, after my time in Spain I decided to know exactly what I was letting myself in for.

Six months in Salamanca had opened my eyes as to how far Catholicism could jump from the gentle teaching of the gospels to the bitter repression of the Spanish Church. I wanted to know for myself, to be sure that my life, the life I was dedicating to international communism, was not going to warp along the way.

This brings me back to the 'ifs' again. Because if I had known then about Stalin's labour camps, or his ethnic cleansing, or his torture cells, I could have lived a different life. If I'd known what would happen in the USSR, in Poland, in China, Romania, Bulgaria and Albania, I would never have fought for what turned out to be their arm of oppression. But I didn't know, and it was the

1950s in a world without mass media. It was nine years after the Second World War. It was only nine years since the Nazis had stopped exterminating not only the Jews but the communists too. Every country that had been occupied by the Germans could bear witness to the atrocities of the Nazis. Every bus conductor in Paris could, and did, bear witness to the heroism of the Resistance, many of whom were communists.

All around me, France was full of Spanish socialist refugees. The Spanish communists in exile all had eye-witness accounts of fascist atrocities. Spain was fascist. I had lived there, and seen first hand what fascism could do to the human spirit.

So, back then, I was a communist. It took me over ten years to discover what was really going on in Russia. And just as I embraced the party and it embraced me, when I left, its powerful machine turned on me with full force. For over thirty years now, my name has been a blend of dirt and excrement in communist circles. I am 'an enemy of the party'. I am a traitor in the eyes of all its hardliners. There have been times when I really didn't know, as I walked down a street, any street, whether I'd be shot that day by a bullet coming straight at my heart, and whether that bullet had been sent by the Right or the Left. I lost most of my friends by becoming a communist, and then later, I lost most of my friends again by ceasing to be one. I never stopped being a socialist, but I came to loathe communism with a vengeance.

But the fact of the matter is that I embraced communism in the 1950s. Socially, in Paris at that time, it was an OK way to be. No one forgot that France had fallen to the Germans in only six days, while Russia (the USSR as was) was constantly being maligned by the Americans. But Russia, it was well known, had heroically beaten the German VIth Army. Russia alone had worn down the apparently invincible Germans and smashed their morale. The Russians had paid a price of thirty million dead. The figure was almost inconceivable. In France, in 1954, some of the greatest minds in the country praised Russia, and were either overtly or tacitly pro-communist.

The Algerians who lived in my neighbourhood told me horror stories of their oppression in Algeria. Only a fool, it seemed, could hear such things and sit back and wait for another Hitler to catch the world unawares. Once these atrocities and injustices were known, surely only a cad could look the other way? I had marched with the Algerians on the 14 July and seen them fall at my feet. There was no time to waste!

But while I was being busy and productive, lies were told about me back in Valera. Venezuelans came and went, dropping seeds of truth into the gossip patch. By the time I was twenty, I had inherited the myths and misdemeanours of every artist and every arsehole in exile from Panama to Patagonia. In a curious biblical reversal, the sins of the son were visited upon the father. I can imagine how much it hurt him. I could fill three chapters with the tales that grew out of my Parisian years, but a few must suffice to give the general flavour.

Supposedly, I contracted syphilis from the prostitutes in Pigalle, and I lived with a negress whose skin was as dark as charcoal, and whose mouth was so wide that we had once been found drunk in a gutter with my entire foot in her mouth. 'If she hadn't passed out, the black giantess would have swallowed him whole, like a boa constrictor.' So the story goes. And it was told 'on good authority' that I sold my backside for glasses of pastis, and when no one would buy me a drink, that I'd give it away.

And it was said that I breakfasted on long, thin loaves of bread, which I cut lengthways in half with a surgical scalpel, with the sinister precision 'learnt from the Schulers'. It was said that I then filled these loaves with live slugs, refusing to eat anything from a Christian menu.

Between these bouts of sex and sandwiches, I supposedly spent my days in an opium den.

And so the stories went, from house to house and town to town, gathering momentum.

Meanwhile, I actually studied law and sociology, and I worked every day for the party. I read Baudelaire and many hundreds of other writers. For those who are interested, the truth is as follows. Occasionally, I visited the zoo. When I did, I was particularly fascinated by the orang-utangs. And I did get pissed on pastis more than a couple of times. I couldn't afford even the most raddled of prostitutes in Pigalle, so I got laid when I got lucky (which wasn't nearly as often as I wanted). I bought a baguette for my breakfast every day. Once in a while I ate escargots (with a parsley and garlic butter sauce), and I loved them. And I loved frogs' legs, and sea slugs, and all manner of vegetables and salads (or what we call 'rabbit food' in Venezuela).

Then once, and only once, some of my Colombian friends and I did fall asleep, drunk as skunks, in the gutter. All the other times, I managed to crawl home, which was pretty miraculous when you consider how unused to mixing my drinks I was, and how hard it is for a Venezuelan to adapt to the French way of drinking. In France, people drink to savour the wine, the brandy and the champagne and a plethora of liqueurs, whereas in Venezuela we drink lager, whisky and rum for the sole purpose of getting drunk. Parties in Venezuela go on until the last man is legless. Sipping and tasting, choosing wines and pacing drinks, was a whole new concept to me. It took me years to be able to taste a really fine wine and be aware of anything other than its alcoholic content. And although a great red wine is one of my greatest pleasures, I still love the old Latin-American style bash, where you end up hugging the lavatory bowl at six o'clock in the morning.

CHAPTER XIX

The worst thing I did in Paris happened in my first week. I sat in Izaguirre's room numb with shock and retrospective fear over what had happened on the march.

On 15 July 1953, the morning after the Bastille march, I went from room to room with Izaguirre and showed my solidarity to the party and to the Algerian hierarchy within it. I paid my respects to the families of the victims and also to numerous walking wounded. I offered my services to the survivors and their organisation.

The deaths were brought home to me, literally, because the shot Algerians had lived in Izaguirre's neighbourhood: two of them had lived on his street. I was sleeping on his floor, but I couldn't sleep. There was a lot more of that unearthly wailing and then there were the funerals.

It was as though Paris had died on that day. My long dark days in Salamanca were not far behind me. My mind was still fragile from them and a smothering depression enveloped me after the march. It got so bad that nothing short of another violent shock could have got me out of it. Then, as luck would have it, some of my mother's rich cousins were visiting Paris and she had given their son strict instructions to visit me and see how I was. So I went from being in shock to being wined and dined by my playboy cousin. Although his parents couldn't bring themselves to come and meet their 'degenerate Red cousin', they footed the bill.

My playboy cousin took me to dinner in a little, hideously expensive bistro. We drank champagne and a number of vintage wines, which were mostly wasted on both of us. I was given the gossip and news from Caracas and some of the latest scandals from Valera, but it was nothing beside the Algerians' deaths. My cousin told me that I was miserable company, and after dinner he insisted on cheering me up. He took me, and the big wad of money he had in his wallet, for a stroll through Pigalle. He was excited by Paris. He wanted to see the Moulin Rouge and the prostitutes, he wanted to get royally laid and be able to go back to Caracas and tell everyone about it. But he didn't dare go by himself, not speaking a word of French. I told him I hardly spoke any either. But he insisted we go together.

At first, I went along with a bad grace. But since I hadn't got my leg over since my first night in Madrid, the abundance of bare flesh in Paris had brought my libido back with a vengeance.

There were so many women on the street, every doorway had one or two, and they were short, tall, thin, fat, blonde, dark, pretty, and sometimes, really ugly. The more girls we passed, the more choosy I became. Since it was a present from my cousin, I wanted to get someone I actually found attractive. After about half an hour of looking and finding fault with this one and that one, my cousin got pissed off. He was the sort of guy who would have shagged a goat if there wasn't a girl around, and he couldn't see what all the fuss was about. We were on the rue de Clichy, just past a little theatre, and there were two women standing in a cobbled courtyard. My cousin pushed me in towards them and told me to do a deal. It worked out that we got the one woman for the two of us.

Because I had done the negotiating, I got to go first. She was a pretty tart, but she had a hard face and she didn't even pretend to be interested either in me or in what she was doing. In Valera, whores always act as though every client is God's gift to women, regardless of what you look like. So I wasn't used to being treated in that offhand way as though I were a bit of dirt. Little did she know I had had to shift my whole mindset to get into this evening out at all. If anyone was going to be marginally indifferent, then that person was me. I resented her bad manners: we were paying for it, after all! Upstairs in her bare little room, she sat down on

the iron bed and didn't even take her clothes off. I got undressed
and she sort of spat at me to hurry up.

There was something nasty about the whole encounter. It was
sordid to the point where I felt my lust waning by the second. I
remonstrated with her in a mixture of Spanish and French, telling
her to make a bit of an effort. Whereupon, she got up off the bed,
came up to me and bit me on the nipple. She bit me so hard it
made me feel sick. Without thinking, I hit her away. She had
drawn blood. It was no playful nip: her teeth had gouged into my
flesh. It was so painful I couldn't see, think or move for a few seconds. When I could, I saw the blood running on my chest. And I
saw the whore lying on the floor with her legs folded under her.

My mind worked very quickly then. Mentally, I replayed the
scene: I had hit her, but I hadn't hit her that hard; so she must
have knocked her head against something as she fell back. My first
reaction was that she was dead. My second reaction was to get my
clothes and get the hell out of there. My third reaction was to
wonder what happened to foreigners who killed women in Paris.
I had seen what happened to people who had disagreed about
something and gone on a peaceful march. It didn't take much to
imagine what the police would do with a murderer. And my
fourth reaction, which was the one that dominated all the others,
was waves of sickening pain.

I hit the street and got my cousin away from the crime scene,
giving him a garbled account of what had happened as we fled
through Pigalle. It took some explaining because he wasn't really
interested in any story of mine and just wanted to go up for his
pre-paid turn. Also, my account was so garbled it was almost
incoherent. My chest was swelling in the most alarming way and
there was blood all over my shirt. It was the latter that finally
brought home to him that we had a 'situation' on our hands.

My cousin smuggled me into his fancy hotel room, and I
showed him the bite. My chest was puffed out like a male pigeon's
and the swelling had gone hard. The wound itself was infected: the
edges were raw and inflamed. (What the hell did that whore have
on her teeth?) My playboy cousin's reaction was mounting panic,
but I was in so much pain I couldn't take in most of his ranting
and I completely ignored his pleas for me to leave his room and

keep him out of it. The pain, far from abating, was getting worse. I obviously needed a doctor, but we both reckoned that would be my quickest route to prison and the guillotine. By dawn, I was semi-delirious: how much from pain and fever, and how much from fear, I couldn't tell you.

At some point, Izaguirre came and got me and smuggled me out in a big overcoat. Over the next week, he also got me some black-market penicillin, and arranged for me to be moved from one safe house to the next. Meanwhile, he scoured the newspapers for news of the dead tart. Day after day, there was no news. Day after day, I cowered in a room waiting for the police to come knocking on the door to drag me away. I wondered what it would feel like to lay my head on the guillotine block. I did not wonder whether I would be brave and, in that detail at least, give my father the satisfaction of dying like a man. I knew I wouldn't be brave. I knew I would weep. Just thinking about it made me weep. And I thought about it a lot because the bite took three weeks to heal.

Nothing ever came into any of the papers, not even about an assault. There never had been any evidence that the prostitute had either died or been seriously injured apart from my having seen her unconscious on the floor of her room. She must have just been knocked out.

My cousin and his family left Paris the day after the incident. (I don't think he has ever been back.) And I not only didn't return to the rue de Clichy for another thirty years, I never went back to a prostitute in Paris. When that episode became known back in Valera, the gossips thought they had died and woken up in heaven. And they only knew about the poisonous bite, not the possible murder!

So, whatever my father's fears, and my Valerano neighbours' gossip, I did not waste my time in Paris. Even the hours spent drinking in the evenings were hours of serious talking and debate. I tell you, I could talk the back legs off a donkey. And do you know something? If I didn't love to talk so much, years later I would never have felt the tumour in my throat, right beside my voicebox, as the discernible, alien presence it was. I became aware of it every time I raised my voice. With my penchant for verbal drama, that was twenty or thirty times a day, and each time I felt a tickle. As a result, I asked a doctor what it was. As a result, the tumour was caught in its infancy. And as a result, I am still alive.

There has been no revenge as sweet as my survival. My continual refusal to die makes my enemies as sick as three cats in a bag of sulphur.

For the record: I have never much liked cats.

CHAPTER XX

I lived in France for five years, quitting just after Perez Jimenez and his dictatorship fell on 3 January 1958. During my French years, I lived like any Frenchman of the Left would have lived, who wanted to be an intellectual and a thinker. Except that I read all our left-wing stuff and also everything from the Right. I read about the Cuban lawyer Fidel Castro's July fiasco at Moncada barracks, and I read his 'History will Absolve Me' speech from his trial.

I wanted to know what was happening all around the world. And because I had access to, and read the press from both the Left and the Right, it seemed to me that I had access to all the news. And yet, the Sorbonne and the party and our café life was as divided into rigidly demarcated factions as the outside world. I prided myself on crossing over the boundaries from one faction to the next and being deeply involved with diverse groups. Yet much later I discovered that I had been at university together with people I never met, and some of them, like Ho Chi Minh and Pol Pot, would decide the fate of entire nations.

Despite my total immersion in French culture and French life, I always felt that the friendships I made there would be almost transitory. I knew I was a bird of passage, that I would never stay in France. Even in my love affairs, I tried not to fall in love there: to keep myself free to go home.

Something in me embraced France, and something in me

rejected her. Even now, I have no vocation for French culture. Unlike Nene, for example, who was always completely immersed in French poetry and who was interested in surrealism, after my initial adolescent rush, I have never really been in the thrall of French literature. When I arrived in Europe, so proud to be there, and feeling (momentarily) so sophisticated, I had read very few French writers.

On the other hand, from my childhood, I had had a great deal to do with German culture. I loved Bach and Brahms and Mozart – Bach in particular. Listening to Bach's *St Matthew Passion* has been one of the great luxuries of my life. My early serious reading was mostly of German origin. I singled out a couple of other French writers and also studied them in isolation, whereas I studied *German* philosophy and *German* thought: Glissen, Marx, Hegel, Heidegger – the lot!

I had (or, to be honest, I still have) a great fondness for German culture. This fondness started in Valera (in the library in my daily forays to its classified shelves). I have already said that I dreamed of Freiburg and Tübingen. Despite the way things turned out for me in Paris and my involvement there at every level, I could not set aside that German dream completely. It remained as an integral part of my future plan. I was ambitious, even then, and getting to Freiburg and Tübingen featured in my ambition. I focused my drive by studying for my law exams as though my life depended on them. I don't know if I was trying to prove some-thing to myself or to the world at large, but at the law faculty I studied hard and fast, with a thoroughness that put me well ahead of my course. This meant that I was able to take some time off, and I decided to use that time to visit Germany: my intellectual Promised Land.

Filadelfo Linares (a hero and mentor of my schooldays) was living in Tübingen, and in the final days of 1953 I arranged to spend some time there with him. I was not exactly to be his guest. We had a pact: I was to cook for him, and because he was a fair man, he was to do the laundry. Being the designated cook was some-thing Filadelfo expected me to take seriously; and since my board and lodging depended on its outcome, I took it very seriously.

Every day, I went out to buy food. It was a slow and laborious process interspersed with conversational breaks. Within two weeks of arriving, my German was reasonably fluent, thanks to the daily viva voce in the market.

I wanted to learn German so as to be able to read the philosophers in the original. Thanks to the months I spent in Tübingen, I have been able to do that, but my spoken German is a curious strand of the language. I learnt an entire lexicon of food. I still remember the names of all the fruits (which I don't know how to say in other languages I speak more fluently). I have culinary German with the soundest of grips on housewives' shopping lists. I learnt to differentiate between the dozens of wurst: to know not only the names but the merits of each tight-skinned sausage. And I learnt to queue.

Nothing is more alien to a Valerano than a queue! Sin, in Salamanca, was what was sensual. The sins of Tübingen, as perceived by its citizens, were against order. The first few times that I queue-jumped, it was done unwittingly. Later, I confess, I did it again and again, to observe the startling reaction my action unleashed. The ritualised greetings and sugary goodwill of entire shops full of people went straight out of the window, to be replaced by lynch-mob outrage.

Also, skin-deep under the placid surface, there was an entrenched xenophobia. But the two responses were not connected. I was not forcibly ejected from bakers' shops because I looked like a Jew. I was thrown out for a crime against order. I am sure that if any one of those Tübingen hausfraus had gone mad and queue-jumped, she too would have been assaulted. I wasn't playing out my infancy there (as I had done by throwing stones in Spain), I was observing something very deep within the German psyche. It threw some light on the national paradox, in a very practical way.

On the surface, Tübingen was the sweetest and friendliest place I had ever been in. It was literally smothered in amicable greetings. You couldn't buy so much as a carrot without exchanging pleasant wishes with whichever stranger had just sold it to you. But once the effusive *Grüssen* was over and done with, there was an undercurrent of racism, which I felt wherever I went. In

France, I was taken for an Algerian because there were so many there and I looked like them. In Germany (where Algerians are thin on the ground), my hairy, swarthy looks and hooked nose meant I was taken for a Jew. Sometimes, among the remorseful sector of the post-war population, this favoured my visit. And sometimes, with those native citizens who felt more resentment than remorse, it did not.

Gradually, as the months went by, I made friends with a number of Tübingers and became that time-honoured figure in German life: the decent Jew. I was the outsider unblemished by the unacceptable taint of other outsiders. I was the person from that lower caste who was actually rather nice and bright and who could safely be invited for a schnapps or even a plate of wurst and potato fritters. Even some quite rabid anti-Semites softened towards me and not only suffered my company, but sometimes sought it.

This was not, as one might think, a reaction to the ethnic cleansing of the previous decade. It was something that had happened even at the height of institutionalised anti-Semitism. Goebbels complained about it in his diary in late 1941. 'This nation is simply not yet mature and is full of maudlin sentimentality.' Again in his diary, he complained that 'all of the eighty million Germans came' to him and that 'each one has his decent Jew!' They made it clear that the others were bastards, but this one, 'their one, was a first-class Jew'. Goebbels claimed that there were actually more petitions for clemency than there were Jews in Germany.

By the following year, it seems that all those hundreds of thousands of friends and colleagues, neighbours and lovers, had accepted that the idea mattered more than the person, but that it happened at all is still another interesting insight into German thinking.

I also saw the 'maudlin sentimentality' Goebbels railed at, and I found it alarming at first, and then deeply puzzling. In Venezuela, men don't cry. It just isn't an option. So, it was astonishing to sit in a café with guys who were (with scarcely any exaggeration) nearly twice my size, bull-necked, hugely muscular, and immune, it seemed, to any kind of sensitivity, but who burst into tears. I would be sitting drinking beer with Filadelfo in

whatever beer cellar was selected for the night, and a Schubert
lied would come on the radio. The bull-necked local drinkers in
the cellar would pause appreciatively and listen to the sweet
strains of the song. Then one of the bulls would respond with a
spontaneous show of silent tears. A big, grown man would stand
there in public while tears rolled down his twitching face. To me
it was as disturbing to witness as to have seen him tear off his own
head. I couldn't believe it.

Little things moved Germans. They were moved to cry at
things like a glimpse of art, or of beauty, or a moment of tenderness. The drinking mates of the afflicted soul would maintain a
respectful silence, staring into their beer steins with surreptitious
pride, as though a member of some elite religious sect had been
blessed, momentarily, with a holy seizure. Then the moment
would pass, and the noisy, beery evening would continue as
though the interlude had never happened.

I watched moments like the above like an explorer in the heart
of Africa witnessing some arcane traditional ceremony.

Filadelfo had a small circle of well-informed friends, mostly
German, who gave me a lot of insight into, and background on,
the war. For instance, one of them, Detlev, with a three-barrelled
surname, told me that the Allies had refused to help the relatively
small German Resistance with any technical aid, information or
supplies. He was very bitter about this and saw it as having been
instrumental in prolonging the war.

We met at a tea party with his brother and a professor of history from Heidelberg. Socially, it was bad form to mention the
war. Even the word was taboo. If it had to be mentioned, it was
referred to as the *Unglück*: the 'misfortune' the war had been to
Germany. When I brought the subject up, Detlev leapt on it. The
others had stared pointedly into their teacups and one had tried in
vain to divert attention by enquiring about a violin recital pro-
grammed for the following week. These tactics merely made
Detlev turn his diatribe from me to the rest of the gathering.

The professor did not agree with any of Detlev's views on the
Resistance, and told him so rather curtly. Then, out of the blue,
tempers snapped.

The professor claimed that the 'so-called Resistance' had always been too divided, too small, too infiltrated and too utopian to have achieved anything, with or without Allied aid. When he added that its patriotism was also questionable, the conversation got so heated that some of the cake ended up on the floor.

Detlev, on his noble hands and knees, was obliged to pick up the crumbs from our hostess's formerly immaculate parquet. Having started the discussion, I felt suddenly very aware of being seen as the uncouth outsider who had ruined the genteel tea party. I didn't know where to look, so I knelt down to help him. He hissed: 'The reason the English wouldn't help was simple: our Resistance was *German* and therefore a suspect enemy force.' As he settled back into his leather armchair, he finished his speech loudly as though defying anyone else in the room to contradict him. 'Every other Resistance movement (with the sole exception of Britain's own Channel Islands, I believe) received help from England. *Our* Resistance was left on its own.'

After the debacle with the dropped cake, everyone else in the room had returned to small talk. No one challenged Detlev von nobleness, but neither did anyone other than me show any interest in his statement. They had glazed over.

The earlier outburst was something I would not see repeated often. In Tübingen, so long as no one jumped a queue, tempers didn't snap in public. There was an even keel; all unpleasant memories and ideas were kept well under the surface. Such was the determination that afternoon to maintain the status quo that the tinkle and clatter of teaspoons and Meissen porcelain almost drowned out Detlev's final shot.

'Some two million "good Germans" were killed by the Nazis. Which is the main reason why there are so few Resistance members left to speak out.'

Detlev looked from one impenetrable face to the next and then addressed himself exclusively to Filadelfo and me.

'People like my father!'

Bringing the personal into his argument was the equivalent of switching the lights out in a London pub. It was the cue for everyone to get up and make their farewells. Filadelfo, whose social antennae were acute, was among the first to leave.

As we walked back to his bachelor's apartment through a warm drizzle, he explained what I had already half realised: no one wanted there to have been a German Resistance. Now that the war was both over and lost, for intellectuals, in particular, the mere notion of any real resistance to the Hitler regime raised enormous issues of guilt. It suited people to blame the German high command exclusively for all its errors. If the leaders were 100 per cent guilty, then they, the people, could be 100 per cent innocent.

I subsequently learnt that this version of history was not just a national whitewashing exercise. The Allies didn't want there to have been a German Resistance either, because it didn't fit their version of the war. The entire war, it seemed, was on a big deceitful loop.

It seemed that the Allies wanted the Nazi atrocities and crimes against humanity to be seen, but then they wanted to blame a handful of high-ranking Nazi officials, and a handful only. The Allies specifically did not want the German *Volk*, the average man in the street, to have known what was going on. The Allies wanted to believe that all German civilians had been terrified and intimidated into cooperating so openly (and so publicly) with Hitler.

England and America wanted to hang the blame on a few leaders, hang those leaders, and then exonerate the rest of the country. The United States, in particular, wanted the average German to be an 'OK sort of guy'. That way, the rest of the world could feel OK about him, and let the war thing drop (once the evil leaders had been hanged and were safely in hell together with their 100 per cent responsibility). Then the world, including the citizens of buffer zone number one, namely West Germany, could concentrate on the real purpose of life: i.e. catching commie bastards and curbing the Red Peril.

It was as though almost everyone I saw or met in Germany went around with a big 'D' for *denial* invisibly stamped on their foreheads.

I was too young and brash and filled with self-righteous fervour then to weigh my findings against the backdrop of a nation who had been brainwashed into not saying what was in their hearts. More than a decade of brutal Nazi rule had bred whole cycles of self-protective mechanisms. What I observed had a value, but its value was distorted by not representing the other Detlevs of the Third Reich. It was safer to talk about sugar and sausages and the cost of living than to risk showing either true feelings or opinions. The wound of the war had made a hard scab, but it had not yet made a scar. When I was there in 1954 it was all too new for most of the people concerned, and it was too much to deal with.

Sometimes, as with Detlev or, later, Georg, I got flashes of insight into the German psyche. Yet this was rarely re the 'Jewish problem'. In fact, the whole 'Jewish problem' seemed to have the same kind of insignificance that, say, swatting a few mosquitoes the day before would have had for a Valerano. Had I, for instance, asked my mother or my uncle Emiliano, 'Why did you do it? Why did you kill that mosquito yesterday?', or if I had asked any of my siblings or cousins who had witnessed the deed, 'Why did you let it happen?', the response would have been approximately the same. The insect-killer would have had a fading recollection, if any, of the act. And what the hell was all the fuss about? Did you have a motive or a plan for things like that? What was the matter with me? What the hell did a few mosquitoes matter? Swatting mosquitoes in the tropics is a minor part of a bigger plan for the pursuit of comfort. Swatting them is a detail, it isn't a profession. It isn't important; it just has to be done.

It wasn't that people denied what had happened to the Jews during the war: they just didn't see that it mattered particularly. With their country in ruins and the wolf at their door, why go on about the Jews?

CHAPTER XXI

What frightens me about German culture is its combination of sincerity and thoroughness. I believe it is crucial to understand that culture to understand what happened to such a large chunk of the entire world in the middle of the last century. It would be easy to dismiss the tears of the big brutes in the Tübingen bars as crocodile tears. But they weren't fake: they were real. Raising the stakes, some people might dismiss the soft side of such an obvious bastard as Adolf Hitler as fake, but I believe it, too, was genuine. For instance, I don't believe Hitler was lying when he told Speer and Himmler, 'I love people so much! I find it insufferable when a car drives through puddles, splashing people along the road ... Beauty should have power over people.' Something genuine in him triggered that response. And perhaps we need to understand that soft side to him to understand the other ruthlessly cruel side. Perhaps to ignore the one is to fail to fully understand the other.

Hitler did not invent the Third Reich alone. He had the support of his people. It is undeniable that he did not have the support of all his people. Yet I wonder how many of those against him would have been so had the little Führer come out of the top drawer socially, had not been the 'little upstart house painter'. It seems clear that there would still have been an opposition, but it would probably have been quite a bit smaller. Be that as it may, the support he did have was massive and it was support so loyal it stuck through thick and thin. He did not gain it through cruelty and slaughter; he kept it despite those things. That kind of allegiance tends to draw on deep wells of fundamental truth. It can rarely be sustained on either lies or greed alone. Hitler had to have really, genuinely cared about certain basically decent things to have won the allegiance of a basically decent nation of people *before* he pressed everyone's fear button.

There you see another paradox, because Germany in the run-up to the Third Reich was far more 'decent' than almost anywhere else on the planet. German thought has been obsessed with what decency is. It has searched for what is good and what is divine. Germany was receptive to great ideas. It was a country with a broad philosophical training; its culture was steeped in reason. It was a country actively trying to get close to God.

Hitler persuaded the German people that his plan for a Third Reich was a great idea.

Having got their allegiance, Hitler whacked them with one great idea after another. In that glorious line-up, he slipped in some ideas whose only greatness was the greatness of their crime against humanity. And he managed to slip them in quite simply because some of his other ideas *were* great. He saw himself as Germany's saviour, as a hero and a power for Good. He managed to make people keep on believing in him because he so totally believed in himself, and his powers of oratory were such that they would have followed him to hell.

I arrived in Tübingen in mid-December 1953, hitting the run-up to Christmas. Despite the pockmarks of bullet holes on the buildings, Tübingen looked like an illustration to a fairytale, sprinkled in snow like icing sugar. The gingerbread and chocolate figurines in the bakery windows, the chiming of Christmas bells, the singing of carols and the intricate models and musical boxes on the toyshops' shelves made an enchanting impression.

I loved Tübingen and its small-town-ness. I love small towns in Germany in general. Perhaps the areas I like best are all the lands along the river Rhine: Köln, Düsseldorf, Frankfurt and Heidelberg. They are the most charming little towns. I loved the coffee shops and the beer cellars with their *Streusselkuchen* and *Kirschtorten*, and their cups of hot chocolate drowning under cream. Under the

auspices of Filadelfo, my compatriot, mentor and roommate, I
had a concrete role to play within the society: every day I had to
go out and shop, and come home and cook. The town was in the
middle of a very specific battle: would the housewives be able to
find and afford the white veal Christmas sausages? And would
there be enough carp to go round all the Christmas Eve dinners?
As a newly appointed chef, I found these worries beguilingly
absorbing.

The formality of the etiquette was intriguing. The elaborate
greetings had to be learnt and repeated on entering and leaving
every space. It was new to me. Together with some shopping tips,
Filadelfo had warned me of the importance of addressing everyone
as 'Sie' and never as 'Du'. Failing to say goodbye to a complete
stranger was a big gaffe. Using the familiar 'Du' apparently was
unforgivable. I was fine with that. In Valera we tended not to say
'thou' to anyone except animals and very small children. And in
the Venezuelan Andes we were used to standing on ceremony to
a certain extent. Our Spanish is archaic, handed down from the
Conquistadores from the days of courtly Spain. What got me in
Tübingen were the bows and the titles and double titles: the Herr
Doktor Doktors. Would a scholar with four Ph.D.s be Herr Doktor
Doktor Doktor Doktor? And would anyone ever talk to him?

Twice, once in Köln and once in Tübingen, I saw two men,
who were obviously old friends, and were sitting drinking
schnapps, stand to attention, bow to each other and link elbows,
while one invited the other to address him henceforth with the
informal 'Du'. For all their strangeness, I loved observing the
small ceremonies.

Well, I spent whole days unravelling the even smaller rites of
buying vegetables and picking eggs from wooden stalls served by
red-faced farmwomen. I got to know the names of all the herbs
and, like my mother, to learn their medicinal uses: fennel tea for
indigestion, camomile for sickness, sage for headaches and thyme
for the bladder. The market women were very forthcoming: they
treated me like an honorary housewife, and were full of tips about
how I should keep my kitchen. During my first month, I jigsawed
the language and a lot of its recent history together by picking
through the market stalls.

CHAPTER XXII

I got to know the town of Tübingen, lane by lane, and shop by shop. I got to know the tower where Hegel had lived. I became a regular at the café where I used to go with Filadelfo. It was a place of sudden intimacy, of beer stains and astonishingly strong plum liqueur. It had a wood-burning stove and an aura of welcoming good cheer. I felt a genuine fondness for Tübingen, whereas there isn't one place in France that I feel as emotionally attached to.

As in every fairytale, the enchanted city was under a spell. Bang in the middle of all that geographical affection, I got to know first-hand some of its darker side. Behind the excessive politeness, the collective amnesia, the clean, bright prettiness of the town, there was a dogged virulence. This went beyond the ignorant nastiness of some people who took me for a Jew, and blamed me for the shortage of beeswax in the shops or the scarcity of oranges. And it went beyond those who looked away from me with such obvious distaste. It went beyond the occasional stranger who came up to me and showered me with apologetic kindness, again, mistaking me for a Jew. It went beyond all those actions (which were superficial) to an underlying ruthlessness such as I have never known.

I came across a few Nazis who were unashamedly loyal to the Third Reich. The *Unglück* for them was more than a stroke of bad luck: they saw themselves as subject less to misfortune than to misunderstanding. Their regrets were limited to a job unfinished: a job that still had to be done. One old guy made a point of telling me that next time around I 'wouldn't slip through their net'.

In Tübingen, I first saw that aspect of the German character which makes them capable of carrying an idea to its ultimate consequences, regardless of whatever human price it might involve. The jump from Valera to post-Nazi Tübingen (albeit via Salamanca and Paris) was a bit too extreme for me to conform to the social niceties as good Germans were supposed to do. I refused to turn a blind eye to the recent past. And I refused to honour the prevalent taboo surrounding any mention of the *Unglück*. I was insatiably curious. I was like a puppy dog, and I found every way I could to get close to people. One of the ways of breaking down barriers was through chess. I used to sit in the bar and play my right hand against my left in the hopes of luring a lonely player across to the board. It didn't work very often, but it worked enough to make it a worthwhile ploy.

One of the punters I pulled in like this was Georg, an ex-soldier. He was much older than me: in his early forties. He had an air of depression about him. And I soon discovered that he lived alone and was obviously lonely. In my unashamedly Latin way, I had got him first to nodding terms, then to the chessboard and then to become my regular twice-weekly partner in the bar. One day (after many hints and hopes) he invited me back to his flat. He lived in two small, musty rooms crammed full of carved oak furniture. It looked as though he had inherited these dressers and the sideboard as family heirlooms from a much larger house. Incongruously cramped, it seemed as though, like Georg, they were trying to tell their story.

As we huddled round his small oil heater, over a glass of schnapps, I plucked up the courage to ask him about the war.

Georg seemed suddenly relieved. He told me he had volunteered for a police corps, and that after his basic training he'd been sent east.

'I was in Byelorussia,' he said.

'What was it like?' I asked. 'What was it really like?'

He paused for nearly a minute, looking into my eyes so intently that it felt as though he was detecting the actual remains of something or someone he had lost in the depths of my eyeballs. It was, momentarily, so intimate, and his look of yearning and loneliness was so intense, that I thought for a moment he wanted to kiss me. He took a step across the trampled brown flowers in the carpet. I took a step back in Andean alarm. (Men do fuck other men in the Andes, but they don't kiss and they don't let other men fuck them.) I had heard that several of the German High Command had been back-door chimney sweepers, and there were rumours that all that Nazi emphasis on blond hair and tight trousers and male beauty had a horizontal slant. And I had, after all, picked Georg up in a bar and done my damndest to get invited back to his lair.

My step back broke some of the tension. Georg stopped and his shoulders went very limp. He looked suddenly quite lost.

'Can I trust you, Oswald?' he asked. 'I mean, really trust you?'

Something in him was broken and I guessed that whatever he had on his mind had nothing to do with sex. I nodded guiltily and then assured him that he could, that the war had passed us by in Venezuela, and meant nothing to us one way or the other.

'Then, Oswald, I will tell you about it. You know, sometimes a man needs to remember.'

I waited while he gathered his composure and went across to one of a pair of hideously carved dressers with crude lions snarling in lieu of handles and misshapen maidens arching backwards into brackets.

Then he opened a drawer and rummaged around in a box of photographs. He came back to me, carrying two of them. They were worn and thumbed the way favourite photos can be. One was of himself, younger, and in uniform. He was posing at the edge of a pit full of what must have been prisoners of war, a few of whom were reaching up towards his trousered leg. One hand, with gecko-like fingers, has grasped his boot. Georg is smiling at the camera, hands on hips.

The second photograph looked as though it had been taken shortly afterwards near the same pit. Georg is standing arm-in-arm with two other soldiers. His face is turned back to the pit, as though the photographer has called him. Georg is caught smiling happily, interrupted as he laughs. They are all in their mid-thirties but they all exude the energy that younger men have.

While he showed me the snaps, a faraway look came into his eyes. I waited for him to speak, to tell me whatever it was he had to say about that death pit and the others like it. His hand trembled slightly as he showed me the photograph and his sagging jowls twitched. Once again, he made time stretch, but this time his eyes were locked on the black-and-white image of his former self. I said nothing, waiting for his moment of truth to come in his own time. The room was so silent I could hear our breathing. Eventually, he sighed and said, 'It was good, you know. We were all together!'

And that was it. What he remembered were the friendships he forged over it and what he regretted was the loss of that camaraderie. What he wanted to confide in me was his nostalgia for those good old days and his sadness and confusion at the silence that had been enforced around them. As I was leaving (quite soon after that), he murmured, 'Some of our Corps died out there, you know, Oswald. Doing their duty.'

And that was the only mention of death or killing that he made in his 'confession'.

I don't think Georg or the majority of Germans enjoyed murder. I know that some found it downright distasteful. But it was a job that had to be done. It was a necessity to make an idea happen. For lonely Georg, it was the time of his life: the one time when he belonged. I spent many hours with him and can vouch for his having very little grip on ideology. There were probably thousands of Georgs, all ready to be swept up by the idealists. And the German idealists were driven by a ruthless determination to carry an idea through to its ultimate consequence.

Occasionally, in history, there have been people who stood out with a similar ruthless determination. It is rare. Lenin, for example, carried out his ideas to their ultimate consequences, and didn't give a shit about the human cost. Hitler and Lenin had something in common; well, maybe not so much Hitler, because he wasn't really an ideologist, but let us say Goebbels or

Rosenberg and all the great German theoreticians. If you compare
the racism of Gobineau with theirs, Gobineau maintained that
there were superior and inferior races; St Hilan claimed that mis-
cegenation weakened a race. They thought it, but they never
arrived at consequences, or carried their theories to extremes.
Their solutions were always theoretical. The German theorists
forced theory into effect: into action. 'Yes,' they claimed, 'racial
mixing is negative, and there is a race which has damaged and
diluted our superior race. Therefore, let's exterminate it – now.'
Full stop. Over and out.

Lenin was a bit the same with the revolution. 'Things must be
carried through to their extreme conclusion, and it must be done.'

That was Lenin. And he never budged an inch. If it is necessary
to steamroller millions of men in the process, that doesn't matter,
because it is the idea that counts.

The idea came from Hegel. It got borrowed by Lenin, Stalin
and Mao Tse-tung; but it came from Hegel. The consequences
that that idea had on the German people were much more honest
and up front than on any other nation.

At Nuremberg, the Allies had hanged a few scapegoats. They
couldn't hang half of Germany! The Holocaust was too great a
crime for its blame to be shared. The blame is shared now, but by
those who were not directly responsible for it. Even most of those
who still seek out the actual culprits waited a generation before
pointing the finger. War criminals tend to be doddery and apparently harmless old men who totter to their trials with the vacant
stares and hazy memories of geriatrics. After the war, the Cold
War made the Reds the enemy. For that to be the case, the
United States needed Germany as its ally: to be a buffer between
East and West. So Germany was whitewashed.

The Holocaust was initiated and perpetrated by Germans. It
could, theoretically, have been initiated and perpetrated by any
other nation. To a lesser extent, elements of the Holocaust *have*
been initiated and carried out by other nations in this century and
even in this decade. Even when circumstances exclude individual
choice – for whatever reason, such as fear, obedience to authority,
the need to please, peer-group pressure – a certain element of
choice remains. That the vast majority of mankind chooses not to

take it, or rather, chooses to ignore it, is not, I think, the prerogative of Germans. It seems to apply to all of us, no matter where
we come from. The exceptions to the rule – the Nelson Mandelas
and the Mahatma Gandhis of this world – are few and far
between.

What I see as the strangest element of the behaviour of the
leaders of the Third Reich is their obsession with and loyalty to an
idea. The pen proved mightier than the sword, mightier than
human emotion, mightier than our innate sense of good and evil,
and mightier than plain common sense in the Great Famine in
China, in the Gulags in Russia and in the Nazi camps. In each
case, there went out a decree and the decree itself, the idea,
became like the will of God. And as with the wrath of God in biblical times, its consequences were suffered as a just necessity.

After the world was reduced to rubble and the dreams of glory
had been shattered and the bitter taste of defeat had to be chewed
daily like a cud of ashes, for many, the idea was still untarnished.
As an intellectual and a would-be philosopher shaped largely by
German thought, I realised that I too was only a step away from
warping. Perhaps we are all only a step away from warping, but as
one fascinated by ideas, I felt more vulnerable than a man driven
by impulse and emotion alone. What was that step? How big was
it? Was it a Monod-ian leap or an imperceptible shuffle? Had
Heidegger, one of my guiding lights, taken a half-step? There
were rumours that he had. If true, where did it leave his work and
where did that work lead? These were questions I asked myself
but could not answer.

In the early summer of 1954, I returned to France with the
German paradox stuck in my throat like a chicken bone. Germany
is the country that has tried the most to understand God and to
understand the sublime in some way. And since the Greeks, the
country that has contributed most to the field of philosophy is
Germany. And the country that has strived most to find an answer
to the questions of Judaism and Christianity is Germany. And yet
it is in that country that the episodes of life in which there was the
greatest absence of God were lived.

Had I followed my own master plan, my choice, I would have

gone back to Germany after Paris and studied at Freiburg. As things turned out, that was not to be.

I re-read Heidegger and Schopenhauer, Hegel and Spengler. When I turned my back on Freiburg and Heidegger and embraced communism and later socialism more fully, the latter was, in part, a reaction to the void left by perceiving the flaws in Martin Heidegger's reason. I think that the years I dedicated to analysing Sartre's work were also a reaction to the disillusion I felt on discovering quite how close Heidegger's ties had been to the Nazis and quite how close his philosophy was to theirs. Sartre's philosophy hatched from the same egg, but Sartre, unlike the Dean of Freiburg, wrote about despair without ever actually taking the step that induced it in others. In the past fifteen years, there have been a number of books and essays on Heidegger the 'Nazi'. There have been apologists for him, claiming that he was a naive who got pulled out of his depth, and there have been accusations that he set the scene and then pulled the Nazis in after him.

One of the hardest things to bear is betrayal by someone one thought of as a friend. Although I have never lost all my respect and admiration for Heidegger, losing his mind as a source of inspiration for my own was as personally hurtful as being betrayed by a friend. I returned to Germany to meet one of my great heroes: Thomas Mann. Not that I knew him before, and neither did he know of me. But in 1955 he was to give a speech and I decided to collar him after it and 'converse with the master'. Then I didn't once go back to Germany in the next twenty years. I worried over that paradox – that search for good and that research into evil – in bars and brothels and jungles all over the world. Only through the life and poetry of Paul Celan have I been able to address the problem. Celan is the poet who has tried most to understand Germany and German thinking. It is important to me, intellectually, to understand it.

> More than the dove, more than the mulberry
> it's me that autumn loves. Gives me a veil.
> 'Take this for dreaming' says its stitchery.
> And: 'God's as nearby as the vulture's nail.'

But I have held another cloth instead,
Coarser than this, no stitchery or seam.
Touch it and snow falls in the bramble bed.
Wave it and you will hear the eagle scream.

CHAPTER XXIII

What else can I say of my time in France? I got my law degree and my diploma in sociology. I got tuberculosis, and spent some months in a sanatorium outside Paris, in a kind of delayed puberty, playing pranks on the nurses with the other TB patients. We had pillow fights and midnight feasts, and confessional friendships like boys in a boarding school. It was like belonging to a very elite club. The closest friends I made in France, I made there. TB sufferers the world over are a bit like Freemasons: they stick together.

Before, during, and after that illness, I continued to militate for the party. I was chosen to be one of the representatives for France to the Youth Rally of International Communism in Bucharest in 1955. Side by side with the very serious aims of the youth rally, and the speeches that all the delegates prepared, was the fact that the hundreds of delegates were under twenty-five, boys and girls together, it was summer, and a lot of us were drunk a lot of the time. It didn't matter that the hundreds of delegates spoke dozens of different languages: communism was about sharing. Running parallel to its political side, it became a gathering of free love. Never, not even in my wildest dreams, had I had so much sex.

For once, the slander that seems to stick to me like burrs was short of the mark. I now realise that those Slav girls were making the most of what might have been the only taste of freedom they

were ever going to get. It was a frenzied interlude during which –
I really don't know how – I staggered onto the podium and gave
a rousing speech. I returned to Paris feeling that international
communism was the most wonderful movement in the world.

And then there was Vida. Vida is the Spanish word for life. Vida
was the only woman I would marry. She was my wife and the
great love of my life; she is the mother of our son, Ramín. She also
drew me into Iranian politics and an involvement in the Middle
East. Vida was central to the opposition to the Shah. She would
later spend nineteen years as a political prisoner. Eventually freed
by the Ayatollah Khomeini when he came to power, she went on
to help lead the Kurdish rebellion against him.

Although she transformed my life, at the end of all that passion,
Vida is a Persian lady who doesn't really like me now. And, if I
am honest about it, she didn't really like me then either. The passion was always one-sided. I first saw her in a café in the Latin
quarter, and I fell in love with her in a way that I have never been
in love with anyone else. It was a coup de foudre.

She was stunningly beautiful. Look how many times we say that
about women. I say it all the time, when I'm in the mood, about
any woman who's halfway good-looking. But Vida was different. I
saw her and was literally stunned. I didn't ever want to let her out
of my sight. I couldn't take in what she looked like. I didn't know
who she was. She was with a man, a ridiculously handsome, tall
man. When I approached their table, I thought, She will see me.
She looked up in a slightly bored way, irritated momentarily by
the interruption. Despite this, I thought, She will know that I
cannot breathe for love of her.

I had been taken to that café to meet her. My sometime girlfriend, Charachu, was Persian, and her friend, another Persian, had
come over to visit a sister who was studying architecture at a private university in Paris. That sister was Vida. Vida had an
imperious manner, which she showed that evening when she
waved us away without nodding more than a cursory 'hello'.
Charachu and her friend left, but I stayed at another table, making
one café filtre last while I stared in adoration at Vida's beautiful
face, neck and hands.

Vida had a stillness about her, a poise that made her stand out wherever she was, and she too was tall. When they walked past my table, she and her friend were talking and she didn't notice me at all. I couldn't understand how she could change my whole life, alter me so profoundly, and be unaware not only of that change, but of my presence. As they went through the door, I stood up and followed them.

They walked for miles.

After I recovered from the poisonous bite on my chest, I had found myself in the embarrassing situation of being part of a group that I knew nothing about. The first thing I had to do was to locate Algeria on a map. The next thing I had to do was read about every aspect of it.

As I followed Vida and her escort, I felt increasingly guilty that I was simultaneously standing up my comrades and friends. During the past year, I had become close to an exemplary Algerian called Ben Bella – the leader in exile of the opposition and probably the most wanted man in France. Some of his inner circle were gathering that night in one of their safe houses in S. Antoine. I was not only invited, I was expected. And yet, there I was shadowing a strange beauty for reasons as far from either politics or Algeria as it was possible to be.

My momentary defection aside, independence for Algeria was the first cause I really felt passionate about. In fact, the plight of that country was my true initiation into politics. Everything I had done until then in Venezuela with regards to politics had involved an element of playing and play-acting. While my comrades and I were discussing Lenin's speeches in a small storeroom in Valera with the net result of my painting a few slogans on walls, the FLN was systematically sabotaging the French colonial rule of Algeria, organising mass insurrections and striking heavy blows against the effective running of the country.

I had never truly believed in what I said or did as a left-wing agitator when I was a boy. And there was always a surreal element to my political activities back home because, no matter what I did, I was partly protected by my family network. I walked a tightrope sometimes, but it was always with a safety net to catch me if I fell.

After seeing the gunning down of the Bastille marchers, and

having begun to understand the root causes of the Algerian people's struggle, I joined them and it. In 1954, at the outbreak of the Algerian Revolution (which would last until independence in 1962), the French settlers comprised only 11 per cent of the population and yet 90 per cent of industrial and commercial activity was in European hands. The so-called Pieds Noirs, the French, owned the best of everything, while the native population, be it Arab or Berber, was exploited, repressed and mostly undernourished. Ninety per cent of the indigenous population was illiterate and only one Muslim child in ten went to school.

The FLN had gained widespread support in the far-flung villages and solid backing in the cities. Algerian Muslims were converted to the idea that there had to be an Algerian nation instead of Algeria continuing as an official part of France.

Under the leadership of Ahmed Ben Bella, the Algerians had nothing much more to lose by fighting to the end. The stakes in the struggle were high and rising week by week, almost day by day. Theirs was a real battle. France, with its massive modern army supplied with the latest NATO weapons, would do almost anything to keep hold of its lucrative playground in North Africa, while the Algerians were fast approaching that unique point in human endeavour when almost every man, woman and child rises up with one voice and demands, and then takes, their freedom.

I think I would have given my life for the FLN had I been asked to do so, but I still had to know the facts, the background and the other side. The turning point in the tactics of the 'liberal' French government's approach seemed to be the Massacre of Philippeville in August 1955. That one drastic act (in which the Algerian insurgents killed 123 people) not only brought about a reprisal in which up to 12,000 Muslims were slain, it also brought about an all-out war with no holds barred and no underlying ethical rules. It gave the Pieds Noirs a propaganda tool to wave under the noses of the French public. That one incident at Philippeville shocked the hitherto laissez-faire French governor-general into asking for repressive measures and France committed nearly half a million troops.

In Algeria, the FLN and its military branch, the ALN, were well-organised, efficient fighting units. In Paris and Marseilles there were tightly organised logistic groups with more than enough highly educated and motivated people to run them.

During the early days of my affiliation to their struggle, all I had to offer was my solidarity. They didn't need me, but I needed them. I needed to feel a part of something.

I was fired by the spirit of the Algerians and their rational plan for the 'conscious construction' of their country according to 'socialist principles with the power in the hands of the people'. The communist bloc and the leadership of the communist and socialist parties of France all steadfastly refused to support or even recognise the FLN. Where I could be most effective was in converting French intellectuals to the cause. Sometimes to do so felt a little bit like ploughing the sea, but, eventually, the atrocities committed by the French in Algeria turned the tide of public opinion in France, and (disgracefully slowly) the rest of the world began to ask embarrassing questions. Thousands of villages were razed in a scorched-earth programme and the battle of Algiers was conducted with a savagery by the French colonialists that was hard to equate with their cultural heritage.

In France, the Algerian Resistance centred around Boumediènne, an elusive, clandestine leader with enormous charisma and vision. He, in turn, worked behind the scenes with Ahmed Ben Bella, but the latter was never more than a mythical name to me in Paris. Boumediènne himself, on the other hand, became a close friend. It was a friendship fuelled by fleeting encounters and our shared passion for his cause.

I thought about a hundred and one things as I followed Vida through the streets that night, and one of them was that my behaviour was hard to equate with my cultural heritage. But no matter how foolish I felt, I seemed to be compelled to keep going.

Remembering back to those early days of my courtship, I am always amazed at my sheer tenacity. Because I didn't 'court' Vida – I stalked her. For months, after that first evening, I followed her through the streets, to the university (where she studied), to her apartment, to restaurants, cafés, to cinemas, theatres, concerts, couturiers', perfumeries, jewellers' and parks. We went to all the places where lovers go, but she was with her

friends, male and female (and, more often than I could bear, with
that handsome bastard!), while I was trotting along behind her as
a more than unwelcome shadow. I look back to all that stalking
and I am amazed that I dared to do it, and amazed also at my stamina. I had weak lungs and the scrawny physique of an
intellectual. Sport was an alien concept to me. I was short and
weedy. When, eventually, Vida began to notice me, she called me
a 'runt'. Such is the power of infatuation that Vida swivelling on
her beautiful stilettos and saying, 'Stop following me, you nasty
little runt!' had the sweet ring of success to my ears. She was
noticing me, seeing me, at last! She had spoken, not to her glam-
orous friends and lover, but to me! She was beautiful when she
was angry: beautiful in a different way.

One of the things people remember most about Vida is that her
eyes changed colour depending on her mood. She had green eyes.
When she was tired, they were the cloudy, dull green of the
pools around the small fountain in the courtyard of her apartment.
When she was happy or excited, they were a clear, brilliant green.
When she was angry, her eyes flashed and transformed to a very
definite grey. When she was moody or depressed (she was often
moody, but rarely depressed), her eyes were a deeper, charcoal
grey. Her eyes were magic, Persian ovals framed by pale, perfect
skin rounding over high cheekbones and a high forehead. Hers was
a regal face. I didn't know when I stalked her (or even later, when
I married her) that the reason she looked so noble was that she
came from royal lineage.

She had the energy of an ocelot. She walked taking long strides
with her shapely legs. And I followed her, getting stronger every
day from my tubercular bout but still, always, struggling to keep
up with her. On the first night, I swear she strolled for six or seven
miles around Paris. The part of Vida's anatomy that I know best
is the nape of her neck, the sweep of her heavy black hair piling
onto her head. Her back was straight and graceful. Her arse was
not large, not small, but tight and swaying from the hips, swaying
in a way that made me drunk with lust. I know Vida off by heart
from behind because, for eight months, that was virtually all I saw
of her, as I dogged her footsteps.

The thrill of her back, on that first summer's night, pulled in at the waist in folds of cream silk, is a sensation I can bring back to this day. It was a sensation that embodied all the elements of my life until then: excitement, curiosity, lust, fear, love, admiration, religion, a sense of destiny, grief, happiness, pleasure and pain.

The pain factor began with an ache in my groin, shifted to an ache in my legs (as they tired from traipsing along the boulevards), and then gravitated to my feet. I was unaccustomed to walking. My feet were pinched in what had been, until then, a perfectly serviceable pair of shoes.

Such was my insignificance to Vida and her playboy escort that it took several hours that night before they even became aware of my presence. From which alone I deduced that this couple moved in entirely different circles from my own. The people I knew were all paranoid. If an old lady doing her shopping happened to walk behind one of us for a block and a half we would log her as a police spy and start dodging into alleyways.

What am I saying? I need a shovel to scrape off some of my bullshit. Vida came from another world and I saw it within seconds of hitting the street behind her. She wore expensive high-heeled shoes. She wore raw silk. Her pencil skirt had to have been cut by a designer. She wore tiny earrings with real emeralds that even to my untrained eye exuded wealth. And her escort was dripping with upper-class understatement. Whenever I got close enough to them to hear what they were saying, their accents were the perfect French of L'Académie Française.

Eventually, they slowed down and the guy whispered something to her. He turned round and gave me a withering stare. The shit! I already hated him with a passion. I didn't care what he did or said, or how he stared: I was going to oust him from his position at the side of the still nameless beauty he was with. I heard her name that night, Charachu had said it and I had heard him say it, and didn't realise that it was a name. And Vida, when told someone was following them, didn't deign to turn round. The combination of their now much quickened steps, their attempts to dodge me, and the critical condition of my feet, ended the evening in defeat. I caught the bus home (well, several buses), feverish with rapidly alternating fits of elation and despair.

Hope won that night. I convinced myself that the mystery

goddess would cross my path again. She had to. We were meant for each other. Many friends have pointed out to me the fundamental flaw in this hypothesis: Vida was meant for me, but I was not meant for her.

Later, when we were together, I knew that Vida loved it when I read aloud to her; she loved my voice. I saw that she was proud of me when I swayed a room full of people or a rally. All the time I was with her, I couldn't believe my luck. I watched her for signs of affection and tokens of esteem — little things, like finding my hypochondria amusing, and joining me in the search for the perfect pillow to appease my allergies. Shopping together for food in markets gave her pleasure because I could talk to the vendors and other shoppers alike, while she never knew how to make quick connections. This shyness often made her seem haughtier than she actually was. She would get visibly excited when we discussed matters strictly related to socialism, sociology or Iran. We used to discuss them for hours curled around each other on a sofa like two cats, and she would lap up my knowledge on counts one and two and then dazzle me with Persian tales. She was thirsty for knowledge and I was the fountain at which she came to drink. Perhaps I should have noticed more that as soon as I strayed from these three designated topics or ventured an original idea, she would instantly end our idyll, dismissing me with a sneer. But I didn't want to notice such things. I was savouring what we had in common, not what kept us apart.

And lastly, although it was a pleasure she struggled to deny, once we finally made love, she was as drawn to me sexually as I was to her. No matter what else she said or did, I saw this physical bond as an absolute proof of her love. I knew her body spoke the truth.

But truths are like gems: they have many facets, and each individual gem is unique. They are not magnetic, and neither do they follow each other through any natural law. Each one has to be mined and cut separately. And yet truth is mercurial: it disperses into numerous separate balls at the slightest impact, but unlike mercury, the balls of truth do not necessarily re-adhere to the same mass.

It was true that I loved Vida and I tried to make her love me.

I courted her in ways that bordered on the insane, and crossed the border into the criminal. I eventually bludgeoned her into living with me, marrying me, and bearing our son. And it was true that she loved our love-making and (three topics of) our conversation. Yet there were also many other truths and these were what others saw so clearly, while I was blind with love. One of those truths was that Vida loathed me with the same, visceral intensity with which I loved her.

Just as sometimes a momentary lucidity would allow me to see the hardness at her core, an almost frightening intransigence, so sometimes would she see a flash of brilliance or wit or attractiveness of some kind in me: the person she otherwise despised.

I only really discovered who Vida was when I went with her to Persia some years later. I had fallen in love with her, whoever she was and wherever she might be from. Her flatmate (who despised me more than Vida did herself) was just her flatmate to me. The flatmate was the beautiful, haughty fashion fool who, by marrying the Shah of Persia, was to become the Farah Diva of Iran. That was the kind of social circle Vida moved in – but I was oblivious to that.

Vida, on the other hand, was very aware of how the world perceived both her and others. Although she had been sent to Paris to refine her education and fill up her wardrobe, she was, as I have hinted, a woman with a mind of her own. Unbeknown to her parents, her flatmate and her friends alike, Vida was leaning sharply towards communism. You might think that Dior suits, everything that Coco-Chanel could come up with and communism were a contradiction in terms, but you would be surprised how many join the party and follow its course from the luxury of their yachts and villas. I even know so-called communists who insist on their servants wearing livery. Be that as it may, Vida was a communist sympathiser and a rich foreigner on the fringe of all the intellectual excitement in Paris then. Although she saw me, personally, as little better than an underevolved reptile, she could not help but be impressed by my involvement and leadership within the party.

I would follow her to expensive restaurants and wait outside for hours while she dined. She would see me, but pretend that she hadn't. And on her way out, she'd never say a word to me. Yet she would attend some of the rallies and meetings we held, and, often as not, it would be me addressing those meetings. Gradually, it became clear to her that I was popular in ways she never could be, and I was accepted in ways she never would be. At these meetings, I was the big shot, not her. She didn't bring her rich friends along with her on these occasions. Her reactionary flatmate would have had a fit if she had known how Vida spent her time. A couple of times, Vida even said hello to me when all the crowd of comrades were around. Then I would introduce her to a few people, and I could see that it pleased her to be taken notice of, even at the price of having to pretend to be my friend.

We comrades always went to a bar after these meetings. I invited her along, but she wasn't ready to be seen in public with us, with me. I have always liked to think it was her thousands of years of high breeding that kept her from accepting my invitations, but perhaps it was just me.

Anyway, there was a bit of cat and mouse going on. After the first two months, I was no longer as in awe of her as I had been. I found the courage to speak. This did absolutely nothing to further my cause, except to hear a few times from her own lips that she found me repulsive, loathsome, undersized, pathetic, ridiculous, preposterous, idiotic and a pain in the neck. I was no closer to making love to her, or marrying her, but it was a dialogue of sorts.

I continued to dog her footsteps. It wasn't possible to keep up my assault around the clock because I had to study and militate. Also, I had to spend a little bit of time with the two girls who did want to have sex with me. And I had to distance myself, from time to time, from the handsome monsieur who had gone from escorting Vida and holding her hand to sticking his tongue down her throat right in front of me, and caressing the small of her back as I followed them.

I had a couple of run-ins with Monsieur Handsome. The first time, he wheeled round and told me in no uncertain terms to fuck off. The second time, he reminded me of the first. The third time, he pushed me against a watchmaker's window (hard). The fourth time, he shoved me off my balance and I fell in the gutter. He was just telling me that that was exactly where I belonged and that he would have had me arrested weeks before if it hadn't been for Vida's insistence to the contrary (interesting and very hopeful!), and was aiming his brown-brogued foot to kick me, when Vida publicly intervened. She told him to leave me alone, and for him not to be so pathetic.

Maybe I exaggerated her response a little when I took this as an open invitation for me to sleep with her. But from the dusty gutter it looked as though Vida had finally surrendered to my siege. I was helped up by a pair of elderly ladies, who assured me that they had seen it all, and apologised profusely for monsieur's appalling manners.

I had been to Vida's apartment block a few times. I had hung around outside, I had watched her tight-arsed flatmate go in and out. I had exchanged dirty looks with the uniformed doorman. And I had suffered some long, unflattering stares from the wealthy people who went in and out. From my first visit, anyone connected to the building assumed that I was a delivery boy. The first bunch of flowers I took to Vida placed me firmly in that category as far as everyone, residents and staff, were concerned. I left my bouquet with a profound note on the coconut mat outside her apartment door. Vida, I noticed, threw my roses unwrapped into the bin.

I didn't have enough money to be buying flowers from expensive florists in the first place. So next time I tried chocolates. I bought a beautifully confectioned box from a fashionable patisserie. These too went straight into the rubbish, from where I retrieved and ate them. The next time I went empty-handed; I was challenged twice and had to run the gauntlet of hostile stares on my way through the building.

My third choice of gift was beautifully packaged bath salts. The box was flowing with gold ribbons and bows. This gift Vida pushed straight back at me as though it was goat droppings. Once again, I was left standing like an idiot outside her slammed apartment door. But now I had an endlessly recyclable delivery, which got me in and out of her building unmolested. Day by day, I flourished the package on my way in, muttering 'delivery' to the doorman. And every time I slunk back out, the bath salts were hidden under my jacket.

It was a minor victory. It doesn't take much to encourage a man in love. I was encouraged by the fact that Vida did not have me thrown out of the building. She threatened me with security a number of times, but she never actually called them.

I am no courtier. I never have been. My conquests have come through lust, tenacity and luck. To the best of my ability I courted Vida. When she eschewed my gifts, I jumped a few stages and opted for an overtly sexual onslaught. I have never used such a tactic on any other woman. My friends, who were often party to my stalking exercises, used to pull me aside and say, 'For God's sake, Oswaldo, what's the matter with you? Can't you see the lady loathes you? And look at her, man! She is a *lady*! What are you doing whispering all this dirty shit at her? You've got to stop it. You're losing your marbles. How can you humiliate yourself like this?'

Well, it was only for her, my Persian princess. I wouldn't (couldn't) have done it for anyone else. The more she scorned me, the more I wanted her. And I had an inkling that my only hope was to fire her sexual fantasies. I knew that Vida thought that just being in the same space as me was a kind of slumming. So I gave it the flavour of Zola: sex, sex and sex. Of course, it would have helped if I had looked more the Lothario and less like a satyr, and it would have helped if I hadn't been half-witted with love. In the end, familiarity erased a modicum of the contempt Vida felt for me. As I have said, I just wanted her to respond; I was indifferent as to how she responded. Her insults, if directed at me, were a sweet palliative to my frenzied desire.

CHAPTER XXIV

The gossips in Valera say I have no shame. They cite endless instances of my alleged depravity as evidence of this. I'm not saying there haven't been shameful moments in my life – there have. But when it comes to my relationships with women (with the noticeable exception of Vida), no matter how badly things may have turned out, I can say with a clear conscience that I have not intentionally acted like an arsehole and I have sometimes actively tried to behave well. Moving away from the subject of sex (which is always hard for a Valerano to do), there have also been shameful moments in my career – many, in fact – which slide from the sublime to the ridiculous. But there is a fundamental difference between the shame you merit and the shame you don't; the shame you seek and the shame that finds you and attaches itself to you like a head louse, breeding in your hair and contaminating your friends and family.

I think there must be shameful moments in everybody's life. No one behaves perfectly all the time, and those few men and women who seem to, who rise to the status of exemplary human beings, only do so by learning to behave well as they make their way up the slippery ladder of life. Gandhi, who dedicated almost every second of every day of his adult life to the good of his people, tells of a shameful occasion when his father was dying.

Gandhi was a young adolescent living at home but also in an arranged marriage that he confesses to having enjoyed with the

gusto of a randy goat. He was little more than a boy, but most of
his thoughts were fixated on the perfectly legal enjoyment of his
conjugal rights. He tells of the last moments of his father's life, of
knowing that his duty and deeper inclination needed him to stay
by his father's bedside as the beloved patriarch crossed over into
death. But he tired of this vigil, and kept longing to satisfy his
pubescent lust. He describes in detail how he couldn't wait to
leave the sickroom so that he could rush off to his own bedroom
and climb back into bed with his child bride. Not only did the
young Gandhi long for this, he did it; his father died while he, the
son, was having sex. He speaks of the incident in his autobiography, dwelling at some length on the baseness of his behaviour as
a source of undying shame.

And yet, Mahatma Gandhi was virtually a saint. He was, if ever
there was one, a saintly person. He lived on leaves and water,
lentils and tea. He later forwent sex and all forms of gratification
the better to concentrate on saving his people. And still he was
aware of having done shameful things. Compared to the rest of us,
of course, Gandhi's lapses in common decency were few and far
between, but thanks to his searing honesty, we know they happened.

In life there are great figures, like Gandhi, the father of India,
and Nelson Mandela, and Marie Curie. They are men and women
whose lives and actions shine like beacons across time and place.
And then there are lesser beings who aspire to greatness but
achieve it at a lower level. Even when their achievements are
spectacular and momentous and transform our existence, they
themselves do not necessarily have that intrinsic immortal quality
that makes them shine. Their actions, inventions and contributions
may be great, but they, the perpetrators, the men and women, are
not touched by the gods. In fact, someone can be a brilliant
achiever in their public life and a complete bastard in their private
one. I think, without naming any names, we can all think of a few
of those.

Sliding further down the ladder, there are people who are far
below the saints and social transformers, but are still high above
the bottom-feeders and high above the mass of doers and followers. They are like a coral reef in a rough sea. They break the

waves and soften their blow before they hit the shore. They have neither the strength nor the power to make this buffer alone. A reef is something that grows organically over thousands of years. It is the combined effort of millions of organisms. Each millimetre of coral is the life's work of a separate builder. Together, they construct a wall. Alone, they would just be drifting bits of grit.

My detractors insist that I am a bottom-feeder. I am not. But neither am I anywhere near to being (nor have I ever aspired to be) a saint. I am not dodging the shame issue. In fact, I am coming to it: because I know that in my unorthodox courtship of Vida I behaved shamefully. And I am ashamed of how I forced myself into her life. I loved her and I wanted her to love me. It has been said that the first duty of love is to listen. I did listen, but it was to myself and not to her. I could not accept that such a huge love as I felt could remain unreciprocated. I was convinced that if I could just open her eyes to me, she would respond and succumb.

With time, she did respond and she did succumb; but I forced the issue. And I know that that was wrong. The way it happened was as strange as the rest of the affair. I had laid siege to Vida. I slept outside her apartment door sometimes, slumped on the floor. Vida would come in and out and step over my prone body with either regal disdain or, sometimes, intense irritation. Particularly when she was with her flatmate, she would berate me. Her flatmate (she who would marry the Shah of Persia) wanted to call security and have me bodily ejected, but Vida wouldn't let her. So, in a bizarre reversal, Vida, who loathed me, also protected me. Of course, I saw this as the equivalent of a written affidavit of her undying love. Long before we became engaged, I felt that we were, because Vida protected me from her hard-hearted girlfriend.

Click, click, click. Their apartment block had a marble floor. Vida and her flatmate wore stiletto heels and they clicked across that stone with an invitation to lust. Click click, click, click click. I felt sure I just had to stay there with my ear to the ground, listening for the correct combination, and then, one day, miraculously, the safe would spring open and let me in. So I stayed there, decoding the clicks.

One night she came in late, alone and in a foul mood. Her flatmate was away in Biarritz or somewhere equally fashionable. Vida broke her usual pattern of ignoring me and told me to get out of her life and leave her alone.

'You are sick, Oswaldo,' she told me. 'And this has to stop. Have you no shame at all? Look at you! You are like a dog! Why can't you understand: I loathe you! What will it take to make you understand that you make me feel sick?'

Then she took out her key and slipped into her apartment. She tried to slam the door behind her, but I put my foot in the door. As soon as I was in the room, I began to take my jacket off and then to unbutton my shirt.

I told her I would transport her to places she had never even dreamt of. I told her that she was sexually repressed and uptight and that I, a Latin lover, could bring out her hidden passions. It was by no means the first time I had given her graphic descriptions of what I and my dick would do to her, but now I said it with an urgency bordering on the insane.

It was the night for surprises. Vida looked at me with venomous scorn and pointed to her bed. Magnificent and enraged, she said, 'Get in!'

I was open-mouthed with astonishment and sure only that I must be hallucinating.

'Get in!' she repeated, and motioned me into her bed. 'Come on, runt, you have been begging for it long enough and if it is the only way to prove to you that I will never care for you the way you want, then come in and fuck me and then GET OUT OF MY LIFE!'

Like so many revolutionary plans, my proposed coup did not have a follow-up. I had besieged Vida and begged her to sleep with me. I had offered, I don't know how many times, to fuck her from here to kingdom come, but when she told me to come on and do it, I ran out of strategy. This was definitely not how it was supposed to happen.

She was in control and very cold. I had glimpsed into her apartment before but had not grasped until I went in how palatial it was. The marble continued in great mosaic swathes. The room was an exotic and daunting mixture of silks and silver and crystal. As Vida clicked across the floor to her bedroom, her heels were intransigent. They bullied me to follow her and her voice almost barked at me to hurry, to follow, to undress, to get on with it, and then to get out.

Despite all I had said and asked and done, I felt outraged that she should be behaving in this way. I may have talked about fucking, but what I wanted to give her was my undying love. And I may have tried to fire her with talk of sex, but it was never meant to manifest itself like this: with her like a brazen hussy. As I hurried after her to her bedroom, I wanted to tell her this, to explain the magnitude of my emotions.

She undressed, clinically, as though preparing for a distasteful but necessary medical examination. I saw that she was even more beautiful than in my dreams. It was summer, so she was wearing only a simple shift and a brassiere and pants, which she peeled away, garment by garment, with irritated gestures of contempt. With each movement, she stared at me, defying and mocking me. She stripped naked and stood before me and I was filled with awe. I was searching for words, for anything that could help me to keep my balance and catch my breath. The result, so Vida told me afterwards, was some incoherent gibbering.

'Hurry up, take your clothes off, I haven't got all night,' she told me as she climbed into bed and lay, bored and naked, on a sheet the size of my entire room. Somehow or other I undressed. I had to make her mine. I had to truly impress her.

But then, most ungallantly, I fell asleep.

I remember lying down and feeling an enormous tremor enter my blood as the moment I had sought and stalked and schemed for was finally mine. I was shaken with relief. My last recollection that night was of Horemheb, general of the Egyptian armed forces, who made a fool of himself for love; and who finally got what he desired but at a terrible price.

In 1300 and something BC when Akhenaten died, his youngest brother, Tutankhamun, became king. Because he was still a child, Akhenaton's former advisors, a vizier and a general, managed the kingdom. Of these two, General Horemheb was the most powerful. Tutankhamun married his sweetheart, Ankhesenamun, and the two children lived out their love as nominal king and queen of Egypt.

Horemheb had lived his entire life for war and battles in the pursuit of wealth and power. But in the afternoon of his life, as regent to the boy-king, he came into almost daily contact with Queen Ankhesenamun and, having never given his heart before, he fell in love with her. Meanwhile, the royal couple were so wrapped up in their own love that they lived only for each other.

Horemheb was chewed up by love, jealousy and lust. He did all he could to gain the queen's favour, but she saw him only as a peasant and, as such, she despised him. When the boy-king died mysteriously, his young widow withdrew into her palace to mourn him. The Regent Horemheb tried in vain to woo her. He went out and won more battles to gain favour with the beautiful and haughty queen.

Without a pharaoh, Egypt was vulnerable. So when the country was saved from an invading army thanks to the valour and skill of General Horemheb, the proud queen was forced finally to notice the elderly warrior. She saw him, but still despised him as a man. But Horemheb was driven by yearning and he dreamt of marrying the queen. He had become so powerful that he had the entire kingdom at his mercy, and he could ask for whatever he wanted. He wanted one thing only: the young queen. He asked for her hand, but she laughed in his face.

The victorious warrior made himself king and summoned the queen. 'Now you cannot refuse me, Queen Ankhesenamun. Marry me or I will put your entire family to the sword and destroy your land and your people.'

She told him that to save her people she would marry him, but it would be in name only because she would never love him and never let him touch her. He said that his love was great and he would wait. They married and lived separate lives, but Horemheb pined for her love and his passion ate into his heart. Day after day and week after week, he wooed her sweetly to no avail.

Then, on the eve of a great battle, Horemheb could wait no longer. His advisors had long been urging him to use force since force was what had earned him all he had in life. Emboldened by wine, and knowing that he might not survive the battle ahead, Horemheb raped his wife.

The next day, full of remorse, he left for battle and was gone for several years.

Week after week he sent runners back to the court with messages of love and gifts for his queen. And week after week she replied that she too had a gift for her husband, but that he must see it only when he returned. Horemheb was a peasant and a warrior; he didn't like surprises. So he asked his spies, 'What is the queen's present? What is the surprise?'

No one dared say that every night, as the sun set over the river Nile, the queen dressed in her servant's clothes and went down to the poor parts of the town. She went to the porters and the beggars, the oarsmen and the charcoal burners; and every night she gave herself to different men. She sought out the lowest of the low and she gave herself freely to them all. For each man she had sex with, she took a piece of coloured glass. Then, back in the gardens of her palace, she had her servants build a pavilion entirely made of this collection.

As the months went by, the pavilion grew to a brilliant sparkling edifice in her orchard. It glinted in the desert sun and was the talk of the town. Everyone knew about it; eventually even Horemheb knew of it too. His heart rejoiced in the gift, savouring it as he waited to return. Everyone knew of the queen's behaviour in the night as well, even far away. But Horemheb was a warrior whose first weapon was fear. And since he never asked what the queen was doing beyond the building of her sparkling edifice, no one told him how the glass stones were gathered.

At last, victorious and full of love, Horemheb, the warrior king, returned. His first thought was for his wife and he brought her gifts that were trophies from all his battles. She thanked him and said, 'Now you must come with me to see what I have made for you.'

Full of delight he followed her into the gardens to the pavilion she had built for him. When he saw the pavilion, he marvelled at its size and beauty. Moved by her gift, he thanked her. And then she told him how it had been built, and what each glittering tessera represented.

I don't know why I was thinking about that story as I climbed into bed with Vida, except perhaps that I was relieved to be lying

beside her by her invitation and not through force. I remember
thinking of the pavilion glinting in the Egyptian sun, of the river
Nile with its pirogues and its sandy banks. I remember drifting and
then ...

I woke up and it was morning and Vida was getting dressed to
go to the university and I had slept all night in a deep semi-
comatose sleep and my window of opportunity was shattered into
more pieces than the queen's pavilion.

The big difference, however, was that Vida had developed a
tenderness for me in my slumber. She found it intriguing that I
had fallen asleep. She found it touching. It was also the one and
only thing about all my behaviour that had remotely aroused her,
and from that day forth she allowed me into her life. Ironically,
had I made love to her, I could never have impressed her as I
wanted. Casanova himself could not have won her heart, so she
said later.

By falling asleep, I unwittingly called a truce. From then
onwards (starting with our coffee and croissants in her grey marble
kitchen) she listened to me. I used the power I had, which was the
power of words. Even the little lust I aroused in her was a mere
reflex. It was the perverse reflex of a worshipped woman who felt
a flicker of desire for the one man who had, when offered them,
ignored her charms.

Looking back, I see that the story of the warrior king probably
came to me for a good reason. It came to me so that I might heed
it. He had loved his princess with a passion and forced her to be
his queen, then he raped her and she concocted a magnificent
revenge. I too loved my princess with a passion, and I too wanted
to force her to become my wife. I raped her with my words,
trapped her in my ideas; when she finally escaped, she too would
react with calculated savagery. In love as in politics, it is unforgivable to force one's will on other people. Eventually, the victim
will get revenge.

I know that now. I didn't know it then. I know the back story now
as well: the story that allowed Vida to marry me.

It turned out that Vida was ready to fall in love with communism. She was also ready to embrace whatever her family would

have most disapproved of. She wasn't ready to break such bonds for a mere man – certainly not for such a puny one as I – but for an ideal, she was ready to rebel; and rebel she did against all the autocracy of her upper-class Persian background. I was merely the key, the combination to her own secret safe. Vida was someone burning with idealism. She subsequently dedicated her life to a cause. She had the sort of fanaticism in her that made her ideally suited to follow Communist Party dictates. She was ready to live and die for her ideas if need be.

She later proved this by spending almost two decades of her life as a political prisoner under the Shah of Iran. Having been flat-mate and best friend of the Shah's wife, the Farah Diva, in Paris did nothing to get Vida out of her prison cell, but perhaps it kept her alive when so many others perished in Iran. I don't know. What I do know is that when the Ayatollah Khomeini came to power, Vida was eventually released along with many other polit-ical prisoners in Teheran. And I know that later still, she walked across the desert with a party of fleeing rebels and was one of the few to survive the arduous journey. She had nerves of steel and a ruthless determination. Somewhere along the line, in Paris, she had decided to become a Red; at some time during my dormant night in her apartment, she decided that I would be her way into the party. I didn't know that then, of course. I thought: At last, she has seen the light and ours is a love that can move mountains.

Ours was a complex relationship, which I lived through and yet knew virtually nothing about. I was a young man in love, engaged and then later (in Caracas in 1958) married. Vida threw herself into the life of the party with an energy that amazed and delighted me. Side by side, we were socialist activists. Side by side we acted like a couple in love: cocooned by the signs and secrets shared by couples the world over who are in the thrall of prolonged and pas-sionate sex. And side by side, when people saw us (even when those people were my friends), they couldn't help asking what on earth we had in common besides lust and the party. Under the sheltering embrace of that party in which all men were supposed to have been born equal, Orwell's quip about some people being more equal than others never held more true than it did for Vida and me.

I have never met anyone more dedicated to the cause, but neither have I ever met anyone who felt such intrinsic demarcations of inherent superiority and inferiority. Vida went out with me, got engaged to me, married me and bore me a son, and in her own way, she even loved me. But she always loved me reluctantly. I don't think it mattered to her that she was so beautiful and I was not. And I am sure it did not matter to her that she was so rich while I was so poor. Nor, to be fair to her intense communism, did it matter that my social status and hers were miles apart. What really mattered was the cultural chasm between her country and mine. Vida was a terrible cultural snob.

With hindsight, it is easy enough to find faults and flaws in my one and only wife. But for well over a decade, she was my guiding light.

CHAPTER XXV

For the first thirty years of my life, there was always my version and 'their' version. There was what actually happened and what people said had happened. By the time I left Venezuela for the second time, aged thirty, my life was too full and too hectic for me to really be aware of what people were saying about me back home. So, when the myth was forming, fuelled by both the right-wing press and the gutter press as well as by word of mouth, and I became the bogeyman, I was one of the few Venezuelans who didn't hear all about it.

Piecemeal, over the years, since my final return to Venezuela and the renewal of my academic career as a sociologist and my life as a journalist and a political thinker, I have gleaned my own oral history as perceived by my compatriots. Thus my story with Vida has been distorted and condensed into the following by popular myth. It is the quick version of our marriage. It is the version that people whisper behind my back.

According to that myth, I cast some kind of malign spell over Vida and duped or drugged her into marrying me. Within weeks, I left her a ruined woman. I set sail for Venezuela to stir up trouble; Vida, rejected by her family for her dishonour, eventually followed me there. Despite the fresh air from the sea voyage, Vida arrived like a zombie. On the way to Caracas from the port of La Guaira, we stopped for a cold drink. As was my wont, I left Vida to fend for herself. A fight broke out over her, and a client in the bar chopped another man's head off, spattering Vida's white muslin dress in the process. Apparently, the severed head rolled like a football to within inches of her feet. Vida awoke from her stupor demanding immediate repatriation, which she continued to lobby for until finally, and only after being forced to bear me a son, I allowed her to leave.

Well, that is what the gossips say. It is even what half my own family believes. Within my family, this is neither strange nor malicious: 90 per cent of the story is true (she did leave and she did take our son and they didn't return). Yet the truth has shifted gear. Perhaps it is interesting to see why and where.

Vida and I lived together in Paris. She studied architecture; I had finished my law and my sociology degrees. In 1958, the dictatorship of Perez Jimenez fell and we both wanted to be in the aftermath in Caracas and do our bit. Venezuela was living a euphoric moment. After nearly a decade of repression, the entire country was bubbling over enjoying the novelty of its freedom. Mine was a country crying out for able minds and willing hands to rebuild it after the ruinous corruption, incompetence and brutality of its previous government. A general election would be imminent. A suspicious and lethargic public would have to be motivated. If the Left were to truly stand a chance at the polls, there wasn't a minute to lose. I felt that moment like a call to me directly to bring all my European experience; my years of giving speeches, rousing crowds and generally militating for the cause of international communism were urgently needed. My country needed me! It was a fantastic feeling. It was both sweet and exhilarating. I had to go home.

However, I was deeply in love with Vida, who was madly in love with communism. Far from trying to hold me back, she couldn't wait to get on the boat herself. But as an Iranian citizen with an Iranian passport, she had to wait for an indefinite time to get an entry visa for Venezuela. Because of the upheaval of the fall of the dictatorship, the visa process had been thrown off kilter. On the one hand, as it was, Vida didn't stand a chance of getting an entry visa in the foreseeable future. On the other hand, as my future wife, she would be able to follow me back 'within five to six months'.

I did not 'abandon' Vida then. We decided that the bureaucratic process necessary for her would work best if she lobbied from Paris, while I could use my contacts on the inside in Caracas to lobby for my foreign fiancée to be allowed to join me. This decision was also reached in the interests of the party: there was work to be done and I could do it. Personal considerations were not supposed to influence a good party member's actions. We were not people: we were cogs in a machine. The right-wing dictatorship of Perez Jimenez had fallen, leaving an entire country ripe for conversion to the cause. The engine of the party machine, the powers-that-be, dictated that I go forthwith to spread the word.

Vida was not like other women for me. She was the light of my life. I don't know what would have happened had it not been possible for her to follow me to Caracas. Given the choice of losing her or losing the chance to help my country, I don't know what choice I would have made. However, I was not forced to choose then.

Later, time and again, I was obliged to choose between my love life, my personal life and my duty to my political career – whether that be the dictates of the Communist Party or the dictates of whatever political struggle I was involved in. Time and again, in the future, my relationships and my personal life would be crushed by the needs of my political agenda. So I was never able to truly test my ability to live my private life to the full. After Vida, I made a choice to give myself to the future, so to speak. By so doing, I know that I hurt myself; but as I have said, I made a choice. Now that I am weighing up my life, what I cannot tell is whether the people I left behind, the women I left, the love I spoilt and the pain I caused them was justified. More and more, I fear that it was not. I try to tell myself that they found other lovers and other loves.

What is harder to come to terms with is my children. They did not find other fathers. At best, they had stepfathers. But they were my blood and I know that they needed me, with all my neuroses and imperfections. I am their father. I know what it is like to grow up without one. The absence of my own was like a running sore through my childhood. As a boy, I swore I would never do what my own father had done to me and leave a child to fend for himself emotionally.

My first child, my son Ramín, was born in 1959 in the turbulent year after the coup that tumbled the dictatorship in Venezuela. He came like a revelation to me. For the first six months of his life, the three of us were inseparable. Contrary to the custom, Ramín was like a 1970s European child: he travelled like a little hippie, strapped to his parents, attending rallies and meetings. I took to fatherhood quite naturally and found new pleasure in the details of catering for the daily needs of a baby. I discovered in myself a love for babies and children. I was as surprised by this as were my friends and comrades.

Again, I cannot know, but I think my life would have evolved differently, i.e. more as a scholar and less as an activist, if my firstborn had stayed with me. I am not saying I would have been a normal family man (whatever a 'normal family man' may be) but I would, I believe, have lived a more settled life. The tie was so strong and it tugged inside me with such strength, I could not have cut that cord myself.

It was cut for me. It was cut and no midwife tied a knot. When Vida eventually left me, three years after arriving in Venezuela, she took our son. She eventually took him to Persia and then her family took him away. Her family, that noble, wealthy clan of powerful Iranians, did not entirely blame me for Vida's transition from Parisian socialite to party member. They blamed me more, I think, for my inability to control her unorthodox and unacceptable behaviour as a Muslim wife than for her conversion to Marxism and her eventual fall. Vida was arrested and imprisoned for her communism in Teheran under the Shah. During her nineteen years behind bars, her family cared for our son. Materially, he lacked for nothing. Emotionally, he had neither a mother nor a father. His family (her family) cut me off. No letters, no telephone calls and no messages were allowed to travel either way. So I lost my son and he lost his father. There is more to this story. (Isn't there always?) Some of that 'more' I will tell later. But that 'more' would involve Vida rather than our child.

In the first flush of parenthood, when all my caring instincts were fully roused, I was formally declared unfit. When Vida left me, I still loved her. The loss of her and Ramín left me with a sense of domestic inadequacy which I still feel to this day. Mea culpa.

I used that wrenching away of my happiness as an excuse for the rest of my life. I am an unfit husband. I am an unfit father. I am leaving you, but you are better off without me and our child is better off as well.

Since this is a balancing act, I must add to the other side of the scales. Given my political involvement, my clandestine and often criminal activities, most women were, legally, technically and probably, better off without me. In the few cases where I have lingered in a relationship and continued to share a lover's bed, those lovers have been forced to share my lot. Ex-girlfriends have been interrogated and imprisoned because of their closeness to me. So moving on, in love affairs, could be argued to have been the decent thing to do. Where the equation falters is always with my children. When I was in prison, of course, I could not be with them. Thus, I suppose, I am 'excused' for many years. But when I was not in prison, I could, I know, have given them more of myself. As a young man, I made a choice. Now, as an older man, I am reviewing it.

As ever, it all comes down to the 'ifs'. With hindsight, I see that 90 per cent of my political struggles were in vain. The time I stole from my children for a higher cause was mostly time wasted. That weighs on my conscience.

Yet my children have grown and flourished despite my neglect.

PART 3

CHAPTER XXVI

Out in the *monte*, when the vultures began circling over my head, there would come a time – years, actually – when I really didn't know why I kept doing what I did. In the early days, though, after the bloody Bastille march, I believed that through militating as I did, and preparing people's minds, we could indeed achieve the true goal of socialism: i.e. the greatest good for the greatest number of people.

We campaigned, and later fought, as I imagine the Allied soldiers fought in the Second World War: convinced that we were fighting evil and righting wrongs of a moral and ethical nature. Being a socialist in the days before communism lost its halo was a bit like falling in love. It made us selfless and brought out the best in us. We lived in a glow of self-esteem, happy in the knowledge that we were helping others (except, of course, in the Romanian jamboree, when we were helping ourselves).

Even without the orgy in Bucharest, I could count as joyous the days I spent based in Paris. We, the Far Left, were intoxicated, at times by our own words. Had we been a community as united in thought, we might have managed to gain some sustainable power. This was not to be, largely through the endless in-fighting and bickering, which has always been the bane of politics in general, but which has been the absolute ruin of socialism. What remained pure and fresh, though, was our passionate enthusiasm for our cause (whichever branch or twig of that cause we passionately supported). We looked at the world through extreme lenses, focusing mostly on good and evil. We were good, of course, and we felt it our duty as disciples of Karl Marx to enlighten and convert the evil. Ours was a righteous crusade cocooned in philanthropy.

None of us knew that communism by its nature was bound to corrupt. None of us knew about the Gulags and the Russian and Chinese genocides. What filtered through to Paris and Lyons, Tübingen and Algiers were images of euphoric collective farmers shovelling mountains of food into brightly painted carts with smiles and cheers. It is easy to see, with hindsight, that, to borrow a phrase, power corrupts and absolute power corrupts absolutely. Back then, nobody saw communism as being a vehicle for absolute power.

I am not sure, but I think that a couple of the Polish and Romanian girls in Bucharest may have been trying, albeit cryptically, to alert us to 'another world' behind the Iron Curtain. One girl even tried to get a couple of us to smuggle her back to Paris. But we were rampant males in our prime, and the girl in question was both ugly and creepy and only got into our circle under cover of dark. Groggy with sex, we all had blue balls and a lot of testosterone and very little compassion. This was compounded by the fact that at the party youth jamboree there was absolutely nothing cryptic about the Eastern Bloc girls' appetite for sex. If they were trying to hint that there was something rotten in the state of Denmark, or Poland or Hungary, they really didn't try very hard, and we barely shared a common language from the waist up.

One of my few regrets on leaving Paris was leaving my Algerian comrades at a time when they were as near defeated in their struggle as they had been since it began in 1954. The number of FLN bombings fell dramatically as the French paratroopers applied dragnet methods to Algiers and the surrounding country-side and then systematically tortured their prisoners. 1957 had also seen the arrests and/or deaths of most of the FLN leadership. When Ali la Pointe was cornered in the kasbah of Algiers, he was the last hope of the FLN continuing an effective armed struggle in the immediate future. When Ali la Pointe refused to surrender, he was blown up. It took another three years of bitter repression before Algeria won its independence. The desperate fighting and the ruthless counterinsurgency tactics that followed my departure were hardly reported in Venezuela.

So it was a bit like being addicted to a particular programme on the radio. I was tuned in twenty-four hours a day for years and then suddenly I lost the wavelength and everything went off the air except for the odd crackle. Other events and other programmes took over and, from our having been as close as family, overnight I more or less lost touch with my North African comrades and their wavelength, and tuned into Radio Venezuela instead.

In 1958, when Venezuela finally got rid of its dictator after ten years of military rule, there was a sense of euphoria. The celebrations in the last week of January 1958 in the Latin quarter of Paris were historic. I heard later that it was the same in every city where there were Venezuelans in exile. All of us wanted to go home but it was almost impossible to get news. Our consulates and embassies were closed. All telephone calls still had to be made via the international operator, and since most of Venezuela was without any phone lines, let alone phones, it was always a miracle to get through even when the country wasn't in turmoil following the fall of its dictator.

When I finally set sail for Latin America, I didn't expect to see my Algerian comrades again. Having followed the rise of Ahmed Ben Bella and Boumediènne, I sent them all messages of solidarity and went home, little thinking that chance would send me to live in Algiers less than five years later.

I sailed back to Venezuela early in 1958, on *El Venezuela*. I arrived at what appeared to be a magnificent, happy and wonderful beginning of a new era. I was met by my family, who were all doing well, and were highly esteemed in their new neighbourhood of San José. During the months before the fall of the dictatorship, there had been serious fighting in San José. My brothers and sisters, who had all joined various factions of the Left, had contributed heavily to those battles.

Everyone could celebrate in the street and relax without having to worry about anything except to argue the pros and cons of this and that party and this and that politician. I had been away from

Venezuela for five years, and both it and I had changed a lot in that time.

In June of that first year of my return, there was a congress of the Venezuelan Communist Party (PCV), in which I participated as a delegate for the neighbourhood of San José. During that congress I was elected to participate in the regional conference (which was more important). The party members who had stayed and fought – the real heroes of the armed struggle, the ones who had not been living abroad – made it clear to me that they saw it as opportunism on my part to have accepted my election.

There was a new kind of aristocracy within the Left, which marginalised everyone else. I tried to make a place for myself within that existing hierarchy. I made up my mind to try to become one of them and not to have an 'exile complex'. But it wasn't easy.

Then, once again, chance intervened and redirected the course of my life.

It was like this: I had been in Venezuela for three months, living with my family in Caracas. They had all got used to the move from Valera, but, for me, home didn't really feel like home, and it was taking me time to settle down. My parents didn't say anything, but I could see that they were getting a bit worried. I wasn't working and I wasn't revalidating my law degree. I didn't say anything either, but I began to feel uneasy about it too.

One day, I was walking near our house on my way to Silencio, when I saw a job advertisement for a bank clerk on a card in a window. I looked up and saw that the bank was called the French-Italian Bank of Latin America. For some reason I cannot explain, this was the first job that had attracted me. I spoke French and had graduated as a lawyer in France, and I had always had a flirtation with Italian culture and all things Italian. I had made it a hobby to study the language and I spoke and read reasonable Italian.

I looked at my watch: it was ten o'clock in the morning. I went into that bank and I asked for a job application form. I filled it out, then I continued on my way to Silencio. When I got home at 4 p.m., my mother was all flustered. With her voice cracked with fear, she said, 'You have a letter from a bank. What is it about, Oswaldo? Do you have anything to do with banks?'

What a premonition! In the light of my future career as a bank robber – what a question! My mother had an uncanny knack of knowing when there was hidden danger in the most innocent-seeming things. She had known intuitively not to let me get my jacket on the day when my political troubles began in Valera while I was still a schoolboy. Heedless, I reassured her.

'No, so far I have had nothing to do with banks.'

But then I remembered I had just asked for a job in one. I reached out for the letter she was holding in her podgy hand. It turned out that I had been granted an interview for the following morning.

The next day, I presented myself to the manager, Dr Carminatti. Both he and the bank itself were very formal. He told me that the bank had three managers. Above them all, in the stratosphere, there was Dr Talei, the overall chief of that French-Italian Bank of Latin America (which had branches in Buenos Aires, Lima, Bogotá and Caracas).

Within the bank, Dr Talei was so important that his name was only mentioned in hushed and reverential tones as though he were God himself. Dr Carminatti was very grand while still retaining a slightly ambiguous twinkle in his tawny eyes. He spoke not as 'I', but as 'we': like royalty.

'We have read your application and we don't understand how, with a curriculum vitae such as yours, you could be asking for just any job. The only vacancy we have in the French-Italian Bank is for the secretary to the secretary of the legal department.'

All I wanted was to be able to go home and say to my mother that I had a job, any job; so I took it.

Dr Carminatti was surprised by my decision and took great pains to explain to me that the legal department had two lawyers: Maglioni, with a degree from Paris, and Bonessi, with a degree from Pisa. Under them there was the Señora Ernestina.

'You, Barreto, will address only the Señora Ernestina. Your job will be to type letters inviting our customers to pay up their debts. There is a module which you must follow. You must not address the managers. Managers form part of the fabric of this bank. There are only three of us. Above us are the chiefs. Below us are all the employees. Is that clear? We run a tight ship here.'

I nodded.

'You will work for eight hours a day, six days a week. The pay is 700 Bolivars per month.' (About $200.)

My new boss, the legal secretary Señora Ernestina, was then summoned to take me to a tiny desk. Her manner was over-brusque. Her welcome was as to something Dr Carminatti had just scraped off the bottom of his shoe. She gave me three cards with the three types of letters I was to copy and I started to work.

Despite her initial concern, my mother was delighted to find that I was gainfully employed by such a prestigious and important bank. During the dictatorship of Perez Jimenez, it had been the bank of all the Italians, and the Italians had been making the fastest money as they monopolised the construction business and a substantial part of the capital's commerce. Founded by two far-thinking Italians, it was the first of a new kind of bank which gave credits and discounts. However, with the fall of the dictatorship, it had lost a lot of clients and a lot of money. So the bank was going through a crisis and it was trying to consolidate its assets by recu-perating as much money as possible from its loans.

It did this by sending letters to all its clients who were in the red. The first of the three types of letter said:

Esteemed Señor,
Given the lamentable state of your account, we would be eternally grateful if you could grace our office with your esteemed presence to discuss this matter at your earliest convenience.

The second said:

Esteemed Señor,
Lamentably, we asked you to come to into this bank and you have not done so. If you do not come into the bank within three days, your account will be transferred to our legal department.

The third said:

Esteemed Señor,
We regret to inform you that your account has now been
transferred to our legal department.

Every day, I had to type out exactly the same antiquated wording,
which to the average customer must have sounded like a joke. One
day, I suggested to the Señora Ernestina that we upgrade the letters. She was outraged. 'Barreto, you are not here to make
suggestions; you are here to write the cards.'

I answered her humbly. 'Very well, Señora.'

From eight until five I made my cards (with one hour off for
lunch), from Monday to Saturday. In the first ten days I was
there, the acting head of the legal department, Dr Maglioni (of the
University of Paris), did not once speak a word to me. He always
dressed very elegantly and it was clear he had honed his performance of disdain over the years. He did, however, sometimes
address my direct superior, the Señora Ernestina, when the need
to share his virulent anti-Semitism got the better of him. He had
lived for many years in Argentina prior to moving to Venezuela,
and he had evolved a conspiracy theory of his own about the
nefarious actions of the Jews. He would say things like, 'Señora
Ernestina, have you noticed any blackbirds outside?'

Thrilled to be addressed at all by a high-and-mighty manager,
she would blush and flirt as though the question had been a com-
pliment or an invitation to hold hands.

'No, Dr Maglioni.'

'Aha! No! And do you know why?' It was not his wont to leave
time for anyone else to reply when he was on his pet theme.
'Because the Jews have slaughtered them all. They did it in
Buenos Aires when I was there and now they are doing it here.'

The issue, of course, was the supposed Jewish plot to wipe out
life as we knew it on the planet. Well, the xenophobic Maglioni
did not once speak to me, though he often paused to scrutinise my
rather hooked nose. I could see him thinking: Barreto Miliani,
Creole/Italian, but could there be a drop of Jewish blood in him?
And I could see him making a mental note to beware, just in case,
because 'they' were everywhere.

On the tenth day, Maglioni came into our room and spoke over

my head. 'Barreto, they have asked for a report on prescription at
the commercial bank. It must contain everything under
Venezuelan law on the subject. I am too busy to do it myself.
Since you claim you are a lawyer: you do it. It must be seven to
ten pages long. It must be written in French. You have one week.'

'OK, no problem, Dr Maglioni.'

He swept out of the room and I continued to type up my cards
on the massive Olivetti typewriter with its worn-out 'a' and 'e' and
its penchant for chewing the ink-ribbon, while the Señora
Ernestina stared at me as though I were a poisonous snake which
had slid out from under a sneaky camouflage. She looked at me as
though I had also stolen something precious from her. I kept
typing my cards and pretended not to notice her.

A report such as that was a piece of cake for me. I went to the
public library and got out the relevant reference books, I looked
up the codes and a couple of minor points and I consulted one or
two cases that had come up as precedents, and then I wrote it.
That same afternoon I finished the report. It was exactly ten
pages long.

Next morning, I gave it to Dr Maglioni. He took it and asked,
'What's this? I told you to take a week.'

'Well, I didn't need a week. There it is, take it.'

I left it with him and went back to typing my letters. 'Esteemed
Señor, Given the lamentable state of your account, we would be
eternally grateful if you could grace this office . . .'

During our coffee break, I noticed that Maglioni had initialled
my report as his own.

About an hour later, Maglioni came into our office with his face
as ashen as the grey suit he was wearing. He came straight up to
my desk and told me in a strangled whisper, 'Dr Talei wants you
to go up.'

The Señora Ernestina began to hyperventilate on the word
Talei. In nearly twenty years she had never been upstairs.

'Me?'

'No, both of us together,' Maglioni told me.

Once in Talei's palatial office, the head of all the heads completely ignored Maglioni and addressed only me.

'How are you, Barreto? I said from the start: you are either an imbecile, or you are ambitious; because no one with a degree from the Sorbonne would come here as a secretary's secretary. But, I told myself, if it is someone ambitious who knows that sooner or later the employees of this bank will have to be Venezuelan, then you started very well. I congratulate you on your work.'

He waved Maglioni peremptorily out of the room and Maglioni slunk out like a whipped dog.

'It is the work of Dr Maglioni,' I lied.

'Like hell! That shit Maglioni! Hmm! I can't make you the head of our legal department because Ciffatti, who is on holiday for six months in Italy, is the head. But while he is absent, I hereby appoint you as acting head of the legal department. Your salary, starting today, is 2,800 Bolivars.'

I was astonished. 2,800 Bolivars was $800: four times my former salary. I was rich! I thanked him and went back downstairs. By the time I got back to the office, Maglioni had already cleared his beautiful, spacious, antique desk. I told him not to bother, that I would keep my old tiny desk. He tried to insist, but I did not allow him to. After all, I was the boss now and I didn't want his desk or to further humiliate him.

Within the city, my job coup was a big thing. News of it spread from bank to bank and office to office. Not only did I now have a good job befitting my qualifications, I was rich.

In the short run, I kept typing my cards, but I had noticed that no matter how many invitations we sent out, for such a big bank, very few people paid their debts. I now decided to investigate this and I asked to see the files of all the debtors.

It turned out that Dr Bonessi (of the University of Pisa) kept these files under lock and key. At first he refused to let me see them, but when I pulled rank, I got them. As I had suspected, 90 per cent of the debtors were paying nothing and clearly had an 'arrangement' with Bonessi. The debtors were almost all Italian and had businesses that either made clothes or sold them. Their shops were clustered in just two zones of Caracas and could all be visited in one day. The sweat shops were on Avenida Urdaneta and the fashion shops were in Sabana Grande.

I explained to Carminatti that I needed to borrow a car for the following day. He lent me his without asking what it was for. I started my tour at one end of Sabana Grande and went from fashion shop to fashion shop to personally invite the owners to pay up.

'Good morning. I'm from the French-Italian Bank.'

'We deal with Ciffatti, the head of the legal department.'

'He's away.'

'Yeah, but there's Maglioni.'

'That has changed. There is an urgent situation. I need you to come tomorrow to regularise your account.'

Before that week, the bank was recuperating 80,000 Bolivars a week on unpaid loans. In that first week and thereafter, it recouped 240,000 Bolivars.

I sent Vida a ticket to Venezuela and told her to come: 'I am getting rich. I have $800 a month!'

I hadn't had much luck getting a say within the PCV or in finding somewhere to put my foot on a ladder-rung within the hierarchy of the Left. It is ironic that I made my name courtesy of my job as a bank manager and the bank workers' union. Each bank had its own internal trades union; a few months after I was promoted to acting head of the legal department, I was asked to become the foreman of our one.

My first concern as union leader was to introduce a five-day working week. Trying to get the members to think about this, or anything else for that matter, was well nigh impossible, because although most of my countrymen *can* think, they don't want to. In vain did I explain: 'We have nothing to lose by working five days so long as we don't have to work longer hours on the other days.'

The bank wanted us to compensate for no Saturdays by loading the lost hours on from Monday to Friday. Eventually, I got all of our lot to grasp it. Then I found out that there were other bank workers who wanted the same thing. We joined forces and founded a union for all the banks. We called it SUTRABAN. Together, we were strong enough to impose a five-day week with less than eight hours a day.

Vida arrived on a three-week visitor's visa. She arrived at La Guaira full of affection for me but within weeks she was numb with culture shock. She took a violent dislike to all things Venezuelan. She didn't speak any Spanish, which isolated her in her early weeks. However, my mother and my sister Graciela developed an immediate affinity with her and, unlike my own bond, theirs lasted.

The only way to get Vida her residency was for us to marry. So this we did, in Caracas on 11 November 1958.

From being a stranger to my country, I now lived in San José with my family and my newly arrived wife and drew a fat salary. When I wasn't at my nine-to-five job at the bank chasing up their loans and listening to Maglioni ranting on about imaginary Zionist plots to do anything from massacring blackbirds to watering down his coffee, weakening his toenails and causing the scattered rubbish to rot in the street, I listened to Vida's daily lists of complaints. After supper, cooked by my mother in quantities sufficient for a small army, Vida and I would go out for a stroll and a drink and to see friends. Then we would come home and she would berate me for the dirtiness of the streets, the poor quality of the wine and the uncouthness of my friends (hardly any of whom spoke French). Then she would curl up miserably in a rocking chair to study, while my small army of brothers and sisters and I would argue about which particular faction of the Left was best, while the tree frogs croaked outside and the cicadas whirred and (with or without Maglioni) there wasn't a blackbird or a Jew in sight.

CHAPTER XXVII

The Venezuelan Communist Party, like its Soviet master, didn't want to venture any further towards socialism. Its role was to uphold the current democracy. It had called upon all other parties to join forces to support the president against the ex-dictator's supporters, who were out for another coup d'état.

It is important to know that I was not alone in believing in a more radical approach than the party; neither was I the one to come up with such a radical approach. Back then, in 1958, people thought that revolutionary movements got the idea of fighting to victory from Fidel and Che Guevara. But long before them, people like my compatriots Douglas Bravo and Ilio Novelino (to name but two) had said, 'Why should we fight to have the right to discuss agrarian reform? Let's do it! Let's make the agrarian reform ... Why should we fight to have the right to talk about reforming the cities? Let's reform the cities. Let's make it so that rich people can't have more than one house, and let's make them share all their apartments.'

Bravo and Novelino and others did not elaborate this theory – it was totally impulsive. This approach was the complete opposite of the French way. The French can't take a step without elaborating a theory explaining how I am going to move my foot for this and this reason. 'What are we going to do in the election?' was hanging unanswered in the air.

Meanwhile, Dr Ciffatti, the rightful head of the legal department at the bank, returned from his six-month sabbatical. Ciffatti was a diehard old fascist. He took over the department while keeping his distance from me. Under him, I had less work and less responsibility and so I took the liberty of accepting the candidacy for deputy in the state of Trujillo. Together with Manuel Isidro Molinas, who was the candidate for senator, we had to go for the electoral campaign in Trujillo. I loved the idea of the campaign, of returning to my home state and my home town. I loved everything about it, in fact, except for how I was going to manage to be in two places at once.

Since my immediate boss was a rabid fascist, I could hardly appeal to him for compassionate leave to participate as a socialist candidate. I finally settled for that time-honoured habit of faking an illness with a friendly doctor and getting a medical certificate to cover me for 'fifteen days of rest due to hepatitis'.

Sometimes as I tell this story, I ask myself, What is it with all these details? There are so many of them; so many names and dates and places lodged in my memory. I would like to think they are there for a reason, but sometimes I think that they are just like old clothes or suitcases with broken handles in an attic. They are things I have grown fond of because we went through such a lot together and because they were once so useful, but they are of no intrinsic use any more. Maybe they are part of a pattern. I hope that if I put all the disparate pieces together and lay them out and see them as a whole, I will learn from them. Maybe.

When I went to Valera to campaign for the election, it was my first time back in the Andes in six years and it felt fantastically good to be home. I belonged in the mountains. The journey took eighteen hours. The last stage of it, from Barquisimetos, was four hours long and consisted of almost constant bends. As our car climbed up round curve after curve of roads flanked by sugar cane, the familiarity squeezed my chest so tightly I could hardly breathe. I belonged in those green velvet foothills.

Before I left Valera, as a boy, I had behaved like a delinquent. My antics had fuelled enough gossip to keep the town animated for years. I wasn't sure what my reception would be.

Our exhaust came loose during the journey so that we clanked into town, thereby drawing even more attention to ourselves. I say 'even more' because our car was pretty noticeable, with 'Vote Red!' slogans painted all over it.

Before I could switch off the engine, someone called out, 'Barretico!' And such a crowd gathered round us that we could hardly open our doors to get out. Manuel Isidro Molinas was even more known in Valera than I was because he had founded the Communist Party of Trujillo, and the local radio, and the baseball team, and the nurses' union, and our first newspaper.

The malice of the gossip from my childhood and adolescence had slipped into popular myth. I was touched and surprised by the warmth of my welcome. It was 'Barretico' here and 'Barretico' there.

Despite all the things I had done and achieved and aspired to abroad, the most frequently asked question, after 'More beer?' was: 'Can I see the scar on your breast where the French tart bit you?' From which I deduced that gossip had been rife. Yet, from the friendly way in which that question was asked, I also saw that I had been forgiven; or rather, that I had been promoted to precious material for the myth-makers.

My fatherland regarded my political antics with indulgence, the way a father is often secretly proud of a rebellious son for having the guts to be such a naughty boy. That indulgence and pride would change into vociferous disapproval and, finally, virulent opposition. But for now, I was welcomed as a prodigal son. Everyone knew us and everyone showered us with hospitality. In fact, we would still be sitting down to lunch at someone's table there today if we had accepted all the invitations we were given.

We held meeting after meeting and gave speech after speech. From an attendance point of view, our campaign was a tremendous success. The halls and squares where we rallied were packed. I remember feeling elated by the response. I had never seen such a mass reception of our ideas. But the people who came to our meetings didn't give a toss about communism – they wanted to see us. They came to see Molinas and Barretico and Barretico's wife.

'Barretico's married an Arab.'

'A what?'

'An Arab – you know, a Turk.'

'Really! A door-to-door saleswoman?'

'No. I've heard she is an architect ([doctor/engineer/acrobat/etc.].)'

'Really? Who'd have believed it! Whatever next?'

'And I've heard she's a heathen.'

'Really! ... What do heathens look like?'

'Come and see for yourself. They put her on show twice a day at their meetings.'

'I think I will ... Does she speak, the heathen?'

'No, she's like a clockwork toy: she doesn't say anything except "Vote red". It doesn't matter what you ask her, she just shouts out, "Vote red".'

'Why does she say that? What is it with red? I saw they have red signs all over their car.'

'I have no idea, but you know Barretico, he's as wild as a goat with a hornet up its nostril. He says it's some political thing, but I've no idea what ... He always did talk a lot of nonsense. Do you remember when he was a kid ...'

After the two-week electoral campaign, we drove back to Caracas and I returned to my work at the bank. On my first day back, Ciffatti was waiting for me in the office. He had very pale grey eyes and he always wore very elegant Italian suits. That day, his suit was the same colour as his eyes.

'Good morning, Barreto. How is it going?'

He said it with such enthusiasm that I was instantly on the alert. Ciffatti's manner was positively ingratiating, and very different from what it had been when I left the office before my bout of 'hepatitis'.

'Much better, thank you, Dr Ciffatti. The doctor has cleared me.'

'No, no, no! How is the *campaign* going? Is there a chance that you will get elected?'

My mind flew to regretting having spent so much of my salary since Vida arrived and in Valera. If I got fired now, I would only have enough to keep us going for a couple of weeks, if that.

I braced myself, but Ciffatti wanted to drag the whole thing out.

I didn't entirely blame him. I had lied to the bank, to him and to all my co-workers. He invited me to dinner and told me to bring Vida. Why bring Vida? I thought. But then he went on, gleefully. 'I need to talk about what you are doing because ...' He paused and his eyes took on a dreamy expression and he smiled fondly, remembering. 'Because that's how I was – once.'

Ciffatti knew everything I was doing in Caracas and everything I had done in Trujillo.

'It pleases me,' he told me. 'In Italy, the fascists then were like the communists now. I used to lie to the bank where I worked to go to Mussolini's rallies. They were wild days: heroic, full of life ... Yes, it pleases me to see what you get up to. So you can count on me. I will cover for you here.'

Ciffatti was as good as his word. He never told anyone about my campaign. So my job and my 2,800 Bolivars a month were safe; which was just as well because I did not, in the end, get elected as a deputy.

I stayed at the bank for several more months and then resigned out of solidarity with one of my co-workers. The Adriatic Insurance Corporation tried to bribe me into leaving the bank. The message to meet the head-hunter in the bar across the street was delivered by one of my co-workers, who had been with the bank for many years and who was next in line for promotion. Although they offered me the astronomical sum of 4,000 Bolivars per month and a penthouse apartment thrown in, I didn't want to make a career out of banking, so I turned the offer down. Within the hour I was summoned by Dr Talei, the head of heads. He knew I had been head-hunted; he knew I had stayed loyal to his bank and he thanked me. He also told me that it hadn't been a trap. There were horizontal connections between the man who tried to bribe me and Maglioni's wife. She told Maglioni and he had gone running to tell tales to our boss, Talei. I went back downstairs with a merit mark for loyalty, but Talei had already shot the messenger.

Maglioni was told that because of his part in the affair, he would now never get promotion. Having only forwarded a message, he found this unjust and without more ado, he resigned. After he had cleared his desk, he thanked me for shitting on his future and spat in my face. When I calmed him down enough to hear his story, I too resigned. As I packed my desk, I saw Maglioni's eyes fill with tears of relief.

'Where will you go?' he blurted out.

'Don't tell anyone, but I have been offered a job in a Blackbird Brigade.'

His whole manner changed.

'You see!' he said triumphantly. 'I know they exist. They have been slaughtering the blackbirds for years. In Buenos Aires there are none left at all. Who is their leader?'

I leant over a little and whispered, 'Ssh! The Zionist Bird Control Board doesn't allow us to say.' I tapped my not un-Semitic nose. 'Loose lips sink ships, Dr Maglioni!'

CHAPTER XXVIII

No matter what my life looks like from the outside, most of it was spent in the kind of routine that occurs in the lives of most men. When I moved to Mérida I lived first as a solitary scholar, and then when Vida joined me I had a wife, and later a child. I had a job and a house; I had a routine; and I had a circle of friends and colleagues.

The day after I resigned from the French-Italian Bank, Vida heard that the University of the Andes (ULA) in Mérida was looking for two communists to work in public relations and the university press, respectively. Vida and I were drinking coffee with Ilio Novelino and I told him how much I longed to be in the Andes again. Novelino said that he, too, would love to move back to Mérida. Then and there, Novelino and I decided to apply for the posts.

We set off for Mérida the next day. All three of us took it in turns to drive and we arrived two days later. I had come armed with a letter of recommendation to the brother of the dean of the faculty of Humanities. Ilio and I were received and interviewed by the dean.

As interviews go, mine was a complete disaster. Not only did I not get the job, but the dean told me that I was a danger to Mérida. Novelino fared much better – they offered to take him on right away. Alone, he didn't want to stay. Just as he was turning his job down, another man came in. Having chucked in my work at the French-Italian Bank, and just got married, and come all the way to Mérida to get a job, I was pretty desperate. I wouldn't normally beg, but I did then. I didn't know that he was the eminent Cuban philosopher, José Antonio Portuondo, who was exiled in Venezuela and was the power behind the throne of the university, when I explained, 'Look, I am a sociologist – I could give a course on the history of sociology; and I have studied literature – I could teach the sociology of literature.' I mentioned Lukacs and his writings on a Marxist aesthetic. 'I could give a course on the juxtaposition he makes between narration and description: the naturalism of Zola and Dostoevsky and the realism of, say, Balzac and Tolstoy; and ...'

When I said that I also knew his literary criticism, Portuondo intervened.

'You know Lukacs?'

'I had the pleasure of meeting him in 1955 when Thomas Mann returned to Germany.'

'Good God, man! You have actually *met* him!'

Then Portuondo and I began to discuss literature Eliot and Alvarez and God knows who else. He stopped almost mid-sentence and said to the dean, 'Ever since Fidel took over, I have been waiting until you found someone worthy to replace me here so that I could hand in my resignation and return to Cuba. Here he is! Now I am not leaving this house until you make him a professor. I resign; he takes over. Nobody knows György Lukacs here. Barreto here is a phenomenon *and* he's a sociologist ... What a wonderful coincidence. I insist! He will carry the torch for my students. He will give them soul and form! Now I can return to Havana.'

So I began my university career in Mérida, where I stayed for three years: from 1959 to 1961. Portuondo returned to his native Cuba to support Fidel Castro and the revolution. There he faded into oblivion. It was a tragic loss of one of the greatest Latin American literary critics and thinkers. Like a cuckoo, I took over his nest.

Even though it was while I was there teaching in the Andes that the armed struggle began, those three years represented my best years – actually my only years – for concrete research. It was there that I could really read. When I began to give my courses I had a general knowledge of the subject. In Mérida I was able to live the scholarly life I had always dreamt of.

At first, Vida stayed in Caracas and continued to study architecture. Alone and undistracted (except by my secretary generalship of the PCV and the occasional flirtation), I studied and taught. And my life moved into a fairly strict routine.

I awoke just after dawn every day and I made coffee and washed and dressed and shaved. On my way to work, I greeted the shopkeepers opening their shops, and I greeted the bus driver with the broken nose and a map of broken capillaries across his cheeks who waited to take his first shift of the day. I greeted the banana vendor as he set up his stall, who spent countless minutes propping up his damaged sunshade, yet never mended or replaced the offending spoke. I greeted Doña Abigaíl on her return from mass, with the lace mantilla that was her pride and joy despite having been assaulted by decades of moths; and I winked at her Timotocuican Indian servant, who slopped behind in her fraying cotiza sandals carrying the heirloom prayer book and rosary and whatever vegetables and poultry her mistress had wheedled out of her wealthy cousins on the daily parade to early mass.

I was always one of the first to arrive on the campus. From 1959 until I had to leave Mérida in 1961, the bulk of my life was dedicated to literature for the first-year students in that faculty, and sociology for the third year of the history degree course. I had my own study/office in the Humanities faculty with 'Prof. O. Barreto' on the door. Well, it was more like a cupboard than an office and the walls were made mostly of glass like a greenhouse, except that much of each panel was frosted. The glass was frosted in a fine balance: it was enough to give some privacy, but not enough to give the privacy required to, say, have a quick one with any of the staff or students. Since a university campus is a hotbed of illicit sex, the glass-cubicle divisions were probably specially designed morality guards. Ingenious colleagues had discovered that it was actually possible to shag in secret if you lay down on the floor between the desk and the back wall (and refrained from any grunting or screeching).

After years of moving and being moved, I felt incredibly rooted in Mérida. I began to gather books around me like never before. I devoured them and enjoyed the luxury of being able to cross-reference my sources as I studied. I spent many happy hours sitting at my battered mahogany desk with its wedge of paler wood propping up one leg.

Mérida wasn't like Valera or any of the other Andean towns I knew. You went to Valera because you were born there, or you had family you had to see, or you needed to do some business with someone who lived there. Mérida, on the other hand, is a tourist attraction. It is the highest town in Venezuela, and with its monumental architecture, its arcades and its two rushing rivers, it is unlike any other.

Helped by its natural geographical boundaries, it has been isolated from the rest of the country since it was founded in 1558. It is close to the Colombian frontier and, in many ways, has more in common with its more Europeanised neighbour's cities than with our own chaotic Tropicana. Because of its altitude, even its climate has a northern feel. The temperature hovers at about ten degrees above zero every night of the year. The pale mountain sun highlights the pastel, furry-leaved frailejones, one of the only plants able to withstand that combination of height and cold on the bare mountain slopes that lead down to Mérida.

Above the city, the spectacular Pico d'Aguilar, the highest point in Venezuela (and, at 15,000 feet, one of the highest in South America), imbues the nestling capital with a natural pride. Actually, the city is more closely overlooked by two other peaks, one of which boasts the highest cable car in the world. But 'Mérida' and 'Pico d'Aguilar' are twinned in the popular imagination. When Venezuelans hear 'Mérida', they think 'Pico d'Aguilar'.

The population divides more sharply between Indians and Spaniards, or, rather, between Indians and families of Spanish descent. There is, of course, the ubiquitous racial mix, but it is, perhaps, less evident than anywhere else in the country. Beyond the city, there are far fewer haciendas with their licence to miscegenate in the time-honoured fashion of feudal estates. Nothing much wants to grow on the chill, bare hills. There are a few coffee plantations and a few fields of wheat, but mostly there are patchwork allotments of cabbages and potatoes and pockets of oats and barley. Since time immemorial, a harsh wind has blown the topsoil away, leaving only the occasional ridges for the ingenious peasants to farm. So Mérida is more a place of small subsistence farmers than big landowners. Its core does not service its hinterland in the way our other towns do. It has a hub of shopkeepers, artisans and, of course, because of its distinguished university, students and academics.

As a place to live, it was as near a perfect intermediary between Paris and Caracas as I could hope for in my native land. Mérida is small by most urban standards, but it is also relatively orderly and alive. Beyond the stately façades of the cathedral and the Governor's Palace and the old municipal buildings, the houses are a tropical hotchpotch of blues and yellows, greens and reds. The windows and doors are, as in the whole of Venezuela, always painted green. I find the vibrant colours of most other Andean towns and villages a fake reflection of their flagging spirit. The multi-coloured houses seem to encase endless little clusters of lethargy streaked with impotent rage. In Mérida, on the other hand, they are more like the pools of light they were originally intended to be. So rather than a small sleepy town, it is a lively place, energised as well, no doubt, by the absence of equatorial heat and all its contingent maladies. In some ways, it looks and feels like a toy town with its market and squares, shops and avenues, its big cathedral and its small hotels and bars. It acts as a magnet for the Indian artisans: mostly weavers and leather-workers. It has, over the centuries, acted as a magnet for some of the finest minds in Latin America. Perhaps there is no connection, but it has also acted as a magnet for some of the finest whores in the country, and boasts a couple of brothels that draw clients over the treacherous mountain road from as far afield as our Páramo and Valera, and also from Colombia.

So it was a model town and I was a model professor. I lived at first in a small hotel called the Hotel Luxemburgo and then I moved to the quarter of Santa Elena. Vida and I shared a house on two floors with my colleague, David Viñas, and his wife.

Novelino was ensconced in his job and his apartment, but as we had hoped, our paths crossed often over dinners that lasted into the small hours with endless cups of coffee and a bottle of rum. We argued loudly yet amicably about everything and nothing. There was one point we always agreed on: and that was that our joint move to Mérida had been an inspired one.

By that time, my work was almost entirely academic because I had been replaced as secretary general of the party. I also had to revalidate my French law degree so as to be able to practise law in Venezuela. This I did in 1961 cum laude, adding yet another, near useless attribute to my name.

CHAPTER XXIX

Vida was immensely talented in all forms of drawing, with a natural flair for architecture and a natural talent as an artist. She could successfully have pursued either career, I believe. She was also (quite unlike me) a brilliant sportswoman. She was a tennis champion in Venezuela (and later she would become a ping-pong ace in Cuba). For someone with as strong a character as hers, it was strange how cowed she was by Venezuela. It was as though the country doused her spirit, particularly after she moved to Mérida to join me.

After my first academic year in Mérida, her father sent us the tickets to visit him. They arrived in the post, just like that: as though Persia were the next town, instead of being halfway round the world.

We travelled to Teheran via Paris. En route, Vida told me that she was pregnant and that she did not want to keep the baby. I discovered later that my sisters had been her accomplices in doing just about everything she could to try to abort. However, when it came to actually checking into a clinic for an abortion, they had refused to help her without my knowledge. I told Vida that I was against an abortion. It seemed to me that we should have both been more careful, but that now, what was done was done. Having been a baby of 'potential abortion material' myself (because if my father had been able to see what was coming, he might well have opted for an abortion), I was particularly uneasy about getting rid of our child.

I have nothing at all against contraception. And I accepted, even back then, that there were cases when an abortion was advisable – say on health grounds. But taking a life for no reason – particularly when that life belonged to my own child – was not something I could support.

We had some gruelling talks about it. I couldn't stop lobbying to preserve what I imagined as a tiny cross between a hairy tarantula – me – and my gorgeous, statuesque wife.

Vida was very unhappy over the abortion issue. For most of the three-month trip we took to Persia, not only did my wife not sleep with me, she wouldn't speak to me either. On a first visit to her family, this (very noticeable) state of play was embarrassing, to say the least.

The visit to Teheran was full of revelations. When I met Vida in Paris, I knew she was a rich Persian girl, but I had no idea what an important family she came from. Neither did I know much about her country, or her character. I intuitively understood that Persian women were very different from other women I knew. Only when I visited Teheran did I see that the man–woman dichotomy we have in the West is inverted there. In Persia, the woman is the strong one, the provider.

I learnt a lot about *how* she was, and also about *who* she was. When we arrived at Teheran airport there was a big crowd of people waiting for someone. I remember looking around to see who was the celebrity or the dignitary who had been on our flight. Only as we stepped forward and the crowd pressed in to wrap itself around Vida did I realise that all those people were there for her.

A convoy of limousines then escorted us, almost in state, through the streets of Teheran to the avenue where all the foreign embassies were. There, in their midst, was Vida's family mansion. It was huge and stately and run by twenty-five servants. That was where we stayed (not speaking to each other). Her family was as extensive as a Scottish clan and it was one of the most important families in Persia. Her uncle Madud was an advisor to the Shah. Despite being publicly shunned by Vida, I got on very well both with her father and her uncle Madud.

After one week with her family, her father invited me to stay on and live with them. I thanked him, but pointed out that I had a job at the university and that I earned $800 a month. He said that didn't matter: he would pay me $800 per month to stay in Teheran. Almost in the same breath, he asked me why I didn't smoke opium 'like a real man' and why didn't we finish our discussion with a visit together to a downtown genuine Iranian brothel?

The men in Vida's family did the male thing and bonded with me (despite my not wishing to smoke their proffered opium or share their favourite prostitutes. I had a phobia about prostitutes ever since the one in Paris took a bite out of me). This closeness with her father and uncle Madud was, I think, not a part of Vida's plan for the trip. Instead, I got the impression that she wanted to lean on her family to get rid of me.

All the while, she was getting more and more anxious to abort. She had asked her father to arrange this for her, but he had refused to do anything without my full consent. When he saw that it was not something I desired – although, by then, I was not actually standing in her way – he refused to help. She was furious with both him and me.

During the three months of my visit, I was in the curious position of being in Iran because of her, of staying with her family and meeting her friends, and yet she and I were not together. In fact, we were so not together that I felt sure our union was over. She did not relent – she would not speak to or acknowledge me. At a certain point, I took the decision to leave and it was clear that her attitude to my leaving was 'good riddance'. Despite the above, I enjoyed my visit to Persia. Quite apart from the opulence in which I stayed, it opened my eyes and mind to a whole new world and a new and ancient culture. Her family took me on several short trips to show me the surrounding countryside. We went to the Caspian Sea and, I remember, to olive groves where the trees were over a thousand years old.

When I left Teheran, alone, I never thought I would see Vida again or ever see our unborn child. She had not bothered to say goodbye and it was abundantly clear that there was nothing left of our marriage, or our friendship, nor really any hope for any kind of future union. I flew back via Paris and had four days there before catching my flight to Caracas.

The day after I arrived in Paris, I was surprised to find Vida's sister at my cheap *pension*. She had come as an emissary for Vida. Vida had changed her mind and was desperately unhappy; she wanted to continue with our marriage. Would I take my wife back?

We had just spent the best part of a year not living together in Venezuela, and a few months living together uneasily in Mérida, and we had just spent three months not speaking to each other in Teheran: what kind of future did that forbode? You would really need to have seen the rage that Vida had exuded during our Persian sojourn to realise how weird this request was. I agreed without any hesitation, so long as she joined me immediately. A man in love, however rational he may aspire to be in other fields, will always be a fool where his lover is concerned. I still loved her and all I felt was joy that she was coming back. I disregarded all the intervening bitterness and non-communication and jumped ahead to making plans for our life together in Mérida. In my imagination, I thought, We will be happy together. We will be a family. She will return my love.

Vida flew to Paris two days later. I met her at the airport and we embraced like two lovebirds. Within a week we were back in Venezuela. Together, we drove for two days along the winding road to Mérida. And once our son, Ramín, was born, we played at happy families there. But we didn't live happily ever after, although for many months I pretended that we would.

CHAPTER XXX

Though I lived the life of an intellectual communist militant, communism dictated that only a few individuals have the right to think and explain things. And there was a strict hierarchy as to where those thinkers could come from. At the top of the ladder there was Russia, followed by France, then Italy, then Argentina, then a tight pecking order, at the bottom of which came Venezuela. In that hierarchy of angels and archangels and seraphim there was really no place for us. And quite apart from that absence of opportunity, we had to contend with our natural disposition.

If there is such a thing as a national character, then ours lies in our fondness for impulsiveness. Although it has been much noticed, nobody has tried to articulate it more clearly or better than the Colombian, Fernando Gonzalez. In his book, *Mi Compadre General Gomez*, the author describes how, after an arduous journey, he reached Caracas, and 'at last arrived in that country of mulattos so unlike the seminarists of Colombia'. He goes on to say that we 'mulatto Venezuelans' overthrow governments in the same spirit with which we throw down women to screw them – or words to that effect. He perceived that all Venezuelans are a force capable of action. He also claimed that 'if there is anything to blame Venezuela for, it is the lack of religious sentiment'.

I don't believe that our weakness lies in a lack of religious sentiment; I think our greatest weakness is not being able to go beyond what we can touch with our ten fingers. That has been our downfall. And that has been at the core of my own analyses: that need to dig deeper. Elías Canetti (despite his Nobel Prize) has never been read as widely as he should have been. He writes a lot about creating a world that goes beyond what you can see and feel – about the memory of things. Venezuela never was about that. We never reflect about ourselves. Even our greatest thinkers, Mariano Picón Salas and Mario Agori, did not tackle that. They were both great thinkers, but they were both superficial. Why is that? Why does Venezuela stand out alone in this respect?

Compared to other countries in Latin America, we have different geographical characteristics. We only have one real neighbour: Colombia, and then the sea. Of course, on a map, there is Brazil and Guyana, but there is virtually no contact at all between us. So we are geographically isolated. Add to that that we are the only oil-producing country in Latin America, and our isolation is reinforced by our solitary petrol-dollar status. The two isolations compound to produce certain atypical characteristics. Venezuelans have a habit of throwing themselves into a fight: not because they believe in or care what it is about, but because it is there and happening. And Venezuela has a history of throwing itself into action and fighting, for no better reason than that the opportunity to do so arises.

At the Sorbonne, I learnt to rationalise every situation and every change, however minor, in its development: 'We have to do this because of this and this. Historically, a similar action went like that and that, so we have to see what this and this and that and that could add up to today given that the changes are such and such, etc.' Rationalisation and precision were my education, but that was not the Venezuelan way.

And so it was in October 1961 that the country found itself in a state of armed struggle. It started in Caracas for no particular reason and then it spread. In Caracas, the Simon Bolivar battalion of the army took over the university as a reaction to armed student resistance. At the same time, but probably with no specific connection, a transport strike commenced in the Andean state of Táchira. This strike triggered uprisings all over the country and paralysed Venezuela. Eighteen people died on the first day of rioting in Caracas.

With virtually no warning, the Left had launched itself into armed combat. In Mérida, we had no choice but to support it. For the reasons I have explained above, we were completely unprepared. Because we had no arms, we had to invent them. Our particular group in Mérida gathered in rifles and shotguns, handguns and very little else. The actual fighting was scattered through the country and reached the Andes in uncoordinated incidents, none of which I was personally involved in.

I kept a pretty low profile, appearing only to fulfil my university work and my domestic duties with great dedication. My political liaison was conveniently undercover on the university campus. My contact was Beatriz Rivera, who was a professor of education and also the key to Teodoro Petkoff, the leader of the insurgents. I shall tell more anon of Beatriz Rivera, who became one of the keys to my life. My cover was almost impeccable. I say 'almost' because it might have been perfect if the level of my involvement had been judged from 1961 onwards. I took the greatest pains to show that every time there was a shoot-out or an ambush or a robbery, then I, Oswaldo Barreto, was nowhere near the scene of the crime. I always had an alibi, and it was always impeccable. Meanwhile, behind the scenes, I led a highly organised network of guides and drivers, of safe houses, ID document forgers and makers of disguises. I applied the meticulous discipline of my French communism to plan and execute ingenious escapes. They could not prove it, but I had personally organised the escape of figures as important as Teodoro himself, who, much later, as leader of the socialist party MAS, would play an important role in future governments of Venezuela.

There is a little cinema in Montmartre called something like La Lumière, which shows a lot of foreign films. Vida and I used to go there sometimes with Izaguirre. It has enormously comfortable seats and immense lights, designed, if Izaguirre is to be believed, by Jean Cocteau. Vida took me to see a war film there: *The Colditz Story*. When I was back in Venezuela, smuggling comrades in and out of the country, I kept remembering scenes from *Colditz*, and I kept telling myself, If those prisoners of war could build a huge

tunnel and a train, forge papers and fool the Gestapo, then I had
to be able to plan some successful escapes when all I had to fool
were a bunch of conscripts to the National Guard and a handful
of CIA clones.

While the army and the secret police were hunting left-wingers
and filling the government's torture cells and concentration camps
with intellectuals, I ran a Creole version of the runaway slaves'
underground railway. Ninety per cent of my task was a cerebral
process, 5 per cent was the human factor and 5 per cent was sheer
luck. Every one of my missions was successful. Every man, woman
and child I smuggled out of the city, the state and the country got
away safely; and not once was I linked to their flight.

The bad news was that I didn't start with a clean slate in 1961.
I wasn't just tainted from my boyhood: I was smeared. There
were fat files on me at the HQ of the two arms of the secret police
(known as the DISIP and the SN). Both branches were in their
element after October 1961. They had a free hand to 'rid the
country of its Reds', and even their peacetime foul means became
fair in war.

Given that the government saw me as a troublemaker, and
given the violent times, it has always amazed me that no zealous
DISIP agent ever came up to me, pulled out a gun and shot me
through the head. In military terms, it just doesn't make any sense:
it didn't then and it doesn't now. I suppose I owe my life to the
ingrained absence of logic that I so often bemoan in my compatriots.

Despite my peripheral involvement in any actual fighting, in
September 1961, on my way home from my afternoon sociology
lecture, I was arrested at gunpoint. Two plainclothes policemen
asked me quite politely (but with a gun in my ear) to get into
their car. I spent the night in prison in a cell no bigger than a
single latrine. During the night I heard shooting. They were troubled times, so you did hear the occasional shot in the dark; but this
was different, much more prolonged. I had no idea what it was
about, but it was evident that something out of the ordinary was
going on.

The next day I was moved to San Cristobal. I tried to find out
en route what had happened in town that night, but my guards

were stony-faced and refused to speak to me. I remember thinking that was the strangest part of my arrest: the fact that everyone ignored me, when, as far as I could see, I should have been the centre of their attention. It was my first proper arrest and I was a greenhorn. Later, I would come to appreciate those few hours or days of calm: the one thing you should not want as a political prisoner is attention.

Many years later, when I was living briefly in London, I found myself going over and over the situation of the IRA prisoners in Northern Ireland. I kept hearing about their hunger strikes and their 'dirty protests', intended to force the British government into giving them political status. Who, I asked myself, in their right minds, would *want* to be a political prisoner? In Latin America, the prison authorities starved politicos and smeared them with shit as part of the 'special treatment' reserved for enemies of the state. Yet in Belfast, there were prisoners safely ensconced in the penal system who were demanding to be given that vulnerable and unenviable status of political prisoner.

My own first experience as a politico was a fairly easy introduction into the special methods of our secret police. The worst thing about that stay in prison was my inability to be of service to my family in a time of need. In San Cristobal, I discovered that the prolonged shooting I had heard from my cell in Mérida was the sound of students returning from the university being attacked by far right Copeyanos (COPEI, the Christian Democrats). Two of the students had been seriously wounded. One of them was my younger brother, José. Having taken a bullet in the liver, he hovered for several weeks between life and death. José survived, but the prognosis was that he would be an invalid for the rest of his life. After he came out of hospital, he was smuggled to Cuba where the doctors performed miracles on him and eventually made him fit enough to lead an active life.

After nine months in prison, I was released in Caracas. My trial had lasted for forty days. I was charged with having helped to arrange the escape of several of my comrades. The prosecution was (quite rightly) convinced of my guilt. But despite my being guilty as charged there was not a scrap of evidence to connect me to those operations.

I was profoundly shocked by prison. I felt, I suppose, how a woman feels when she is raped: I felt violated. I suppose I can thank my stars that I was not, like many, actually raped in forced homosexual penetration, but the cells of my flesh were violated systematically and the experience did things to my nerves to the point where I have never quite felt the same since – never quite felt safe again. Despite its public enactment, there is nothing more private or intimate than torture, not even sex. Although I would tell all my secrets, I don't feel comfortable talking about torture. I have managed to block it out and I see no point in resurrecting the memory of it. Let it suffice to say that I had done my job well and I was lucky enough to get off.

Within the Barreto family, that was the only bit of luck we had that year. On 18 January 1962, my sister Blanca Dalia died after being accidentally shot in the throat. It happened at home, when her brother-in-law was innocently cleaning his gun and it went off at the precise moment that Blanca Dalia was coming down the stairs.

We Barretos were ten brothers and sisters: Graciela, Irma, me, Blanca Dalia, Bertilio, José, Ivan, Marina, Gledis and Jesus. Just a few months earlier Blanca Dalia had told me, 'You shouldn't be surprised that José has been shot, in a country with so many people dying. There are ten of us, so surely one of us has to go.' At the time, it didn't seem that José would recover.

The family was still stunned with grief when, only two months later, my brother Ivan was killed in combat in Portuguesa. I have said that all my siblings drifted to the Left, but Ivan was the most intrepid of us all. Unlike me, Ivan had been at the spearhead of the armed struggle and a commander in the field. This armed uprising by the Left against our corrupt and repressive right-wing government would gradually come to be known less as 'the struggle' and more as 'the Guerrilla'. My brother Ivan had led one of the first guerrilla units with acts of bravery that became legendary within fighting circles, even though, at the time, his feats went unrecorded.

The Ministry of the Interior was more effective at silencing all publicity about the armed struggle than it was at quelling the insurrection. Nothing about the guerrillas got into the press or the media. There was almost continual fighting for six years, but every action was construed as criminal rather than political and every activist was labelled a common felon. The public saw a wild increase in armed robbery and street fighting, in brawling, assault, kidnapping and murder. For those who naively did not grasp that Venezuela was living through a guerrilla war, it must have seemed that the world had gone crazy and delinquent overnight. Even the name of the guerrilla army, the FALN (Fuerzas Armadas de Liberación Nacional), was forbidden to be mentioned in the newspapers. Thus, Commander Ivan Barreto, my brother who fell in the field of battle against the army, was merely reported, some weeks later, to have died in a fight.

All ten of us Barretos formed our own groups or affiliated to other different groups, thus while all being part of the struggle, we were separate. We sometimes became enemies within our one family, despite our fundamental belief in socialism.

Our greatest unifying factor was Camila, our mother. But none of us ever fully recovered from the family drama of 1961 and '62. (Camila survived all the horrors visited upon her family until 1991. I was in Paris at the time and I had just returned from a hospital visit when my sister Gledis called from Caracas to tell me that Camila had died. By a strange coincidence, the chemotherapist had that day told me that my cancer had disappeared.)

For the eight surviving Barreto Miliani brothers and sisters, the intentional violence of the near death of José and the actual death of Ivan changed everything too. Until then, the movement had been a romantic one for us: it was happy and sociable, exciting and fun. After March 1962, it became a situation that was both hard and dark. All we knew was that we had to keep fighting. This realisation, which was brought home to my family by the death of Ivan and the temporary loss of José, was also brought home to thousands of other households across Venezuela. People died. People disappeared. And people came home damaged in ways we had never been able to imagine before.

After I was released from prison, I wanted to go back to Mérida, to Vida and our infant son, Ramín, but that was not to be. Rómolo Betancourt, our president, had recently decreed that anyone charged with a political offence in one town could not return to that town after his release. I was accused of a political offence in Mérida, which meant that I was forbidden to return there. Apart from my job and my work at the ULA, and picking up my political activities and my friends, this caused an enormous upheaval in my relationship with Vida and Ramín. My jail sentence had, in some ways, been harder on her than it had on me.

She was a foreigner in Venezuela at a time when there were few foreigners there. On top of that, Persians of Vida's class and education have exquisite manners and an enormous ingrained spirituality. Vida found our oil-rich, nouveau-riche society philistine. She strongly disapproved of our propensity to boast and our obsession with malign gossip. She despised the way we got drunk and brawled and the way the most serious among us would drop everything to party or to trawl through the bars and brothels.

Now that 'the revolution' had started in all seriousness and people were dying as battles were fought, she could not understand our national mixture of passion and levity. In Paris, political life had been deadly serious. Nor could I explain it to her. In many ways, I shared her impatience at many of my compatriots. But a party is a party, and although I was prepared to give up my life for The Party, there was no way I was going to insult my friends by turning down their hospitality. And if one drink led to another, as is so often the case, and the night were to include some good talk and some music along the way – that's life, isn't it?

Before my arrest, in the shared sleepless nights inherent in caring for a newborn baby, we talked about these differences of opinion long and hard. Yet day by day, like water dripping onto stone, our lax and innately violent Creole ways wore down not only her desire to stay in Venezuela, but her wish to stay with me. I see this now; I didn't see it then. After Ramín's birth, we seemed closer than ever before. I found enormous pleasure in the chores that she found a burden, particularly in the first weeks of motherhood.

My love for Vida was complete. Maybe she had what Huxley called 'a Madame Bovary syndrome': an ideal for her life which was unsuited to her gifts; and thus she would always be bound to feel disappointed. But I did not see her in that light then. Who was I (in my quest to become the saviour of my people) to criticise anyone else for their unrealistic dreams? Vida was serious about what she did, and I loved her for that. I saw her exactingly high standards applied first to herself and then to others, and I loved and respected her intransigence. She was giving herself to the cause: to international communism.

Initially, I had been Vida's shoehorn into communist circles. I served a purpose and, at a personal level, I suppose I became a habit. Vida got used to my company and my presence and so seemed to be close to me in ways that, actually, she was not. During the nine months of my absence in jail, I stopped being that habit and she stopped being used to my presence and my company. When I was released and we were reunited, I was too blinded by my own feelings to see hers. Maybe, if I had understood her better, I could have saved our marriage. I have often wondered if that is the case. I have often tried to convince myself that it is so. There are always 'maybes', but in this case, the older I get, the more I see that we cannot change people: we cannot make someone be in love with us, nor can we make them be like us. If true love could talk, I think it would say, *Vive la différence!*

Increasingly, when Vida and I talked, it was to compare recriminations. I blamed her for not loving me enough and she blamed me for not being someone else. That is hardly the stuff of diamond jubilees!

If we had stayed in France, *if* we hadn't gone to Venezuela, *if* we had lived out our political lives in a sphere of intellectual talk rather than in action, *if* we had stayed in Teheran with her family around us instead of mine, *if* instead of having to take on hundreds of my compatriots – each one of them a walking vessel for our national sins – Vida had only had to take on me, then maybe she would not have left me. But, on the other hand, I would never have spent my entire life away from Venezuela. I was drawn home as to a magnet. And I could not have stayed away from home in its hour of need.

I do not feel bitter about her leaving. Even at the time I did not feel bitter: I just felt stunned, and emotionally exhausted; then I felt sad. Looking back, it is still sadness that enshrouds the memories. I feel sorry that I didn't make her happy, couldn't make her happy. I can see her still, standing in our tiny kitchen in Mérida with the cracked white tiles over the stone sink, staring out through the slatted window at the muddy street below. On the concrete draining board there was always the iron tripod that supported the primitive cotton 'sock' through which we strained our coffee. All Venezuelans make coffee this way, and the coffee is delicious. Vida, however, saw our coffee-making method as indicative of our level of civilisation. Her lip would curl whenever she saw the damp, stained object in question. As I prepared my lectures at the kitchen table, I would watch her from the corner of my eye and sometimes I would catch traces of her fleeting disdain. At the time, it made me smile to see how that Persian princess despised our ingenious local filter.

She would stand and watch the rain for hours as she rocked our baby on her shoulder. I used to think it was a cameo so beautiful: mother and child framed for posterity. In her maternal pacing I failed to perceive her desperation to get out. In her apparently vacant stare, I did not see her loathing of the rains – and, by extension, her loathing of the place and all things Venezuelan.

While I found Mérida a pretty town, she found it ugly. While I found it intellectually stimulating, she found it stifling. When I was fulfilled, she was pining. And all those things that I found comforting – like the relentless rainy season, the simple Andean cuisine, the slapstick humour of my comrades, their obscene anecdotes, the rustle of cockroaches in the shower, the friendly squalor of some of our friends' houses – Vida found loathsome. When she clutched little Ramín to her shoulder, her embrace and her rocking alike were less of a signal for him to sleep than a silent promise to bring him up far away from here.

By the time I came out of prison, there was very little left of our marriage. My boyhood mentor Nene had taught me 'to live a great love'. My two grave errors were my refusal to see the one-sidedness of that great love, and my failure to see that the sands underneath it were shifting.

Looked at another way (her way), I could say of our union that Vida stuck it out for three interminably long years. With a baby to care for, she put up with a hundred and one inconveniences and dangers beyond the call of any wife. She stood by me while I was in prison and waited for me in Venezuela even though not only did she hate being there but she was tarred with the same communist brush and therefore at risk herself. She did her best to adapt to a totally alien culture. She moved from the lap of luxury to relative squalor; she went from a world-class metropolis to a Third World backwater. Despite her obvious talent for leadership, she was constantly sidelined and thus unable to contribute anything to her host country. In a society that thrived on spiteful gossip, she was the butt of endless malice. The family she was taken into was torn apart by grief. Her husband worshipped her but never understood her. And then, as a last straw, after nine months of absence in prison, no sooner was he released than she was forced to uproot and move back to Caracas – which she really hated – only to be abandoned once more while he went off to fight in the guerrilla war. Stranded, bored, frustrated and constantly at risk of being arrested herself for her connection to myself and my family, she fled back to the safety and comfort of her family.

Somewhere between our two versions of life lies the truth. As a communist, Vida was not much safer in her country than she was in mine. In fact, her subsequent nineteen years in prison there prove my point. Also, had she been a loving wife forced to flee she could have stayed in touch. Had there been no real personal animosity, she could, at least, have let me stay in touch with my son.

It hurt me very deeply when Vida left. It came as a complete surprise. As a result, I never quite trusted love again, or happiness. The hardest part of all, though, was losing Ramín.

I had already seen what a prolonged absence could do there. I had felt the intense pain of reaching out to him in Caracas as Vida carried him off the bus and turned him to face my proffered embrace. He had shied away from me, refused to let me kiss him, and when I tried to take him, he protested so loudly that everyone turned and stared. Nine months is a long time for a toddler. I had become a stranger to him. No punch or kick in jail hurt as much as that rejection. Vida explained to me that after twenty-two hours in a sweltering bus, he was bound to be grouchy. It took me nearly a month to woo back his confidence. It was a slow and laborious process. So I knew that every week away from him in the future would tear away at the fabric of his trust.

Of course, I had no idea that I was to lose my son for his entire childhood, his boyhood and his youth. Nor could either Vida or I have known that the war of attrition she began with such stubborn silence would be continued by her family while she was in jail. Had I known then what was to follow, I think the knowledge would have unhinged my brain. The loss of Vida and Ramín were two separate losses: they were two separate wounds that festered for many years.

One of the things that affected everyone in Latin America either directly or indirectly was the Cuban Missile Crisis. In the autumn of 1962 it seemed to turn the whole world on its head while triggering mass hysteria in the form of pathological fear. Before the Cuban crisis, we Latin American communists felt that if the going got really tough – as in, if truly faced with annihilation – then Fidel would do something to save us. After the missile crisis, we knew with as much certainty that he wouldn't.

I feel sure that it was not just a coincidence that Vida left shortly afterwards. I don't know if my departure to fight in Puerto Cabello had anything to do with her decision to throw in the towel on our marriage, but I don't suppose it helped.

I was sent first to Valencia and then to Campanazo to join up with three comrades. Together we were to wait for reinforcements to arrive and then help to relieve the guerrillas at Puerto Cabello. My three comrades were Pampero, Hernan La Riva and Florencio Ramirez. We spent weeks together without actually managing to join the fight. No support arrived so we spent a lot of time talking and doing surveillance. In my case, I spent a lot of time observing the labour and organisation of ants.

CHAPTER XXXI

It was in the *monte* and in prison that I got really close to the insect world, that underworld that coexists parallel to our own. In Venezuela, we call little things that creep and crawl bichos. Despite what certain papers say, I have never eaten a bicho, but I have observed them closely.

Entomology has been the secondary effect of my 'interesting life'. You see, an interesting life like mine leaves hundreds of hours for reflection in the interstices between one drama and the next. It was my time in the wings, waiting to be shoved on stage, which gave me first the opportunity, and then the desire, to study insects.

I can almost see a circle of faces mouthing, You pretentious git – pretending not to know what an insect was about until the good Lord confined you to quarters with a brigade of them! As though I hadn't grown up like everyone else with cockroaches scuttling across my face at night, ants in my pants and flies sticking to my fingertips.

Once again, let me clarify. In my infancy (when, technically, I was an innocent), I came across insects at every turn. My reaction was a single and immediate response: I screamed in abject fear. As I grew older, my single response changed: I killed them. I squashed, squeezed and trod on every bicho that came within my range. Now that I am that hardened criminal, that beast (supposedly squashing and treading on every form of human life), I have become squeamish about killing insects. Once you've seen the kind of set-up they have in their nests – babysitters, workers, look-outs, butchers, trailblazers, messengers, you name it – it makes you think twice before upsetting their eco-structure.

Sometimes, though, it's more like an aftermath to an end of the world movie, like *Alien 2*: a what-is-the-point reaction. There are so many insects, and they are so organised, so united – what is the point of killing one or two? Unless, of course, we are dealing with mosquitoes, and then the sheer pleasure involved, the gratifying revenge, is an answer and reward in itself.

My fascination with bichos started in the east, when we shipped in from Cuba in 1967. The diversity of world insects had stung, bitten and annoyed me until then, but they had never commanded my attention. On average, under every acre of earth, there are hundreds of thousands of insects. However, they are not equally distributed. Some acres are more equal than others. In the east of Venezuela (out in the *monte*, with vegetation so dense you can only cut your way through it, step by step, with a machete), insects congregate as to a bicho jamboree.

When you are part of a fully trained, fully armed guerrilla army, primed for action in the middle of a subtropical jungle, you discover how little action there is, and how much sitting around. I don't know how much time you've spent sitting in a jungle, but let me tell you that within minutes the hundred thousand little creatures that could inhabit that average acre crawl in to share the square yard where you're sitting.

If my kids were to ask, 'What did you do in the war, Daddy?', the most truthful answer would be: 'I watched ants. I spied on spiders. I looked at lice.' And these were not one-off occasions. I did a lot of it. I put in years of fieldwork.

Before I move on, I want to digress. Before I do that, here are some points to remember: they are ones I will return to. They are names more than points, names that will reappear. It's the loop: life in concentric circles. Getting deep: there is our solar system. There is the loop of civilisations, and the loop of revolutions. There is the cycle of life and the circle of sex. There is that endless turning of the wheel of fate. Getting smaller, there is the cycle of our mistakes and misdemeanours. In the jungle, there was that perfect analogy, just going round and round in ever-decreasing circles. And in my childhood, stuck like a scratched record, are the novels of Sir Walter Scott.

When it comes to loops, he was the Loop Master: the king of straying from a given point and then returning to it. Sometimes, halfway through a novel, I would think, This time, he's lost it — he's wandered so far from the plot he will never get back to the point! But if there is one thing you can be sure of in this life, it is the Loop Master's ability to get back to the plot. Churned in with all my early ambitions was a yearning to emulate the Scottish bard: to keep going back to the beginning, to keep touching base. I have worked on that. So whoever thinks, There he goes, rambling, and this time he'll never get back, remember that there are centuries of Scottish history, footnotes of fifty pages, sidetracks that take you on the scenic route to John O'Groats and Norway, and still those central stories circling back. And when it comes to who killed whom, and why, the Scots are way more barbaric than we Venezuelans. So I'm not lost: I'm circling.

I'm circling around the ants and the spiders, the beetles and the lice. On one of life's many intersections (where my loop momentarily crossed that of another), I ran into Rusián Schmitter. Rusián made me think about the meaning of things, almost as much as anyone I have ever known. Sometimes someone opens his heart to you, and just looking gives you a sense of vertigo. Rusián was like that.

And this (in Caledonian tradition) is his story. His family came from Eastern Prussia via the Colonia Tovar, the only foothold Germany has ever really had in Venezuela. Colonia Tovar is the forgotten fruit of an eighteenth-century error. The King of Spain tired of Venezuela and sold it to a German bank, the Wechsler Bank. The Wechsler thought the country should be settled with good German peasants, and shipped them out, only to find the Spanish king had sold the country to them in the first place because it was a nightmare to manage.

The Wechsler, in turn, got tired of their project, and sold the country back to Spain, leaving the colonists stranded. To this day, their descendants are out there: blond, inbred, beer-drinking, strawberry-growing Protestants who live like bichos in a foreign land. The Discovery Channel could have a ball with the Colonia Tovar, opening up that particular anthill to the world's curious gaze. Meanwhile, there are a few tourists and a lot of strawberries.

Rusián's grandmother found her way into this clearing in the bush. She found the struggling colony about as interesting and worthwhile as its banking founders had, and hightailed it out of there as soon as she found herself a husband blind enough to mistake her tyrannical smile for love. Rusián's grandfather was the owner of a vast estate in the plains of the Orinoco river. After a simple wedding, he set off to manage his cattle lands, there to discover he had married a monster. His despotic new wife allowed him to sire her some children, and then took a leaf out of the praying mantis's book, and killed him off.

When Rusián was about four years old, the old lady chose him to be both her heir and the object of her love. So Rusián grew up surrounded by violence, abuse, torture and (when the spirit moved her, or when anyone's table manners slipped) murder. They were his bread and butter. Despite the in-house insanity, Rusián grew into quite the little gentleman, with a passion for architecture and haute cuisine. Unlike his Prussian granny, Rusián showed no signs of insanity. In fact, he was one of the most reasonable chaps you could ever hope to meet. Well, he would have been, if he hadn't, like his granny, had a penchant for killing other people.

There was always logic behind Misia Schmitter's terminations. She set rules, she advertised them, and she systematically punished everyone who broke them. Transgression in some households results in disappointment, groundings, the docking of pocket money, even the odd beating. Misia Schmitter was always more direct. She dispensed with the intermediary retributions and jumped straight to that final solution. Her grandson was different. Most of the time, he was a placid, easy-going man. Just sometimes, he was not.

By the time I met him, he was well into his forties. It seems he'd had a flash of temper less than twelve, and more than seven, times by then. In a lifetime, that really isn't much. Unless, like Rusián, you shoot someone each time it happens. His family were powerful and rich, which helps when it comes to glossing over crime. And they were in Venezuela, which helps too. Once, though, in 1937, he did have to leave and stay out of the country for a year or so while things cooled off behind him.

One day, Rusián was having lunch in a roadside restaurant. I have mentioned he was a gourmet. He prized fine food, but was not averse to a simple peasant meal so long as it was well cooked. Had the boiled rice, fried plantains and steak been suitably cooked, he would have eaten up, paid and left, as he had done on dozens of other occasions.

It was a bad day for everyone. The cook burnt the rice. Rusián shot the cook; and a diner, who witnessed this and remonstrated with the killer, was shot for his pains. One of the things Venezuela has in common with Asia is rice as a staple. Arepas (corn cakes) are our bread, but rice and little black beans pop up on everyone's menu every day of the week. So you learn to cook rice shortly after you learn to walk upright. When Rusián told me of this particular incident, he regretted it. Not, as one might think, for overreacting to the cook's mistake, but for having shot the witness. In Rusián's book there is no excuse for burning rice.

'If anyone is such an idiot that they do burn it, then they shouldn't insult anyone by serving it.'

No, what really upset the man they dubbed the Slayer of the Plains was that he'd lost control of his temper for the split second it took him to fire the second shot.

The second shot (which lodged between the eyes of the passing diner) landed the trigger-happy Rusián in jail.

'It was as though Granny was there, watching over me. When we were growing up, no one ever managed to do something wrong and get away with it. Granny knew. She never had to see things or even be told about them. She just knew. She could read thoughts and see visions; and she never missed a trick or failed to perceive a misdemeanour. The one time when I lost control, it was sod's law: the guy's brother was a general!'

In Rusián's case, the reputation preceding him into the court-room did him no good at all. It isn't often that a rich man gets tried for homicide. The press and the public turned his case into a circus. They scavenged for dirt, and they were so gratified and excited to find it that they insisted an example be made of him.

I don't know whether Rusián's previous victims' families chirped up spontaneously, or whether the press sniffed them out and paid them to add their mite. People stood up on fruit crates in the most obscure parts of the country and reminded their co-citizens of their civic duty. Civic duty was synonymous with lynching Rusián Schmitter in a manly and upstanding way; or, if this option were to be denied them, then ensuring that he was locked up in perpetuity and that the key be thrown away.

Housewives with breasts drooping round their midriffs, who had not had sex for several decades, became orgasmic upon discovering new crimes committed by the well-born slayer. The country was buzzing with self-righteous indignation.

In saying this, I don't wish to excuse or make excuses for Rusián's execrable behaviour. I am merely showing the context, the arena, in which his crimes were committed and then condemned. And I suspect that a good half of his blood-bayers would have killed or had tried to kill or already had killed people themselves.

Had he shot seven, or nine, or even fifteen people for attempting to shag his wife or daughter, none but the victims' immediate families would have batted an eyelid. They turned against him for caring – 'Goddammit! Can you believe the balls of the great pansy!' – and actually speaking about something as thoroughly unmacho as haute cuisine.

Some countries mete out long prison sentences: life sentences that outrun the lifespan of any man outside of the Old Testament. We don't do that in Venezuela. Our sentences tend to be short and sharp or, if you are rich, not at all. Our prisons are neither built nor run on liberal lines. No one is sent there with the hope that they might rehabilitate or reform. People are sent there to suffer. If you are tough enough, and lucky enough, you might survive a year or two and finish your short term. If not, you die like the miserable scum you are legally deemed to be: beaten to death by either a guard or a fellow convict, or starved or raped to death.

I tell you all this to illustrate the extraordinary legal precedent set by the thirty-year sentence given to Rusián Schmitter for shooting that general's brother through the head in a roadside diner. Perhaps it was an accumulated sentence for all the unsung murderers who were the scions of rich and powerful families and got off scot-free over the years. Whatever the reasons, he got thirty years.

CHAPTER XXXII

Thanks to the truckloads of provisions his family sent him, and to his own penchant for cooking, Rusián made more than a few friends inside. The cheapest way to cater for prisoners is not to feed them at all. This policy has helped keep families united even while a loved one is locked away, and it has encouraged the growth and evolution of free enterprise. In a nutshell: either your family feed you, or you terrorise another prisoner (whose family is feeding him) into feeding you, or you starve. Imagine how popular having all that fine food made the generous Slayer!

About eight years into his sentence, though, the therapeutic properties of gourmet cooking began to pall on the master-chef and he decided to escape. Rusián was a clever and enterprising man. He could do most things he set his mind to; and he did them well. The escape was no exception. Despite being held in a jungle fortress, he ganged up with a couple of hardened criminals, and masterminded their break to freedom. He sprung himself, and them, out.

Three weeks after the escape, Rusián and one of the other fugitives were recaptured in the jungle.

There was uproar at the time of their escape. Like a TV star, pop singer or presenter, Rusián had caught the popular imagination. He was the man everyone loved to hate. He was the man who did unspeakable things to women in their dreams. He was the best subject of gossip for twenty years.

He was a spoilt patrician being hunted by the police. While the manhunt was on for him, my comrades and I could not only venture out of hiding, we could visit our children, go to shopping malls and discotheques, and get our teeth repaired. It was as though we were invisible – every available policeman was out searching for Rusián.

The magazines and newspapers were full of him, which made many of us subversives suspect that the government was probably dipping its fingers into the country's till again and didn't want anyone to notice. That was usually the case when the press went to town on a story and got quite so alarmist. As soon as whatever crisis needed to be covered up was covered up, the decoy drama or scandal would slip back into the fourth dimension, never to be heard of again. UFOs and aliens were a favourite standby. The skies over somewhere in the country would supposedly be alive with spaceships and flying saucers every time some major government corruption came to light and every time some dirty deal was being concluded.

Since Rusián and his cellmates escaped at precisely such a need-for-a-cover-up-diversion moment, the newspapers went berserk. The gutter press turned Rusián into the sort of serial killer who scarcely pauses to take breath between one vile murder and the next.

They endowed the man with the energy of a marathon runner. They gave him a tally of killings that ran into four figures. Not that I look at Rusián and see an innocent. The blue-eyed boy took the lives of more than seven (and less than twelve) people. He snuffed out other people's futures. And when he played God, it was not to a master plan, but out of pettiness. His story led me to places I could not enter. They were rooms in the labyrinth of his mind in which only he felt comfortable.

The chance to wash the dirty laundry of the rich and privileged was what really held the country under the spell. It had to be that, because 'Murderers on the loose!' was the stuff of every day. Most murderers were on the loose: they never got arrested, let alone convicted.

However, whipped up by the media, this time the general public rose up in arms, barricading their women and children into their houses, the men organising themselves into vigilante groups from Amazonia to the Caribbean. The government found itself obliged to actually pursue the escaped convicts, despite its perennial inertia. The army was called out to help find the escapees. Members of the National Guard were seen crawling under bushes and searching chicken coops from Maracay to Mérida. The real search went on in the jungle. That was where the government troops eventually stumbled upon Rusián and Co.

The next point of the story is the bit that has always baffled me. It is my big question, the mystery, the knot that will not untie. Three men escaped. Three weeks later, in the jungle, two men were found. The body of the third convict was never discovered, with the exception of his left leg, which Rusián Schmitter was carrying over his shoulder. The police reports reveal: 'The severed leg was semi-decomposed. The temperature that day was 36 degrees centigrade. When escaped Model Prisoner 2965: Rusián Schmitter was asked where the rest of the body was, he replied, "I ate it".'

Under torture, all that the erstwhile Slayer of the Plains would divulge was to repeat, twice, that he had eaten the third convict. The other escapee, who lost all credibility in the public eye when he ungamely died under interrogation, had issued dozens of conflicting statements, all of which were incoherent and inconsistent. According to him, the three of them had been abducted by aliens, aided by water nymphs, kidnapped by man-eating Indians, raped by a gorilla, held hostage by manatees – and so many other improbable stories that all he did was incense the lynch-mob mood of the country.

With two down and only one to go, it was felt it would not be enough merely to return the Slayer to prison. He must be made to suffer in a very public way. Killing people in those days may have been common in Venezuela, but eating them was not. After all the usual punishments had been meted out, it was decided that Rusián should be branded for what he was: a cannibal.

Historically, branding was a time-honoured punishment distributed far more readily than alms to the poor. Slaves, of course, were routinely branded, but that was to establish ownership and facilitate commerce. Branding as a punishment was something else. Branding was inflicted on those convicted of seditious libel, blasphemy, counterfeiting, criminal fraud and a host of other crimes. In the past, I am sure the branding irons were readily available in all the appropriate shapes and sizes. Not so in the 'Swinging Sixties': one had to be made specially for Rusián. The new branding iron was a large one. There was no point in a tiny, illegible brand that would have ended up looking like a love tattoo. His 'CANNIBAL' was supposed to disfigure, to mark for life, to be visible from a distance even by those who were slow readers or semi-literate.

Within the very serious arena of Rusián's crimes and punishments, an element of farce keeps recurring. The barbarism of his branding was not left unscathed by farce. There is a regrettably high instance of illiteracy among the peasant class in Venezuela; and because the bulk of the army recruits come from that class, and 95 per cent of the burden of our 'obligatory' national service also devolves upon them, there is a very high rate of illiteracy within the army. Anyone with a few dollars and halfway decent connections can get their son off the call-up list. As a result, most soldiers are not only dispossessed and socially put-upon, they can neither read nor write. This makes a mockery of dispatches and letters of safe conduct, etc. It is a well-kept secret covered up even by higher ranks as promotion jacks non-readers into positions of relative power.

In the years when I was active, I owed my life many times over to the illiteracy of the National Guard. The DISIP, our would-be SS, or the CIA or central government could signal our whereabouts to military outposts as much as they wanted. But if the message came by tickertape, by telegram or letter, someone had to read it – and the chances were that no one could. Even telephone calls or radio messages could fall short. I know that in my case, a name was once wrung from the dying lips of a torture victim and hot-lined through to my known vicinity. My cover was blown. But a security agent rang up the relevant roadblocks and spelt my telexed pseudonym down a laborious one-way radio.

Spelling was synonymous with panic. Spelling was something the average soldier couldn't and wouldn't do. So I could slip through the army's net because one of its men couldn't read the name on my identity papers.

Sometimes a soldier could be talked into taking one of the literacy classes on offer to the military. An officer would have to lose his power and humiliate himself by admitting his shameful ignorance. Officers were free to drink, whore, party, spend lavishly and take other men's lives. Why would any of them voluntarily give both up by joining a literacy class? Literacy classes were despised and, by association, literacy itself was despised. All men linked to books were seen as alien bichos. Spellers of words and all people linked to learning were regarded as a dangerous sub-species which had to be destroyed.

(Lest you were wondering, my loop does have a relevance to the rest of my story. Have faith and bear with me awhile.)

It was decided that Rusián would be branded across his back at shoulder level. An experienced cattle-brander was hired for the day to do the job.

Cowboys in western films talk about righting wrongs and slaying robber barons, and about building towns and educating their children. In Venezuela, cowboys talk about cows, whisky and women, in that order. They talk about the art of lassoing, the finesse of branding, the perfect edge of a master brand, parasites and other cattle-associated points that might well pass the average city-dweller by. Over the years, I have spent a lot of time hiding out with cattlemen, so I know how they pride themselves on a job well done.

Rusián's brand was a masterpiece of its kind. His flesh had been allowed to sizzle for just the right time, to the split second, so that the brand would scar him for life and yet make each letter of that scar clearly legible. The edges were so neat that cowboys boasted about it for years to come as the perfect example of their craft.

After all the fuss and the pomp and the ceremony, the solemn repetition of the sentence, the moment of proffered religious solace, the public pain and the triumphant revelation of the branded man: 'Cannibal' was spelt wrong.

For those who could read, the humiliation of having been party to a barbarous and public branding of a native patrician as a

'CANEBAL' was hard to bear. The only person to benefit from the misspelling was Rusián himself. It probably saved his life. Instead of progressing to the obvious next stage of systematically flogging him to death, he was thrown into a cell in some out-of-the-way dungeon to keep him and his back out of the public eye.

And then, with the usual muddle of unread and wrongly spelt paperwork, no one knew where he was for the next five years.

For weeks after the branding fiasco happened, though, there were dog days in the army. After that branding session, the buck was passed so many times, the eastern sector got to be one big rodeo. Careers were ruined, feuds began, duels were fought, abuse was slung, and several soldiers died mysteriously in a series of explosions all involving hand grenades from the specific issue of the barracks responsible for capturing and punishing Model Prisoner 2965: The Enemy of the People, Rusián Schmitter.

For weeks after the branding, the press was full of gory details. There were eye-witness accounts of what singeing human flesh smelt like, and the calibre of the prisoner's groans and sighs. Papers reported the 'true expression in those murderous blue eyes'. What the priest said to Rusián – 'Repent' – and what Rusián said to the priest – 'Fuck off!' – expanded into a pious tract of Catholic repentance, published in instalments in the gutter press and then sold as pamphlets by the Society of Jesus. The proceeds of these sales were sufficient to fund a new wing for the refectory of the Little Orphans of Saint Teresa, plus a bacchanalian inauguration for it the following year.

In the editing, the Man of God's single word ('Repent') was lengthened into a convincing speech so moving it brought the Man-eating Beast back into the fold of the Church. And Rusián's own rather ungracious comment ('Fuck off!') was metamorphosed into something altogether more readable in the drawing rooms of Caracas and Trujillo.

You know those old black-and-white films in which someone gets shot in the chest in the heat of the battle, but then lies in his buddy's arms, expiring over a speech so protracted that the battle, in real time, would have no end. Well, the pamphlet of the branding of the Slayer of the Plains showed a scene that must have gone on for hours and hours while a big crowd of dignitaries waited under a broiling sun for the priest to be done with the prisoner's reconversion. Apparently some of his supposed speeches were fifteen pages long!

I, of all people, know that the gutter press prints what it will.

In Rusián's case, despite all the reporting and the digging and the so-called truths of the case, the mystery remained unsolved. Why was Rusián carrying the severed leg of the third prisoner over his shoulder? Why? That is what I want to know. All and sundry, from press to public to judge and army, accepted that Rusián did, as he admitted, eat the third man. What makes the case so thoroughly mysterious to me is that it is a known fact that Rusián was a gourmet. The man was an eater so fastidious that he felt himself justified in shooting a chef for burning his rice.

The jungle was full of delicious fresh game: it was almost overrun with succulent wild pigs. There are over a dozen pretty delicious species out there. I cannot believe any of them would have been less appetising than the rank remains of a peasant, whose own eating habits made him the land equivalent of a bottom-feeder. Anyone who has been to a funeral in the tropics must know that the corpse goes off within hours. So the severed leg would have been putrid from one meal to the next. Rusián wouldn't have liked that. He wouldn't have eaten it: not roasted, grilled, or soused in his famous lime escabeche.

If it wasn't for food, what was it for? Why did he carry that heavy souvenir? I won't say it kept me awake at night, but it puzzled me. When he told me the story, I really wanted to know the answer. Surviving the vagaries of my own life, I have learnt a few things about prudence. So, when this charming man opened his heart to me and drew me into his world, explaining some of the triggers that had led him to flip for those few moments in which he eliminated another one of the seven (or twelve), I was pretty keen not to bring his quota up to eight (or thirteen) by irritating him.

With time, I felt those blips, those homicidal blind spots, had definite culinary links. I felt safe enough, eventually, to ask him why he had hung on to the severed leg.

'Why did you keep his leg?'

Rusián gave me a look of complete candour, and told me, 'I don't know.'

I still don't lose sleep over it, but when I happen to be awake and thinking, my thoughts loop back to Rusián and that 'Why?' The more I think about it, the more analogous it seems to my own life: wandering around in the jungle with a heavy festering load over my shoulder which I could put down but won't. I know it is rotting and that it is a magnet for flies and unwanted attention, but I will not let it go.

At the beginning, I carried the severed leg because I believed in it. After a while, though, it started to go off. Gangrene is not something you can pretend not to have noticed. It has an unmistakable sweet-sickly smell. I went round in circles for most of my life lugging a decaying ideology around. Why? No matter how much I ask that question, I really don't know the answer.

CHAPTER XXXIII

We were not any Latino country fighting, we were the one and only oil-rich country in Latin America, and under no circumstances was the United States going to let it turn Red.

It was at the time that I became a fully fledged freedom fighter and the armed struggle began to really spread, in early 1963, that Vida left Venezuela. My fighting or not fighting probably didn't have anything to do with her final decision to go.

Partly because of my sense of responsibility to my wife and child, and partly because I have always believed that I can be of most use as a thinker rather than as a combatant, I had held back from the real fighting. The extreme cowardice I felt as a small boy diminished as I grew older but it never entirely left me. My nature is to shy away from violence. It pains me to see a chicken or a dog suffer, let alone a man. Intellectually, I was clear about who we were and what we had to do within the movement, but I did not see the wisdom of fighting then without the ant-like organisation necessary for military success.

'Warfare is the greatest affair of state, the basis of life and death, the Tao to survival or extinction. It must be thoroughly pondered and analysed.' Our actions were contrary to every rule of strategy from Sun Tzu to Liddell Hart. Alas for our cause, we had not, at that time, read *The Art of War* by Sun Tzu. Perhaps because I have always been so aware of my own lack of bravery, I have always admired the raw courage and the physical virtuosity of certain men like Elias, my future friend and ally.

And yet, despite my inherent cowardice, in 1963, after Vida upped stakes and left me, I joined the Guerrilla and threw myself into the fray. There was an average life-expectancy of less than six months in that world of ambushes, skirmishes and raids. This did not deter a lot of volunteers from setting off to join the FALN. They would turn up by the dozen and declare themselves ready to fight. Most of them were sent home bitterly disappointed. What the FALN needed were strong, resilient, skilled and trained fighters with the balls of an elephant and the stamina of a camel. Most people didn't qualify on any of those points. I have to include my weedy, delicate, squeamish and rather cowardly self. The difference between me and the average volunteer was that I was known to the leaders and I could be relied on to substitute brain for brawn. I joined a fighting unit of the FALN and was given the codename 'Otto'.

Within days of my joining up, our unit was involved in a minor skirmish in the hills. It didn't last for more than fifteen minutes because we were outnumbered and forced to make a disorderly retreat. A man named Alfonso, who had been in the unit for a couple of months before I arrived, was shot and bleeding heavily. Our side not only had more enthusiasm than arms, it was also seriously short of medical personnel. As luck would have it, Alfonso still had his beer belly from happier times, and since he weighed about 140 kilos, neither I nor our two other comrades could carry him back to camp. For two days we hid in a disused shack and were divided from our unit.

Although Alfonso didn't look anything like José, with his each groan and murmur, I felt for him a protective tenderness so great it was as though he was my younger brother. In the afternoons the tin roof of the two-room mud hut we were hiding in was so hot we could have cooked on it. Crawling with flies and impregnated with goat's piss, the shack was altogether as far from sanitary hospital conditions as one could imagine. A small hole in the mud wall served more to attract bugs than to ventilate us. I wasn't wounded, but I was covered in Alfonso's blood. While our two comrades kept watch, I sat on the dirt floor with the patient, my nerves in shreds as every leaf rustling and every cockroach scuttling made me imagine either Alfonso's death rattle or the arrival of the army, or both.

I have rarely felt more helpless than I did then. Alfonso begged us to get him to a hospital. To have done so was not only against our orders, it would have been suicide. Perhaps because I looked so unlike my bigger macho comrades, and perhaps because it was I who sat with him and swatted the flies from his face and bathed his brow, he singled me out for his pleading.

By the second day his voice was hardly more than a thread, but he kept wheedling. Before he joined the FALN, he had helped his father run their small, family-owned shop. It had been Alfonso's job, he had told me earlier, to go in and out of Maracay to replenish their stock. From his early boyhood, he had become a consummate haggler, bargaining like a Turk for every sack of corn and every stick of tallow. As he lay on the compressed mud floor, seeping blood, he bargained to be taken into town. Hour by hour, day and night, he offered me everything he owned and everything he could imagine owning if only I would get him to a doctor.

Like my interrogator in the months before my trial, he alternated between sweet reasoning and menace.

'Listen, Otto, I've got a 1958 Chevrolet back home. You can have it. The engine is souped up and it was resprayed last year. It's a beauty. The keys are in my room, inside my baseball glove. I'll write you a note to my brother and, I'm telling you, it's yours if you get me to the hospital. But we have to go now! Look how much blood I've lost. I can take pain. I didn't even call out, back in '55, when a sack of rice fell on me from the deposit and ruptured my spleen. But this isn't right. I'm dying here. You've got to help me. I've got three spare tyres for the Chevy and my brother has a Winchester rifle. He wouldn't give it to me, but he'll give it to you. Listen, man, you have to do it ... What kind of a man are you? You miserable faggot! Look at you! My family will break every bone in your body when they find out about this. I tell you, you'd do better to shoot me through the mouth right now, because when I recover, I'm going to snap your ribs like chicken wishbones for this. There won't be anywhere in Latin America where you can safely hide. I'll come and find you, you bastard! Son of a rabid whore ... I've got a little shack by the sea, a shag pad, you can have it. It's got half a hectare of coconut palms in full production. You won't have to work again – just sling your hammock between two palms and watch the waves. It's yours, Otto. I swear on my grandmother's grave, may she rest in peace, you can have it, just get me into town.'

At the end of the second day, we were found by a scouting party of ours with a jeep. It was an enormous relief. Alfonso was delirious on the ride back to the rest of our unit. The jeep bounced over the potholes in the dirt track and my patient began bellowing like a wounded ox. Had we had to pass a normal road or, God forbid, a roadblock, we would have all been for it.

Luckily, the main camp, only three kilometres away, had a doctor. Within a week, Alfonso was back on his feet, looking tired, haggard and resentful.

For the next month, he avoided me when other people were around, but every time he got a moment alone with me he would make it clear that I was not the owner of his yellow Chevrolet, and I couldn't have his spare tyres, and his shag pad on the beach was his and his alone. His memory of what he had said and offered and given away was hazy, but he knew he had been trading and he wanted to make it quite clear that all deals were off.

'Did I say anything about my brother, Juan?'

'A bit.'

I wasn't going to give away anything unless he brought it up specifically.

'If you tell anyone about what he has got, you'll swallow teeth, is that clear?'

We had a terrible shortage of weapons, so his brother's Winchester rifle was a desirable asset which Alfonso ought to have begged, borrowed or stolen before joining up. Now he knew I knew it.

'You didn't help me out there, you bastard. You were going to let me die like a dog. Now you had better keep your mouth shut!'

Friendship is a strange thing. Since he had lain in my arms, since I had swatted a thousand flies from him, mopped his brow, cleaned his shit and held a wet rag to his lips, I would have thought a glimmer of gratitude was called for. Instead, I had a young macho man who hated me for having seen him reduced to weakness.

But I had stayed with him, stuck by him, and probably thereby saved his life. That, it seemed, counted for nothing to the fallen warrior. The others he forgave more easily. Me, he saw as the worm that could have eaten into his grain store, taken off with his precious Chevy and ended up, illicitly, with his shag pad by the sea.

CHAPTER XXXIV

People say that if women knew how painful childbirth is they would never get pregnant. Perhaps the same applies to war. If people knew what they must endure as soldiers, they would never join up. Day by day, the reality of combat expanded my definition of what I could bear to a breaking point. In this I was not alone, but I was, perhaps, as a fastidious intellectual, uniquely ill-equipped psychologically and physically to live under the harsh conditions of a guerrilla fighter. After the first harsh initiation, both mothers and soldiers seem to take to their tasks with a masochistic pride.

Joining battle was the most practical lesson of the distance between thought and action I have ever had. On the one hand, the distance was minimal: you heard a sound, you thought, Danger: I have to take cover, you ducked and a bullet whizzed over your head. That was the quick response. The slow one meant that you thought, paused, and died. On the other hand, there was the bigger picture; and, as with so many of life's lessons, it took a long time to understand. It was as though there were too many reasons for reason itself to prevail.

Once the armed struggle had begun, there was no choice other than to be for or against it. In my case, to have stood against it would have been to betray my side. And later, as I ran like a hamster inside the wheel of fortune, it was about keeping going, about keeping running. The famous lines of Euripedes about war and peace ran through my mind as I kept going.

When the people vote on war, nobody reckons
On his own death; it is too soon; he thinks
Some other man will meet that wretched fate.
But if death faced him when he cast his vote,
Hellas would never perish from battle-madness.
And yet we men know which of two words
Is better, and can weigh the good and the bad
They bring; how much better is peace than war!

Unlike a regular army, death does face a guerrilla fighter when he casts his vote. And 'casting votes' is too democratic a process to describe how we were swept along.

I was the most unlikely freedom fighter I could imagine. I was small, weak and tubercular. I was physically timid, cowardly and squeamish. When I set off for Falcón to join up, I was militarily untrained. And last but not least, I was meticulous and obsessive with my things and neurotic in my ways. I was a fussy eater and a fussy sleeper. I needed my papers and books and notes to be just so: to be undisturbed and untouched by others. I needed a lot of time to think in peace and quiet. I needed entire libraries at my disposal and I needed to bounce my ideas and thoughts off other curious thinkers.

Healthwise, I suffered from weak lungs, heartburn, indigestion, constipation and various allergies (including virulent reactions to mosquito bites). There were a hundred and one foods that I couldn't eat. To ignore my rebellious digestive system was to invite acid attacks and bile. My joints have ached since their first racking (hung by my wrists and then by my ankles from a worm-eaten rafter) on my first term of questioning in prison. I was never good at carrying weights or walking for long distances. I can swim, but not very well and not very far. I have always found loud noises acutely painful (probably because my eardrums burst at birth and are scarred). I have always slept very little and cannot do so properly without a nightlight. This is a legacy of my infant phobia about the dark. If my shirt or my trousers are a tiny bit too loose or too tight, it bothers me all day and produces a state of neurasthenia. And I absolutely *hate* it when people refold a news-paper with even a millimetre out on its crease. I hate disorder. In short, I am a monster – a walking collection of petty requirements, all of which had to cease to exist in the Guerrilla.

I joined up and I made do with what there was. *I* did not complain, but my body did. My feet were so chewed up by fungal infections that the skin cooked and bled into my boots. I shall not describe the smell! The saga of my feet could fill an entire chapter. I was so constipated that I think we had more battles than I had bowel movements out in the *monte*. I slept so little and so badly, I was half crazed with sleep deprivation. And the fear of capture and the fear of death were secondary to the night-long terrors of the natural darkness. I became a lunar expert merely because the few days on either side of the full moon were such a welcome respite whose anticipation I savoured during the intervening nightly blackouts.

I am not, naturally, a man's man. I have to find my way into a group of men like a worm on a computer. I have to sneak in and gradually take over; and that takes time. And yet I am not naturally a solitary scholar. I have always wanted to be part of a group: to fit in organically and to contribute socially as and when I can.

When you live in a small group in which imminent death is one of the members, there is not only the chance but also the necessity to 'belong'. My experience with the wounded Alfonso was an exception to the rule: on the whole, being together in the Guerrilla, even for a few weeks, bonded us more closely than years shared in peacetime. That camaraderie was the upside of the struggle. On the downside: our casualties were high. No sooner had a new friendship been formed than it would literally be ripped away.

1963 was the most intense year of guerrilla fighting in Venezuela. It was the year the army came out with tanks and entire battalions to thrash our ragged units. Despite our lack of arms, our lack of ammunition and, more importantly, our lack of any overall strategy, one thing we were never short of was wild, raw enthusiasm. We were cannon fodder on any battlefield. The FALN did not have the horses of the Polish cavalry when that old-school regiment made its tragic charge at the German Panzer division, but on one memorable occasion a couple of units of the

FALN charged blindly into enemy fire, throwing men at machine guns and mortar. Our men chucked Molotov cocktails in beer bottles at a line of advancing tanks.

Astonishingly, many survived even such a suicidal gesture. The FALN started out with a nucleus of only about twenty men in Falcón but then the rural guerrilla fighters expanded to some 300 men in the state of Lara with Petkoff and about 150 men under Douglas Bravo in Falcón. We were, of course, inspired by the example of Fidel Castro and Che Guevara and the mini revolutionary army they led to victory from the Sierra Maestra. Once the smaller units, or focos, had been formed and given the logistical support of three local landowners and their peasant workers, the FALN had an effective force with which to continually harry the army and commit acts of sabotage.

As the United States was to discover to its cost in Vietnam (although our haphazard efforts were hardly on a par with the brilliantly organised Viet Cong), no matter how strong an army is, it cannot beat a guerrilla force. So long as we remained hidden and struck out only at random times and in small numbers, we were able to keep going and to keep regrouping. The amount of damage actually done by us was relatively small and the areas of fighting were also relatively contained.

Meanwhile, from the middle of 1962 until his arrest in March 1963, Teodoro Petkoff left the *monte* and returned to Caracas to form part of the Venezuelan Communist Party's military section. The urban commandos were the ones that attracted attention internationally because they pulled off some truly spectacular stunts.

We might not have been as organised as the Viet Cong, but they were so impressed by the unique guerrilla tactics of our urban commandos that some of our comrades travelling abroad were pressed by the Vietnamese revolutionaries into dictating exactly how we planned and executed such operations as the kidnapping of De Stefano, the Spanish-Argentinian football star, the theft and voluntary return of an entire exhibition of French Impressionist paintings in Caracas, and last but not least, the kidnapping of the US military attaché.

It made front-page world headlines when the FALN captured a

US military mission's HQ. The international press featured a US colonel in his underwear. Another time, the FALN hijacked a plane and dropped propaganda leaflets over Caracas and then looped the loop low over the rooftops to the mixed delight and terror of the populace. It was the FALN's tactics that made them popular the way, say, the Tupamaros were popular in Uruguay. The early stunts of our urban commandos were ingenious, and bloodless. They made fools of the police and the government and had maximum political impact.

Although at first we were intoxicated with the propaganda and the triumph of the Cuban Revolution, as Teodoro Petkoff said, 'We first thought the rural guerrillas were the most important battlefront, but events themselves transformed the city into the main fighting front. Caracas was like an echo chamber, and a firecracker exploding on a downtown street corner had more political impact than a pitched battle between the guerrillas and the army in the mountains of Falcón.'

Venezuela had switched within the half-century from having had a largely rural population to having a largely urban one. So it was in the cities that there was most social contradiction and political tension. Our vanguard of only 500 men kept going for two years in Caracas because of the support from the urban population.

Out in the *monte*, on the other hand, the fighting continued for a lot longer than that, but it was an uphill struggle. And 'uphill' is the operative word, because we would come down from the hills, hit a target and retreat with the army in hot pursuit. No matter how high up we went, the soldiers came after us. Our casualties were high, our supplies were erratic, our weapons were both scarce and inadequate, our organisation was continually damaged and our morale rose and sank with dizzying speed.

Politically, we may not have moved the earth, but emotionally, we were like magnifying glasses directing the sun onto dry grass. We were high on emotional energy and every kind of stress, which we relieved by frenzied coupling. Because of our high casualty rate and our incredibly short life-expectancy, we tended to cram everything we had into the slenderest of attractions.

When I joined the Guerrilla full time, I was reeling from having been dumped by Vida. Out of a mixture of desperation and revenge, I went for good, bad and ugly sex, so long as the person at the other end of my penis was female. The effect of those hasty liaisons, other than contracting a very painful rash, was to compound my loss and lack of Vida. That is, until I fell in love with Beatriz Rivera.

I already knew her quite well because she was a professor of education at the same university. As a university professor, I had been able to move in intellectual circles without arousing suspicion, thus I could appear to meet her as a colleague rather than as a communist contact. Beatriz was under surveillance. We became close friends and had a great influence on each other. She had an open spirit, which I, as a fairly orthodox Marxist, did not. It was she who persuaded me to put prejudice aside and to re-read Freud, and she set me on the path of thinking autonomously, even within the parameters of Marxism.

Quite apart from that, she proved herself to be infinitely more independent, autonomous and creative than anyone else in Venezuela. She wasn't like a conventional wife, or housewife, or the mother of her two children. Without any of the trappings of feminism, she felt herself completely free to live her life as she saw fit. Her husband, Teodoro Petkoff, was the founder and leader of the Guerrilla. They had a son and a daughter together, who lived largely with her parents. While remaining a loving and tender mother, she acknowledged no ties. She was with Teodoro and she was with the party because that was what she wanted and not at all because she felt obliged to follow either as wife or militant. To behave like that, at that time, and there, was extremely rare and also extremely courageous.

She was the youngest student ever to have graduated from any Venezuelan faculty of psychology and education. She was wild and funny and stunningly pretty. And she was also far more courageous than I was and had about ten times my stamina. She was two years younger than me.

I loved Beatriz Rivera. I didn't have to pretend to be someone else, to be either better or worse, more or less than I was. We lived a life so stripped of normal trappings and hypocrisy, and so close to death, that we were able to reach an extraordinary closeness of a kind and quality I have rarely experienced since. Her sweet, feisty love helped to heal the wound of Vida's leaving and made the loss of my son more bearable. And it transformed many of my days in that armed struggle into some of the sweetest moments of my life.

I had had no news of Ramín since he and Vida had left. At first, I attributed this to the precarious postal conditions under which we lived. As time passed, though, it became clear that not just as a husband, but also as a father, I was to be shunned. And I imagined that it was as a bicho that my estranged wife saw me: like someone out of Kafka, metamorphosing from man to insect. The more I thought about bichos, the more of them I saw. The *monte* was full of bichos. To name but a few, there were the ubiquitous mosquitoes and there were midges, flies, scorpions, giant bees, wasps, burrowing worms, poisonous spiders, lice, and cattle ticks that bloated on our sucked blood to the size of cherries. Compounding our discomfort, the heat was oppressive and the washing facilities were few and far between. We had to crap in the bushes and sleep wherever we could. My inability to take a crap in public exacerbated my life-long struggle with my slow intestines to the point where I had to make hot mallow poultices and apply them to my distended gut. Once, it got so bad that one of our unit risked blowing his cover and went into a village to get me a bottle of castor oil and some laxative pills. We laugh about it now, but the indignity at the time was like the last straw.

These were my personal trials. There were others that plagued us all. The undergrowth, for instance, was a constant problem. Most of the time, we didn't climb hills, we crawled up them, cutting our way through tangles of thorns. With bad food, insufficient sleep, physical fatigue and our nerves constantly frayed, we often bickered and bitched about tiny things. The habitual fevers and infections of the tropics took a heavy toll and our sick and wounded had such a hard time of it that no one malingered.

But we felt we were doing something heroic, something good – even essential. It was a form of passionate romance and the feeling was mirrored by our behaviour. Those who were not actually lovers were close friends. Although we spent a lot of time indulging in our national pastime of malign gossip, even that was more good-natured than the verbal assassination we practised at home. Almost everyone had a great sense of humour – those who didn't did not survive for very long! Some of the time we were overcome not by the enemy but by laughter. And when we were encamped on, or by, one of the haciendas that gave us the bulk of our logistical support, then we lived like the bandit kings we had all fantasised of being.

Some of our few allies within the country at that time were the Italian communists. Most of the world's communist parties, including (increasingly) factions within our own Venezuelan branch, were staunchly against our armed struggle. The Soviets didn't want to upset the status quo and so with self-serving hypocrisy they condemned our fighting initiative. Our own PCV did little but criticise and gripe, but the Italians offered their total solidarity. They were the group least expected to do so because there had been a general anti-Italian feeling for at least a decade when the entire construction business shifted into their hands during the dictatorship of Perez Jimenez. The small comforts of our life in the wild were often thanks to the help of the Italian community.

Then, public opinion turned against us, and, as I have said, the government censored any mention of our political activities. Uprisings and strikes were reported as criminal riots. Our people disappeared, formal arrests were for felonies rather than dissent. The press wasn't just gagged, it was used to nullify us. This news blackout of what we were doing meant that we were getting less and less support from the peasant population. There we were fighting for the peasants' rights in the belief they were right behind us, and there they were, half the time, right behind us but turning us in. It got so that we had to hide from everyone: friend and foe. Without even the tacit support of the peasants and the rural villages, we were bound to fail. We couldn't see that yet, or maybe we wouldn't see it, but it was so.

One by one the men around me fell or disappeared. Beatriz Ribera was seconded to the urban commandos, leaving me desolate. By the end of 1963 the chances of any one of us surviving for a prolonged period of time out there were virtually nil. I knew it.

We all knew it. The government net closed in further. Our already meagre supplies got fewer and our manpower dwindled with our morale.

It was at this point that the PCV intervened on my behalf and ordered me to leave. To my enormous relief, I was pulled out and sent away to continue the struggle somewhere else.

At the time it seemed like a miracle. I see now that it made sense. I was sent to a sanctuary to keep me alive so that later I could keep the party going in Venezuela. Many of our finest leaders and finest minds had been killed or were in prison.

The unit I was with was wiped out one week after I left it.

As you can imagine, there were a lot of retrospective accusations of desertion and cowardice from my detractors over my having been saved, as it were, for posterity. Even the left-wing press has gone to town about it. And what can I say? I am guilty as charged of not having died in the Guerrilla. I didn't ask to be pulled out but I was more than glad to be given a break.

In the past, communists could get away from persecution in their own country by going to Cuba, or to Russia or to a friendly Arab state. Algeria, newly liberated from France and running on the first steam of its utopian goals under the guidance of my old friend Ben Bella, was a haven for anti-imperialists from all over the world and was also the destination chosen, by chance, for me.

I was taken like a human package and zigzagged back in the boot of I don't know how many cars en route to the port of La Guaira. The plan for my escape was that El Chino Valera was going to smuggle me onto a ship and get me out of the country. El Chino Valero was a genius at smuggling. He was the sort of person who could put a cat in a fish tank and make people believe it was a goldfish. I knew very little about either my escape plan or my mission except that I was to stop over in France, and that before I set sail I would get a chance to see and be with Beatriz again.

She and I spent two days together. Forty-eight hours laced with an intense imprinting of each other. As members of a forbidden movement, there could be no letters or telephone calls or even messages; there would be no future for us as a couple. So when I finally left the small squalid room with the broken shutter in the safe house where we had our last meeting, I was also leaving her.

Up until 1963, I had been pretty much free to choose to have a life of my own, independently of my political life. Now I became a cog in a political wheel. My internal battles were no longer to love or leave: I would always leave; to settle or roam: I was obliged to roam; to continue or stop with the Struggle: I was doomed to struggle on to my death. Time and again I would have to break my own personal ties and, with no notice, leave what I had and move on like a marionette pulled by the strings of first the Communist Party and then circumstance.

I have spent most of my life learning to know my enemies and my heroes. I have not, until now, spent much time getting to really know myself. I used to think there is never enough time for me. I now think that was my mistake. '... one who knows the enemy and knows himself will not be endangered in a hundred engagements,' wrote Sun Tzu. I am seventy years old and I have survived at least a hundred violent encounters without becoming 'unconquerable' in the sense of Sun Tzu's teaching that 'being unconquerable lies with yourself, being conquerable lies with the enemy'. Time and chance have patched up the cracks in my armour. This narrative, I hope, will mend some of the fissures inside.

When I set out to tell my story, it was my intention to relate my way through my life year by year and incident by incident. But I see now that I needed to go round in circles to find my path. Sometimes, as when we invaded the east of Venezuela from Cuba, we had to literally go round in a loop, but even when I seemed to be following a straight path, I see now that I was still running round in circles. As anecdotes, many episodes in my life can stand alone. They may make you laugh or they may surprise you, but that is all they are: anecdotes – remembered moments.

Most of them have no place in this book. Once I have given a flavour of how it was, you can multiply it into dozens, if not hundreds, of scoops of a similar taste.

Because I have spent my life with people who made decisions that affected entire nations; and because, occasionally, I myself was called upon to make such decisions; and because it was often I who advised the leaders who took them, I need to retrace my steps along the road we trod. I could say, *If something had not happened, then something else could not have happened and something else would not have happened either.* But the If Road is mere conjecture for the past. Where it serves a purpose is to shed light on the road ahead.

Here is an example of that. Although I am not a fanatic, I have sometimes lived with fanatics and worked with fanatics, and often been in a position which fanatics aspire to. And I have been high up in organisations that go out of their way to recruit fanatics. *Had* I been a fanatic, I could have been a powerful destructive force. How does someone become a fanatic? How do people forgo any moral obligation? Why do people give their lives for a cause? Why do humans become inhumane? At what point do we stop listening to other people; and at what point do we stop thinking for ourselves?

You might assume that such a life is not just for anyone: that it could not be yours. And yet history is full of those 'anyones' who rose to the call or were pushed into the breach by circumstance. I am a prime example of a man won over. I had no interest whatsoever in politics and no desire to fight. When I was a boy, the last thing on my mind was armed struggle, and yet I became a militant activist and then a guerrilla fighter. I am a thinker who became a man of action. That is a very big jump. If it could happen to me, brought up in an Andean backwater, it could happen to anyone, anywhere.

Despite my being an atheist, and Paul Tillich being an evangelical Lutheran pastor, I used to enjoy reading his work. Certain of his ideas became like part of my luggage. 'A self which has become a matter of calculation and management has ceased to be a self. It has become a thing.' The shambolic nature of my life is probably as good an amulet as any against overcalculation or management.

Meanwhile, via my mother, Vida had finally contacted me. She and Ramín were fine and living in Paris; she wanted to sever the last legal ties between us. There were divorce papers for me to sign, and she wanted to know where to send them. My being sent to Algiers via France at the precise moment when Vida needed to get the documents signed was the one time when I was able to combine something I needed to do for me with something I needed to do for the movement.

Vida arranged to meet me off the boat. Because I knew we were meeting only to finalise our divorce, and because the eighteen months since I had last seen her had given me time to realise how intrinsically without a future our union was, and also because I was in love with Beatriz Rivera, I was not unduly excited at the thought of seeing Vida again. But I was excited at the thought of being reunited, even for a day, with Ramín.

I walked down the gangplank of *El Flander* to the quayside of Rhennes on a sunny day in August 1964. I couldn't help noticing that Vida stood out like a siren. It wasn't just that she looked beautiful, she was tremendously chic. She had style and everything about her radiated class. What distinguishes women like Vida isn't their beauty or their clothes, their wealth or their jewels: it is their grooming. Some women are meticulously groomed. This isn't the scrub-down conversion, that alchemy that so many women can miraculously achieve, transforming themselves from scruffiness to splendour in less than an hour. Grooming takes many years. Grooming is a combination of taste and time. In Western society, it is the almost exclusive prerogative of the upper classes. In Africa and parts of Asia it is communally achieved. In Latin America, it happens rarely that the right recipe of taste, wealth and leisure combine to produce the truly groomed effect. In Vida, it came naturally and made her stand out in the waiting crowd at Rennes like an exotic star.

To my surprise, she was very affectionate with me. We sat in a café and drank pastis and she told me that not only had she missed me, but that she wanted to continue some kind of relationship with me.

I don't love her anymore, it is certain,
But maybe I love her . . .

And I didn't really know what I felt about her any more. I was still in the thrall of my recent traumatic leave-taking of Beatriz. Stalling for time, we drank a lot more pastis than either of us had a head for; and within a couple of hours we ended up in bed together in a small *pension.*

Later than night, I told Vida that the only way that we could be together was if she came with me to Algiers and my mission there.

So it was Vida and I as a couple who set sail shortly afterwards for Algiers.

PART 4

CHAPTER XXXV

We sailed to North Africa in the autumn of 1964. I still knew nothing of my mission except that I had been told to present myself to the Cuban ambassador there, Jorge Sergera, known by everyone as 'Papito'.

I had read hundreds of reports and heard I don't know how many accounts of what it was like during the revolution. I had absorbed the sultry, gloomy atmosphere (rather than the geography) of Camus' novels. I had eaten in countless Algerian cafés in Paris and visited numerous Algerian comrades in their Parisian homes. So really I felt like quite an expert before our battered tub of a boat arrived at the dock.

But I had not taken into account the barrage of smells that would assault me on arrival: that heady blend of charcoal and grilled lamb, spices and sweat, mint and jasmine, petrol and goat shit, fresh bread and coffee, oleanders and tangy sea air. I thought the city would be licking its wounds – as Tübingen had been a good eight years after the end of *its* war. I imagined Algiers would have a strict, disciplined air and a very serious, intellectual atmosphere, like the intense meetings we used to hold in Paris during the war of independence. But although I knew that Algeria had become a Mecca to anti-imperialists the world over, I hadn't realised how this would translate into the milling, multicultural ethnic jamboree that paraded daily on the boulevards and streets as Ghanaians, Tuaregs, Congolese, Chinese, Indonesians, Koreans,

Senegalese and Mozambicans, Eastern Europeans and Mongolians, Finns and Tanzanians displayed their diverse roots in fantastic exotic displays of fabrics and hats.

The Mediterranean glittered and sparkled as a dazzling backdrop. The port was a hub of noise and colour, the beaches bubbled with people. The palatial architecture of the three-tiered city rose impressively, from the French colonial sector with its grandiose arcades by the sea, to the bustling, lively commerce of the old Spanish quarter, to the ancient Arab city and the kasbah. It was a place full of grace and gaiety. Cascades of bougainvilleas trailed over balconies and roofs, banks of oleanders and jasmines trellised into ornate railings and geraniums grew with a kind of wild abandon.

Even the kasbah, that tragic tomb of Ali la Pointe, was crammed full of colour and shouts of laughter. It was a city gleefully celebrating its triumph. Nothing, in fact, on first impression, gave any sign of the recent war, the bitter struggle or the million deaths of the recent revolution.

Since so many of the two million displaced persons had returned to the city of Algiers, the sudden overpopulation turned every street into a mini souk and every street corner into a party place, seriously hindering Ben Bella's recovery plan for his country.

I was completely disorientated. I had just spent a year in the Guerrilla being hunted like an animal. The contrast was so enormous that I wandered around in a state of near-stupor for several days.

On closer inspection, the stucco was pockmarked with bullet holes and there were open spaces between buildings that had no business to be there. Numerous shops and small factories were boarded up and closed and others showed signs of having been abandoned and looted. Despite these, the pervading spirit in the centre was allegro, and outside the town on the slopes terraced with magnificent olive trees, the pervading spirit was calm.

As the muezzin raised their evening call to prayer and a red disc dropped behind the waveless bay, and the last gulls circled our house and the night-scented jasmine – so redolent of my childhood – smothered my senses, Vida, Ramín and I were cocooned in domestic bliss.

Papito was my age – born in 1933 to my 1934. He came from the same town as Fidel Castro and he had been a guerrilla on the Cuban second front with Raul Castro. During the revolution against Batista, he was one of the youngest commanders. Afterwards, as public prosecutor, he condemned most of Batista's henchmen to death.

His embassy in Algiers was the least conventional diplomatic mission Cuba had; sometimes his ambassadorial meetings seemed more like those of a baseball player meeting other members of a baseball team than the functions of a diplomatic corps. Sometimes he even received his fellow ambassadors in boxer shorts. For all his apparent casualness, Papito never forgot the tribulations of Cuba, his allegiance to Ben Bella, his reverence for Fidel, or his role in the international community. Although entitled to it, he didn't want to live in a big house, and chose instead a modest apartment just outside the city.

He explained to me my delicate mission. A quantity of arms from Korea and China was to be sent to Latin America and I had to find a way to smuggle them there. Cuba was under such close surveillance that it had no real chance of directly supplying arms to Latin American fighting units. The organisation for this indirect transport via Algiers was under the direct control of Che Guevara. Representatives from other Latin American guerrilla movements were on their way to join me. Our combined headquarters were to be in the Villa Susini in the hills overlooking Algiers.

Villa Susini was large and lovely with gardens shaded by gnarled olive trees and speckled with hibiscus between great splodges of purple bougainvillea. It was assigned to us by the Algerian government for symbolic reasons, because it used to be the torture centre where hundreds, if not thousands, of members of the Algerian Resistance had met their deaths.

We had a lot of weapons waiting to be shipped: rifles, machine guns, '125s, grenades, anti-tank mortars – the lot. They were all American.

We decided to buy an enormous number of giant olive-oil barrels and conceal the arms in false bottoms. We would ship the olive oil to Venezuela. For this we needed two companies: an

Algerian export company and a Venezuelan import and export one. My job was to set all this up. The paperwork for these companies took me the best part of six months, until the spring of 1965.

The truth about arms supplies for the guerrilla movements in the 1960s is only really coming out now. Officially, the Soviets didn't allow any Soviet weapons to appear in Latin America. The international political consequences would have been enormous. But, behind the scenes, the Soviets were prepared to help us with, for example, an entire shipment of Asian arms.

Cuba similarly couldn't afford to be the country that was seen to be supplying arms to us. What we did get from Cuba, though, was every other kind of help. For instance, I personally witnessed a deal in which Fidel gave 10,000 tons of sugar to Ben Bella for the Algerians to sell so that the money could be given to Latin American guerrilla fighters.

In February 1965, there was to be a conference in French, in Algiers, and Che Guevara was invited to participate. Papito asked me to translate Che's speech.

I met him at the Cuban embassy. Thanks to our discussions about that speech, I got to know the profound isolation which was inside the complex communist world of Che. He was not aligned to the Soviets nor to the Chinese nor even to the Cubans. He seemed to be waving a solitary banner. He didn't come across at all as someone who had lost his nerve, but (at least in private) he did come across as someone who was beginning to lose his faith.

The speech itself was a new departure: admitting not one, but numerous mistakes. The exact wording was so crucial to Che that I got the impression this speech was as much of a confession to the world at large as it was a plea to Fidel himself to at least see the error of their ways, and it was also an auto-da-fé. When he gave it, it put the audience in shock, regardless of faction. At one extreme were those, like Papito, who thought 'the show must go on'; so, in public at least, swear blind that the revolutionary whitewash of all Fidel's government's actions is the truth, the whole truth and nothing but the truth. At the other extreme were Cuba's equally adamant detractors. In the middle were many ardent supporters of Fidel and his revolution who just wanted to know the truth.

Che's speech was an open challenge to Fidel and also an avowal of independence and integrity. Fidel saw it as a stab in the back for himself and for Cuba. And he saw it as evidence that not only could el Che no longer be trusted, but, ironically, that of the two of them it was Che who was bordering on the insane.

In a nutshell, it wasn't just any moment or any speech, and working on it together made us close. Generally there is something very direct about Cubans, and in fact about most Latin Americans. We tend to be loud and hearty and as friendly as puppy dogs. Some people are good at breaking the ice socially – Latin Americans tend to just ignore it and crash in. Che wasn't like that. He was more shy and reserved, mixed with spontaneous outbursts of excitement. But because we were communicating through his speech, we got to know each other quickly.

Che was excited by the idea of intervening in Africa and he spoke openly of his plans to take Cuban troops to help the liberation movements there. We agreed to further discuss this possibility later.

For several weeks after he left, I was fired up by the thought of us going to equatorial Africa together. In preparation, I deepened my ties to the various African diplomatic missions and their entourages. I found that, intrinsically, Latinos and Africans share a timescale governed by emotion and circumstance rather than clocks; that we party spontaneously; that our societies are both fundamentally tribal; and that the Caudillismo of my native Andes was the bread and butter of African politics. Having not quite regained my stamina after my year in the *monte*, however, I also found that my liver was unable to sustain the gruelling party marathons of the African delegations. So as the spring progressed and the almond trees blossomed in the garden, I withdrew to my shell at the Villa Susini and returned to the tamer gatherings of my Latino comrades.

Che was pleased with the plan for shipping the arms but displeased by the bureaucratic slowness involved in starting the necessary companies. He didn't hold with the Latino mañana: he liked everything to be done yesterday. He was very aware of time and as punctual as an Englishman. Later, when I got to know Fidel (whose sense of time, particularly in his own speeches, was positively rambling), I wondered how the two men could be so incompatible and yet have stayed such close friends.

During the next year, we met again and talked some more but although we discussed the need to intervene in Africa, the opportunity to work together there fell by the wayside. Che was preoccupied with other things, not least of which was his renouncement of the national leadership of the Cuban party, his post as a minister, his rank of major in the Cuban army and his Cuban citizenship. From the end of April 1965, my mission ceased to be controlled by Che and fell under the direct control of Papito.

If the arms smuggling plan was to work, then absolutely all its paperwork had to be in perfect order. So there was nothing to do but wait. During that period of waiting, we at the Villa Susini kept busy by setting up a number of other import-export companies all over Latin America; touring olive groves and buying up vast quantities of olive oil and enough giant barrels for the eventual shipping. We also had a number of soldiers being trained secretly by Cuban instructors within the villa complex.

After the new year, which was scarcely celebrated locally (what with Algeria being Muslim), an undertow of unrest, which had began to become apparent, broke out in a number of ways. The most significant of these were the strikes by the industrial working class in January 1965. Although this sector accounted for less than 1 per cent of the population, it made itself heard, and its voice was loud enough and angry enough to stir up a much larger malaise towards the neo-colonialist forces within the government.

When the colonialists left en masse in and before 1962, they closed down most of their companies and factories. Ben Bella's plan was that these would reopen and begin production again under the control of self-management committees. To a large extent, this did not happen, because of the lack of trained personnel.

After the Liberation (that is after 1962), the Algerian people expected to be rid of the French completely. Ben Bella, on the other hand, knew that he had to honour the agreements made with

France and the rest of the world regarding not only the remaining colonialists but also Algeria's number one asset: oil.

Despite the occasional strikes and rumours, Algiers continued to feel like a safe haven. It was like a honeypot buzzing with life. I regained my health and my strength and began to look forward with renewed enthusiasm to the day when I could return to Venezuela to finish off the fight that the Left had started there, but which had subsided into a state of stalemate. One by one, my brothers and sisters had all joined that fight. They had fought together, briefly, to bring down Perez Jimenez' dictatorship and then they affiliated with this or that branch of socialism. News filtered through that at least two of them had joined the Guerrilla after I left. Irma, my eldest sister, began to rise in the PCU and would remain a hardline communist all her life. Paradoxically, thanks to all the embassies and their diplomatic bags, it was easier to get news from the outside world and from home than it was to know what exactly was going on within the country we lived in.

We didn't really see or sense quite how much intrigue and ill-feeling was floating around downtown. Ours was a satellite community, composed largely of exiled Latin Americans who gravitated around the bright star of Papito.

The city was warm and beautiful, the beaches were fantastic. The company was stimulating. Not being hounded was the greatest luxury of all. Being able to stand at my window without fear of being shot, to walk out of my door and say hello to people I met on the street; being able to take a dump without fear of death or capture – all these things were like a balm to my system. Able to eat proper meals, to drink wine, to listen to music; to write and think in peace, to buy and read newspapers and to have access to books and journals – it was an enormous luxury.

Vida took to Algeria. She made friends and found a niche for herself. For several months we were able to live as a family. For the first and only time since he was a baby, I was able to get to know my son. But in the spring of 1965 – just before I left for Prague – Vida's second shot at having some kind of relationship with me fizzled out. This time round there were no big scenes or fights of a personal nature, nor were there the lists of grievances we had split up over before. Our relationship was like the cliché my mother and her generation used to murmur to each other when their husbands and sons mistreated them for the umpteenth time: 'Men! You can't live with them and you can't live without them!' And, as it turned out, Vida and I could not live together and yet we could not live for long apart. Time and again we would separate, only to reunite months or years later. Vida decided to stay on in Algiers while I went to Prague – but in our pattern of reunions and separations she would later change her mind and join me in Czechoslovakia. Then, Ramín went on holiday to Vida's family in Persia. Having gone for a two-month visit to his doting grandparents and their clan of relations in Teheran, our son never came 'home'. The 'holiday' kept extending and would continue to extend not only until Vida herself returned to Iran, but until Ramín himself, as a grown man, left Teheran to study Communications in France.

CHAPTER XXXVI

In April 1965, with no warning, I was sent to Czechoslovakia as the Venezuelan Communist Party delegate to the editorial conference of *Co-inform*, the official communist magazine, at its headquarters in Prague.

At the editorial conference, there was a strict pecking order. Depending where a member country stood, delegates either could or could not decide or vote. At the top of the tree were the founder members: the Soviets, parties of popular democracies in the Communist Bloc, plus Italy and Argentina. They could take decisions over the content of the manifesto and finance. Secondly, there were combatants: member countries involved in armed combat. In 1965, Venezuela was the only member country that qualified as such; so I was in a category all of my own and could vote.

In Prague, I was astonished by the material luxury that surrounded me. I was given a stupendous apartment while the Czech people I met were sharing the most cramped and squalid housing. The apartment I had would have served four entire families had they been Czech citizens able to pull strings in the party. And while I, for attending two editorial meetings a week, had my pockets full of party money, the locals had to work for a subsistence wage in whatever factories or jobs were assigned to them, regardless of their status and qualifications.

While living on the inside of communism, I saw it was a false society, a nightmare society. Like when you dream something bad: you are run down in a street and you don't know how you got there or how you got to the point where a lorry ran you down. You are both protagonist and phantom observer and yet still you don't know how you got there or why or where that lorry came from. You cannot make sense of your dream and when you wake up you are still dreaming so you cannot get out of it. It plays on in shadowland, and it will not stop. That was what it was like to live under the Soviets: like living a nightmare, for the young Czechs in particular.

Against the grim backdrop and maybe as a reaction to it, some of the friendships I made in Prague were very deep. One of the most important of these was with Rocce Dalto, who arrived in Prague at around the same time as I did to the editorial conference as an observer delegate for El Salvador. Rocce had the same kind of charisma as men like Fuchs and Lorca must have had. He appeared to be as much human as divine, as much male as female; he was both young and old; he even managed to represent both the Left and the Right politically. In short, Rocce Dalto was like a god: a person of irresistible attraction. During the months I was in Prague, his companionship opened up the city and its society.

During our editorial meetings, Rocce was on my side, but since he was a non-voting observer, it was, by necessity, mute solidarity. Thus among the Latin American delegates, I found myself alone championing armed struggle for us within Latin America. Internationally, I was not entirely alone because of the support of both Algeria and (carrying more weight within the conference) Italy. I much appreciated Rossi, the extremely intelligent and astute Italian delegate.

Approval by the Soviets, though, was a battle lost before the conference even began. Theirs was a policy of submission. They put up with their heritage of Stalinism; they put up with the Cold War; they went as far as to go along with the alliance Khrushchev had made with Cuba; but they wouldn't go one single step further.

They had a terrible economic crisis within the Soviet Union, which they tried to conceal at all costs. However, they did not say, 'We cannot go further – we are broke.' They said, '*You must not go further – it is wrong.*' 'We cannot' came to equal 'You must not'. I saw what a difficult position the Soviet Union was in: they didn't have the capacity to support any movement capable of carrying out the Marxist idea. Nor could they offer themselves as an example. Living inside the Soviet world in Czechoslovakia, I could see how false this world was.

Twice a week, week after week, the debates continued, smothered more by what was not said than by what was. Everything was cocooned in hypocrisy. At the end of each meeting, we stuffed ourselves with fine food and wines and then went back into the streets of Prague as privileged transients in the grim grey reality of that lost city. The smell of boiled cabbage and stale beer lingered in the streets. The suburbs were a maze of dour concrete apartment blocks while the centre was an array of grand façades. No matter what the buildings looked like, they all smelt of old cabbage and they all emanated a sense of gloom. The people were shadow men and women with pasty ashen faces. Some days the people of Prague looked as though they had all been hit over the head with a stun gun.

Tell me who, who are these travellers, more fugitive, even,
than we? Who, from the very beginning, seem driven
and forced by a will – and whose is it? –
which unrelentingly wrings and bends them
hurls them and swings them; tosses them, catches them
back.

As they shuffled and waded through the miasma of rules and lies, they looked downtrodden and bewildered.

To understand what it was like, you have to see the huge difference between being Czech and being a Soviet. Communism was like a lens made opaque with dirt. With a little rub, with a little perception, one could see through it to the real society that had been created in Czechoslovakia. That was a society so different from what I had believed in until then, and so different from what we were fighting for, that I finally lost my faith in the Communist Party.

Having said that, I should clarify that I didn't actually break away from the party there and then – for a number of reasons, not least of which was that I had a shipment of much-needed arms in Algiers. Also, at the very point when I became disenchanted I was asked to help prepare the Tricontinental conference in Cairo and then to attend the Conference itself, to be held in Havana in January of the following year.

While I was in Prague, the semi-idyllic Algiers I had left the previous April had undergone yet another phase in its revolution. On 19 June 1965, my good friend President Ben Bella had been ousted in a military coup by Colonel Hourari Boumediènne. Ben Bella himself had 'disappeared'.

Subsequently, it would become known that he had been taken prisoner and would remain locked up for fifteen years. At the time, though, my own principal ally in Algeria (next to Papito) was out of the picture. I no longer had a home there; and news of the new regime was less than reassuring. Besides which, my 'work' at the editorial conference was supposed to keep me in Prague until the autumn of 1965.

The Cubans in general, and Fidel Castro, Che Guevara and Papito in particular, were outraged by the coup. They had been staunch allies of Ahmed Ben Bella. For them (as for me), he personified the Algerian Revolution: he had been the central leader of the FLN and president of the revolutionary workers' and farmers' government that came to power following the victory over Paris in 1962. It was the Cubans who had come to Ben Bella's aid when Morocco invaded Algeria and tried to overthrow him in the Tindouf campaign. The quick intervention of Cuba – by sending a tank battalion and several hundred troops – had sent the Moroccans running. Cuba had political grounds and Castro had ones of personal friendship for backing Ben Bella. The Cubans declared openly that the coup had 'no possible justification' and thus risked a diplomatic break with Boumediènne. Castro even stated that if Boumediènne's government 'should break relations with us, they should not be the first military regime to do so. We are thinking of the future, and we do not act as opportunists ...'

No one could say the same of China, who rushed to endorse the new government only one day after the coup!

A link emerged later between our Latin American arms-smuggling activities at the Villa Susini and the fall of Ben Bella. Apparently Che told Ben Bella that they had 'just been struck a serious blow. A group of men trained at the Villa Susini have been arrested at the border' and Che was 'afraid they might talk under torture'.

Che was worried that their mutual enemies would discover the true nature of the import-export companies we had set up in South America. Shortly afterwards, Che Guevara left Algiers, but he warned Ben Bella to be on his guard.

Ben Bella was a good socialist and a good man, but he wasn't a saint and he wasn't infallible. He made mistakes; he failed to establish local militias and fell prey to his own army. And he failed to communicate sufficiently to the masses *why* he was doing a lot of what he was doing. This lost him their true support.

'The Tao causes the people to be fully in accord with the ruler. Thus they will die with him, they will live with him and not fear danger.'

The masses of Algerian peasants were so *not* fully in accord with Ben Bella as the ruler that they allowed him to 'disappear' without kicking up much fuss. They even saw the military coup by Boumediènne as just another leadership intrigue.

CHAPTER XXXVII

Although I wasn't sorry to leave Prague, I was sorry to be leaving my friends there without a chance to say goodbye. And I was sorry to leave Vida, who had arrived to join me only eight weeks earlier. I packed up my spacious apartment. I did not know where the next step in my life would take me, nor whether I would return to Prague.

I boxed up my new collection of books, taking some and leaving most of them in store with a friend. The world is full of my abandoned belongings – mostly books – that I have never been able to catch up with. Over the years, I have been the butt of much ridicule thanks to my penchant for travelling as a combatant with paperbacks stuffed into every pocket of my commando jacket; but I am unrepentant. Not many of my compañeros had read much philosophy, but some of the ones who had travelled knew Lao Tzu's saying: 'A scholar who cherishes the love of comfort is not fit to be deemed a scholar.' It was one of the quotes beloved of fortune cookies in Chinese restaurants around the world. But books have always been my comfort. Wherever I am and whatever the conditions – be they a prison cell or a dug-out in Falcón or a slum attic – I am in a comfort zone if I have my books with me. As to Lao-Tzu, all I can say is he must either not have been referring to books, or things were different back then in 500 BC, or he was just plain wrong.

I took my leave of Vida, not knowing when I would see her

again. We were still in the honeymoon period of our reunion so it was a fairly emotional farewell. I think I have mentioned this before, but because it was one of the most striking things about her appearance, I will say it again: Vida was like a chameleon in some ways. Her eyes changed colour. This wasn't something that happened once or twice: it happened often. They not only changed according to her mood, they were affected by place. She arrived in Czechoslovakia with bright grey-green eyes in which the sparkling emerald predominated. She had been green-eyed during most of our sojourn in Algiers. In Prague, it was as though her pupils soaked up the sombre slate grey of the city. This made her look less exotic, and less feline, more sombre, yet still very beautiful.

At the airport when I looked back to wave a last goodbye, Vida's chameleon-eyes looked dark as charcoal. I was so struck by this new hue that I wanted to stop for a while and ponder quite what a remarkable beauty hers was. But I was already through the barrier and my flight was boarding; so I had to leave her to fend for herself while I flew away to Egypt.

Because I missed Vida, I remember that I wanted to feel sad – or at least subdued – on the plane, but I was so exhilarated by the idea of Egypt that nothing short of a tragedy could have doused my traveller's euphoria at the approach of a promised land. Few places on first sight could live up to such high expectations as I had of Cairo, and yet it did not fail to delight me. It would be hard to imagine a bigger contrast than between Cairo and Prague in 1966.

I looked out of the plane window at a landscape of desert and pyramids. The pyramids! There were two whole pages devoted to them in the public library's children's encyclopedia I had so loved as a boy.

The battered taxi honked its way through one bustling, exciting, exotic street after another. En route to the apartment where I would be staying with the two other Venezuelan delegates (both of whom were old friends of mine), the Arabic splendour seeped sleaze. I was enchanted. Every time the rusty taxi slowed down, I felt tempted to jump out and buy a bunch of postcards to send home to say, 'Look where I am!' In the Guerrilla, the cult book was *Justine*, from Lawrence Durrell's very daring (for that time)

Alexandrian Quartet. Having read *Justine* was more important than having read Marx. Alexandria and Cairo were both Egyptian and therefore near enough to impress anyone from my former unit, my former schools, my family, or, indeed, me.

Of course, I didn't send any postcards either from Egypt or anywhere else. A letter or card from me in those days would have been like posted poison to the recipient. I was a wanted man, and any connection to me was certain trouble.

But I didn't get much time to be a tourist and see the sights because, unlike my sporadic work in Prague, helping to prepare the Tricontinental conference turned out to be a marathon taken at a sprinter's pace. But even so, the air was deliciously warm and my starved skin absorbed the heat and metamorphosed me back from reluctant Czech to tropical creature again. But what I revelled in was the light: the absence of gloom.

The Tricontinental was the brainchild of Mehdi Ben Barka, a Moroccan socialist who was nicknamed 'Dynamo' for reasons which will become apparent. I had heard of Ben Barka in Algeria; he was well known as a daring politician. He had been the leader of the movement to free Morocco from the French. But when that happened in 1956, the Moroccan royal family frustrated his dream of a free and open state by retaining all the power under French guidance. Ben Barka then led an opposition movement.

He had four really striking things about him. The first was his size. He was tiny, really tiny: not a centimetre over 150. He had a tremendous energy. It seemed to buzz off him to such a degree that when you shook his hand you expected to get an electric shock. He was extraordinarily intelligent. And lastly, he exuded power. He had an innate authority. I mean huge authority. Visualise someone hardly bigger than a manikin treating all those warring delegates and bigwigs as though they were small children and making them all jump to attention – literally! – at his every command.

There had been an association of countries in Africa and Asia that had had an armed struggle fighting for their liberation since the Second World War. By 1965 this included Vietnam, Egypt, Indonesia, China, Algeria, Morocco and many more. Ben Barka's idea was to join the existing bicontinental Frasiatica to a third continent: Latin America. The three continents – the three 'A's – would then unite to help each other to liberate themselves from the industrial countries of North America and Europe. The problem was who the Latin American delegates would be. Ben Barka asked Fidel Castro and Lázamo Cardenas to decide which Latin American countries really were revolutionary and had the support of their people. Anyone can say, 'I am a revolutionary.' But if you don't have the support within your country, then you are not representative; you are not a real revolutionary, and certainly not a leader. On the other hand, you might have everyone's support, but you might not be at all revolutionary. Because it was October and the conference was to be in the following January, Ben Barka needed to decide quickly who was in and who was out.

Cardenas said that it was not for him to decide who was and who was not a revolutionary. Fidel Castro said that he would nominate only those countries that had a history of or were currently involved in armed struggle. This meant that in Latin America, only Chile, Uruguay and Venezuela could qualify, together with Cuba.

For Venezuela, three delegates were elected: Marcano Cuello, from the PCV (Communist Party of Venezuela), Ector Ruiz Marcano, from MIR (Movimiento de Izquierda Revolucionario), and me. From the moment we arrived in Cairo, everyone was at each other's throats over China not being in agreement with Fidel, and China not being in agreement with either the Soviets or the Arabs. The bickering began to get out of hand. It was at that point that it became apparent quite how much power Ben Barka had. It was he who settled the squabbling and he who personally decided everything. People talked about him over and above China and the Soviets. We were used to hearing: 'This and this is happening because the Soviets have said so.' In Cairo, though, it was all 'Ben Barka has said' and 'Ben Barka has decided'. And everyone accepted it without a murmur because Ben Barka *was* the boss.

The aim of the conference in Cairo was 'to put all the resources of the three continents together to stand up to the industrialised countries'. With delegates and translators from three of the four corners of the globe, the only thing that everyone agreed on from the outset was the impossibility of covering our huge agenda within the given time.

We gathered on day one and Ben Barka took the stand. Microphone in hand, he looked more like a travesty of Edith Piaf than a great leader, but from the moment he started speaking he mesmerised his audience. He talked rapidly, enunciating every word with a precision that went rat-a-tat-tat like bursts of machine-gun fire. He spoke in both English and French.

His opening sentence was: 'We have the honour to be here for the Tricontinental. We have two days to get through the agenda, but we could do it in four hours!'

His speech was very short and it flicked from point to point, whiplashing them into line. 'First point: to define the Soviet and Chinese Pacific Conference. Second point: to define . . .'

One by one he controlled every one of us. We stood open-mouthed in a mixture of astonishment and admiration. He was like a puppet master or a headmaster. His tiny stature became formidable. A delegate would rise to speak and as he approached the podium, his mouth shaping for his opening bid, Ben Barka would strafe him with instructions like, 'I hope you are going to talk about Cameroon, because if you are not, you may as well say nothing – don't you think? NEXT!'

Before we knew it, it was evening and the entire agenda had been covered. And that was that. The next day we started work on the manifesto. Again, Ben Barka was so able, so clever: he knew that the Cubans had fallen out with the Algerians (over the overthrow of Ben Bella who was a friend of Castro's) and he wanted them to make up. Well, Ben Barka announced that since the three countries who had had the most recent liberation struggle were Vietnam, Cuba and Algeria, it was they who should work together to prepare the manifesto. It was a good idea, but the Cubans opposed it and proposed Venezuela instead. Ben Barka said,

'No problem. Oswaldo Barreto, I choose you.'

Then he hardly paused for breath before he launched into the work. I have never seen anyone work as Ben Barka did. He was a dynamo, a phenomenon!

He said, 'OK. We are all here. Right! First phrase: "We, the countries of the world." Are we in agreement with the first phrase? Right! Second phrase: rat-a-tat-tat-tat ...'

And away we went, rushing through that manifesto for the Tricontinental conference to be held in Havana. If I, or anyone else, interrupted him, he would say: 'Compañero, that's great what you are saying. I understand completely; but I disagree completely. So: rat-a-tat-tat-tat!'

And away he would go again.

Because I had been working with the Soviets on the magazine in Prague, I knew their point of view and what they thought. I knew that they would never vote for a lot of what Ben Barka was saying and I told him so. I was the one who interrupted him most, but he wasn't brooking any interruptions. Despite that, he and I worked fairly closely together because I was seduced by his mind and his manner. Serious as he was, he still found the time to joke. He would say things like, 'We are here to do some work and then we are going out to lunch.'

So we'd do the work, and then he'd say, 'Good! Now for lunch!'

He would look from one to the next of us in his bird-like way, like a bobbing sparrow with bright currant eyes.

'What shall we go for? Any suggestions? Let's eat, compañeros!' He said it with such enthusiasm that it made my mouth water. Someone would come up with their favourite dish; another would suggest a good restaurant. And then without twitching a muscle, Ben Barka would say, 'Overruled!' And on cue someone would arrive with eight sandwiches and eight Coca-Colas, and we would work on.

When we finished the manifesto (in record time) he said, 'OK. Now let's read it.'

He then proceeded to read out our joint manifesto from the fresh galley proofs. To our astonishment, the text was completely different. Unabashed, Ben Barka stood up and addressed us.

'As you can see, compañeros, this movement has come up with a great many ideas which would have taken too long to formulate. Whereas, they actually condense into something far simpler — and here it is!'

Well, it wasn't what we had discussed or suggested at all. It was a more radical version of what he personally believed and wanted, and he was much more radical than any of us. And there it was in black and white: done. The Arab runner with a bootlace moustache was waiting impatiently by the door to take it back to the printing press. As we delegates exchanged astonished glances, Ben Barka was thanking everyone for their collaboration and wrapping up the meeting ready to set off to organise the film he wanted for the opening in Havana. The other delegates were speechless; but, as I have said, I was not intimidated by Dynamo, and the Tricontinental was a big thing which I believed was important, so I spoke up.

'Look, excuse me, but this manifesto does not reflect either our ideas or our opinions.'

Ben Barka stuck out his chest. 'Come on! Are you really going to interrupt the liberation of entire countries of the world to quibble over some little point about who said what and how you spell it? That's a minor point, don't you agree?'

'No, not at all, as I've said —'

'Compañero, you are splitting hairs. There is work to be done: the Revolution has started. Don't you agree?'

The fact of the matter was that it made no difference whether we agreed or not (for the record: we didn't). The thing was printed the next day and there was nothing we could do about it.

When the Tricontinental Manifesto was finished I returned to Prague, the Soviets asked me a lot of questions about who had voted for what, and yet they were surprisingly easy-going about the manifesto. I had thought that maybe they were going to pull out of the Tricontinental, but they seemed more determined than ever to be there for it in Havana.

A few days after I returned to Prague, Ben Barka arrived. I think he had come via Havana. He didn't stay at the International Hotel; he came straight to my apartment, suitcase in hand, to stay with Vida and me. He could not have been more amiable. In fact, when Vida opened the door to him he was positively expansive to my Muslim wife. But I was still pretty angry at the stunt he had pulled in Cairo with 'our' manifesto.

'I want to explain something to you, Oswaldo,' he told me. 'The Soviets and the Chinese know everything about us: and I do mean *everything*. But I also know the story of each of you delegates. So I know that the delegates for Mexico and Cameroon are Soviet agents; and I know that the ones from Nepal and Bengal are paid by the Chinese. If there had been too much arguing and imbroglio, then different countries would have withdrawn from the conference, and we can't have that. The only thing that matters is that as many countries as possible attend. We need them all: Benin, Mali, Rwanda, Ghana, Sumatra – I tell you, there is no island too small! Now, because the manifesto is so radical, the Soviets and the Chinese will insist that all their satellites go so that the satellites countries' delegates can be in Havana to vote for the points of the manifesto that the Soviets and Chinese want approved; and the Soviets and the Chinese will go to monitor it all and to make sure that everyone toes the party line. So, you see, I had to do what I did with the manifesto.'

I had to hand it to him: he was a master strategist. He had been so utterly convincing in Cairo that he had taken us all in. His speediness was not an act, though. He was speedy all the time. Ideas flew out of his head like shrapnel. Some hit their mark while others just scattered.

He stayed with me and Vida for a couple of days, during which he was a charming but eccentric guest. During his visit he accomplished several missions and tried to instigate another which came to naught. The latter was his attempt to incite Vida into getting rid of the Shah of Persia. His insistence on it made it clear that he really was a lot more radical than me (or Vida, for that matter). He kept urging her to do it with him. Every time there was a lull in the conversation, he would start it up again with, 'Let's kill the Shah. One day he is going to die; and when he does, it will be a disaster for Persia. Mark my words, he has to go quickly.' First thing in the morning and last thing at night he would say, 'Come on, let's do it: let's kill the Shah!'

Ben Barka's main reason for coming to Prague, though, was to appoint me head of all the eligible Latin American countries that did not have old established Communist Parties, and to ask me to visit them in rapid succession to set up committees there to send delegates to the Tricontinental. Having delivered this mandate, he set off for Paris to set up the film about national liberation movements in the three participating continents. It was to be called *Basta!*

He had an appointment at the Brasserie Lipp, on the Boulevard Saint Germain, with a film producer, a journalist and a scriptwriter. There was very little time to get such a film together, but he was confident that it could be done if he threw his own energy into the project.

Simultaneously, I set off for a whirlwind recruitment tour of the Caribbean and the three Guianas (British, French and Dutch). While I was in the Caribbean, Ben Barka's name was headline news. Much of the following story was not reported at the time; to this day, some of what happened to him in Paris is still a mystery. It is a famous story.

On 29 October, he set out for the appointment with the film people at the Brasserie Lipp. One of his own group shadowed him at a discreet distance. En route to Saint Germain, Ben Barka was stopped in the street by two French policemen, who showed their ID and asked him to accompany them in their police car. Quite calmly, Ben Barka complied.

The 'shadow' saw that there were other people in the car, and he was sure that one of them was an 'honourable correspondent' (an agent of the SDECE, which is the French secret service). The car moved off in the direction of the southern suburbs of Paris. Ben Barka's shadow man managed to follow it and he saw it stop in front of the house of the notorious French gangster, Georges Boucheseiche. After that, all certainty ends and only mystery and speculation remain. Mehdi Ben Barka was never seen or heard of again. He had been abducted, and it is assumed he was assassinated, but his corpse has never been found. It is rumoured that his body was taken secretly to Morocco with the compliance of Mossad and the French secret police.

The known facts of the case are that on 29 October General Oufkir, the Moroccan minister of the interior, was informed that the 'parcel' had been delivered. His deputy, Commander Ahmed Dlimi, was also informed. The next day, they both arrived in Paris. Investigations carried out in Israel, France and the US confirm the involvement of Mossad in this affair. From 1967 onwards, revelations in the Israeli press about the involvement of Mossad in the assassination of Ben Barka indicate that this led to a serious crisis in the government and even to the resignation of the Israeli prime minister at that time.

There is no concrete proof that the CIA was involved in the assassination, although *Time* magazine revealed that in April/May 1965, the Moroccan authorities submitted an official request through the US embassy in Morocco asking the American government for help in 'picking up' Ben Barka. There is no trace of the answer to this request. However, his family and supporters, by making use of the channels opened up by the Freedom of Information Act, learnt that the CIA archives contain, under the name of Mehdi Ben Barka, some 1,800 documents of three to four pages each. These documents are classified and their release has been deemed 'harmful to the national security of the United States'.

It all happened over thirty years ago and yet despite a lawsuit for 'kidnapping' having been filed in the French courts in 1965, and another for 'murder' in 1975, and despite General de Gaulle's personal written pledge to Ben Barka's mother in late 1965 assuring her that everything would be done 'with diligence' to bring the truth to light, nothing has been done except to pile more and more lies on top of the existing scandalous evidence of the murder of a great man.

The immediate effect of Ben Barka's abduction and subsequent disappearance was that we, his delegates, all travelled to Havana without him. The entire Tricontinental conference had been his idea and his plan. Yet, in the end, it took place without him. There was no film called *Basta!* to show at the opening and there was no Dynamo to preside over the opening ceremony or to keep order during the following days.

PART 5

CHAPTER XXXVIII

I reached Havana at the end of December. I flew there with Vida, who was also attending the conference. It was the first time I had visited Cuba. Already, by the level of my collaboration in the setting up of the Tricontinental, I was marginalised from the Communist Party. I was clearly aligned with those groups involved in armed struggle and clearly at odds with both the Soviet and the Venezuelan party line. This would have serious consequences later, but during the conference, the 'favouritism' that Ben Barka had showed to me in Cairo and his declared confidence in my capacity and opinions meant that I was listened to by the delegates. This was just as well, given the pig's ear the conference threatened to turn into.

Quite apart from having its guiding light extinguished, our conference got off to a bad start. Without any of the delegates knowing it was to happen, Fidel doomed the Tricontinental on the day before it opened. He did this by giving a speech in la Plaza de la Revolución on 1 January 1966. He savagely attacked the Chinese. By doing so, Fidel sabotaged Ben Barka's idea of uniting the three continents of Asia, Africa and Latin America. The Chinese, obviously, could not ignore such an open attack from Fidel Castro himself, so there was an immediate schism. Furthermore, the speech seemed to align Cuba with the maintain-the-status-quo policy of the Soviets. Fidel appeared to be against guerrilla fighters anywhere.

As a result, when we sat down for the conference the day after Fidel's speech, we had no unity. Until, modesty aside, I came up with a speech that partially, at least, solved that breach.

I stood up and I told the assembled delegates, 'I have just come from the Caribbean – see for yourself, there are the Antillean delegates.' I pointed out the (mostly rather startled) new Antillean recruits; and then continued. 'When I was in Guadeloupe and I asked, "What is the most important revolutionary movement in Martinique?", they didn't know, despite the fact that they are both French Dependencies. When I asked, "And who is there in British Guiana apart from Cheddi Jagen?", they didn't know. When I went to British Guiana and I asked Cheddi Jagen in person, "Who are the revolutionaries in Surinam?", he said, "Well, I know one chap, but other than him, I don't know." And in Surinam, they didn't even know there was a Cayenne; and they weren't in the slightest bit interested. Now I want to ask – for instance – any Bolivian here today. Can you stand up and tell me the name of the most important Colombian revolutionary? And one of you Venezuelans: can you name me someone from Ecuador?"'

Everyone was silent.

'OK. That is my point. We are compartmentalised and that is exactly what the United States wants. Yet, if we united, we could be a force to be truly reckoned with.'

I gave an example of collaboration and how it had helped. I mentioned, of course, that uniting for the Tricontinental had been Ben Barka's dream. In short, I gave them a rousing speech which shoehorned the Tricontinental into some kind of spirit of cooperation.

The next evening, two men came to find me to go to Fidel. When I arrived at his house, there were a dozen people waiting to see him. Of these, I knew Regis Debray (the young French journalist) and a fellow Venezuelan, Luben Petkoff (the famous guerrilla fighter who was also Teodoro Petkoff's brother), and Tuzio Lima. Our joint meeting would be at 6 p.m. and we were told to stand by.

Fidel didn't turn up until 9 p.m., by which time some of the group had grown either sleepy or restless or both. Most of us had travelled from afar and were still jet-lagged and exhausted from the flight. Added to this, on the opening night of the conference there had been a reception and a sort of rum-a-thon. We were all hung over. There was a lot of snoring and going in and out of the waiting room to piss and going out to have a smoke and coming back in. Everyone was pretty annoyed by the time Fidel finally arrived. He apologised for keeping us waiting. He said he had been busy with something else. Since we all knew that keeping his visitors waiting was a tactic he had used successfully since the Sierra Maestra, from the time he was interviewed for *Life* magazine by the legendary Herbert Matthews, we couldn't tell if his delay was genuine or planned.

A lot has been said about that *Life* interview, in which Fidel stressed his anti-communism. Matthews reported that Fidel had greater strength and power and far more organisation and arms than he actually had. Herbert Matthews made Fidel Castro famous worldwide. Fidel deliberately tricked the gullible US journalist. Where the debate heats up is whether Fidel lied about not being a communist.

Fidel had no support from the communists in the Sierra. His call for a general strike in April '58 had been a failure, he had only 500 men in total and the Cuban communists had denounced him as a 'petty bourgeois putschist'. I would say that Fidel was not a chameleon: he did not change his colour to suit his background. He changed not once, but several times. And when he changed, he changed radically. He changed body and soul. When he was not a communist, he really was not one. When he became one, he really became one.

He was a man who did everything to excess. He didn't know what a half-measure was. He had a passion and a single-mindedness of spirit that were inspiring to most of the people he came into contact with. He had charisma and what they call 'presence'. People admired him: we all did, because he said what he believed and he did what he said. When, ultimately, history judges him, that will probably be his downfall. In his most famous speech, given at his trial after the failed attack on the Moncada Fortress in 1953, he said, 'Condemn me. It does not matter. History will absolve me.' Had he stepped down in 1959, or even 1960, or – pushing his luck – 1965, he would probably have been right. As it is, history tends not to absolve tyranny, particularly when it lasts for nearly fifty years.

Back in Havana, though, it was January 1966. That was still soon enough after the actual Revolution and the routing of Batista for Fidel to retain his saviour's glow almost intact. He arrived wearing a short-sleeved white shirt and combat trousers when we met for that first time, but metaphorically he was still wearing his saviour's halo and his warrior's laurel crown. To repeat his initiative and victory, first in some small village and then nationwide, was the aspiration of every guerrilla fighter. Fidel Castro was our inspiration.

If this were a tape, I would say, 'Please, stop there and rewind it. Go back and bring out a fanfare of trumpets, a war dance, a rain dance, a low bow, a frame. "Fidel arrived" – I make it sound so matter of fact. "He walked in; he was wearing a white shirt." It was no small moment for me. Fidel Castro was my hero. (*Was*, note; not *is*.) My knees weakened and my heart pounded as I followed him and the group into another room. It was the kind of moment a Catholic can have upon meeting the Pope or a courtier upon meeting his king.

Fidel sat down on the edge of a small table and without any preamble, he announced, 'Look, my friends, I know you are all anxious for revolution in your own countries. I am going to read you something that I think will help you on your way. They are some letters that I wrote from the Sierra Maestra up until we triumphed. Until April 1958, when we were in the Sierra, we had some people scattered here and there, and we had some weapons at different points – but as you probably know, not many. We had the odd shoot-out and a skirmish or two and we did a lot of training and talking. Then we heard that Batista was preparing a serious invasion, and that it was going to liquidate us. So I began to write letters.'

Fidel waved his right arm and a woman came in carrying a large box which she placed beside him on the table. She was like a shadow, very thin and dressed all in white. Fidel took a sheaf of letters and postcards from the open box and began to read out loud while we, the thirteen members of his audience, sat on our thirteen small and uncomfortable wooden chairs in that bare, hot room and drank in his words. By sheer chance, I was sitting so close I could almost have touched him. Thus, I could actually read each handwritten letter as he finished reading it out loud.

'This is the first one, it is to Cuevas: "Cuevas, the army is not coming from the mountains, it will arrive by sea. It will disembark at the foot of the hill where you are. The army will then climb up that hill and you have to watch out because there is a spot in such and such a place which they will pass and you have to dig a trench and place a nest of machine guns in such and such a spot."

'Then I wrote to Rivas: "Rivas, I told Cuevas to put a machine gun in such and such a spot; but he is a bit distracted. Since I told him you would take him two more machine guns to place in such and such a position, go and check that everything is OK and set up there."

'Then to Albenga: "Albenga, take the new recruits to train with Che and tell him not to give them any of our new ammunition. We have to use up the old surplus first."

'To Che: "Che, Albenga is arriving; so put out the ropes to dry."'

Fidel read on and on and we listened, fascinated, as letter followed letter for hour upon hour. Only gradually did it become apparent that the box beside him was full of letters and he was going to read us every single one of them.

He had every detail and every man on a strategic grid. He knew everything and checked and double-checked everything. Nothing was too insignificant to escape his control. Hundreds of letters into the box, we were struggling with thirst, the heat and our fatigue. We were struggling to keep up; but Fidel's letters showed that he forgot nothing. His memory and strategy were phenomenal. He knew everything that was going on.

'"Cuevas, what the fuck are you: a revolutionary or a faggot? Yesterday I went to you and you hadn't dug a single trench! Not one!"

'"Rivas, what the hell are you waiting for to take the arms to Cuevas?"

'"Camilo, stand by at dawn to man your machine-gun nest."

'"Che, I told you to use the surplus ammunition. Why haven't you? We need the 54s for our offensive. I know you have the others because I saw them in your armoury."'

And so it went: on and on, rat-tat-tat-tat. Like a machine-gun burst of instructions and orders and more orders. And he read letters, and more letters, and more letters still.

"'Rafael, I have seen your trenches and they are no good. You have to dig real trenches of at least 1.40m so that a man can stand up in them. No one can fit into yours.'"

"'Che, so and so is waiting for you at 11 a.m. on Wednesday. Be there.'"

Three hours went by and he was still reading. When I sneaked another look at my watch it was 2.30 a.m. He had been reading for four and a half hours. By that time, only Tuzio Limas, Luben and I were still awake. The rest of the audience had shuffled and shifted on their chairs for the first two or three hours and then, like flies sprayed with DDT, they had nodded off one by one, leaning chin on chest or heads on each other's shoulders. The chairs were primary school seats and were small and incredibly uncomfortable. We had all had two long and intense days of the Tricontinental conference plus our jet-lag and post-party trauma. Both Che and Fidel scorned comfort and later Fidel was to prove himself no stranger to methods of torture. Yet I had the firm impression that the Big Man, Fidel Castro, was sincerely trying to help us by his reading the secrets of his tactics out to us.

There was so little oxygen in the room it was like being on a Third World airline or a cheap charter flight. By 3 a.m. I was the only person of the thirteen who was not fast asleep. I had, perhaps, the unfair advantage of suffering from almost constant insomnia ever since my spell in prison in Caracas. But apart from that, the sheer excitement of being given the key to how to succeed in what had become my life's mission and my dream would have kept me awake for as long as the Master Guerrillero kept reading. Fidel had been convinced from his youth that he would be the saviour of his country. And I had been convinced that I would be the saviour of mine. Each was a near sacred mission. He had achieved his goal and I had not yet begun to tackle mine.

From the letters, it became clear that Batista's troops had invaded exactly where Fidel had said they would; and Cuevas hadn't heeded Fidel's advice and subsequently was forced to make a detour, thereby sacrificing some of his men. Then a game of lies and cover-ups followed. Fidel created the illusion of strength and the simulacrum of control. Because I had read reports of the entire campaign, I could compare what actually happened with what Fidel had predicted would happen. It was uncanny how Fidel was almost always right.

Ignoring everything but the sound of his own voice and the proof of his own brilliance, Fidel read on. Like the great strategist he indubitably was, he had saved the best till last. He read out his finest letter. It was a masterpiece addressed to the commander of the government troops, which had got the rebel army by the short and curlies. Fidel's adversary was ignorant of the rebel army's untenable position. He was also ignorant of the fact that his 6,000 troops had actually encircled less than 120 rebels and that 120 men was the total size of Fidel's revolutionary army. So cleverly had Fidel given the impression of having at least ten times more fighters than he actually had that he was able to trick his enemy into surrender. A handful of the rebels had managed to remain outside the enemy's net and this helped to persuade the enemy commander that Fidel had surrounded him, instead of vice versa. In fact, Fidel's 120 guerrilla fighters were not only surrounded by 6,000 highly trained soldiers and facing imminent defeat, they were also facing total liquidation. But Fidel had a handful of fighters on the outside, and Fidel had balls.

If there is one thing both friends and enemies of Fidel Castro agree on about him, it is that he is the most stubborn man on the planet. His almost insane refusal to accept defeat enabled him to lead his revolutionary army to victory. The same almost insane stubbornness has driven him to hold on, using the most unheroic and unjust means, to the power he won so heroically.

Against all the odds and anyone else in the world's better judgement, he saw a chance of victory in his defeat. And he achieved it by means of a letter. It is a famous one and has been widely published. Fidel read out his masterpiece letter to the enemy commander. I cannot remember it verbatim, but the gist of it is as follows.

Comandante Guerrero,
    You are surrounded and I have the certainty of victory.
But the honey of that victory is to defeat the only
honourable adversary in the army that I have ever known.
    Do you remember that we met when we were students,
and we discussed the Constitution; and you said that you
would do whatever it took to uphold our Constitution?
This is your one opportunity to do that; but instead of
taking that opportunity, you are ignoring it.

He went on to tell him not to sacrifice his men in a lost battle.
Fidel had seen the chance to break out at a point held by over 400
government troops. By chance, he knew the enemy commander
personally and thus he knew that he had a chance with his letter.
It is a great letter! It is so great, in fact, that his adversary surrendered both his troops and 415 weapons to Fidel and his 120 men,
and thus not only did not crush the Revolution, but also gave it
the means to win.

Back in the hot airless room with Fidel, it was getting on for 4
a.m. and Fidel showed no signs of flagging despite having come to
the last letter in the box. He read it out, placed it carefully on top
of all the others and then launched into a detailed strategic
account of his revolutionary campaign. He described it day by day
and week by week down to the smallest instruction.

His voice was decisive and enthusiastic as he rolled back over
his recent military history. What he said was underscored by a low
snoring, a concert of heavy breathing from the twelve sleeping
delegates. He ploughed through the formation of the second front;
he told how he sent Che to fight at Santa Clara; how he sent
Camilo somewhere else; how his logistic support came in; how
much that was, and when and where it was delivered to each
camp and by whom. Fidel showed no signs of fatigue as he
marched on towards his triumph in Havana, either in his story or
in the stifling room in which he narrated it.

Then at 6 a.m., with the same drop of sweat (that had formed
well over an hour before) still in place on his forehead, he
looked up for the first time and actually noticed us. From the
way he looked at the sleeping heaps of listeners it was hard to

tell whether he was offended or quite indifferent to what anyone thought or felt.

After slowly scanning the room, Fidel's beady eyes settled on me. He frowned and looked momentarily surprised. Although he is much bigger than me, we look quite like each other. I thought I saw him considering for a second whether he found this a problem. His brow cleared and he announced (as though it had been we who were keeping him), 'Well, I have to go now – I have a meeting with the Chinese at seven.'

And he left.

I nudged a couple of the others awake and they then nudged and elbowed each other until we were thirteen baffled people wondering sleepily what our 'meeting' had really been about. Once it became clear that I had stuck it out to the bitter end, everyone wanted to know that answer from me. 'What did Fidel say?' When I told them that it had just been several hours more of the same, they were astonished.

'Why the hell did he send for us?'

'What does it mean?'

I shrugged. I could hardly say that while they were snoring, it had meant a lot to me. When we stumbled out of the building, the sun had just come up over the city and the conference was restarting within a couple of hours. The first thing we needed to do was to drink a lot of water because we were almost dehydrated. Then we drank coffee and ate breakfast and made our way back to the Habana Libre Hotel (where we were all staying) so that we could at least take a shower and change our clothes.

CHAPTER XXXIX

Next day, I was up in my hotel room with Vida discussing how on earth someone could have such superhuman energy, and how sad it was that most of my comrades had missed the crucial bits of Fidel's nine-hour monologue, when the phone rang. A man told me that he was at reception and that he wanted to come up to my room.

'Who are you?' I asked him.

'No,' he said, 'it's not me who wants to come up, it is el Comandante. He is on his way now.'

A few minutes later, there was a knock at the door. Vida opened it, and there was Fidel in his combat gear. He shook hands with Vida as he came in and said, almost in passing, 'So you are the Moroccan wife.'

Way back in Jajó, I first got into communism because it was an -ism and I was already into surrealism and impressionism and existentialism. Well, it was probably just as well I had all those other -isms up my sleeve, as it were, because the surreal aspects of my life as a communist might otherwise have been too bizarre for me to deal with. As you can see, my early meetings with Fidel Castro were positively surreal.

Fidel gave a cursory glance at the seaview and sat down. He addressed Vida almost exclusively, and apropos of nothing he said, 'Eye contact is very important, you know: the ability to communicate without speech – but also when you don't make eye contact and there is a flash of recognition – do you know what I mean?'

Vida has never had any hairs on her tongue, as we say in the Andes – she just comes right out and says what she thinks. So she said, 'No, I don't know what on earth you are talking about.'

Fidel laughed loudly and told her, 'Then you have no idea how we live here!'

After that, they sat down to talk about it. Vida told him that she had lived in Venezuela and knew quite a lot about Latin Americans. Fidel was unbelievably friendly as he jumped from one subject to the next. He always let Vida have her say in the most democratic way. I joined in a bit, but it was really their conversation. Since Vida and I had both heard that power was going to Fidel's head by then and that he brooked no opposition, we were surprised both by his openness and by his being there in our hotel room in the first place. Vida was determined not to let this opportunity pass without having a good dig at him, so she kept probing.

Bearing in mind the Comandante's supposed tetchiness about being crossed, I was slightly worried by her directness. At one point, I thought she had gone too far when she said, 'You know, when you were in the Sierra, you were disrespected.'

Whoa! That went down like a rat sandwich! He reacted in a completely different tone of voice.

'What do you mean: I was not respected? How dare you!'

Vida was unfazed as she explained, 'When someone has authority over someone else and the leader tells his subordinate to do something; if that subordinate doesn't do it – then in Venezuela we call that disrespect.'

Fidel relaxed. 'Aha! So that's what you mean.'

Then they talked about life in Venezuela, Vida's time in Mérida. From the conversation, there was no clue as to why he had come.

At a certain point, he got up, took his leave as though we were all three old friends, and left.

Later that day, I was again summoned to him and I went to his house. This time, I was alone with him.

He said, 'That was a good intervention you made at the

conference. But it isn't that. There is something I have to know. It is a mystery I need to solve: why didn't you fall asleep when I read out the letters? I was watching you and you were the only one who didn't fall asleep.'

'No,' I said, 'I don't sleep much anyway – and then: how many times in my life as a revolutionary fighter will I get the chance to learn, step by step, how to conduct an entire war? I've been in the Guerrilla with Luben Petkoff, and I know that the key to success is to know the terrain and then to know your own and the enemy's strengths and weaknesses.'

'That's it!' he shouted. 'That's what I wanted to say with the letters: that any revolutionary fighter who wants to win has to be that thorough, that persistent, that dedicated. Winning isn't about luck – although it helps – it is about being prepared.'

Sometimes I go over incidents in great detail. Perhaps it is too much detail, but without it who would believe the haphazard way in which my life was shaped? For instance, I owe my Cuban years (which were to follow the above encounter) to my sleeping habits. I stayed awake while others slept and thereby gained the friendship of Fidel Castro. It is true that I *wanted* to stay awake; but I was also *able* to stay awake. Luben Petkoff and several of the other delegates *wanted* to stay awake but they physically couldn't. Fidel knew who all the delegates were whom he had convoked to his letter-reading, but he never held it against any of those who slept through it.

My true closeness to Fidel, the confidence he had in me and our ensuing friendship were due in no small degree to the following. Fidel Castro knew that he was a superman. Even when he was a young lawyer in Havana, and then as a deputy and the torch bearer of Eddy Chibas (the 1950s Cuban martyr to truth and purity), Fidel believed he was the saviour of his country. Chibas had a popular radio programme in Havana in which he fought the corruption of Batista's dictatorship. Every week, on air, Chibas and his Ortodoxo Party promised to come up with concrete evidence to prove his accusations. When that proof failed to materialise on time, Chibas shot himself dead, but live, as it were, on air. His death was seen as a symbol of purity. Fidel was part of that Ortodoxo Party. After the public suicide, Fidel wanted to follow his hero's example, but instead of killing himself, he formed part of the campaign that set out to vindicate Chibas and fight government corruption. One of Fidel's tasks (ironically, with hindsight) was to write letters. But since he did everything in excess, instead of writing 1,000 letters as he had been asked to do, Fidel wrote 10,000 letters. That was how he was: always better than anyone else. He was almost prosecuted for that. He didn't care!

Here is another example of how excessive his nature was. There is a famous bell in Cuba. It is a symbol of freedom, which every year is carried by relays of young men into Havana. They raise this incredibly heavy bell onto their shoulders in groups of two and three and take turns in shifts to carry it the fifty kilometres into the capital. When Fidel was a boy, he went to help carry that bell. He picked it up and he said: 'Leave it to me. I'm going to carry this by myself.'

And he did for fifty kilometres. Alone! Fidel is a man who is able to accomplish the greatest excesses. Everything he sets out to do, he does.

That is the terrible aspect of Fidel, as opposed to Che Guevara. Che knew that he was exceptional. But he didn't think that God made him like that or that he was like that thanks to any particular intrinsic gifts. Che *made* himself be a superman. He made himself strong when he was weak. He forced himself to be better than his peers. That is not the case with Fidel. Fidel accepts that he was born exceptional. That he is, if you like, a divine being. Che, on the other hand, was less tolerant: other people *had* to be able to keep up with him, to achieve what he could achieve, because he knew that a man could learn and train (as he had) to get there.

At the time that I met Fidel, he was not a classic tyrant figure. It would be misleading to label the man I knew as a vulgar oppressor. He was much more complex than that. Besides which, back then he didn't force people to do things his way. He was tolerant in that he always used to say: 'Do it your way.' (Well, rather: 'Do what I say, but do it your way.') There are a few notable exceptions, but in the early days his tolerance was a noticeable strand of his character. He understood the weakness of others, as opposed to his own extraordinary strength, stamina and capability. That was the aspect of his persona that I understood.

Later in 1966, Fidel asked me to form a team of ideologists to make sense of the Revolution in a more open way than orthodox Marxism. As part of the faculty of philosophy at the University of Havana, I dedicated myself to forming and then leading that group. All the members were young and brilliant and ready to look at what had happened and was happening in Cuba in another way. We did this with the guidance of texts by Lukacs and texts against Marxism and by pooling our own thoughts and ideas.

Within that group there were people who are now famous anti-Castroists and counter-revolutionaries, for example, the dissidents Diaz and Avenas. My entire group comprised people of the Left who thought with a certain freedom. José Martí, Cuba's almost sacred hero, said, 'The first duty of every revolutionary is to think for himself.' Fidel (like all Cubans) was very keen on Martí and never missed an opportunity to invoke him and somehow link his own thoughts and words to those of Cuba's greatest national hero. Later, the more despotic Fidel became, the more he tried to mask his words and actions as 'sanctioned by Martí'.

So far so good, but as a maxim for a national leader to follow, it gets dangerous if the leader goes mad. It is one thing to have twenty-two like minds and to stubborn out a revolution, but when a man stands entirely alone in his thought train, and then he forces everyone around him to climb on board his train, and that train is the equivalent of a cattle wagon, and no one is allowed *not* to board that train, and no one is allowed to get off once they are on – then we each have the second duty to think about what we are thinking.

It was a fine gesture for Fidel to have asked for such an alternative think tank. And it was extremely democratic of him to have allowed us to gather and brainstorm. For us, the ideologists, it was an enormous responsibility and one which none of us took lightly. What was not clear was that we were supposed, ultimately, to affirm the rightness of Fidel's own ideas and not have new ones of our own.

It is possible that when I was asked to form the think tank, Fidel genuinely wanted to see further than he could alone. It is possible that something happened in between the start-up and the result of that brainstorming. It is possible that he took that step that warps, that he crossed the line. These are questions I cannot answer. These are mysteries that – unlike the 'mystery' of my wakefulness that originally brought Fidel and me together – no one can explain.

CHAPTER XXXX

Immediately after the Tricontinental conference, in January 1966, I stayed on in Havana and began working on ideas with Fidel as a consultant and advisor. Then I worked on my ideology think tank directly for Fidel. Vida and I continued to live in our room in the spacious, twenty-six-storey Habana Libre Hotel as guests of the Cuban government. We became connoisseurs of its menus, and friends with its staff. Everyone who was anyone visiting Cuba in 1966 passed through the Habana Libre. The first-floor bar was about as cosmopolitan as anywhere I have ever been. Major issues were discussed there and major deals were made. When entire countries were not being hypothetically liberated or enslaved or national budgets actually being sunk or saved, an enormous amount of conversation hovered around the subject of Coca-Cola and Pepsi-Cola.

Latin Americans might squabble about politics and everything else under the sun, but they are all in agreement about (and pretty much addicted to) one or other of the Colas. There are those who are passionate about Pepsi (most Venezuelans, for instance, were Pepsi fans in those days) and there are those who favour Coke, but we all drink vast quantities of it as a part of our staple diet. The national drink of Cuba – the cocktail that every visitor to Havana asks for automatically – is a Cuba Libre: rum and Coke with loads of ice and a twist of lemon. Well, after the Revolution, you couldn't get real Coca or Pepsi-Cola in Cuba any more. There were all sorts of revolutionary factories making Coca-Cola substitutes – the most famous of these drinks being called Son – but it just wasn't the same. It wasn't the real thing and everyone knew it. Each time someone ordered a drink, the issue came up again. What was the secret ingredient the Yankees had? Why couldn't it be reproduced? No matter how much a Cuban loved Fidel and the Revolution, they also loved Coca-Cola and the lack of it was like a rat gnawing away at their morale. Even el Comandante Che, who in those days didn't have a word to say against the Cuban Revolution or anything revolutionary, was said to have picked up a bottle of Son and commented, 'Son una mierda!' – a pun on the name and the shitty quality of the fizzy drink. ('Son' is Spanish for 'they are' and 'Son una mierda!' means 'They are shit!')

Every few weeks, Fidel would come up with a request for me to do something more. Usually what he wanted was for me to do missions – errands, if you like. He would send me to talk to people, to negotiate with people – both in Havana and abroad. Sometimes the missions would involve delivering or fetching things. I became halfway between a delivery boy and a secret agent, but I also became Fidel's confidant. If he asked me to fetch or deliver things, it was usually because he was doing it behind everyone else's back. When money was involved, in particular, it seemed to me to be a reasonable precaution to keep people out of the way of temptation. Not many people can resist dipping their hand into the cash box when that cash box contains millions of dollars.

At the beginning and the end of each of these missions, Fidel and I would talk for hours. We shared many ideas and we shared insomnia, or rather, the need for very little sleep.

One day, he called me over and asked me to work with him on a plan dear to his heart: to export the Cuban Revolution to other countries in Latin America. He made me the director of a group of twenty-two guerrilla fighters from all over Latin America, with the task to take them into the interior and turn them into invincible commandos. He told me that the number of recruits was symbolic: that it was the number of men who survived the ambush when he and his 26th July Movement revolutionaries disembarked in Cuba after sailing from Mexico on the rickety yacht, *Granma*, to oust Batista. It was odd, because I had always understood that the *Granma*'s passengers were mowed down almost on arrival and only twelve escaped to the Sierra, but who was I to argue about somewhere I hadn't been, with someone who had?

I liked the idea of taking a guerrilla group to train. In fact, the timing of his request was curious, because Vida had been asking me for some days prior to it to speak to Fidel about the possibility and the advisability of reuniting the Iranian exiles who were scattered around Europe and bringing them to Cuba to be militarily trained. Since Vida was never one to give up an idea once she had got it into her head, she had talked about it incessantly. So my mind had been running along a similar sort of training track for days.

Later, a group of Iranian revolutionaries were invited to Havana, and they too went into the wilderness to be trained by the Cubans – but that is another story.

Fidel had absolute confidence in his plan. He told me that our aim was to be ready to embark, probably for oil-rich Venezuela, within a year and to start, carry on and win a series of copycat revolutions in mainland South America.

That was the core of his plan. What he wanted to do afterwards was expand it to train many more guerrilla fighters in order to send them to as many insurgent groups as possible in as many different countries in Latin America and the Antilles as possible.

I wondered why he chose me to direct this operation. Of course, I had been in the Guerrilla in Venezuela and he knew it. But he wasn't a fool, so he must have also known that I wasn't a military type. So I think he chose me because he knew how much I believed in armed struggle as an option for Venezuela, and because I had just been in the Antilles, and also knew Latin America a bit, and because Che and Papito had spoken highly of me to a number of people after we worked together in Algiers. But I think the main reason was probably because he knew that, like him, I could stay awake for days on end and, like him, I would attend to details.

The first step of this project was for me to ascertain which of the countries who had participated in the Tricontinental wanted to send men to be trained in Cuba.

That was in the middle of 1966. He gave me no further information at that stage and no further instructions except that if it was necessary to bring any of the various men into Cuba right away, then I was to do so. Other than that, I was to do as I liked. I had full power to do everything as I saw fit. I accepted the task.

It was after that meeting that I contacted someone who was very famous within the Cuban Revolution: Piñero. He directed the activities and supplied all the help to the revolutionary movements in Latin America. Piñero was in charge of another of Fidel's dreams, that is to say: to export the Cuban Revolution to Cuba's next-door neighbours. I began to work closely with Piñero, and beyond our work, a friendship formed.

The thinking (above all, of Fidel) was that the Cuban world could not exist in isolation and that it needed the support of Latin America – a socialist Latin America, in which a country like Venezuela, with natural resources, was key. Cuba's policy was to emancipate Latin America from imperialist control, and then to form a close socialist alliance. Fidel knew that a socialist country cannot maintain itself in isolation. If the Soviet Union with 22 million square kilometres couldn't do it, how could Cuba hope to, with a surface of only 110 square kilometres? The initial success of the Cuban Revolution would be impossible to sustain without outside support.

By that time, Che Guevara and Fidel had begun to see the Cuban Revolution differently, but they still agreed wholeheartedly on the need for outside support. To this end, Che was globetrotting for Cuba. With hindsight, it becomes clear that his diplomatic mission served the additional purpose of keeping him out of Fidel's way. Also with hindsight, I see that Regis Debray and I were filling the advisory gap that Che had left behind, and that Piñero assigned several delicate missions to me that would probably have fallen into el Che's lap had el Comandante Che not offended Fidel's Soviet puppeteers.

During that summer and autumn of 1966, Piñero used me; and I say 'used' in the strict sense of the word. He kept calling me to tell me things like: 'It is essential that you talk to so and so [e.g.

Savaleta from Bolivia]. We want to talk to Savaleta, but the time isn't right for *us* yet, so we want *you* to talk to him.'

Or there would be some Argentinian passing through Havana, and Piñero would say, 'Oswaldo, we want to tell him about our plans for Latin America, but we want *you* to tell him.'

Since I shared Piñero's point of view, I was happy to be his spokesperson.

While I was in Havana, I worked closely with a good friend. This was someone whom I had introduced to Latin America when he was still very young. He had first arrived in Venezuela in 1963 and he had gone straight to visit me at the university. He had brought with him a letter of introduction from Simone de Beauvoir and Jean-Paul Sartre (neither of whom I knew yet, but both of whom knew of me from other Latin American revolutionaries). Their letter of introduction asked me 'to treat the bearer, Regis Debray, with absolute confidence'. I did.

In 1963, when Regis Debray came to me, he was virtually unknown internationally as a writer, a journalist or a thinker, but after his visit, he went back to Paris and published an article which became hugely famous, called 'The Long March of Castroism in Latin America'. In that article, Regis suggested that the real road to take was to copy Castro's example. This contradicted the existing policy of revolutionary movements, which concentrated on urban groups instead of on rural guerrillas. He wrote of the need to encourage rural guerrillas, and thereby became an influential spokesman for the armed struggle.

Later, in Cairo, Regis Debray was one of the people I had worked with to prepare for the Tricontinental conference. During that preparation, we had expanded that 'rural versus urban' guerrilla theory. Together, we'd had various meetings, for instance with Salvador Allende. And later we were sent to various countries, including the Antilles, Brazil, Uruguay and Argentina, in the hopes of those countries sending delegates to the Tricontinental who were partisan to the cause of rural guerrillas. It took some searching, but Regis and I did find some people: Guadaloupe promised to send four delegates, Uruguay four, Brazil ten, and from Argentina we were unable to get any promise of anyone. I remember that I personally had to buy the tickets to Havana for all these new delegates – and that it was almost harder to organise their flights than it had been to find and recruit them in the first place.

The conference delegates recruited by me and Regis Debray were to be the core of the commando army I was asked to oversee. We were a very mixed bag: there were Bolivians, Guadeloupians, Uruguayans, several Brazilians. Then, besides these Tricontinental recruits, there was a group of Venezuelans, two Cubans, one Mexican, one Chilean, and me. They sent us to train as guerrilla fighters for several months in the interior. I was the head of that group, which, as Fidel had desired, numbered twenty-two in all.

We went out in an army lorry to the Oriente, the east of the island, and established a camp in the middle of nowhere. There were twenty-two of us, our Cuban instructors, and about 22 million mosquitoes. We had a radio connection back to Havana, and several of us had transistor radios. At night, the sound of our combined radios was often drowned out by the squadrons of mosquitoes. We were out there for months, and despite the very professional training we received, I knew on arrival, and I still knew when I left, that I was not of soldier material.

Some people are brainy and some people are sporty. I was of the brainy sort and sport had always passed me by. Vida would have fared much better than me out there. She was a natural athlete. Because I was the director, and the confidant of Fidel Castro himself, I got by. Without such perks, I would never have passed the training programme under my own steam. Some of 'my' group of twenty-two rather admired me for the things I had achieved and the connections I had made through my brain power. They did not believe that the pen was mightier than the sword, but they accepted that a pen could be effective. After all, Fidel Castro didn't keep calling *them* up on the radio, he kept calling *me*. Others of the twenty-two despised me for my physical weakness. Several of them thought that people who read books were homosexual (in this belief, in militant revolutionary circles, they were not alone). Be that as it may, we trained, I directed, I continued to study and to read poetry and philosophy; and whatever the other twenty-one men in my group called me behind my back, to my face they called me 'el Profe' (the Professor).

The training was pretty intense (the rest of the group found it fairly easy, *I* found it intense) and comprised physical education, continual marching, target practice, the use of explosives: everything really that is needed as a soldier. We had mostly US weapons and a few Soviet weapons. Each of us was numbered. Because I was the director, I was number 1. The two Cubans were 21 and 22. The instructors never called us by anything other than our numbers, and even among ourselves the numbers were used a lot, or we used codenames. I was the exception: I was Number 1, but I was always called either Oswaldo Barreto or I was 'el Profe'. No one else kept their real name. It was the one bit of dignity I managed to retain in what was otherwise a humiliating daily reminder of my physical inadequacy. The instructors cited Che Guevara's extraordinary physical prowess and stamina as a galling example of how the weak could be strong 'if they only wanted to enough'.

'If el Che could do it with his asthma, why can't you, Barreto?' was a question that came to irritate me almost as much as the mosquito attacks.

After the first day (the worst), and the first week (when I thought I was going to die), I gradually became a lot fitter and stronger. The training was invaluable and has, subsequently, saved my life several times over. We all knew that a certain number of months ahead we would set off in a boat as the effective nucleus of a revolutionary army.

People talk a lot about the dangers of boatloads of revolutionaries being sent out from Cuba, but you never hear about boatloads of revolutionaries *invading* Cuba. Yet in 1966, while my team of twenty-two would-be rural guerrillas were in training, a boatload of 120 radical Venezuelans (armed to the teeth and raring to enter into mortal combat) arrived clandestinely in Cuba. The boat carried the revolutionary pilgrims to their political Mecca.

This 'invasion' of militant Venezuelans was not displeasing to Fidel. He had a special plan for Venezuela. What he proposed was that instead of there being various fronts, there be only one. So the people from the MIR, from the PCV (communists) and

Douglas Bravo's Comandancia General, all unite as one single group, and that that group be guided (rather than, say, 'led') by Cubans. These Cubans would enter Venezuela at a point on the east coast to bring the local units into contact with the methods the Cubans had tried and tested in the Sierra Maestra. In other words, Fidel didn't think that the Venezuelans had sufficient knowledge or tactical experience, and that they needed Cuban guidance. Well, anyway, the 120 Venezuelans who arrived on the boat were led by Ojera Negretti: he was the fighter of most prestige back home. He had fought in Falcón together with Baltasar Ojedin, codename Elías (Cuban codename Eliazar). Both of them were very experienced fighters who had spent years in the Guerrilla. The other 118 'boat people' had also all had experience in guerrilla combat and some of them were pretty high up in the political scene.

At that time, Fidel valued fighting technique over politics. He was very fond of coming out and personally showing us some of the techniques he had devised and used successfully in the Sierra. These included a type of ambush or trap which involved the ingenious use of a hosepipe. It was a technique that had worked wonders in Fidel's war and he gave us a practical demonstration to show us how good it was. I was fascinated by it, not least because it was so simple. We, my group of twenty-two, were all impressed. But when the new boat people – the veterans – arrived, they refused to be impressed with Fidel's techniques as a viable option for Venezuela. The most outspoken of the new men was Elías.

Though Elías was always known as Eliazar in Cuba, his story intertwined with my own so closely from then on that his name will keep cropping up; so to avoid confusion, I will call him Elías both in Cuba and elsewhere, since that is how I knew him.

When Fidel repeated his 'hosepipe trap', Elías said, 'No, that's no good for us: that won't work in Venezuela. First of all, because our roads in the east of the country don't have bends in them like yours do. Roads in the interior of Venezuela have been constructed taking the eventuality of such attacks into account. And then the enemy there are expert shots. Just with their first shot, they could knock out such a plan.'

Well, Fidel didn't like that at all. He didn't like being contradicted; and he particularly didn't like being contradicted by someone who was an experienced guerrilla fighter. That little disagreement happened within a week of the boat people arriving. From then on, the clashes didn't get better – they got worse. Their group of 120 was divided into two units. There were those who were to train as urban guerrillas, and those who were to specialise in rural combat, Cuban-style. The latter group, the new rurals, who were all experienced fighters and veterans of our armed struggle, kept arguing with Fidel and Fidel's ideas. There was almost daily conflict with the Cuban instructors and with the underlying tactical ideas.

The Venezuelan veterans insisted that they had no lack of capacity but a difference in conditions. Some of them, Elías in particular, maintained that ours was a different sort of fight and the fighting conditions had to fit the mould. They argued that it was not a matter of technique or of their level of training, neither was it a matter of commitment. They were all ready to die for the struggle and they could all cite their guerrilla records to prove it, but the Venezuelan peasants did not have that national revolutionary sentiment that the Cuban peasants had.

Elías kept making this point: 'Will someone please listen! Quite independently of Fidel, the Cuban people wanted to be free of their North American yoke. The Cubans were sick of being controlled by the Americans. In Venezuela there is no such awareness, no such feeling, no such potential support for rural guerrilla groups.'

Elías knew what he was talking about, but nobody wanted to listen, not the instructors, not Piñero, not Fidel's brother, Raul and certainly not Fidel himself. A theory of guerrilla warfare had evolved in Cuba whereby there was no need for revolutionaries to have political or social roots. Nor did they have to have a relevance to the society they were attempting to revolutionise, or to be part of the mass movement. This was music to the ears of some Venezuelan militants, who could not be bothered with ideology of any kind. If all that was required was the will to make the revolution, then they had it. 'What are we waiting for? Let's go!' These trainees were not worried about popular support; they were worried about paramilitary training. Fidel wasn't worried about the politics of his exported revolution either, so long as each outcome would benefit Cuba. And me: what did I think? I believed absolutely that given the peculiar circumstances of Latin America at that time, armed struggle was the only solution. I believed it was the only way to uproot the corruption. I believed (in my ignorance) that because I *thought* a lot, others did too. And I believed (in my arrogance) that I could study for everyone and somehow communicate the results of my studies so that common sense and common decency would prevail.

I also believed that our eventual disembarkation on the east coast of Venezuela would take us into a country that was, in some ways, prepared for a change to socialism. We were not bursting onto a foreign scene as Che Guevara had done in the Congo. We were not rushing in with blind euphoria to impose alien concepts onto a primitive tribal society. We would be infiltrating a government of corruption and repression in order to liberate the descendants of the very people who had risen up to follow Simon Bolivar in the War of Independence 150 years before. Back then, they had overthrown their Spanish colonial yoke to gain freedom, but they had fallen under the rapacious stranglehold of the USA and been kept a hostage to the fortunes of oil. We the revolutionaries would give the rich and beautiful country of Venezuela back to its people. I didn't think it would be easy to rally the peasants' support back home, but I did think it would be possible.

CHAPTER XXXXI

One day towards the very end of 1966, I was called into Havana from my training camp in the *monte*. Actually, two of us were called in: me (Number 1) and my Number 2. Number 2 was my second-in-command and a young man of Spanish origin who looked like a conquistador. His real name was Rojas and he was dedicated, serious and capable. We travelled to Havana together and enjoyed the enormous luxury of not marching and not arms drilling.

As we drove into the city, I began to fantasise about being given some mission or other that would give me a few weeks or days (but preferably months) of respite from the physical training. There were women in the street and the sight of them awakened my desire for a fuller life again. Sex was 'out' in the training period. It was 'no sex, no beer, no rum, no leave, and no rest'.

The road to Havana was dry. Our ex-Russian army jeep, and every stick of sugar cane and every shrub on the verge beside it, was covered in a red layer of dust. The sun beat down relentlessly. The idea that everything in Cuba was involved in the Revolution seemed to have permeated even the crops. The parcels of maize and the vast cane fields beside the road were visibly struggling. We approached the city from Bacuranao and Guanabo along the sea road with its swathes of white sandy beaches and its sprawling villages which, despite the Revolution, still defied any appearance of order.

We stopped in Vedado at the house of a friend for a cold beer. His small kitchen (buzzing with flies) felt like a five-star hotel compared to where we had just come from. His wife cooked us a Spanish omelette, and to this day, the smell of fried onions and the taste of that simple dish puts it high on my list of 'great meals I have eaten'. Our pit-stop was in the suburbs of the city. Two related families shared the ramshackle cottage and seemed to have added corrugated-iron extensions to accommodate new additions to the crew of small children who stood in the doorway and stared at us for the full half-hour of our visit. From a rickety iron balcony, I could see the beginning of the sweeping Boulevard Malecom.

We thanked our hosts, kissed the cook and made our way along Malecom past the Habana Libre Hotel where Vida and I had lived until I was thrown to the mosquitoes in the *monte*, and where I still had a luxurious room which was empty while I roughed it in unspeakable discomfort in the training camp. The Habana Libre was famous for having been the revolutionary HQ after the fall of Batista. With its false balconies and twenty-five storeys of towering concrete, it was by no means the most attractive building in Havana, but it was historic within the Revolution. As though to prove this, it had stamps of approval all over the place in the form of posters of Fidel waving his fist. Its ground floor looked a bit like a hall of mirrors at a fun fair – with Fidel's face cloning on every available surface.

Rojas and I had an appointment with Piñero, exporter-in-chief of the Cuban Revolution. I was pleasantly surprised to see Sol Ortega already in the office with him. We said hello to each other and chatted for a few minutes, and then Sol Ortega got up and left.

Piñero made some joke about my having lost weight. I was on the bone from the combination of endless bullet beans and rice, hours of physical training and, at best, a hammock and, at worst, the bare ground to sleep on at night, both of which left me a martyr to mosquitoes.

Then he told us that we were being pulled out of my training group. 'To be effective as of this moment,' he said.

I was relieved that my physical torture was to stop. I immediately began to fantasise about returning to the comfort of my hotel and the line-up of Cuba Libres I would consume nightly (regardless of the poor-quality Coke). I wasn't too happy, however, about not having had a chance to say goodbye to any of the men I had spent twenty-four hours a day with for the past several months. I tried to point this out, but Piñero was in Fidel-mode and didn't let me get a word in edgeways.

'Instead, you are to be integrated into the group of 120 boat people. These, if you recall, have been divided into two categories: Urban and Rural. You two are to join the Rural group. You already know two of the men in that group, and we know they will be sympathetic to your ideas. Use them. They are Sol Ortega – who has just left this office – and Luben Petkoff.' Then he turned to me and said, 'Oswaldo, Fidel wants to see you before you head back. In fact, you had better go to him now. He is waiting. You and Number 2 will be picked up here at twenty-two hundred hours to be taken to your new training camp. Your gear will be waiting for you when you get there.'

Rojas and I stood up to leave. As we reached the door, Piñero called after us, 'And, Oswaldo, good luck with the new training. It's a bit more ... *rigorous*, I believe.'

So much for my fantasy of a mission! And so much for my fantasy of a hot shower at the Habana Libre and a proper bed with my Sea Island cotton pillow and cocktails at sundown. And how, I wondered, could the new training be *more* rigorous? What I had been doing for the past few months had already nearly broken me!

As it turned out, Fidel did have a mission for me; it just wasn't the mission I would have chosen for myself. Fidel explained to me that of the 120 Venezuelan veterans who had arrived as boat people, there were now approximately ninety left. Piñero's parting shot had been: 'Ideologically, only two of Douglas Bravo's people – Sol and Luben – think like us. The training is *rigorous*.'

Fidel told me, 'You have personally fought side by side with Luben; and Sol fought with your brother. Independently, both men have the full respect of the rest of the group and both are extremely popular. You have a connection to each of them. The communists and the MIRists are in the other camp – doing the urban tactics – so you won't have any trouble with them. You have to train with the Rurals. You have to integrate into their rigorous programme and I am counting on you to convert them to the Plan.'

What is it with the word 'rigorous'? The Plan, which was Fidel's plan, was to 'rigorously' and specifically train a group of approximately 120 men to disembark in Venezuela and, with a Cuban back-up, fight its way inland from the east coast. That was Fidel's dream: that a group of 120 men could gather an army and fight their way cross-country to victory. Actually, although he was telling it to me as though it were top secret, it was exactly the same plan as that devised for my own group of twenty-two men the year before. The only difference was that the new plan had a significantly bigger group, and the training was to cover methods of disembarkation.

Fidel never cared about things like repeating himself. He announced the plan as though it was a revelation. Even in those relatively early days, he had a fondness for the sound of his own voice and the trumpeting of his own ideas that was remarkable. Everyone knew that a meeting with him could, and probably would, become a verbal marathon in which thousands of words were marshalled into his monologue. Even his 'history will absolve me' speech after the Moncada fiasco was five hours long. Think about it. He was on trial as a terrorist at a time when most of the other members of his group had been either summarily executed or tortured to death. Why did Batista's kangaroo court allow the young Fidel to speak for five hours? If his enemies heard him out when he was powerless, what chance did his friends stand against his oratory once he was all powerful?

Four and a half hours later, I came reeling out of Fidel's house. It was ten minutes past eight and I had to rendezvous with Rojas outside Piñero's office to be picked up and escorted to my new training camp. I still had to cross town, which meant I would have a maximum of twenty-five minutes to do what I pleased. I needed and wanted and longed for a hot shower in the comfort and privacy of my hotel room. More than that, though, I needed to feel a woman's touch. My relationship with Vida had fizzled out again and she had sailed back to France. So I had a hotel room I could call home, but no wife and no lover. All along the road into

Havana I had been plotting how, where and for how long I could escape from the imposed celibacy of my training.

With twenty-five minutes in hand, and no appointment set up, however loosely, to jump into bed, by the time I got to a bed I would have under twelve minutes with a wild rush at either end of it, a scramble to get back to the rendezvous on time (Piñero was out to prove single-handedly that Latin Americans can be punctual. He was an absolute stickler for time). Fitting in a shag also meant forgoing not only my shower but any kind of visit to the Habana Libre to replenish my stocks, check my mail, etc. Needless to say, I didn't pause on any street corner while I weighed these pros and cons. Instead, I raced towards my twelve-minute-long sexual firework option; and I remain eternally grateful for the sweet release of that hurried interlude. It was to be the only sweet release to come my way for a long time. There was nothing sweet at all about my other releases at the beginning of 1967.

By the new year of 1967, as if being isolated from my group of twenty-two (and thereby relieved of my command) was not sufficient a trial, I was thrown in with the sharks in the newer group of boat people. I had wondered what everyone meant by referring to the boat people's training as 'rigorous', and I soon found out. The new training was ferocious. It was horrendously harsh in ways I will describe.

First, though, I need to say that in that period of isolation in which I was truly the odd man out, I was expelled from the Communist Party, by the Venezuelan Communist Party, for being 'divisionist'. From one day to the next, they chucked me out without so much as a red cent of compensation for all the years of hard labour I had put in. I had been pretty sickened by communism for a good two years before they expelled me, but that wasn't the point. For a party that was all about workers' rights, as I said to Sol Ortega, my first reaction was: 'At least when they fire you from a factory, you get some kind of recompense. You know, so many years of work equals so much severance pay and pension fund contributions. Well, not so with the What-about-the-workers Party. They chucked me out: just like that! I entered when I was fifteen and now I am thirty-three. Sixteen years!'

I had wearied of communism in Prague. I had had serious doubts about its underlying ideology. But in 1967, to be a socialist militant and be expelled from the Communist Party was a tricky and dangerous position to be in. Luckily, as it happened (and no thanks to the Venezuelan Communist Party), I had found a niche in Cuba.

I hated almost everything about my period of training with the 'big boys' – the veterans. The 'almost' was the notable exception of some friendships I made there: for instance, with el Negro Manolito – the man with the sweetest singing voice I have ever heard. One by one, I managed to convert about a dozen of the group of forty veterans to Fidel's and my cause. It wasn't that the men didn't want to fight in Venezuela: they did. It was that they wanted to fight their way: in isolated groups with a departure point from their existing *focos* of armed resistance. Fidel and I favoured using the element of surprise. We wanted to simulate an element of chaos and then to systematically move from the east with a few men and a big plan.

My task at the camp was not made any easier by my two main allies, Luben Petkoff and Sol Ortega, being removed from the group with a handful of like-minded men only two months after I joined it.

It seemed clear to me that whatever we, in the Venezuelan Guerrilla, had been doing up until then had been a pretty dismal failure. We had to do something different, something dynamic and also organic. An armed struggle had been taking place in Venezuela since 1961. By 1967, that meant there had been six years of fighting. The government and the rest of the world could pretend that it wasn't happening, and the press could censor the name of our armed groups and the names of our leaders as much as they liked, but that didn't mean that they didn't exist. For six years we had fought a phantom war and we, the insurrectionary fighters, were like phantoms. Our forces had been beaten back to next to nothing. The 120 veterans had escaped by the skin of their teeth. Hundreds more had died for our cause. The reason why we were out there risking our necks in the first place had not changed. The corruption within our country was as rampant as ever. Our only hope was to unite and, I believed, the only way to do that effectively was if we did it soon.

There was altogether too much in-fighting and bickering going on in socialist circles back home. We did not have a real focus or a united force. Individual and isolated acts of heroism (like those of my brother, Ivan, of Luben and Teodoro, Sol, Ojera and Elías) were all very well, but if they resulted in the continuous sacrifice of lives, we would, eventually, just run out of heroes without achieving anything.

Back in the veterans' training camp, though, everyone had their own ideas based on their own isolated experience. They didn't want to know about an overview. They wanted to practise old tactics and learn some new ones. They wanted technical tricks to take back to their old stamping grounds. What they didn't want was a weedy little professor who read poetry books telling them what they should do.

The fact that the weedy little Prof was in direct contact with Fidel Castro did not impress them as it had my group of twenty-two. The veterans were like those people who judge the merits of paintings exclusively on their personal taste. It was good if they liked it. Once the initial romance of the Cuban Revolution had become their daily reality, and once the aura of Fidel Castro had worn a bit thin, and once it became clear that Che Guevara was not going to return from his global wanderings to personally train them and join them, there was an undertow of disrespect towards our Cuban hosts, which many of the veterans took no pains to disguise. The conflicts both within the group and towards the Cuban instructors were escalating. Like the craquelure of an old master painting that has been given a quick dab of new varnish to keep the flaky surface in place, the rifts and resentments were constantly visible.

The growing lack of respect for Fidel himself was born not so much from what he said as the time it took him to say it.

'Bloody hell! Maybe he didn't fight any battles at all. Maybe he just *talked* his enemies to death. Give the guy a loud-hailer and throw him at the enemy with one of his speeches and entire battalions will surrender. Fidel's special weapon is boredom. He can knock anyone out with it.'

Such talk elaborated into a long and ever-expanding joke. That other men, wiser by far than Fidel or I, had mastered certain rules of strategy was neither here not there. That the Chinese, over two thousand years ago, had known more than we could ever hope to learn about the subject was not something the veterans wanted to know. 'What the fuck have we got to do with the Chinese?'

I had, some years before, begun to read Chinese literature in translation. Despite the political shenanigans of the People's Republic of China, I found myself very attracted to certain aspects of their culture. In Algiers, on Wednesdays and Fridays, in a kind of ritual, I used to drink coffee with a veritable sage called Mr Wai Kit. He was both a scholar and a connoisseur of life. We began to become friends by discussing coffee. If you remember, I grew up in San Cristobal de Torondoy surrounded by coffee plantations, so I knew a little bit about the subject. Wai Kit, on the other hand, had grown up on the banks of the Yangtze river far from any such plants, but he knew the history and the properties of coffee and he verbally tracked it from Arabia to the Orient and from Arabia to Sicily, and then via Naples to the Western world. From coffee, we progressed to revolution (as one does) and Wai Kit introduced Confucius as the first revolutionary thinker. Wai Kit's manner was always grave and his head moved backwards and forwards on his neck with the darting movement of a gecko. His erudition was so dazzling that whenever he spoke, everyone around agreed with him. Although his neck movements were a nervous tic, they looked like a pre-emptive self-congratulatory reaction to his own brilliance and thus sometimes distanced other potential listeners. As someone easily drawn into discussing coffee, I was lucky enough to get beyond his restless surface to the extraordinary depths of his mind.

Anyone watching us might have thought we were a pair of young lovers, so infatuated were we with pride and pleasure at his literary and philosophical revelations. Week by week, he would lend me books to read and then guide me through the subtlety of their meaning like a teacher with a chosen pupil. Nodding and darting his chin and converting all 'r's into 'l's, he asked in his gentle, almost breathless French, 'Now you have read Sun Tzu, do you find his work remarkable?'

I told him, 'If only we had had his *Art of War* as a manual in Falcón, things might have been very different.'

'Yes, Mr Oswado, but Sun Tzu is only about rules and governors. It is important for you to read Sima Qian, China's most important historian. On Wednesday, I will bring it for you.'

I thanked him and yet I could never thank him enough as, tome by tome, Mr Wai Kit guided me expertly through thousands of years of civilisation, from Lao Tzu to Confucius and Chang Tzu.

One day, he said to me, 'Mr Oswado, from now on: only Confucius.'

Which I took to mean that it is better to understand a single line than to name-drop a thousand books.

From then on, for several months, on Wednesdays and Fridays, between 5 and 7 p.m., we studied Confucius, who was the first to comprehend that power does not come by right of birth, but by how able you are and how much the people like you. Meanwhile, all around us in the little bar, dozens of militant Marxists and Maoists quoted revolutionary propaganda to each other over glasses of muddy coffee and mint tea. Although I did hardly more than dabble in Chinese culture, it was enough to see that while we were taking years to reinvent the wheel, and then more years greasing that wheel with our blood, sweat and tears, the Chinese had solved the problem before Christ was born, and moved on (such as through the thought of Confucius and Laozi's *The Book of Tao and its Virtues*) to heights we Western plodders could not even imagine. Very little real news was coming out of China, but I was filled with curiosity as to how a revolution would evolve in such an enlightened culture.

Meanwhile, back in Cuba, for the rank and file of the veterans, being expected to accept Cuban ideas was bad enough; being asked to even consider Chinese ones was ridiculous.

Simulated chaos is given birth from control; the illusion of fear is given birth from courage; feigned weakness is given birth from strength.

Order and disorder are a question of numbers; courage and fear are a question of strategic configuration of power; strength and weakness are a question of the deployment of forces.

Thus one who excels at moving the enemy deploys in a configuration to which the enemy must respond. He offers something that the enemy must seize. With profit he moves them, with the foundation he awaits them.

Nearly 2000 years later, the rules of strategy were almost unchanged. I did not, of course, go spouting pages of Chinese thought at the men. Yet some of the underlying purity would always challenge what was in my own head.

A couple of months before I left again for Prague, Mr Wai Kit stopped coming to the bar. In fact, no one saw him again in the city. Papito said it was common practice for the various Chinese attachés to disappear. When I suggested that I might ask after him at the Chinese embassy, Papito dissuaded me.

'They have a different concept of civilisation these days. For all you know, asking for him might plunge the poor bugger into ten years of re-education and hard labour in Qinghai Province. Let it go, Oswaldo, because, believe me, every step those Chinese take is an irrevocable historical act. Give your Mr Wai Kit an epitaph from Confucius; and move on!'

Two years later, in Cuba, it was in large part thanks to Wai Kit's teaching that I managed to convert a few of the veterans to adopting one well-ordered plan of invasion from the east coast. I did this not so much through argument as through incidents: things that made me liked by the men.

While I was in training with my group of twenty-two disparate revolutionaries, I had found the physical strain hard to bear. While I was with the veteran Venezuelans, the ferocious nature of the training very nearly killed me. The new training consisted scarcely at all in the use of arms and explosives, and almost all in disembarkation techniques. We were being specifically trained to disembark on the rugged east coast of Venezuela. The sea would be rough there; the channels would be treacherous to our boat; the coral rocks would graze and slice us. There would be sharks and waves, darkness, currents and just about every other conceivable danger. The purpose of our training was to prepare us for the worst-case scenario conditions of disembarkation by making them as realistic as possible.

The rigour of our training consisted in our being taken to between five and ten kilometres out to sea on a little boat and then being thrown overboard with a small pack on our backs. We were made to practise on an isolated bit of coast way beyond Havana without a light in sight and in the middle of the night. This exercise was repeated several times a week. We were left in the water and we had to make our own way back to shore. 'Simulated chaos is given birth from control.' There was nothing simulated about the chaos on those nights, particularly when the sea was rough.

I think there may have been something punitive in the Cubans' control of those exercises. We Venezuelans, en masse, were too cocky by half. We disrespected our hosts, we refused to treat their revolution with the reverence they themselves held it in. At night, as we sat round our camp fire, we took the piss out of their leaders. I do not cite my own reaction to the training methods as proof of their excessive nature (although I would like to). Instead, I cite the fact that later two of our group died while training. Add to this that no other groups were training like us. Add the fact that even on a good night, there were waves and sharks, currents and pitch darkness; and the boat that had dumped us always just buggered off. Lastly, add to this the fact that even the 26th July Movement revolutionaries who came over from Mexico on the *Granma* never underwent such a rigorous training, and I really begin to wonder if our preparation wasn't blended with a punishment for insubordination.

Although later el Che became a martinet, putting people through their paces and pushing them beyond the limits of human endurance, that is another story – and Che was notable for his absence at that time. In fact, he was so unaccountably absent that along with almost everyone else in Cuba I missed his presence. Che had been roaming the world singing Cuba's praises as he spread the word and drummed up support for Cuba's revolutionary road. Then, from the autumn of 1966, he seemed to drop off the face of the earth. My training period coincided exactly with this mysterious disappearance. Whereas a lot of other people were asking where he could be, thanks to our talks in Algiers and a subsequent sporadic and cryptic correspondence, I knew that he was in Africa and probably in the Congo but possibly in Mali, Guinea, Ghana, Dahomey or Tanzania. At the Villa Susini in Algiers he had asked me to go with him to Equatorial Africa to assist the revolutionary movements there. At the time, I was seriously interested. His deep voice and utter conviction were very persuasive. On his adoptive island in the Caribbean, I sometimes half regretted not having done so, because instead I was about to drown for the *Patria Grande* – for an America with a capital 'A' of Che's vision.

Conflicting stories began to circulate as to where el Comandante Che was; there were endless 'sightings' of him from around the world. In the summer of 1967, some of the mystery behind Che's absence was solved when his farewell letter to Fidel was made public (by Fidel and against Che's wishes).

He must have taken the decision to split from the Soviets (and thereby to distance himself from Fidel and therefore probably have to leave Cuba) before he came over to Algeria for the second economic seminar of the Organisation of Afro-Asian Solidarity, because he made his disaffection for the Soviet Union known there. And maybe because it was such a momentous decision, he talked about it a lot in the run-up to his speech. He had also talked at length about what he would do afterwards: about Africa and our America, which had been mocked for almost 500 years. What struck me most about him (apart from his intense loneliness, his wit and charm) was that his mind was still open to ideas and open to change. He was absolutely serious and dedicated 100 per cent to work and integrity. He was naive and stubborn. Proof of both is that he was convinced that he could motivate an entire nation to work like dogs for the pure joy of the moral ethic rather than for gain: thus confusing the temporary manifestation of love, loyalty and solidarity of the masses with the long-term problem of what they actually wanted. He didn't see that the sacrifice of the Cuban people was a gift to him and Fidel and the Camilo Cienfuegos of this world (Camilo Cienfuegos was one of Fidel's henchmen from the early days). He was sometimes stubbornly slow to admit his mistakes, but he was always able (eventually) to do so. That is a mark of greatness. He wrote (in the speech that I translated for him) and he believed that: 'There are no boundaries in this struggle to the death. We cannot be indifferent to what happens anywhere in the world.' He was a just man who lived by and died from his own passionate belief that 'it is better to die standing than to live on your knees'.

Because Che became such an icon after his death, you might expect me to say more about our friendship now. Yet the fact remains that I didn't go to Africa with him (or to Bolivia, for that matter) and our paths didn't really coincide again. We were two ex-communists who had communism stuck like a fishbone in our craws; which left two Marxists who believed deeply in socialist revolution and who had very little support around them and found some in each other's ideas.

So Che was away from Cuba while I was there being trained to jump through the circles of hell. Disappearances seemed to be the order of the day: even Regis Debray had left Havana and dropped out of circulation. I fondly imagined Che Guevara still to be in Africa when he popped up in Bolivia, followed hotly by none other than the ubiquitous Regis. There were rumours that Regis had been arrested in Bolivia and counter-rumours that it was all lies and he had not. It was the middle of May 1967 before Fidel confirmed to me that Regis was indeed awaiting trial in Bolivia together with an English journalist. It was surprisingly hard to get any information on what was going on with Che and his tiny band of guerrillas, but from what little I could glean, it sounded like a disaster. While all the Guerrilla Manual's 'don'ts' were being enacted out there by its author, our total immersion into indoctrination of the 'dos' progressed relentlessly in Cuba.

Before I go any further with my deep-sea training experience, though, let me add that I am not a good swimmer. I never have been. I had never even splashed around on a beach with a snorkel and mask.

My first dose of this painful medicine occurred when I was completely exhausted from the first full day of training under the new (sado-masochistic) regime. Our crowded launch chugged into the Gulf of Mexico across a slightly choppy sea. I am not much of a sailor and could thus compound my misery with seasickness.

Had the day ended then and there, I would have needed two days' complete rest and a medicinal cure with the miraculous waters of Santa Maria del Rosario to have recovered from it thus far. I was huddled up on deck brooding about this and watching the veterans leap into the sea, when some bastard came up behind me, picked me up and threw me overboard. It is pointless to say that I wasn't ready.

Everyone has their own worst nightmare, and that was mine. All my infant fears returned: water, sharks, the dark, drowning, being unable to breathe, being lost, being alone. I completely panicked. It was about ten o'clock at night. There was very little moon. I couldn't see anyone else. As the boat had turned to chug away, I tried in vain to be rescued by the Cuban instructors on board. They completely ignored me and by the time the dimmed lights were blocked from my sight by the waves and the night, I was close to drowning.

God knows what I was saying or sobbing. I can't remember *what* I shouted, just that I was shouting. I do remember thinking with complete certainty that I was about to drown. I did not have the clarity of mind to be aware of my actions, but I had the consistency of mind to carry them out. I had always lived under immense protest. Since I was about to die, I had obviously decided subconsciously to do so under immense protest too.

While I thrashed and flapped around screaming and gulping huge mouthfuls of saltwater, the veterans swam confidently out of my hearing towards the distant shore. Then, like a guardian angel, one of the veterans came back, cupped my chin above the water while I caught my breath, and with a vice-like arm held me as still as he could.

'Hey, *profe*!' he shouted into my ear. 'Don't worry, stay calm. You won't drown. And don't be nervous. Do what I do; and just follow me.'

He was a mere boy, not a day over eighteen. When I couldn't swim, he pulled me; when I gave up, he encouraged me. That night, without a doubt, he saved my life as he guided me through the Gulf of Mexico to the shore.

His name was Marco Rubén. From then on, he became my friend. He protected me endlessly, letting up on his task only some months later when Elías took over his protective role. Meanwhile, the instructors continued to throw us into the sea, and Rubén continued to life-save me.

On turf and surf, he was a good guide to follow. He knew instinctively where to move and what to avoid. He seemed to have antennae alert for danger. He was like an insect – a bicho – out in the wild. He was also naturally intelligent, but he had very little formal education and regretted it. As he grew closer to me, he picked my brains about everything and everyone. Through teaching, I was able to repay a fraction of the debt I owed him. Sometimes, though, he taught me a thing or two. Conclusions that had taken me years to reach, he sometimes jumped to with sheer common sense. He was very good at pinpointing the weaknesses of communism and Cuba and its revolution.

I remember one day when he and I were out in a lorry fetching supplies. We stopped at a roadside café for something to eat and drink. In Venezuela, roadside cafés sell everything from pork fritters to the kitchen sink. They sell sweets and snacks and cold drinks, whisky and milk shakes, hot dogs and sacks of oranges and corn. They sell live chickens and grilled chicken. They sell books and records, T-shirts, and hams, spare parts and batteries, magic potions, plaster statues of St Anthony, DDT, and edifying tracts by Dr Gregorio Hernandez. In Cuba, on the other hand, the roadside cafés had one or two wretched stalls standing forlornly in a long patch of dirt. On a good day, they had some fresh papaya juice, and maybe (but never count on it) a cup of coffee. And that was it!

We pulled up in a cloud of dust and several women and children in flip-flops got up from where they had been sitting on the ground around two broken plastic chairs to offer their wares. It wasn't a good day, there was no coffee.

Rubén looked long and hard at the one shrivelled papaya on the stall, then took me to one side. He whispered a little nervously, 'Between you and me, *profe*, is this socialism quite what we want in Venezuela? I mean: is this what we are fighting for?'

Touché. That was Marco Rubén.

Not that I called him that in Cuba. He had a pseudonym like all the other trainees. In the 'rigorous camp' real names were absolutely forbidden. Everyone knew my full name, Oswaldo Barreto Miliani, but the others were all supposed to be anonymous. If anyone ever doubted that men can keep a secret, the fact that by the time we reached D-Day everyone knew at least what everyone else's real first name was should be evidence enough that they can't. And this was despite the draconian penalties applicable for such a security breach, plus the obvious future risk if any of us were to be caught and tortured.

I don't know for sure what happened to Rubén. I heard that he didn't make it. One of the saddest aspects of my life is the long list of my friends and comrades who didn't make it. In my line of work, it isn't feasible to keep an address book, and it isn't safe. If I did have one, though, it would be full of little crosses beside the names of all the friends who have died before me.

Tell me who, who are these travellers, more fugitive, even,
than we? Who, from the very beginning, seem driven
and forced by a will – and whose is it?

CHAPTER XXXXII

The head of our entire group of veterans was Elías. He was to be the leader of our expeditionary force. He was in his early twenties, extraordinarily dynamic, and as handsome as a movie star. He had joined the Guerrilla as a teenager in search of action and never much cared for politics. Although he was our commander, during our rigorous training he was nowhere to be seen. Literally: we never saw him because he had the mumps and was sick in bed with his bollocks swollen to the size of a couple of honeydew melons. Apart from the fact that it is a bit ridiculous for any man to have elephantine balls, it was a bit ridiculous that as we men prepared for our finest hour, we had a leader in name only. Such was the power of el Comandante Elías's name; and such was his fame that he kept hold of his power by remote control.

We all knew that we were on standby to sail to Venezuela. We were waiting for our marching orders from one day to the next. Everyone's nerves were taut and frayed from the mixture of exhaustion and tension. Every time a jeep or a truck approached our camp we all jumped: 'This is it! It's time to go!' Someone would overhear the radio operator saying something about Venezuela, or the east, or the coast, or a boat, or the sea, and immediately begin to spread the rumour that the order was about to be given. Every time we were told to take our full packs with us, we all thought: 'It's D-Day.'

Weeks went by like that with our adrenaline peaking and nothing happened beyond the gruelling training sessions. Then one day the order we had been waiting for arrived: 'Everyone get your things together – we are leaving tonight!'

It would be our moment of destiny: to live or die attempting to carry out what we had prepared. That is a singular moment when at last you get what you want. It is not the same thing as meeting your destiny unprepared. When you do something on impulse or you run into it – that is very different from consciously planning an act and then carrying it out.

It is hard to explain adequately, but it is a rare moment. While you prepare for action, immediately before it, you feel very much a man, but when you execute your plan you can feel like a god – by knowing what you were going to do, you did.

The atmosphere was so intense it induced silence. We looked at each other and that was all. Our every move seemed to freeze into memorable frames. The camp was struck quickly and efficiently. Still hushed with excitement we climbed into the back of two trucks and sat knee-deep in waterproof bags of weapons. Every sensation was amplified. Every sound was significant; we devoured everything with our looks. Some of us might be living our last day and seeing our last sights, hearing our last sounds. That knowledge filled even the most uncouth of us with a kind of reverence.

Since our expeditionary force was to make a sea crossing, we obviously needed to head towards the coast. I have never had much of a sense of direction, so I had no idea where we were, but some of the other guys were certain that we were heading in the wrong direction. Inside the trucks, people began to talk; mostly to ask each other where they thought we were going. We had to drive south so as to embark opposite the coast of Venezuela, and yet we were heading north. Instead of approaching Havana, we seemed to be heading away from it. Half the guys in my truck maintained we couldn't be approaching Havana, and the other half insisted that we were. An argument broke out, which would have turned into a fight had it not been for a large road sign which clearly stated 'Havana 15km'.

We were lulled back to silence and just stared out of the canvas flaps at the back of the lorry as it lurched towards the capital.

Then, without any explanation from the Cubans, after approximately five kilometres, we turned off the road and were driven to a deserted army barracks called Punto Zero. It had something sinister about it. In fact, it looked like a concentration camp with four hugely long, poorly built, barn-like buildings and a small hut for the commander and one at the gate for sentries. Great strips of dying creepers and lianas hung from the barbed wire.

A huge iron gate in a high fence topped with barbed wire was opened by a couple of Cuban soldiers. Once the entire expeditionary force was inside, the gate was closed behind us. Two of our instructors opened up the back of our lorry and told us to get out. Nobody wanted to. This wasn't what we had come for. When we were told to overnight in the barracks, there was a spontaneous and mutinous chorus of 'No way!'

We had all braced ourselves for death or victory. We certainly hadn't cleansed our souls to jump down into some dusty parade ground to overnight in some derelict tin shacks. We all talked at once, asking the Cubans why we were there; what was happening; why we weren't at the coast; when were we shipping out? But the Cubans were stone-faced and monosyllabic. Not one of their monosyllables answered any of our questions as to why we were there at Punto Zero. We noticed that their silence was democratic: they didn't answer any of the queries from the urban commandos either. They didn't even answer el Multi, the most excitable and obstreperous member of either of our groups. El Multi could argue the back legs off a donkey. He was as insistent as a nagging child, and he divided his time equally between taking offence and picking fights.

El Negro Manolito (who was our acting commander and temporarily in charge) and I exchanged anxious looks when our Cuban escort locked us all inside that semi-deserted barrack compound. El Negro went off to see if he could find whoever was in charge, while I stood around in the heat and dust with the men. We grumbled for a bit and then, gradually, in twos and threes, we went off to explore the barracks. There was a huge tin-roofed hut with eighty camp beds inserted into the dust and cobwebs. It was obvious that our hosts had been hardly less ready in preparing Punto Zero for our reception than we were to be received there.

Outside the dormitory, at a distance, there was a small hut for our commander. Then there was a tin-roofed, open-sided refectory, and a rusty barn where the Cubans were (like ours, theirs had plants growing through the walls and banners of cobwebs from the high roof).

There were also two empty barns identical to ours and the Cubans'; lastly, there was a quartermaster's area from which an endless stream of cursing emanated, together with a strong smell of burning. Three cooks had a 'kitchen' behind some canvas screens. The cooks hated us. I think they had been hauled off some really jammy assignment – like being billeted somewhere with pretty girls and a swimming pool – to become our camp cooks. They had no idea how to cook. They managed to burn the rice and serve the beans as bullets. They swore constantly and prided themselves in not giving away one word of orientation as to why we were there or what was going to happen. In fact, they were three of the nastiest Cubans I ever came across. Huddled over their cauldron on an open fire at twilight as bats swooped around them, they looked like Macbeth's witches.

El Negro Manolito returned from the Cuban side of the barracks and he made it clear that he had no idea what was going on. As night fell, we were brought beans and rice by the ungracious cooks and dozens of bottles of Cuban Cola. The latter made up for its lack of taste by a surplus of bubbles. We waited in a huddle in the yard, ready to be picked up and taken to the sea. We thought up and discussed a hundred possibilities as to why we were there instead of where we were supposed to be. El Negro organised a sort of boy scouts' sing-song round the campfire and we filled in a few hours getting drunk. As it got later and later, we left two men on guard and the rest of us went to sleep.

Next day, food continued to be ferried from the quartermaster's favela (rice and beans) but no news came from anywhere as to what the hell was going on. El Negro Manolito was as mystified as the men. Everyone was asking what no one knew.

I was an outsider in that group because I had big-shot connections which the other men deeply resented. My friendship with Fidel, far from winning me any favours, was looked at with suspicion. Who the hell did I think I was? What was so fucking brilliant

about me: the most pathetic soldier in the entire group? And
having a room at the Habana Libre Hotel, and being friends with
the leaders, and being an old buddy of Teodoro Petkoff, and
friendly as hell with el Negro Manolito *and* Sol Ortega *and* Luben
pissed all the other veterans except Rubén off to the point where
they would have gladly killed me. To make matters worse, I was
a famous intellectual in Latin America and the more intelligent of
the veterans resented me for that. They really hated me. I was a
sneak in their eyes: someone on friendly terms with all the leaders, great and small. I was someone who got special favours they
thought I did not deserve. They had all stayed and fought while
I was making my way as an intellectual from the safety of France.
They were great warriors and I was a fraud. They saw me as a
cuckoo in their training camp whose every breath stole something
precious from them. The mute hatred of their stares burnt into my
back every time I turned it; they never lost an opportunity to rub
in how much they despised me. A few days after my arrival in the
training camp, I had overheard one of the veterans sum me up to
his peers. He said, 'I don't know this *profe* guy from Adam, but he
certainly talks a lot of bullshit and he doesn't look anything like a
warrior. You have to remember, if a thing looks like shit, and
smells like shit, then it probably is shit.'

Notwithstanding any shittiness, by the end of our second day
locked into that barracks, and despite their hatred, more and more
of the guys were sidling up to me to ask what was going on. After
all, I was the one close to Fidel and Piñero.

'Come on, you must know something. Why are we here? What
the fuck is going on? Since you are in the know in Havana, you
have to know.'

There was no telephone, no radio and absolutely nothing to do.
With every hour that passed, the sense of anticlimax worked like
a slow poison.

Because of our intense training, we were more like a troop of
regular soldiers than a group of revolutionaries. We adhered to
strict military rules: we wore uniforms and had to keep them
spotless. Our boots had to be polished and our weapons cleaned
and ready for inspection at all times. We saluted our superior officer (el Negro) and stood to attention for his inspection night and

morning. Maintaining this routine kept us busy for an hour or so each day and acted a little like glue, giving some cohesion to the hardwood we had been and the sawdust we were turning into.

At dawn on our second morning there, an army truck arrived with over a hundred cases of ammunition. A young major with a very straggly beard told us it was for us and got us to unload it. While we did that, we felt a momentary elation. It was OK: we had been waiting for extra ammo. The Cubans were taking care of us after all. We'd be on our way that day. We prepared ourselves again: *patria o muerte!*

The major said, 'You can shoot here at your discretion. I have been instructed to tell you that you can use as much ammunition as you like.'

Once the truck was empty, he left. We fired off a few rounds while we waited for our own trucks to return to collect us. Then we fired off some more and some more until by midday, I think, each of us had fired off more ammunition in one morning than that used in Venezuela during the entire armed struggle.

Everyone stood in the yard and fired round after round into the air, into the fence and into a breeze-block wall with a basketball net at the southern end of the barracks ground. So many bullets went into that wall that it eventually collapsed. The men were so hyped up and so bored that little things provoked enormous rage. The fact that there was a basketball net but no basketball was something the men had found particularly annoying. There had been a few desultory attempts at a game using rolled-up shirts and Y-fronts as a ball, but the clothes kept spilling out. All our pent-up fire and courage, our passion and our anger, burst out of our weapons in those pointless volleys.

While the firing was happening, currents of animal savagery exploded in that yard. There was shouting and snarling, screaming and yelling and every foul-mouthed oath you can imagine. When the wall crumbled, there was frenzied cheering and then a growing uneasiness crept back over us. Why were we there? What was going to happen? And when? By midday, we had wearied of firing. Not even the machine guns were fun any more. We were like kids at a fun fair who have grown bored and jaded after they have been on all the rides.

After lunch, the daily lethargy of the dead hours drove us back into the shade of the barrackroom. It was like an oven under the tin roof, but it was also baking out in the yard. We stripped to our underpants and lay down for a siesta. From our narrow iron beds we stared at each other, at the rusty roof, at the concrete floor, at the cobwebs over the window vents. We stared in almost complete silence until, gradually, everyone started to talk to his neighbours. The talk was mostly wild conjecture and gossip. It was the nastiest, most foul-mouthed, lowest level of gossip I had ever heard – and as a Valerano, I had heard a lot!

That gossip was like a snake slithering between the beds, encircling first one of our comrades and then another. Of course, I came in for massive attack, but no one was spared. One by one, our characters were demolished; our sexual habits were dredged up and ridiculed. So much was invented that each and every one of us was pronounced a homosexual, a whore, a paedophile, a rapist, a ne'er-do-well, a liar, a coward, a sneak, a cheat and a thief.

We were eighty-one men in all, plus el Negro Manolito, who was in the commander's hut, and Elías, who was supposed to follow us to the coast but hadn't. We had been informed that Elías had recovered from the mumps. Even his balls had deflated, but he was in conclave somewhere with the Cubans and thus absent at the moment of our departure from the training camp. There was a lot of ill-feeling about our leader not being with us, but there was also a lot of hopeful conjecture that he was 'sorting things out with the Cubans'. When he didn't join us on our second day at the barracks, there was also a lot of conjecture about how game-worthy his swollen balls would have been if cut off and used as a basketball. In all, there had been ninety-five of us veterans (but, if you recall, shortly after my arrival some had left with Luben Petkoff and Sol Ortega). Thus there were eighty-three boat people left plus Rojas (my former Number 2) and me. In case anyone is counting, the maths includes the two poor sods who died in training.

On our second evening, after an interminable day, el Negro Manolito came in and gave us a pep talk about being patient and everything going to be OK if we just kept our heads. He was pretty good, but his talk could not lift either the despair or the listlessness of his expeditionary force. He had done a good job the night before, keeping us going with a sing-song round a campfire to keep the mosquitoes at bay. By pooling our stashes of rum, we had managed to get pleasantly drunk. Without those stashes any more, there was nothing to relieve the mixture of tedium and the nerve-racking suspense.

El Negro and I were friends from before our Cuban days (something the other men added to their long list of resentment against me). El Negro was, I remember, reading Faulkner's *The Sound and the Fury* at the time. He was so taken with it that he spent every moment he could in his hut immersed in that Deep Southern prose. I had been a couple of times to speak to him and discuss what he thought was happening: why we were here; how long we could stay and what our best- and worst-case scenarios could be. He was as baffled as we all were by our delay and pseudo-abduction.

Days and days went by. The long hot afternoons were the most deadly times. For me, it was hard to read or study, think or sleep with so much venom in the air. A few mosquitoes droned overhead, weighed down with fresh blood as they made their greedy rounds from one enraged and disappointed soldier to the next. Some of the men managed to doze off, most stayed awake and drowsily raked over every petty incident that had occurred during our training, and allotted blame with such arbitrary nastiness that I shuddered for our future endeavour.

Everything was distorted at Punto Zero. Even our food tasted like regurgitated bile. No one came to tell us anything. Nothing happened except that the anger and resentment levels of all of us rose to the point were we began to crack. Triggered by tiny things, we all began to snap. One day it was over the arrival of new crates of Cola. El Gordo, named for his gargantuan beer gut, took a tepid bottle from the crate, de-capped it with his teeth and then swigged from the bottle. 'Fuck it! I'm so tense my head is like a shaken bottle of this shit! Why the fuck can't these goddamn revolutionaries make a decent bottle of Coke? '

Rojas came up with a complicated answer about how the Yankees didn't allow the Cubans to have the top secret ingredient any more for their Coca-Cola factories. 'You know: the one that gets delivered in person in a briefcase chained to the courier's wrist. It's a secret formula and —'

'Fuck the formula! And fuck you! And fuck this godforsaken place!' el Gordo shouted, ending with a protracted scream on the word 'place'. After he said his bit, white froth formed at the corners of his lips and he took off from nought to about 25 miles an hour running straight at the perimeter fence. He charged it, collided at speed and knocked himself unconscious. He lay there for over an hour with blood drying on his face and hair. Then he came round, got up, shook himself and acted as though nothing had happened as he joined the group siesta and lay down in his grubby Y-fronts to join in the daily character assassination. The training had reduced el Gordo's once legendary belly to a tight six-pack veiled by folds of flaccid skin, but his name had remained despite his change in girth. Most days, he was one of the most amiable of the veterans; the one who came up with the wittiest comments and dirtiest jokes to pass the time.

During the siestas at Punto Zero, the most harmless time-filler was a game we played called Animal, Vegetable or Mineral? We had played it a lot at the training camp so it was a game we all knew. One man at a time had to go outside. Then another one of the group had to select an object and hide it. Everyone inside knew what had been chosen, but they were not allowed to say. Then the man outside was called back in and by a process of elimination he had to guess what it was that was hidden. He could get clues by asking twenty questions. The first question was always: 'Is it animal, vegetable or mineral?' If he failed to guess correctly what the object was, he would be given a draconian forfeit. The forfeits were chosen by the group as a whole and the fun of the game was in watching the loser carry one out.

Since most of the men were quick-witted and good at this familiar game, hardly anyone lost, so there were few forfeits. This made it rather dull and increased the prickliness of everyone's temper. With all the adrenaline of our *patria o muerte* call jammed into our systems, everyone's senses were heightened and their wits sharpened. For several rounds in a row, the contestants had guessed the object on their third question. Sixty of us were playing the game. The other twenty were outside and we could hear the odd shot or volley of gunfire or ribald laughter muffled by the barrack walls. Rojas was doing the guessing. He had just asked his second question, which after 'Animal, vegetable or mineral?' was always, 'Is it a container or is it contained?' The answer was, 'Contained.'

With an inspired guess, Rojas shouted out, 'Coca-Cola!'

He was right, and everyone hated him for it. He flopped back down on his bed under a barrage of insults.

When the hullabaloo died down, the next contestant was sent out and it was the turn of one of the best fighters in our group to choose what to hide. Without any actual rank within the unit, he was one of the leaders. He was an ex-marine and unbelievably tough. He was also a famous bank robber and one of the few intellectuals in the group. He stood up and paced between his bed and the next, thinking. Then he leapt over the bed (high-jumping over a prone Gordo without so much as grazing the raw cut on el Gordo's forehead) and he took a Cola bottle filled with petrol out of a case on the far side. He held it up in the air triumphantly.

'With this, he *will* suffer! Start thinking up a forfeit; and make it wretched.'

The bottle was duly hidden and the contestant was called back in. The first question, for some reason, was switched.

'Is it a container or is it contained?'

'It is contained.'

The men were all exchanging sly looks, convinced at last that they had a loser before them.

Then the contestant asked, 'Is it animal, vegetable or mineral?'

Without any hesitation, the ex-marine said, 'It is mineral.'

Without thinking, I said, 'No, it's not a mineral.'

And the ex-marine turned on me and almost spat: 'Shut up!'

Somebody else said, 'Of course it's a bloody mineral, you retard!'

I turned to that person and said calmly, 'No, it's not a mineral.'

'What the fuck is it then? A Martian?'

The ex-marine was furious. He came over to me and accused me of sabotaging his turn, of betraying his secret. I told him that I wasn't betraying anything, I was just pointing out that it was misleading to give the wrong answer. When I said 'wrong answer', the words were hardly out of my mouth when he exploded. The game was over and he was shouting, 'So, *profe*, are you trying to tell me that our national product, our national *mineral* product is not a mineral? Are you trying to take the piss?'

I spread my hands in denial. I wasn't taking the piss. I was just quoting a fact. 'It's a hydrocarburate. It's organic: so it's animal, not mineral.'

The ex-marine's response was instantaneous. He shouted, 'You fucking faggot!'

A magenta stain flushed onto his neck and began to race up to his forehead. The veins in his neck were bulging like chicken's guts as he shouted, 'I am sick to death of you!'

He jumped onto his bed and did an impersonation of me, repeating my words in a high-pitched camp voice with accompanying gesture. Most of the men laughed. His act was underscored with a homicidal violence. It was more of an announcement of his intention to kill me than a moment of mockery. Some stood up and began yelling their support of the ex-marine, but a couple of others supported my 'animal' stance. Rojas stuck his neck out and yelled, 'Technically he's right. Petroleum is a hydrocarburate, and hydrocarburates are organic.'

His were the last clear words before the whole room burst into a frenzied discussion as to whether petrol was animal or vegetable. Was it organic or inorganic? Both sides were vehement and both sides hurled insults and wild threats. The noise was amplified by the concrete walls and floor and the tin roof. 'Fuck you!' and 'Shit!' jumped out of the jumble of accusations and counter-accusations. All the bitterness and rage of the past several days welled up and exploded in unleashed fury. The men who had been outside came back in, drawn by the noise. Within seconds, they too had joined either side and were yelling with the best of us. Over the next few minutes, the eighty-one men divided as though by an invisible command into two sides. I was, of course, on the animal side. The ex-marine was the self-appointed leader of the mineral side.

At a certain point, there was an uncanny lull in the shouting. The ex-marine took advantage of it to grab his rifle and release the safety catch.

'Right!' he said, pointing it at my head from across the divide. 'Eat shit!'

The words 'Eat shit' acted as a subliminal command. It was as though he was our commanding officer and he had said, 'Take aim,' because everyone reached for their weapons. There were a couple of minutes of scrambling and rummaging and taking aim and then the Venezuelan liberation army's expeditionary force of eighty-one men lined up in two groups facing each other. Our automatic weapons were aimed at each other's chests; as a prelude to our intended mutual massacre, we were squeezing in one last round of abuse.

At that very moment, our acting leader, el Negro Manolito, came through the door. He was carrying his Faulkner novel in his hand. He looked at us for a split second. And then he barked, 'What the fuck is this?'

About twenty people began shouting each other down to explain to el Negro why we were about to mow each other down in that dormitory. During the moments they spent talking, the killer instinct in the men died down enough for el Negro to placate them. He grabbed the soldier in us and pulled rank. He got everyone to lower their weapons and thereby avoided the discussion being resolved in a rain of lead. His timely intervention stopped eighty-odd revolutionaries from killing each other at Punto Zero that day. He put the Faulkner paperback in his pocket and took full control. Within five minutes, it was over and we soldiers were out in the yard, drilling.

But it wasn't over entirely. Something ugly had surfaced. After the near fatal fight, nobody trusted anyone else again. No one liked another; the unity was gone. That unity had been there when the veterans had fought so valiantly in Falcón. It had been there when they helped each other reach the east coast; and when they found a boat; and when they sailed to Cuba. It had been there during the gruelling training suffered only the better to re-embark as an expeditionary force to liberate their countrymen and right the wrongs of Venezuela. And it all evaporated in half an hour over a silly word game. We had entered Punto Zero as a battle-ready fighting unit. After playing Animal, Vegetable or Mineral? we would never be that again.

We could have fallen out over anything. We could have fought over any subject under the sun. How ironic it is that we did so over petroleum: our national product. As one of the leading oil-producing countries in the world, the history of Venezuela is soaked in petroleum. Everything we Venezuelans do and are is impregnated with petroleum in some way. Our entire domestic and foreign policy is governed by it. It is the source of our wealth, the root of our power, the mainspring of our government's corruption and the heart of our woes. And, as though that were not enough, in Punto Zero in the summer of 1967, it also became the reason for our rift.

CHAPTER XXXXIII

Just a couple of days after the animal, vegetable or mineral fight, Elías arrived to take up his command. His presence had an almost miraculous effect on the men. His word was law; no one stepped out of line in front of him. Not only did everyone obey him implicitly, I never heard any one of his comrades have a bad word to say about him behind his back. Elías was a man of action, purely and simply; he did not have time for squabbles. Every time he spoke he had our full attention, and such was his magnetism and charisma that no one dared interrupt him.

He was not tall, but he looked tall. He was powerfully built and extraordinarily strong. His skin was the cinnamon-colour of the tropics and his features were chiselled like a Mayan statue. People talk about Elías sometimes as though he was a mythical character, and others think that it is all exaggeration. It isn't and it wasn't. Elías had certain qualities, which I never saw, before or after, in anyone else. For instance (and I know this sounds silly, but it is true), he could move without appearing to move; and when he was actually still, there was something hypnotic in his presence. Often, when he did speak (and he was not a man of many words), it was to joke and make light of a given situation, no matter how dire it seemed to others. And a reprimand from Elías had the effect of a beating by anyone else; a word of praise was positively uplifting.

Within minutes of arriving, he took command and he took control and all the men were calmed by his presence. When he addressed us for the first time, it was quite formally in the yard. The second time, he joined us as we were finishing our lunch of rice and beans and sitting at trestle tables in the 'mess' (the high tin roof on four poles at the back of the barracks). Elías came in with el Negro and told us that we would, while waiting for whatever it was we were waiting for, continue our training, starting at 15.00 hours that same day. The only one to question this news was el Multi, who jumped up and called out, 'What's the point of going on like this? We—'

Without changing the amiable expression on his face or the enthusiastic tone of his voice, Elías said, 'Sit down and shut up or I'll punch you in the face.'

Multi sat back down abruptly. His mouth was open and shaped for his next word, which he mouthed silently.

'And stop your nonsense, do you understand?'

Multi nodded. He looked stunned as though someone had just punched him in the face. And that was it. Under Elías, we never heard a squeak out of Multi again and, I tell you, Multi had been a royal pain in the arse since the day he arrived in Cuba. From that moment, he fell under Elías's spell, as we all did.

Days and days passed and absolutely nothing happened and then, out of nowhere, two ex-Russian army trucks arrived with a Cuban escort to take us to a party. I can't explain why we were invited to a party. I just know that it happened and that, unlikely as it may seem under our bizarre circumstances, the army trucks were there to take us to dance.

The party was about eight kilometres away and it was one of those national holiday celebrations when everyone gets drunk and dances in a town square with several hundred of the locals. As our truck swerved round the endless bends in the narrow road, blasts of salsa music came and went for several minutes before we got there. It was hard to tell what was most exciting: being let out for an evening from our semi-prisoner-of-war camp, or being able to have sex after months of abstinence. We shagged like gods, that night, like kings (and also, I suppose, like goats). Somewhere between all the frenzied coupling, someone sidled up to me and slipped a piece of paper into my hand. That note was the key to our mysterious abduction. It was about the

MIRistas, the other group of the veteran boat people. It said: 'MIRistas got there before you. Got caught with Cubans. One Cuban dead. Two captured, one talked. Block against Cuba.' It was signed: 'a friend'.

When I showed Elías the note, he said, 'We have to find Sol Ortega immediately.'

We skipped the party in the town square and made our way to Havana. We walked for about seven kilometres under the stars with no sign of anyone in pursuit. We located Sol without any difficulty. Around midnight he was always in his favourite bar in Vedado. He told us the following: 'A couple of weeks ago, Fidel sent a boat to Venezuela with Luben Petkoff and a handful of MIRistas and eleven Cubans. Among the Cubans was Captain Arnaldo Ochoa.'

Ochoa was Cuba's most brilliant commander, who would later become a celebrated general, and later still be executed by his own side on a trumped-up charge of treason and corruption. I came to know him very well and, for what it is worth, I can vouch for him as one of the most decent, upright, loyal and honest people I have ever known.

'From day one, it all went wrong. The MIRistas were ambushed practically as they disembarked. The casualties were high. One of the Cubans had been killed too, another, Manuel Hill, was captured, and another of the Cubans has not returned and is believed to be lost or captured. When news leaked out back in Cuba, the other MIRistas were furious. These MIRistas said that Fidel had acted out of favouritism and they insisted that some, at least, of their own group get escorted back to Venezuela too.'

Sol wasn't sure what had happened next except that he thought there had been a second, smaller venture and that it too had been a fiasco. Far from finding the missing Cuban and making a fresh start, it seems the second boatload was ambushed soon after arrival.

There were endless rumours. What was known was that most of the MIRistas were dead, and one of the Cubans had been killed, another captured. As a result, there was an international outcry against Cuba. Fidel Castro had decided that no one else was going to be sent to Venezuela from Cuba.

*

A few days later, Fidel called me, Sol Ortega, Elías and el Negro Manolito to talk with him in Havana. It wasn't really a 'talk' he wanted. He wanted us to listen while he told us: 'In the light of the fiasco of the MIRista landings, our hands are tied ... We cannot send all those people to Venezuela. We cannot send any of you to Venezuela. Nor can we allow any of you to disembark from Cuba on your own without our support. You must stay here – you have no choice. It will be for a minimum of one year – probably for two. Only then will we help you. To do so any earlier would be to risk Cuba incurring dire sanctions.'

End of 'discussion'.

We didn't talk on the way back to Punto Zero, not least because we had Cuban escorts. One of the Cubans who was sitting in the back with us had ears the size of bed pans and was obviously listening to our every word. When we got back to the barracks, the men crowded round our truck for news. Elías convened a meeting then and there. As soon as the Cuban truck had left the premises, he began to explain what Fidel had said. We all listened. It was one of the rare moments when our entire group was silent. When he had finished recounting how we were being told to stay and wait for at least one, but probably two years, there was a murmur of discontent.

I stepped forward and said, 'That's all very well, but we can't wait for two years – or one year, come to that. We have to do what we set out to do; and that never did depend on the political climate here in Cuba, and it cannot depend on that now. We have to go forward. We have to do what we set out to do. That means, comrades, that we have to leave.'

Elías said, 'I agree. Who else agrees with us?'

A handful of men stepped forward. The majority of the men stood their ground as their faces became vacant and their eyes avoided any contact with any of us.

Elías seemed to press an invisible charisma button. He took a small step forward and asked again, almost joking, as was his wont, but deadly serious as we all knew, 'So, who else is with us?'

A few more men wavered, glanced hastily at the ex-marine and stepped forward to stand with us. Then there was a moment of intense silence.

In all, we were twelve who were prepared to go on with our plan on our own without the help (or the permission) of Fidel and the Cubans. That is: twelve out of eighty-three. A few days later, four more men joined our group, making a grand total of sixteen.

I informed Piñero of our decision. After I had told him, his manner to me changed. He suggested we reconvene the next day with 'the others'. By 'the others', he meant his others (the Cubans) not mine. Until then, meetings with Piñero had always been amiable and semi-informal. When I returned with Elías the next day, the Cubans were seated in a line as though for a court martial. There was nowhere for us to sit. I repeated what I had said to Piñero the previous day.

The Cubans listened gravely and then said, 'We cannot agree. Fidel wants you to wait.'

I told them that we could not do that. That good friends as we all were to Cuba – something that I, in particular, had proven in deeds as well as words – we had come to Havana to further the needs of Venezuela and we had to return.

There were a few beats of quite nasty silence followed by a pronouncement: 'We wash our hands of you. If you go, that is your business. We will give you a passport and $800 each and then you are on your own.'

From that moment, we, 'the divisionists', were completely ostracised in Cuba. I never saw Fidel again in private, and the one time I saw him in public, he ignored me. When I approached him, he barely acknowledged me, as though I was seeing him for the first time. His infatuation with me was over and I was out on my ear.

A couple of days after the meeting with Piñero and his junta, I went back to my room at the Habana Libre Hotel and found that after nearly eighteen months it wasn't mine any more. My bags had been packed and brought down to reception. I was no longer a guest of the Cuban government. Before I became persona non grata in Cuba, I had dozens of friends and I would have been able to stay with any number of them. The moment Fidel ceased to know me, so did most of those 'friends'.

I took my bags and moved into a cramped little hotel room with one of the sixteen divisionists and we turned our attention to how to re-equip our loyal but reduced group now that the Cubans had confiscated all our arms. There were sixteen of us ready to embark and carry out our plan, but we didn't have a weapon between us.

Back in 1966, the boatload of veterans had arrived in Havana laden with their own arms, which had been handed over to the Cubans before training began. After our schism, a delegation of our divisionists went to Piñero and asked for their weapons back. For a couple of heady days we were all quite hopeful that this would happen, because they had been told to put in a formal written request to Piñero's department, complete with an inventory of said arms. There was a lot of discussion about this list and who owned what and who had carried or swapped what. In the end, their claim was for: 12 single-shot rifles, 15 assorted hand-guns, 2 Garands, 2 M-14 automatic rifles plus 1 Belgian FAL, 6 grenades, 15 machetes, a garrotte, 10 flick-knives, 3 trip-wires and a harpoon. There was a six-hour discussion and a great deal of passion spent over whether to put the harpoon in or not.

Once the claim had been formally delivered, the harpoon banter evolved into jokes about why we didn't use bows and arrows or Goajiran blowpipes. And then there were many hours of waiting for a reply in one or other of our cramped boarding-house rooms. During those hours – which became days – we discussed how best we could use our little arsenal and build on it. Some of the weapons were old, but we were confident that we could still do a lot with them.

Finally, the answer came. Like the request, it was also written. 'Eat shit! And remember who paid for your training.'

In what felt like an endless game of snakes and ladders, we were, once again, back to square one. As I leafed through all my notes and papers for possible leads, I noticed that I was not the first person to have looked through those papers, and also that many of my notes were missing. It was one thing to be in Havana as Fidel's special friend; it was another to be there as his enemy.

CHAPTER XXXXIV

The night I moved into my new, shared hotel room downtown, there was a storm over Havana. The lights kept going in the hotel and somewhere on the building a window shutter was banging against the wall: *Bam! Bam! Bam!* Each crash had a mocking finality: *It's over! It's over!* I was alone – I recall that the others had gone to a dance – but despite feeling so afraid and low, my stubborn streak kept telling me: It can't be over! My fortunes were at a low ebb, but my inner voice was as strong as ever. It was crying out that my life was my mission, and it would only be over when I died.

I lay on my bed, which was hard and narrow and reminiscent of the camp beds at Punto Zero, and, very much alive, I reviewed my life so far. None of my achievements to date satisfied my soul. I had a specific goal: to liberate Venezuela. I was still determined to do it. All we needed were some arms and some luck.

And, as fate would have it, I suddenly remembered a stash of weapons in the Villa Susini in Algiers. They had been stuck there since the military coup by Boumediènne. Hardly anybody knew they were there, but I did, and I knew exactly where they were hidden. Technically, if they were anybody's, they were mine. So, if only I could get them back, we'd be set to go.

I remember going out into the rain to find Elías and Sol to tell them this. I was drenched through and the wind was so strong it was hurling roof tiles into the street and beating me against walls, but I didn't care. Potentially, we had arms! Of course, the others were delighted: all we needed now was a new sponsor. The logical choice, once the Cubans abandoned us, was to turn to the Chinese.

Back in January 1966, during the Tricontinental conference, I had been in daily contact with the Chinese delegation and also with the embassy staff. During my stay in Havana, because of my privileged position with Fidel, Chinese embassy people had stayed very friendly with me. One of them was a cousin of the sage Wai Kit, my mentor from Algiers. I felt that I knew him well enough to pose our problem to him and see if his masters would give us at least our airfares to China and Algeria.

I went into the embassy on a Wednesday and asked for this help. By Friday of the same week, I had two tickets in my hand from Havana to Paris via Moscow. In Paris, the Chinese embassy would give us ongoing tickets to Beijing, and in Beijing we would be given our flights to Algiers.

The relief was enormous. Since I left my cushy job in the bank long ago, the party had been my protective house. Party officials were as dependant on a fixed salary as any clerk or minor civil servant anywhere in the world. I had never had to earn the money to pay my expenses or buy my flights. I had never had to worry about how to pay for my plans. My entire adult life had been covered by a very modest but very stable expense account. When I was expelled from the PCV in January 1967, the impact of that expulsion in financial and logistic terms had been nil. I was under the full protection of the Cubans. Whatever I wanted or needed, the Cuban government paid for. I was Fidel's protégé, his favoured advisor. In return for my services rendered to the Cuban Revolution, the Cuban treasury picked up my tab.

But in the summer of 1967, when Elías, Sol and I broke away with our splinter group of revolutionaries, there was no one behind us: no one at all. We had no sponsor and no protector. There was no one to pull strings, no one to pay our bills, no one, more seriously, to provide us with intelligence, issue documents, give us passports and visas, arms and boats and ammunition. In our group, we were sixteen. Sixteen able-bodied people can each get a job and earn enough to pay their own costs, so if push came to shove, we could eat. OK, after meeting with the Chinese, we could get them to buy us two air tickets, but that was still only a fraction of what we needed. And what we could not do in the foreseeable future was earn enough to finance a revolution.

We needed weapons, and we had weapons in Algeria, but we also needed a big boat to transport them to Venezuela. If we were really to succeed, what we needed was a new protector.

One of the main purposes of our trip to China, apart from asking for the means to buy the boat, was to find in the Chinese such a protector. The deal was that we would go to Beijing and explain in person exactly what we were doing and what we wanted and why. To this end, we were given two tickets to China. The two envoys chosen from our group were Sol Ortega and me.

Sol was chosen because he was the most representative of the group. He had been a guerrilla fighter since the start of the troubles in Venezuela. He was also educated and articulate (he was a geologist who had never once practised his profession because instead he had dedicated himself to war). I was chosen because I was an intellectual and, to some extent, a polyglot – I spoke French, Italian and German; and I had travelled and made a name for myself in serious left-wing circles. So I had some solid credentials.

Sol and I stopped over in Moscow where we had a meeting set up with some students. The Soviet Union had given a great many scholarships to Latin American communists in Moscow. They were very generous with them and paid for fares and accommodation, university fees, books – the entire package. My brother José was in his third year of geology at the Lomonosov University on just such a scholarship, and was one of the student leaders there in Moscow. By chance, José was on a field trip in the Urals at the time we passed through, so we didn't get to see him. Despite his absence, he had rallied a great deal of support for us on the campus and our meeting was well attended. One of the students – a brilliant young mathematician called Miguel (Miguelito) – was so enthusiastic that he dropped his studies, joined our group and came with us to Paris.

In Paris we had been told to present ourselves at the avenue Victor Cresson at the consulate of the People's Republic of China and to ask to see a Mr Zhang. Because I was an honorary Parisian, Miguelito and Sol left it to me to guide them to the address in Issy-les-Moulineaux on time. I knew from Havana that the Chinese were obsessive about punctuality, so we left our *pension* with at least half an hour in hand. Having been topographically challenged for my entire life, I managed to get us lost. It was only thanks to a last-minute taxi that we got there in time. Mr Zhang gave us two tickets to Beijing with a departure date five days away.

The $800 dollars each we had been given in Cuba was running very low, so even the cheapest hotel was out of the question. I tracked down some friends from my student days and found that my having been expelled from the PCV had altered several of those friendships. In some quarters, I was about as welcome as a leper. Fortunately, there were others who welcomed me with open arms. We ended up boarding and lodging with two of them, and they also offered to look after Miguelito while Sol and I went to China. The five mornings of our five days in Paris, from 9 a.m. to 12 a.m., were spent in the Kafkaesque pursuit of our Chinese visas.

We arrived in Beijing (which in those days we called Peking) in the late summer of 1967, bang in the middle of the Cultural Revolution. I had been warned that the Chinese would be very cagey. The inscrutability of the Chinese is an old cliché, but one I was told to expect at every turn. We were braced to expect that no one would say what they thought or befriend us because, apart from the reticence of their national character, they were all shit scared about being reported for political incorrectness.

Therefore, I was doubly surprised when the man who met our flight told me in perfect French and as an opening gambit, 'Welcome, comrades. Alas, you have arrived in a moment of anarchy. There is only anarchy here: nothing else! China is in chaos. Let us see what comes of your mission; but I can offer you no hope at all.'

PART 6

CHAPTER XXXXV

Next to his stripped-down essentials, in the luggage of every revolutionary there is always a vast supply of mindless optimism.
Without it, we would all give up. After we were dropped off at
our hostel, I translated the Chinaman's words for Sol and then
together we extracted positive signals from our meeter and
greeter's gloomy prognosis and our presence there in Beijing. On
the way in from the airport, our Chinaman had slumped into a
morose silence, so we decided that he was probably suffering from
a clinical depression. Since our mission had consisted of getting to
China and then persuading the Chinese to buy us a boat, the fact
that we were already in Beijing meant that we had already been
50 per cent successful.

As Sol pointed out: 'They wouldn't have flown us here if they
weren't interested. We are not part of their chaos. If we play our
cards right, between us we will persuade them to help us again.
The main thing is to make sure that they see us.'

On that point, we need not have feared. We were given an
audience the very next day. In fact, we were given an entire programme. Everything was explained to us in words of one syllable.
The purpose of our daily programme was for us to explain to a
panel of Chinese assessors exactly what we wanted and what we
needed. The assessors, in turn, would then say what they thought
of our plan and a decision would be made for or against it at the
end of these sessions.

Day one began with a wake-up call at 5 a.m. At 6 a.m. we were invited to spend two hours in the press room to keep abreast of both Chinese and world news. At precisely 8 a.m., we went into session with the Chinese assessors. This lasted until 12 noon. Between midday and 1 p.m. there was a break for lunch. At exactly 1 p.m., the session reconvened and lasted until 6 p.m. By that time, both Sol and I were wrecked. Our hosts informed us that our fatigue had been anticipated. From 6 p.m. until 9 p.m. we could relax and be entertained. This took the form of an interminable caterwauling opera illustrating key moments in the People's Revolution. At 10 p.m., we were delivered back to our rooms with strict instructions to be in the press room on the dot of six the following morning.

I collapsed into bed and was too tired to sleep properly. Day two was identical to day one, with the possible exception of the opera, which may, or may not, have been a different one. Day three was the same. And so it went on at a gruelling pace for twenty-two days without a break. It was a world of rigid control focused absolutely on the Chinese belief in the three great sources of power: the Front, the Party and the People.

Day by day in our sessions, I, 'comlade Oswado', and 'comlade Sol', explained our aims. Our Chinese jurors were all low-ranking officials but each of them came into the bare concrete room we worked in and sat at the huge bare table, notebook in hand, armed with a grave, unsmiling expression and a million questions as though they were celestial beings, hanging judges or the Spanish Inquisition reincarnated. Whatever we said, the Chinese made some objections.

Neither Sol nor I had twenty-two days' worth of requests. What we wanted fitted into one sentence: we wanted money to buy a boat. The longer version was that we were asking for the money to buy a boat so that we could take the arms from Algiers and our group to Venezuela to continue the revolution there. We could expand this to add that we would be loyal to them, the Chinese, who were the only party in the world who had continued being revolutionary. The rest was all background to the armed struggle in Latin America and in Venezuela in particular and our position within that struggle. There was my Algerian story and there was our more recent Cuban story, but there wasn't much else to tell. Of course, since the sessions were scheduled, we continued to fill in our turns to talk, but, as I said, the Chinese panel kept swatting us down with their objections.

In our 'show and tell' sessions, we got to go first, but we didn't even get to tell our own story. The panel showed from day one that there was nothing we could tell them that they didn't already know. They went over the history of the Venezuelan Communist Party and every one of its members. Their knowledge was incredible. They said things like, 'Since 1936, the PCV has been opportunist because it has confused political struggle with the press. Its main desire has been to have a newspaper: an organ of speech. In 1939 so and so, in his speech on 16 August in Caracas, underlined this opportunism when he said . . .'

And they could quote him. Methodically, they sifted through the entire history of the PCV right down to the last man and the last detail. And they knew the history of each of our political parties: when they were founded, who by, how many members each had, and what they were doing. They talked as though they were reading out endless lists in which each name was an accusation, and each date and event yet another mistake in a long list of grievances.

'In 1936, the PRP was founded. In 1936 Jóvito Villalba founded the Federation of Venezuelan Students, plus Rómolo Betancourt founded ORVE. In 1941, AD was founded. In 158, COPEI began. The MIR was founded in 1960, the FDP began in 1962. Each of these parties . . .'

They listed founders and founder members, schisms and publications. They knew the complete history of the CTV, our biggest trades union, and, I tell you, they knew how many cups of coffee every delegate drank, who was missing a button, and who went to bed with whom. From memory and without notes they quoted Sol to Sol and me to me. They knew the names of my brothers and sisters; and they knew more about what they were doing than I did. For instance, my older sister, Irma, was in Bologna, but I only learnt from them that she was connected to the Istituto Frantz Fanon.

Our Chinese assessors knew every speech I had made and the

date and place where I had made it. They knew every pamphlet I had written. And they knew the names of every girl I had fucked (which was more than I did); and they knew every meeting I had attended.

My memory is good, but theirs were inhuman. They were like walking computers. They knew the politics and the history, the geography and the economics of Venezuela and they knew them better than we did. They knew every mound and stream of Falcón where so much of the fighting in the armed struggle had been. They knew the terrain (our terrain) in the way that Fidel had known his terrain in the Sierra.

Arduous and frustrating as those sessions were, it got so that we did not want them to end because no sooner had they finished for the day than it was time for the rest and relaxation Chinese-style. Sol and I were frog-marched by an armed escort to the opera. There followed three hours of inhuman screeching and banner-waving hysteria. Verdi, Puccini, Mozart and Bellini must have squirmed in their graves as Sol and I were visually and verbally abused on a nightly basis for twenty-two days.

And at 6 a.m. every morning we were in the press room again, being bombarded with yet more facts and figures as we were updated on Bolivia, East Timor, Moscow, Maputo, Marseilles and Madagascar, and what seemed like every city, village, islet and grain of sand in between. Reeling from this news battery, we then sat through the day's sessions and the Chinese appraisal of our national incompetence.

Whenever either of us managed to get a word in edgeways, we would remind the panel that we were only there to ask them for a boat.

As a counterpoint to our own lack of action, back in America (with a capital 'A', the *Patria Grande* that Che dreamt of), during that summer of 1967, tragic events were taking place and we were drip-fed updates of them during our dawn sessions in the news room. After Che's disastrous venture in the Congo (Zaire), he had set off to Bolivia with a small group of Cuban revolutionaries on a venture which he hoped would kindle the masses into revolution. While we struggled with our Chinese interrogation, he was struggling through the Bolivian jungle in what I imagined to be similar circumstances to the ones I had experienced in the east of Venezuela with Sol Ortega when I first joined the guerrilla from Merde. The Bolivian Communist Party had flatly refused to cooperate with him in any way. Thus, far from heroically leading a revolutionary army, el Che was trudging through mud with a group of twenty men and women in a hostile terrain while 2,000 Bolivian soldiers trained by the US Rangers and the CIA tracked them down.

My close friend, Regis Debray, had been out there with him. Regis was a French citizen and an accredited journalist, but indiscriminately aimed bullets don't recognise press passes, so day by day I read the news fearing to see an announcement of Regis's death. Stories began to come out of Bolivia at the end of April that year that Regis Debray had been arrested together with Ciro Bustos (a painter and reluctant revolutionary whom Tania, a heroine of the Cuban Revolution, had recruited in Buenos Aires as part of an emergency reinforcement). Being a painter was not a great qualification for the harrowing march Che had put him on, but when Ciro was caught, his artistic skills enabled him to draw an exact likeness of each of the other fugitives from justice. It was confirmed that Ciro and Regis were in prison in Bolivia and awaiting trial. All through the summer there was talk of Regis, who had not helped the police and the CIA, getting the death sentence. Regis was really young – twenty-six – and I felt responsible for having got him into the whole revolutionary thing in Latin America because ... well, because I *had*, since the day he had arrived in Caracas as a greenhorn and had gone straight to me.

On day one of our visit to Beijing, Sol and I were asked what we would like to eat during our visit to the People's Republic. There were two choices: Chinese or European. Sol, with his innate diplomacy, chose Chinese. I, with the never-ending soap opera of my digestive problems, chose European. Our food in China was a twofold mystery. The Chinese food was horrendous. You might (as we did) imagine trays of gorgeous little nibbly things, gourmet finger-foods and all those dishes beloved of Chinese restaurants the world over, but there was none of that. For twenty-two days,

Sol (and the panel) were served variations on the theme of chicken's feet. These were cooked and served in ways so unpalatable that Sol used to beg me for bites of my meagre European sandwiches. Because for 'European' read 'sandwich'. These were filled with fat, gristly ham or dry, tasteless cheese. What passed for bread was two thin slices of something that looked and tasted like cotton wool.

The only time during our entire visit when we saw a decent meal being served was when we were wheeled out to a lunch for a foreign delegation as token Latin Americans to illustrate the open-mindedness of our hosts. We shook hands with a nameless horde of Korean dignitaries while we eyed greedily a dazzling array of local delicacies heaped on a long and elegant dining table behind the Korean guests. It was about two weeks into our Chinese torture and Sol and I were both ravenous (although poor Sol, who has a much bigger appetite than I do, was really suffering on his share of my ration). There were glazed suckling pigs, baked river perch, lobsters, crabs, shiny roast ducks, basins of rice, and stacks of steaming bamboo baskets of what we imagined were dim sum.

After the brief introductions in Chinese and a lot of hand shaking and saluting and nodding and smiling, Sol and I were ushered (that is, pulled reluctantly) away. So when I say we 'saw' decent food, that was literally it. On the way out of the banqueting suite, I whispered to Sol that I wished, at least, we could be treated like dogs and be given the leftovers to chew on later.

Sol murmured back, 'They eat dogs here, you know. They put puppies in a sack and beat them against a wall and then boil them up with bean sprouts. I have heard that it is quite a delicacy.'

I can understand that if your culture contains a genius such as Confucius, it makes sense to quote him as much and as often as possible. And if your country has evolved politically, economically and socially through the strength and genius of a single leader such as Chairman Mao, then his words and sayings might become a crucial guideline. I had seen how full of himself Fidel was with a relatively small island to rule and a relatively small population to entrance. In China, the egotism of its leader had increased in direct proportion to the vast expanse of its territory and the size of its population.

That meant we were constantly smothered in sayings. Having spent time there, I quite understood how everyone could quote Mao's *Little Red Book* off by heart. After twenty-days days, I probably could have done so too. Since everything was couched in a saying, a proverb or a cliché, it came as no surprise that our interrogation should end with one.

The spokesman of the panel raised his hands and stood up. He bowed his head to us and then said, 'Comlade Oswado Baweto and Comlade Sol Otega, all good things must come to an end. You have discussed your case very seriously with us and we thank you. There has been a reunion inside the competent organ of the Communist Party of the People's Republic of China and also with the Communist Party of the People's Republic of China and our decision is the following.'

Sol and I waited with bated breath as visions arose of a small boat bobbing across the Atlantic en route to Venezuela with an Algerian flag waving in the wind and a hold stuffed full of olive oil.

'You and your group are bandits, militarists and opportunists and your request for assistance from the People's Republic of China has been denied.'

I realised this was our last hope. Although I really didn't like them at that moment, we still needed them, so I said very humbly, 'I quite agree with you, Comrades, but perhaps you could tell us on what basis you have come to this conclusion. You and the spokesman for your national party are two people speaking for two billion. I ask for one further session to discuss your decision.'

When this request was denied, I said, 'It is true we are bandits, but Mao Tse-tung was also a bandit when he began your revolution. And it is true we are militarists, but a revolution is never made by the army, it is made by the party and the people. And it is true we are opportunists: we came here for your help to get a boat, which is the only thing we are asking of you, so that we can liberate our country. Is your decision truly the choice of two billion people?'

The Chinese panel stood up, 'It has been a pleasure. Goodbye.

We will not talk again unless you agree to come to China with your entire group to be re-educated in the proper manner. We will pay for you. The process will take two years. Your ideas are wrong. A pleasure! Good-day.'

Next day we were on a plane to Algeria, eating our little plastic in-flight meals with the sort of relish usually reserved for the creations of great chefs.

CHAPTER XXXXVI

Unlike our visit to China, our visit to Algeria was a success. The day after we arrived in Algiers, I asked for an appointment. I got it the next day, and was treated with respect. When I asked for my arms back, the competent government official said, 'We have no problem giving you the arms, but you will have to work out how to take them away.'

How exactly was I going to do that? I went to the bookshop I used to frequent when I lived in the city to look for some inspiration. After several hours of zero inspiration, I ended up buying a secondhand paperback of *For Whom the Bell Tolls.* Then I linked up with Sol and took him to the café where I used to meet up with Wai Kit. When I told Sol that it was there that my Chinese infatuation had begun, he choked on his coffee and insisted we leave. I looked up a woman I had been flirting with in 1965 and found that life was not treating her very well. When I left for Prague, there had been a definite spark and an unconsumed flame between us. After a lot of mysterious arrangements on her part, we managed to forget our mutual woes for a few hours in my hotel room. After she left, I went through the by now familiar ritual of assessing my losses.

I cannot stress how decisive the year 1967 was for me. It was the year when I became an individual and a man alone. I had no party and no protector: I had nothing and nobody. I had no one to rely on and no one I had to contact. All I had was my life's mission; and if I was to succeed, I had to come up with something.

For a couple of days, Sol and I strolled around Algiers and sat under palms and racked our brains, but we couldn't come up with a solution. On his own, I knew that he would not be able to help. I am not saying that Sol wasn't a capable man, because he was. He was inventive but not enough to come up with a plan from scratch. Sol was a team worker. We all were, really. We were all used to having a comrade or a friend to do things with. *What* we did was worked out by a team; *how* we did it was approved by a committee. Within the party, the support was always there – you got used to never really having to rely on yourself. So there we were in North Africa, alone, but institutionalised.

It was so tiring to remember the fourteen men who were waiting for us in Havana, plus Miguelito from Moscow who was still billeted in Paris. They were counting on us. They had given their loyalty and trust to us and they were offering us their lives. It was a depressing time for a number of reasons, and each one hammered home that we were on our own. In September 1967 Regis Debray was sentenced to thirty years in prison for his part in Che's Bolivian adventure. Tania and her splinter group of Che's guerrilla fighters had been ambushed and killed. Meanwhile, Che himself was running for his life with a tiny group of fighters and nothing short of a miracle could save him. I alternated between a sense of guilt towards my own waiting group, and immersing myself in the pages of *For Whom the Bell Tolls* with all its camaraderie and generosity of spirit.

It was by thinking of such solidarity that I recalled how when I lived in France we used to help people in Paris and Algeria and in Venezuela. We used to empty our half-empty pockets for them out of revolutionary solidarity to help them out of a fix. Why not ask them to help us now, I thought. We are revolutionaries – we need help.

I told Sol, 'I have a plan: you go back to Cuba, and I will go to France and get what we need.'

I took a night ferry from Algiers on 8 October and arrived in Marseilles the next day. I stayed in a cheap *pension* and got up early the next day to drink my coffee and buy a newspaper. The photograph of Ernesto Che Guevara's half-naked corpse was on every front page.

I sat in a smoky bar and drank pastis and grieved. I recalled our talks and his writings and all the fine things and some of the stupid ones he had done. After everything he had learnt and taught, his campaign in Bolivia had not met his own basic criteria for conducting a guerrilla war. There had been a possibility of his going to Venezuela instead of Bolivia and I wished that it had been so. He had a boyish grin and a sense of humour that was as quick as a gunshot. After a couple more drinks, my shock turned to anger. Why *had* he gone to Boliva and got himself killed by the Bolivian army?

After another pastis and a little flirt with the waitress who had a dangerous smile and an alluring chip in her front teeth, I felt able to leave. The revolutionary fabric was getting threadbare: el Che was dead and Regis Debray was in prison for thirty years. Fidel had dumped us, the Chinese had snubbed us, and the party had shat on my head.

I sat on the train from Marseilles to Paris and mused on Che's revolutionary 'bible'. He had written a manual for the likes of us.

We consider that the Cuban Revolution contributed three fundamental lessons to the conduct of revolutionary movements in America. They are:

1. Popular forces can win a war against the army.
2. It is not necessary to wait until all conditions for making revolution exist; the insurrection can create them.
3. In underdeveloped America the countryside is the basic area for armed fighting.

The master was dead. Now it was up to me, his apprentice, to carry his torch. I had arrived in France full of fervour, which I more or less regained on that train ride. I went round France and Italy with my begging bowl. My sister, Irma, was in Bologna at, as I had learnt, the Istituto Frantz Fanon, so I called her up and asked her, and them, to lend a hand. Together, we contacted everyone we could think of who might help, everyone I had studied with and everyone I had worked with. I came straight to the point.

'This is our situation: we are a group of revolutionaries. We need arms. Can you help us?'

The response was immediate. They said yes. Then we needed passports. Within one week we were given two dozen passports, all of which were either French or Italian and all of which were valid. We had only seventeen people in our group, so twenty-four passports was an overkill – but we had them. And we also got offers to fund a boat, to buy more arms, and to fully equip ourselves. It was fantastic!

I went back to Cuba and told my divisionist comrades the good news. We began to plan how to return to Venezuela. I could say how to return *home*, but one of our group, Miguelito, was a Canary Islander and Pierre Goldman was a French Jew. Pierre was our Foreign Legion, our one-man International Brigade. His not very original codename was el Francés. Everyone was so happy. We felt like gods.

Elías was still well connected in Cuba. His fall from grace had been less hard than mine and he still had friends. Among these friends was a pair of identical twins (and I mean *identical*) called Tony and Patrizio de Laguarda. Under Batista, they had been at the apex of high society. They had been playboy racing yachtsmen, both of them fabulously rich. After the Revolution, Fidel had met them at some regatta, made friends with them and made them revolutionaries. The Laguarda twins were like peacocks. Young and handsome, athletic and virile; and nobody could tell them apart – not even their women!

Miguelito flew to Havana to join us and we had a party to celebrate. With our new supporters in France and Italy, it seemed simpler to forget the Algerian arms and re-equip ourselves locally, thus avoiding the logistic nightmare of taking a boat across the entire Atlantic Ocean. We didn't need a ship to take seventeen men across the Caribbean; what we really needed were arms and a small boat.

Elías asked the Laguarda twins to help us out. He took the precaution of asking them both together, because one at a time there was no guarantee which one you had spoken to.

They said, 'No problem. We will find you arms, but you have to find a way to move them out of Cuba.'

They fixed us up with a captain who was doing some wheeling and dealing; the next thing we knew, we had an arsenal of first-class weapons stashed under our beds. The next step was how to move them. We had been told that under no circumstances could we set out from Cuba and go directly to Venezuela. We had to go via Europe. Since there were seventeen of us and since we were taking an individualistic route, we decided that each man would fly to Prague as a tourist, fly on to Paris, gather in a safe house in Bologna and then embark in Marseilles and then set sail, again as tourists, for Trinidad. At its nearest point, the island of Trinidad is only twenty-two kilometres from the east coast of Venezuela. From Trinidad, we would charter a boat in Port of Spain and sail to our destiny.

When I say we decided, I should add that we operated as a military unit under the supreme command of Sol Ortega. I shall say more about this leadership a little later. For now, bear with me; and remember that Latin America is the home of magic realism with its weird and wonderful distortions of logic.

There was a guy from Guatemala there in Havana who was famous for making caletas (a caleta is a box or case with a hidden compartment). Don't ask me why, but Guatemalans were specialists in making them, and the one in Havana (who was supposed to be the best) was a friend of a friend of mine. My friend arranged a dinner at his place for me to meet the master case-maker. I arrived early because I was nervous. That was something that never went away. I know it's silly to be on the one hand an arms smuggler and a guerrilla fighter and a bank robber (which I have yet to relate), while on the other hand remaining the sort of person who breaks into a cold sweat at the thought of meeting criminals and breaking the law.

Lying and cheating
Deserves a beating

The products of my strict and proper upbringing were inescapable. Not that I haven't lied and cheated, defrauded, smuggled and stolen many many times, it is just that I have never done so easily. So I got there early and started drinking rum and Virgin Coke with my friend and his wife – who was obviously in on the forthcoming meeting because she kept up a lively patter about caletas and arms smuggling, interspersed with more frivolous topics. A clock over a framed photo of Fidel was ticking with a nagging insistence. Celia Cruz was giving it her all over the radio, but the clock was louder than her voice and the orchestra behind her.

My friend lived in Alamar, a suburb of Havana that looks like a Czech housing estate of drab concrete blocks transposed to the tropics. The sound of other radios playing and of dozens of babies crying came in from all sides: through the walls, the floor, the ceiling and from out on the street. Meanwhile, the clock kept ticking, and I kept sweating anxiously in the anticipation of doing a deal with the case-master, and my friend's wife kept up her running commentary of life and its hidden compartments, but the Guatemalan case-master didn't show.

Quite late, we ended up eating supper on our own. The good news of the evening was the wife who never stopped talking was a great cook. The bad news was that I left that house, full and satisfied with one of the best carne desmechadas I have ever eaten, but back to square one in the arms smuggling department. Comandante Sol Ortega would not be amused.

A ship cannot go to sea without a captain, and in all matters merchant or military, there must be a chain of command, and someone must be at the head of that chain. There were seventeen men in our group, so we were short on troops, but we were over-blessed with leaders. There was Elías and there was Sol Ortega and both of them were tried and tested commanders. Then there was el Negro Manolito, whose capacity on the field of battle had also been proven; and then, less tried and less tested, but still with some experience, there was me. Given the competition higher up, el Negro and I stepped out of the running for the military command of our new group. I was the strategist: that was my role. In the presence of Elías, it would have been absurd for me to have even considered being the overall commander. (You have to remember that we were seventeen planning shortly to become several hundred.) When we triumphed, my powers of leadership, for what they were worth, would be far more useful leading our future government. I was in the endeavour for its result and not for my own personal glory. Having been demoted from commander of my own group of twenty-two trainees to humble foot soldier within the veterans' group, I was OK accepting orders from the others. That was part of the package: we became a military unit and we lived by military rules.

It came down to a power struggle between Elías and Sol. Alas for the outcome of our expeditionary force, Elías didn't have a petty bone in his body. He could take orders from Sol, but Sol had a few problems taking orders from Elías. The logical choice was Elías because he had been in charge of all the rural veterans, and since our divisionist group was born at Punto Zero, twelve of us were under his command anyway. Sol, however, saw it differently.

He said, 'It's like this: I used to be in the Rurals and that means that I used to be under Elías's command. But I'd been pulled out of that group by the time you guys went to Punto Zero. Fidel was going to send me separately, you know, with my own unit and a Cuban back-up. Believe me, I was as fucked as you lot when the MIRistas got routed and Manuel Hill got captured in Venezuela. OK, Manuel wasn't carrying a Cuban passport, but he was carrying a Cuban accent and he admitted to being Cuban and the entire training programme got smothered in shit! Whatever. What counts is that I am not, *automatically or technically*, inferior to Elías in rank within this group.'

El Negro and I tried a lot of oil-on-troubled-waters tactics and unruffling of feathers and bowing to pride, but it was no good. Sol wanted to be the leader. Since Elías was OK with that, and Sol also had a huge reputation as a warrior and guerrilla leader, he became our commanding officer.

This is to explain how we had a virus in our system even before our mission began. Some of the routes we took were unnecessarily circuitous, and some of the precautions we took were plain stupid, and some of the things we didn't do, and precautions we didn't take, were just plain wrong. But we suggested and our CO decided. Week by week, as we suggested, Sol rejected, while his head swelled up with power. Often, that 'we' meant I or el Negro, because we were, after all, the thinkers; or it meant Elías, who was the tactical, practical expert and also the king of common sense.

Now you have the picture, so when you think: But how absurd! Why did you do that instead of this? Or why did you go here instead of there? – suffice it to say that many (not to say most) of our army of seventeen would have welcomed Logic as a new recruit in our unit, and for Common Sense to have joined us too.

The big question remained: how could we transport our small arsenal of weapons to Venezuela from Cuba on our indirect route? My contribution was that we make our own caletas.

CHAPTER XXXXVII

Our group of seventeen divided up; and one by one and in twos and threes we flew to Prague at the beginning of November 1967. To test the route, the first to go would travel empty-handed. Our travel was sponsored by our own French-Italian Bank (that is, by our friends in France and Italy). The first to go was Constantino. He was the ace pilot of the Cuban air force. He was only eighteen, but pilots are old by the time they are twenty-four. Constantino was a Venezuelan of Canary Island origin. If he arrived safely and unsearched, he was to signal this back.

Then Tumuza and Elías, el Negro, then me, and then the others would follow at the rate of two or three a day, every day. In Prague, we were to collect our bags (which were our DIY caletas stuffed with the contraband arms) and proceed to Paris and then to our rendezvous in a safe house in Bologna.

Each of us was in high spirits when we left. I can still remember the song (by Tonia la Negra) I was singing as I boarded the plane. My bag was cleverly packed with an M23, which was pretty light, and a machine gun and three hand-guns plus a pistol I had in my jacket pocket as hand luggage. It was 1968, the days before X-ray machines and metal detectors came into use in airports. So getting through immigration and customs either end was just a matter of not looking suspicious and not having the bad luck of the random search.

As the plane was about to land in Prague, I went through my

usual 'Oh my God! Jesus Christ!' nerves, but my adrenaline levelled out before we disembarked and immigration was a piece of cake. I went through to the luggage hall and collected my two big bags from the carousel. I was being met by a philosopher friend of mine from 1965 and a whole group of the people I had worked with while I was there. As we embraced, one after the other, with big hugs, I saw my big fat bags moving round towards me on the conveyor belt. I left our emotional reunion to collect my luggage. My former colleagues went with me to the carousel.

I grabbed my first outsized bag with a feeling of elation. But from the moment I lifted it off the belt I knew that something was wrong. I forced myself not to look around me, not to make eye-contact with any of the soldiers and guards who were in the hall. My knees felt week and my head was spinning, but I had to stay calm and collect my second caleta. I spotted it and dragged it off the moving belt. I noticed the same thing and I felt so sick it was all I could do not to vomit my whisky and peanuts.

'What is it? What's the matter?' my friends asked.

'You look as if you've seen a ghost. What's up?'

I had no choice but to laugh it off. The baggage hall was full of soldiers, customs officials and guards. The philosopher offered to help me with one of the bags. Sol had given strict instructions not to do that: not to let anyone touch the caletas on pain of death. What the hell! What did it matter now?

I couldn't do anything there at the airport, but as soon as I reached my hostel I opened both the bags and confirmed what I already knew: they were empty.

I had personally checked them in in Havana, and they had been full. Yet when I picked them off the carousel in Prague, they were empty. Why? What the hell was that about? I racked my brains to work out who had done it. Who had stolen my share of the guns? Was it the Cubans or the Czechs or had an airport thief got lucky? Why did they leave me the cases? Had I lost the arms through my own negligence? When did it happen? Why hadn't I been arrested? Was I going to be arrested there in Prague? Why hadn't I been arrested already? Were the authorities waiting for me to make contact in the city so they could arrest the whole gang? Where did that leave my friends: the poor buggers who had come to greet me at the airport?

I didn't sleep that night and I didn't eat. The more I thought about it, the more of a mystery it became. And the more I thought about it, the more implications I saw and the more dangerous the whole scenario became. The worst thing of all was that I had been carrying about 10 per cent of our weapons: 10 per cent of our chances! The most frustrating part of it was that there was absolutely nothing I could do. You can't go to the police and say, 'Excuse me, I am an international arms smuggler and some bastard has just stolen my shipment of arms.'

It was a disaster. It was dangerous; and it was so *unfair*!

I remembered an incident from my boyhood in the Andes, when I was living with my sister Graciela and her schoolmaster husband, Guillermo, in Mendoza Fría. As I've told you, I was at war with Guillermo: I despised him and he hated me, and it was all very open. Graciela, rightly or wrongly, always sided with me; together we made his life hell. When I did things that I should have been punished for – like spilling ink on Guillermo's papers, getting home late, or not doing my homework – my sister sometimes went as far as to lie to cover me. She was my ally and I trusted her implicitly.

Then, one day, Guillermo lost an important form from the educational board, and he turned the house upside down in a rage trying to find it. He kept saying that he had put it in a safe place. He was not accusing me of touching it. He just wanted us both to help him locate it. Graciela, who had her marital ups and downs, was all lovey-dovey with him that day, and she was searching diligently with him. She was bending to look under his desk, when she stood up suddenly and announced, apropos of nothing, 'Oswaldo had it. He has probably hidden it.'

Then she turned to me and said, 'You had better not throw it away, you know, because it is important.'

In the same instant, Guillermo delivered to me a tremendous cuff round the head which clocked straight into my left ear. Before he could box my other ear, I ducked and ran out of the house. I ran up the steep, cobbled street outside, past the church and the little square, past the last of the houses and onto the Camino Real flanked by sugarcane fields and patches of coffee and pink-tasselled grass. When I was exhausted by running and my heart felt compressed from the mixture of anger and hurt, I threw myself onto a patch of soft grass and pondered the injustice.

My ear had swollen up like a cauliflower and my head throbbed. What Graciela had done was below the belt. It was so unfair! And it had been so sudden that it took me completely by surprise. I was so upset that if there hadn't been *quite* so many insects and if it hadn't been *quite* so dark, and if I hadn't been *quite* so afraid of the bogeyman, I would have stayed out all night just to spite her. As it was, it was days before I could bring myself to speak to her. When I did, there was only one thing I wanted to say: 'Why did you do that? It was so unfair!'

She said, 'Life is unfair, Oswaldo. You are born and then you die: so try and fit in something valuable in between.'

I boarded a plane for Paris the next morning without anyone stopping me at the airport. In Paris, I was supposed to go straight to the Gare du Nord and take the slow train to Milan. On arrival in Italy, my orders were to report to Elías and deliver my two bags of weapons to him and the others.

For the whole journey, I kept remembering my sister's prophetic words. They were my life summed up in two lines. I had lost the weapons. What more of a bitch could life be than that? I had tried to fit something valuable in during the years I had had, but now I was going to die. In the Guerrilla, you got shot for a lot less than 'losing' a shipment of arms. I tried to look at it from the point of view of our group and I knew that they would never believe me. How can anyone just *lose* two big bags of weapons?

I crossed the Alps with lead in my veins. I thought of Valera and Mérida, I thought of my friends scattered all around the world like broadcast seeds, I thought of Ramín, the son I hardly knew, who was living somewhere in Persia and whom I would now never see again. I thought of Vida and the troubled graph of our love, I thought of Beatriz Rivera, and Charachu and a litany of other girls I had liked or loved and left. I thought of my brothers and sisters, my mother and father; and of all the things I could have done if only I were not going to die on arrival in Milan.

I was on the slow train, but it didn't feel slow enough. As soon as I reached Milan central station, I could walk as slowly as I liked through its monumental Fascist architecture, and I could dawdle over the hundreds of steps, but this time around, Chance had played me a very dirty trick and there was no way out of the death sentence that awaited me at the end of it. In the tram en route to our safe house, I wondered if I would be given a last request. That tended to be something they did in the movies – in real life, someone just shot you through the head. Well, I told myself, it depended on who did the shooting. If it was Elías or el Negro, since we were such good friends, surely they would grant a last favour.

As the tram stopped and started along the Naviglio Grande, I wondered whether the old army joke had ever worked. The one where a condemned prisoner stands up against a wall in front of a firing squad and an officer asks him, 'Do you have any last request?' And the prisoner says, 'Yes. When you say, "Ready. Take aim. Fire!" could you leave a space between "Take aim" and "Fire!"'

'What sort of space?'

'About twenty years?'

By the time I got to the apartment building in Milan where we were supposed to meet up, the lead in my blood had gathered in my feet so that I climbed the stairs like an old man. I thought that my one and only hope was to come straight out with it and own up right away and throw myself on their mercy. But even so, I didn't think that they'd believe me.

Elías answered the door. He was sick with conjunctivitis and his eyes looked terribly swollen and red. My heart sank as I lost my last shred of hope. Elías in a bad mood is no laughing matter. I started talking as soon as I crossed the threshold and words tumbled out of my mouth. I know I started off with, 'There's something I've got to tell you.'

Then I tried to tell it all at once: explanations, excuses, events and the whole story. Elías held his hand up as though to break a crazy horse.

'Whoa! Before you go any further, compadre, don't tell us about the arms. We know what you're going to say. The same shit happened to all of us!'

He laughed and then the others laughed, while I stood and stared in disbelief.

'Everyone left with their bags full and arrived without a single weapon. We haven't got one gun left between us ... Nothing! Not even one!'

At which point I produced the Browning pistol I had been carrying in my jacket since Havana and suddenly I not only felt incredibly proud, I had also turned into a hero. That Browning was our only gun and I was the only one out of all of us who had run the risk of carrying one as hand luggage.

The seventeen of us were travelling on false passports. Not all of us stayed in Italy, but we were all needing places to stay where the police wouldn't look at us too closely. M, an Italian we met, gave us a safe house in the historic centre of Bologna. Meanwhile, thanks to the funds that had been donated to us by our French and Italian sponsors, it wasn't hard to find some more arms – you could virtually buy hand-guns on the market. The bigger arms were more difficult and the going was slow. While we sorted this out, our main problem was keeping a low profile. That was partly because we were Venezuelans and Venezuelans have a tendency to be loud. And it was partly because some of our group were party animals and others, including Elías (and myself, though with less success), were rampant womanisers. Even lunch in a café could seem like a small riot when we got together.

Vida had followed her own path since leaving the Habana hotel and, luckily, she was in Paris in 1968 and she seemed to welcome a peripheral involvement with our group. It was she who found most of our rooms for us and who kept a watchful eye on the more boisterous members of the group while Sol and I did the wheeling and dealing to re-equip us.

One night in the run-up to Christmas Vida arrived late at my hotel in Paris. She was very concerned,

'Come quickly, Oswaldo, you have to talk to Albertico. He's in the bar by his hotel and he's drunk and he's telling everyone that he's in a military unit which is going to invade Venezuela.'

Between us, we got him back to his room, and I stayed with him that night. In the morning, he woke up with a terrible hangover and a boyish grin, wondering what the hell I was doing in his room. I explained to him gently, but firmly, that he couldn't talk to anyone.

'It's a secret, Albertico. You have to say you are a kid who studied at the high school in Tenerife and that now you are going to Venezuela to study Maths. You are good at Maths, so if anyone tests you, you can hold your own. Have you got it?'

He nodded enthusiastically, and I knew he would talk again. He was just seventeen and good friends with Miguelito, the Maths student from Moscow. But Miguelito was the soul of discretion, while Albertico was as friendly as a puppy dog and so talkative and so excited about our mission that he was just dying to spill the beans.

He was a good kid in every other way and a good soldier who could also fly a plane. I decided to keep his indiscretions to myself. After all, only two of us had a pilot's licence. Under military code you get shot for talking the way Albertico had – but we had to be different and we had to think for ourselves. If each of us was judged for our errors and indiscretions, then we'd all be dead already. I wasn't sure how sympathetic Sol would be to this way of thinking. The further away we seemed to be from reaching our goal, the more authoritarian he was becoming. So I found the boastful boy a minder in the form of a famous nuclear physicist who had lost a leg in the war and who was 'of the Left' and had a big apartment in Montparnasse. I moved Albertico out of the Parisian *pension* Vida had found for him, and I billeted Albertico on him and his wife, who were both getting on in years and a little bit lonely.

I had a harder problem trying to persuade Sol to send some of our group over to Venezuela to provide a local base for when we arrived. I suggested that Constantino and Miguelito be the ones to go. The former could get a job as a pilot and bring us in a plane, and the latter could rustle up some support for us from among the students.

As was to happen in most debates, Sol won by overruling everyone else and we ended up being seventeen guerrilla fighters billeted in France and Italy.

Elías took command of the Italian faction and filled in his time seducing the wife of one of our main sponsors there and getting her pregnant. Such was Elías's charisma that he remained friends with the cuckolded sponsor.

Back in Paris, in February, March and April of 1968, the logistics of shipping out became my full-time occupation. At the very end of April, in the middle of some crisis or other over one of our many abortive arms deals, I received a call from the nuclear physicist's wife inviting me to dinner as a matter of urgency. She was very formal and very polite and very insistent. I thought, Jesus Christ! What has Albertico done now?

I went round to their palatial apartment and the table was set rather grandly and a major dinner was served. I noticed that there was an empty place, but we didn't wait for whoever it was for. Over hors d'oeuvres of coquilles St Jacques, the wife came right to the point.

'It's about Albertico,' she said and nudged her husband under the table so hard that he dropped his scallop. He cleared his throat and looked embarrassed.

'Excuse me,' he said, 'if I am going to interfere a bit in your affairs, but I am a communist and a war veteran, and this child you have sent to us cannot go to fight as he says he will. You can't have him. You can't take him. We have ... we will ...'

Overcome with emotion, the physicist stopped. My throat contracted and I couldn't swallow my mouthful of food. What had I done? What had he done?

He gathered himself and continued without any tremor in his voice, 'We want to adopt him and pay for his studies.'

'You what?'

'Albertico, the boy: we want to adopt him. And ... my son is going to go with you in his place.'

The wife beamed broadly and nodded blissfully at Albertico as though he were a prizewinning baby. I stared at the boy I knew as a fully trained guerrilla fighter. He hadn't shaved that day and had a faint boyish stubble on his chin. He shrugged and grinned.

'Your son? How come?'

'My son is twenty-seven years old, while Albertico here is still a baby. My son loves planes, ever since he was a boy he has loved planes and he knows everything about them.'

The physicist made a stage cough and then another and his son appeared on cue from behind the door. We shook hands and the son took a seat rather sheepishly at the table. The physicist had warmed to his subject and seemed almost annoyed by the interruption. He gave his son a professorial look and continued explaining, but in the tone of a lecturer.

'Some days ago, when my son here was having lunch with my wife and me, your boy started talking about planes and missions and –' he paused momentarily to flash an indulgent smile at Albertico – 'quite frankly, he was talking rubbish. My son told him this, but your boy is stubborn and he braved out the argument, insisting that he knew more than us. At which point, my son told him that he is a flying instructor. In fact, he is *the* flying instructor here in Paris. Your boy was still unimpressed. He said, "I am a pilot" and then, Oswaldo, he spilt the beans ...'

The son half rose from his seat with excitement. 'And what beans! You have to take me with you! Please! I have to go! I am a military instructor: French air force. And I can get you arms: all you want. I can get you anything you want. I just want to go with you.'

We already had one foreigner in our group: el Francés, Pierre Goldman. With the physicist's aviator son as well, it meant that over 10 per cent of our unit was non-Venezuelan; enough, percentage-wise, to call them our International Brigade. The fact that it was a brigade of two men didn't matter: when your entire army numbers only seventeen, two is a lot! Once again, everything went into fast forward. So once again, we were on our way.

CHAPTER XXXXVIII

Within a week, we had a new arsenal at our disposal. Within another week, it was 3 May 1968 and Paris itself was on the brink of revolution. Tens of thousands of students took to the streets, while the workers and the Stalinists and the Trotskyites and the Maoists, in a bizarre volte face, became the reactionary forces of law and order.

The city was bursting with euphoric young people who had risen up spontaneously and taken control. The atmosphere was incredible and nobody talked of anything other than revolution. By sheer chance, that was the fortnight in which our group got everything organised and hence its green light to go for Sol and Elías. So we were packing and making our last-minute plans while all around us there was a spontaneous explosion of revolutionary fervour. On the sidelines, looking on in absolute terror, the Parisian bourgeoisie hid inside their houses while the police reacted with waves of tear gas and violence and then, like leashed and muzzled Rottweilers, strained at their leads waiting for the signal to attack.

There were slogans painted on walls and trees, on shop windows and pavements. And there were also posters everywhere. A lot of the posters were of el Che. The slogans said stuff like: 'Only the truth is revolutionary.' 'Beware of the Communists stealing our Movement.' 'Forbidding is forbidden.' 'Culture is disintegrating. Create!' One that was all over the place said simply, 'Creativity, spontaneity, life.'

The eleventh to the fourteenth of May were the last days I spent in Paris before we took the train to Rotterdam to embark. The physicist had got us two tickets on a merchant ship to Martinique via Trinidad. Sol Ortega and I were going to sail as two travelling sewing-machine salesmen; we would carry our arsenal in our luggage disguised as sewing-machine parts.

There were a hundred and one last-minute preparations to make, and because of the May revolution, there was a general strike. So not only were the streets blocked with joyful anarchists, there was no transport at all and no way to move around the city other than on foot. I realised I hadn't walked so far in an urban environment since I had stalked Vida years before. We all walked our feet off during that strike, squeezing past groups of entrenched demonstrators, gathering all we needed, and meeting everyone we needed to see. Stacks of cobblestones were student arsenals and endless burnt tyres littered the streets. Despite the logistic nightmare, the sight of a million Parisians up in arms on the eve of our own adventure filled us with the certainty that we were sailing into success.

11 May was a Saturday. We were out as a group in a bar in the Latin quarter, confirming our unity and plotting our destiny. The last of us to arrive in Italy had joined us and we were intent on getting drunk. Georges Moustakis came over the radio and some students in the bar sang along but changed the words into a popular satire. Just before midnight, Mr Pompidou, the prime minister, came on the radio and broadcast to the nation. Not just the bar, but the street (and probably the entire city and country too) fell silent. Overruling his minister of the interior and his minister of education, Pompidou announced that the police would be withdrawn from the Latin quarter and that the university faculties would re-open on Monday the thirteenth. He also said that the law would 'consider' what to do about the students who had been arrested the previous week. It was a massive climb-down. It proved that armed struggle worked. Concessions had been won through direct action which had not been obtainable by any other means.

It was as though the bar, the street and the city exploded. There was a frenzy of hugging, kissing and cheering. Then the streets were effervescent with whooping Parisian braves and bright young things, hippies and tourists and (at every turn) communist militants trying to be a part of something that had very little to do with them and which their party had betrayed. The students won their concessions *despite* the communists. The students had marched and made demands while the communists had spat on them, insulted and blocked them.

It was a very strange moment to live through. It was the nearest France had come to a revolution in the twentieth century. Ten million workers supported the wildcat general strike. Ten million! That makes it the largest wildcat strike in history. Paris had been steaming since the Second World War and the students lifted the lid off an already pressurised pot. The city changed and the people changed: individuals and sectors that were previously completely uninterested in politics politicised. Even footballers occupied their union and chanted 'Football to the footballers'.

13 May was our last supper before leaving on the red-eye train to Rotterdam. It was also the day of real triumph for the Parisian students and their supporters. They had beaten the government, beaten the police and beaten the army and they were celebrating with the kind of wild abandon usually only seen in Paris during the notorious, bacchanalian quatre-arts balls. I think ours was the only sombre group in the city that night, certainly the only group of people who were not talking about the march of a million demonstrators and the general strike and the Renault workers and the CTG and the Sorbonne and the students' leaders, and their demands and triumph, their fight and their victory. Only a few years before, I would have gladly been in the thick of all that. I would have marvelled at the uprising and joined in at every twist and turn. As it was, though, our sights were set on a distant goal, and once again it was 'do or die' time.

Sol and I each had two enormous outsize suitcases full of arms. I have never lifted anything so heavy in my life. I shall never forget the face of the porter at the Gare du Nord who loaded them onto the luggage van of the train. Thank God for porters! In Rotterdam, we embarked with our leaden suitcases as cabin baggage and sat back to enjoy our voyage. Once we passed the Canary Islands, I began to get my sea legs and be able to enjoy the

long evenings on deck reading, after weeks of having done nothing but rush around.

The ship would call at Port of Spain in Trinidad for a nine-
hour stop-over. Our plan was to transfer some of the arms into our
hand luggage and to carry them ashore. We would check into a
small hotel, unload the arms and return to the ship and repeat the
exercise. Thus, bit by bit, we would ferry the entire arsenal into
our hotel room. Then we would jump ship and stay in Trinidad
until the rest of the group could join us.

Meanwhile, Albertico had baulked at being adopted and insisted
on coming with us, and the physicist's son had become so excited
by the revolution on his doorstep in Paris that he had decided to
stay at home after all. There had been an emotional farewell
dinner chez the physicist, which came to a bit of an anticlimax at
the goodbye stage because Albertico wasn't going anywhere yet.
The real son only looked in on the dinner because there was so
much excitement out in the streets that he could not bear to miss.

Albertico would be staying on with them for several more
weeks. It was I who was leaving first, not him, but the dinner had
really been for him: the curly-haired boy with the cherubic face
and the big mouth whom they had come to love.

The first part of our plan worked like clockwork. Our ship sailed
on to Martinique without us and within ten days, el Francés,
Elías, el Negro, Albertico and three more of our group had joined
us in Port of Spain. Our stash of arms was safely ensconced with
Sol and me at the Hotel Britannia, and Sol and I had become reg-
ulars at a little calypso bar in downtown Port of Spain. We spent
our evenings drinking dark rum and chatting with fishermen and
smugglers in the hope of finding a suitable boat to take us to
Margarita and then across the strait to Venezuela. But despite our
having quite a lot of money, we could not find such a boat.

In mid-July, after we had reunited as an almost complete group,
we sent Sol Ortega on ahead to Margarita to get a boat there. He
volunteered to go because he knew people on the island.
Meanwhile, we kept waiting and two more of our group joined us
in Trinidad.

A week later, Sol returned empty-handed and told us there was no boat that we could either buy or hire on Margarita either. At which point, I went to Margarita and looked up a Mexican guy (whose brother had been killed in the Guerrilla) who smuggled whisky from Port of Spain to Margarita. As Sol had said, he didn't have a boat for us, but he took me to a Bolivian who did. This Bolivian had six daughters and a very amiable wife and between them they made great food, which was served as a constant buffet twelve hours a day. So whatever time I went to the Bolivian's house, there was always a hot meal on the table. I must have made about five visits there when the Bolivian said one day, 'You seem really nervous — what's the problem?'

I explained that I needed a boat to get from Port of Spain and back, and that I couldn't find one for love or money.

He said, 'No problem.'

The next day, just after sunset, two guys took me back to Trinidad in a boat big enough for our group. The two men did the sailing, leaving me free to lean over the rail and feed the fishes on the last of the Bolivian ladies' delicious meals. I knew that one of the most difficult waters in the world was the entrance to Port of Spain. There are four mouths, but only one of them is OK to navigate; the other three are lethal. As we neared the island, I asked, as a matter of curiosity, 'Which way are we going in?'

The two Margaritan sailors both looked at me blankly. 'You are navigating.'

There were four mouths: three led to certain death and one leads you into the port. I had no idea which one to take. The two sailors were adamant: they sailed the craft but they did not know the Trinidadian waters and they refused to hazard even an informed guess as to which mouth we should take. What irony that the outcome of all our endeavours should depend on *my* navigating! I chose one of the four mouths at random. By telling this tale it is clear that I made a lucky guess. The sea did not swallow us up that night and smash us against the rocks. 'Guided' by me, we navigated the treacherous approach to Port of Spain.

On the next day, Miguelito and el Bravo flew into Trinidad and that same night we all set off for Margarita and thence for the Guerrilla. We were full of weapons and we had a quite a lot of money on us.

We sailed under cover of night with two very different guys from the one who had brought me back from Trinidad. They came from another world and had another agenda. The exuberance we felt at the official commencement of our campaign was not shared by them. They were laconic and a little bored with life. They had seen all they wanted to see of the good and the bad ferrying contraband across the Caribbean, island-hopping with cargoes of illicit whisky, tobacco and rum. They didn't care where we came from or where we were going or who we were. We were merchandise to be picked up and delivered; like true professionals, they picked us up and delivered us exactly as planned. The only interest they took in their human cargo that night was a sailor's concern of who sat where to balance the boat.

There was a new moon, so it was almost ghostly out at sea. We reached Margarita just after dawn. For the last half-hour, several of our men had talked themselves out of steam and were dozing against the rail and on each other's shoulders. I leant back and watched them and identified in each man all the little things and habits, the quirks and flashes that made them all who they were. Behind them, flying fish were leaping out of the sea in balletic arcs. After all the talking and shouting, blustering and joking, cursing and boasting, there was something beautiful in the still calm of that morning.

After arduous years of preparation: this was it! There is nothing more real than war. I hoped that each man in that boat was there because his heart had held conference with his head and told him to be there. I hoped that no one was in that boat because they had been swayed by my power of speech alone. (An orator, if he so desires, can talk a sane man into jumping off a cliff to his certain death.) We as a group were not jumping to our certain death, but it was probable that many, if not all, of us would die in the next few days or weeks. As I watched the sun rise and bleed scarlet and orange splashes across the horizon, rose-tinting the flying fish and their fluorescent ballet, I felt incredibly happy and privileged to be alive. I knew what had brought me to be where I was, but I wondered again what exactly had brought each of the others. I watched the sun rise in a quick red leap from the horizon to the sky as though it were a red balloon on a string that someone had jerked upwards.

I thought about death and about dying, not just as 'some other man will meet that wretched fate', but as I, Oswaldo Barreto Miliani, faced with death and casting my vote for 'battle-madness'. As we sliced through the shallower water, skirting along the coast to the smugglers' cove, I cast my mind back over some of the doubts that had been forming ever since the absurd debacle at Punto Zero. I had been convinced that armed struggle was the only way to combat my country's ills. An inner voice was nagging me: given that 'peace' was always a better word than 'war', was I, or anyone else, justified in starting a war? Then my alter ego would rear up and reply that we were not starting a war, we were starting an armed uprising. We were triggering a reaction and then laying down our arms to organise the equivalent of a city state. We were seeking a regional and not a national response. Our offensive action would be swift and effective. We would surprise our enemy and take over and the example we set would fire other regions to follow. With the mass of people behind us, further war might not be necessary. Even in Paris, a million people had taken to the streets and seized their rights. We didn't need a million people; all we needed was a groundswell of popular support and we could do something that was needed, that was worthwhile and sustainable. It was worth trying. If we needed to die in the attempt, then so be it!

As the skipper and his mate pulled our boat onto the beach, the other men awoke and rubbed their eyes to see what could be their last ever morning. We were all excited. We were going home. Margarita was already Venezuela; when we set foot on the sand, we would be touching our home ground for the first time in years. Yes, the nagging inner voice continued: But how do you know the people will fall in behind you? How can you count on their support?

And that was my main problem. I knew I could count on support in the Andes, but I knew nothing about the east. Everything hinged on what the others were saying about it. Whenever I brought it up as an objection, they waved or shouted me down. The east was right, according to them. The east was the place to start. The east was where the Guerrilla had a track record. Yes, my inner voice insisted. But after all your studies and your own experience, when did what others vouched for ever turn out to even approximate the truth?

I was last out of the boat, lost in reverie. A couple of the group called to me from the beach.

'Hey, *profe*! Come on! This is it!'

CHAPTER XXXXIX

We left Margarita on a ferry to Porto La Cruz, a sizeable town on the east coast of Venezuela. It was early August 1968. Our Bolivian purveyor on Margarita worked in the ferry company and he got us ferry-workers' overalls and smuggled us aboard as company employees. Four of us went on the advance party: Sol Ortega, Elías, el Francés and me. The others stayed on Margarita ready to join us once we had chosen and established our base. Between us we were carrying two modern machine guns and a hand-gun each, plus our basic equipment and also some high-protein tablets we had bought in Trinidad.

We entered Venezuela via Porto La Cruz for the following reasons. I believed that it was best for us to arrive somewhere where we were not known and wait until a problem arose – probably of a peasant nature – and when, of its own accord, it came to a conflict, we, as a group, would join their fight.

I had suggested that we enter in the Andes, in the zone where I came from, where we could have been covered by small landowners who were my boyhood friends. I knew we would have been both safe and supported there. Some of the Andean landlords, like Jaime Terán, were 100 per cent behind us and their power and influence within their own state would have brought us an immediate stream of recruits. The advantage to this plan was that I knew the terrain, and I knew the people, and I knew that what we had in mind could work. However, I was the only Andean in our group and the only one of us to know the area, so the plan was completely rejected because there was no tradition of the Guerrilla in our Andes.

Also, Sol Ortega was determined to go to the east – where he came from and where there had been a prolonged history of guerrilla fighting and where there were still some very small groups of fighters from the MIR. It was an area that Sol personally knew very well. As our commander, he insisted on personally knowing the terrain, so he was adamant about our starting there.

Once we docked in Porto La Cruz, the plan was to take to the hills immediately and cross the mountain to Bergantín, where other fighters were said to be. In town, we took only the time needed to get rid of our overalls before we slipped behind the hospital and started to climb away. It was a swelteringly hot day and our packs were ridiculously heavy for any kind of prolonged march. Although when we left Cuba we had been fighting fit and fully trained, the intervening months and the French desserts and waiting around in various parts of the world had not done any favours to our condition. Sol and Elías were naturally fit and athletic, but el Francés and I were really only skinny armchair intellectuals. Within twenty minutes of starting our ascent, we were both struggling to keep up. After we had all climbed a fair distance and felt safe enough to stop and review our situation on our first day, we realised that we were missing a number of crucial things.

For instance, we hadn't had our tetanus vaccinations or our typhoid vaccinations, nor had we brought any anti-malarial tablets, and last but not least we had not taken any drinking water – not even enough for the following day. So one of us had to go back down and get what we needed. It was decided that of the four of us there – Sol, Elías, el Francés and me, I was the least known of the three Venezuelans and the best able out of me and the Frenchman to buy and bring back what we needed without arousing suspicion. This decision was made despite my terrible lack of any sense of direction.

Well, I went back down, and of course I got lost. I was halfway up a steep hill and carrying my entire pack, the weight of which was seriously hindering me, not least by playing havoc with my balance. I fell over more times than I care to recount. Then I tried to do what we had been taught in the Cuban training camp: that is, to dig a hole in the ground with a knife and hide my gear in it. The ground was solid. My two first attempts hit rock and my blade made sparks. I remembered our Cuban instructor's voice, explaining how the hole should be at least 25cm deeper than what you have to hide.

Ha ha! I couldn't get my blade to do anything other than scratch the surface. I was on my hands and knees, sweating like a pig and cursing under my breath, when I heard someone approach. I held my breath and waited, not daring to look round. I was hoping against hope that the person or persons wouldn't see me. In a childish way, I imagined that if I couldn't see them, then they couldn't see me. The next thing I knew, someone was right behind me, lightly kicking my foot. I turned round slowly.

It was Elías. He said, 'Otto! You idiot! I knew I could have waited a year and a half for you to dig a hole and get back to us, so I tracked you. That, my friend, is not how you dig a hole.'

Needless to say, Elías sorted it out and got us into town. I bought the stuff we needed, and together we got it back to the others.

Then our horrible adventure in the mountains began.

To start with, Sol Ortega did not know the terrain. He led us into a zone of impenetrable undergrowth. It was so dense that we could only hack our way through it with machetes step by laborious step. Despite the balmy weather on the beach of Margarita and the blistering heat on the hill beyond Porto La Cruz, it was the middle of winter. That is, it was the middle of our tropical rainy season, in which torrential rains beat down for hours at a time day after day. The mosquitoes ran amok, and most of our things were damp for most of the day. It took us, on average, an entire day to make 500 metres of progress. We had an M16 machine gun and an AK-47 and four hand-guns, several grenades, two explosive sticks and God knows what else, but between us we only had one machete. We were down to virtually no drinking water, and for food we were reliant on the high-protein tablets we had brought, but we had no carbohydrate or other nutritional substance. So we were wet, thirsty, hungry, exhausted, frustrated and lost.

Despite this, day by day, Sol kept insisting that he knew where he was. With my sense of direction, I could hardly remonstrate, but I could see that it made no sense to be trapped in a thicket and suffering as we were that early on in our campaign. Elías, like Vida, had no hairs on his tongue and made it quite clear to Sol that on two occasions we had actually gone around in a circle. Sol invented some bullshit about it having been a 'tactical necessity', but the one thing we really didn't have were any tactics there. So we went round and round as we stumbled and crawled and struggled through that mountain of thorns.

When at long last we arrived in an area that was not of impenetrable bush, we were all desperate and broken. During the long nights that followed, we made forced marches under cover of dark towards a valley from which we had seen smoke emerging. El Francés (who was Parisian and very much a city person and who had never been out in the wild like this) was going quietly insane behind Sol. Next in line was Elías, who was permanently enraged. And far behind, there was me.

In the Guerrilla, everyone had to do their bit: we had to keep up and keep going, carry our packs and be responsible for ourselves. If someone was injured by the enemy, then it was the unwritten law that we all helped our fallen comrade. If someone was injured through their own clumsiness or carelessness, then they were at fault and they were not allowed to slow the rest of the unit down. It was our duty to keep up and to keep going. Much the same rules applied within our domestic society in Venezuela. There is very little sympathy for illness or weakness in general. Illness slows a family down: it drains its resources. Perhaps there is something about the tropics that makes life harsher. Death is endemic, fevers sweep people away and natural disasters rain down thick and fast in the form of earthquakes, hurricanes, landslides, plagues of locusts, floods and droughts. Survival is strictly of the fittest, and nature itself does the pruning.

Our 'march' through the mountains of the east was horrendous for all four of us, but it nearly killed both Pierre Goldman and me. When we reached the 'easier' terrain, when we could walk without having to battle through impassable thickets, Pierre and I did a role reversal as I became more at risk than him. We marched in the dark and were forced to rely on the stars and our sense of direction to keep up with each other. My position, as appointed by Sol, was in the rear. My orienteering skills, as appointed by my genes, were nil; so the stars were of no use to me. I couldn't keep up, I always lagged behind and I couldn't steer my way, so I would, without a doubt, have been lost and left there. It was on those night marches that I came to truly appreciate Elías. Not only did he probably save my life, he saved my face; he did it in such a tactful way that not even he acknowledged that he was doing it.

You see, he had watched me in Cuba and in Paris and Trinidad, and he had realised how truly hopeless I was at finding my way. Well, Elías had one of those great big show-off Rolex watches with a luminous face which showed up quite clearly in the dark. Without saying a word, and without letting anyone else see what he was doing, he held his arm up, every minute or so, and thus signalled to me where they were. It was a tiny thing, and yet, to this day, it is one of the gestures that most touched me about him. All through the night, every night, he helped me like that. With hindsight, I see that his kindness was what kept me going. Long after my dream had been torn to shreds, all I had left was my loyalty. Elías believed in me, so I couldn't let him down.

As they told us in China, all good things must come to an end, and after many weeks, we eventually came to an area that was sparsely populated. In little clearings, there were isolated peasant huts. Through holes in their crudely thatched roofs came the ribbons of smoke we had seen from high above. For several days, not to mention weeks, it had looked as though our expeditionary force was going to perish on that mountain. And yet there we were within fifteen minutes of food and shelter. My sense of achievement was immense and equalled only my sense of relief. We sat in the wet grass in a group, and for the first time since I left Salamanca in 1953, I found myself thinking, Thank you, God!

My jolt back out of the arms of the Church was delivered by Sol: 'We can't let the peasants see us, because if they did, they would betray us to the army. So what we have to do first is get to know the terrain before we get into any kind of fight.'

Elías was more pragmatic in his approach. 'Fuck that! We have to eat!'

El Francés was in shock from our recent trauma and had not spoken for several days, but he rallied faintly and whispered, 'I need food.'

'They are right,' I said. 'We are completely depleted. We have to eat and build up our strength or —'

Sol cut in, clipping his words so that it was clear he was pulling rank. 'You have to know the terrain. After that, I will decide what steps to take. For now, avoid all contact with the locals. If you see one of the peasants heading our way, hide. I want zero contact. We can forage now, then we rest, and at 06.00 hours we will start to get to know the terrain.'

End of the discussion.

Despite our near starvation, the results of our foraging that day were: Sol – nothing; me – nothing; el Francés – two possibly edible mushrooms and a crow; Elías – an armful of maize cobs (scrumped intrepidly and against orders from a sorry strip of plants on the edge of the nearest clearing). Fearful of being detected, Sol forbade any fires. None of us was up to tackling the raw crow, el Francés, after a lot of deliberation (some of which, I thought was suicidal), discarded the fungi as poisonous, so we chewed on the raw, bullet-like corn-on-the-cob to ease our hunger. The injection of carbohydrate was welcome for the first half-hour, but the diarrhoea that followed for the next two days was not.

I was in a pub once, not so long ago, in Oxford, not far from the Banbury Road, when a middle-aged man with a face like a bloodhound, who had been slumped over a pint, looked up, looked me in the eye and started to sing. 'Oh! The Grand old Duke of York, he had ten thousand men, he marched them up to the top of the hill, and he marched them down again. And when they were up, they were up, and when they were down, they were down, and when they were only halfway up, they were neither up nor down.'

When he had finished, I wanted to shake his hand. (Being in Oxford, though, I decided against it and bought him another drink instead.) I wanted to say to him: You understand – *that* was what it was like in the east! Because, in order to 'get to know the terrain', Sol marched us up and down that hill for over two weeks. Like four prize idiots, we paced up and down the ridges and ditches and the strip fields and wasteland, communing with the ground. We were seriously hungry and perilously fatigued and we were still carrying our heavy packs. Had anyone seen us, we were an army of four complete nitwits, marching up and down the same hill day after futile day. Nobody did see us, though, because on Sol's instructions, we fled and hid at the least hint of another human being.

After the first week of that pointless marching, our high-protein tablets began to run out, so we could only take them every other day. This meant that our hunger turned to malnutrition. Meanwhile, Sol insisted that he had a plan and that our seemingly useless marches were a crucial part of it. Since we were a military unit and Sol was our commanding officer, his word was law; but as the days wore on, his words and his laws and our behaviour seemed more and more absurd and insane.

Gradually, our marches got shorter and shorter as Sol himself began to flag from the lack of food. He lifted his ban on lighting a fire so long as we were several kilometres away from the nearest inhabited shack, so if we were lucky, now and again, we got the odd sweet corn-on-the-cob, and from the woods we gathered a few wild guava fruits.

Sol continued to insist that he had a master plan; and in the evenings, he talked almost obsessively about how close the army was and how at any moment it would ambush us and how we had to be ready and prepare ourselves by being familiar with the terrain. I knew that what we were doing was completely ridiculous. I bitterly regretted the years I had wasted preparing for such futile nonsense. As we marched, I thought a lot about the waste both in effort and time. I thought of all the women I had loved and left, I thought about Vida (whose memory always sweetened in direct proportion to how far away I was from her presence). I thought about Ramín, who was growing up somewhere in Persia and who probably didn't even know my name. I thought about my family: about my brother Ivan who died in the Guerrilla, and about José and Irma, Marina and Gledis and Graciela and everyone else who had fought in the Guerrilla. Had they fought and died for this?

I desperately wanted our mountain adventure to stop, but I had put everything into it. This was my one chance of making a difference and if I had to suffer the nonsense orders of Sol, then suffer them I would in the hope that he would come to his senses soon and we could get on with what we were there to do: i.e. to fight. Elías was absolutely furious. I heard him mutter several times that he could not believe he had forgone the command of our unit only to fall into the hands of such a complete nincompoop as Sol. El Francés, meanwhile, continued to prove himself particularly ill-suited to those marches and counter-marches. He kept tripping and falling and day by day, as we all wasted away, el Francés became more and more impatient with our leader. Each night, el Francés remonstrated with him. But each night, Sol merely insisted that he and he alone knew what he was doing and we just had to trust him and he continued to scaremonger the proximity of the army and his certainty that the peasants were on the army's side. He did not elaborate on how he knew this; he just insisted that he did. Since we were marching under military law as a military unit, we didn't have much choice but to trust him. To have done anything else would have meant getting shot for insubordination, mutiny or any number of other treasonable charges.

One evening, when Sol had been going on again about how any contact whatsoever with the locals would result in our immediate betrayal to the army and our almost certain liquidation, el Francés got up and wandered away to the clearing in the bushes where I had made my makeshift camp. I followed him.

He said, 'I've had enough! That's it! I am going to make contact with the locals. I don't care if they betray me. I hope they do. And I hope the army does turn up; and I hope they fucking kill me because I can't stand this any more. Death would be a welcome break! But, Otto, in case I fight them and survive – where the fuck am I? I mean, I know I'm in Venezuela, but that is all I know. I am a Frenchman, a foreigner, and I didn't exactly get a tourist visa to come in.'

It was a good point. I told him that if he needed, he should make his way to the nearest town and telephone a mutual friend, Fernando Gonzalez, who had studied with him in France, and who could sort him out. And then I sort of naturalised him. I gave him a Spanish name and some Venezuelan money (because, of course, he didn't have that either, not even enough to make a phone call). We said goodbye, and I went to bed. When we weren't on guard duty, we went to bed at about 7 p.m. because there was bugger all to do out there and we were permanently exhausted. Bed was too fine a name to call the flattened patch of grass I lay down on. It was damp and cold and crawling with bugs and humming with mosquitoes. And yet for all that, over and above its restorative qualities, sleep was doubly welcome in that time because it was our one action which seemed to have a point to it. It was the one thing we did in all that time that made any sense at all.

Next morning, I woke up with the sensation that I was not alone. I opened one eye and saw Sol's boot beside me. That in itself was strange because we had got quite picky about whose 'room' was whose. So we tended to keep out of each other's chosen space. Sensing that something was wrong, I sat up.

He said, 'Come with me, and leave your weapon; I want to talk.'

That was very strange. I got up, and I left my gun and I went with him. His face showed signs of resignation and fear at the same time. About 100 metres from the camp, he began to talk about my brother Ivan: about his life and death, and about how close a friend he had been. Then he told me how much he cared about my family. And then I realised what this 'talk' was about.

I told him, 'Sol, I see that we are "taking a walk" as they say. Since you are about to shoot me, save me the foreplay and tell me what this is about.'

He took out his gun and released the safety catch; and he said, without looking at me 'Otto, you know that defeatism is an offence punishable by death. I know that yesterday you gave information to the Frenchman that will help him escape, which shows that you are guilty. There is no point denying it, because I have heard it all.'

I replied, 'I, too, have heard speak of you, Sol: of all the ridiculous things you have done and all the stupid mistakes you have made, of which this expedition is just one more. But before you kill me, before I die, I convoke a meeting in which you must explain exactly what the point is of marching up and down this hill slope day after day. Because it makes no sense. You talk of defeatism: what defeatism? The only defeatism here is your own!

It is you who will not make any contact; and you who refuses to fight.'

He swivelled round to face me and asked, 'Do you really think that?'

As soon as he said it, I knew that the moment had passed. He was no longer going to shoot me. On other occasions, in other places, I know that men had been shot in the Guerrilla for less than my offence. Regardless of what had gone before and whatever there was to follow, he lost my respect as a man that morning. It seemed to me vile to resolve his own problem by taking my life. His problem was, quite simply, that he didn't know what to do.

We sat down on the ground, which was still wet and glistening from the morning dew, and all his insecurities tumbled out. 'What can we do, Otto? We *can't* show ourselves. We are in a dead-end alley. There is no way out. What can we do?'

He had switched from tyrant to supplicant and from intransigence to putty in my hands. I knew that I had to press the moment if we were not only to do what we had come for, but also to survive. 'What can we do, Sol? We can find a way out! We can *make* one! We have to go down to the nearest village or small town and find some people with whom we can form a base that makes some sense. We are not boy scouts, for God's sake! This is a political problem. We have to act *with* the people. We are here, now. We want to do something – not with the country as a whole, but with the region, this region: your region, Sol. We need to join forces with an existing group and help them to solve an existing problem. That group has to be as local as possible. *That is why we came here!*'

He was completely deflated. He said, 'OK – let's do it. I'll stay here with the Frenchman, while you go into the village with Elías and start to make contact there. Talk to a few people to see what we can do.'

He gave me some contact details, including that of his brother, who lived in Porto La Cruz. Then we wandered back to the camp like the two old friends we had been, like the two guys who had known each other for years: in Venezuela, in Cuba, in China, in France and Italy, in Algeria, in Trinidad and now here.

He was cheerful with the others and told them the plan as

though he had carefully worked it out himself. When we left for the village, he squeezed my elbow affectionately. I set off down the hill with the blood in my arm tingling from his comradely grip – and the blood in my brain still churning savagely from his comradely desire to have executed me only hours before.

CHAPTER L

Elías and I made our way back to Porto La Cruz by another route. The return journey took us a relatively easy three days as opposed to the harrowing three weeks on the way out. Because Elías was such a famous Guerrilla commander, Sol had insisted that he could not show his face; so I left him in a little boarding house while I made the contacts. As luck would have it, I knew a lot of people in the east. Years before, I had been a Communist Party delegate for the east and I had an entire network of friends and contacts. Besides that, there was Sol's brother and also some of Elías's family. A contingent of our own group joined us from Margarita, and within a couple of weeks, between el Negro Manolito, Albertico, il Pirocco (of whom more anon), Elías and me, we had organised a network.

A supply chain from Margarita was arranged (via the guy who had got us the boat and the ferry crossing). He ferried us all the logistic support we needed, supplying anything from money to dried fish, food, explosives, batteries and medicines. Our group began to grow in Porto La Cruz. Sometimes it branched out in surprising quarters. For instance, there was a woman of about sixty-five who was a dedicated supporter of the party. When I met her, she put everything she had at our disposal. Since she was the madame of two brothels, this meant we had free access to the prostitutes plus the use of their rooms. That madame was the best cover we could have and the prostitutes themselves were also excellent recruiters and purveyors of information.

Quite soon after we made our base in town, Sol's brother told us of a man who was willing to rent us his coffee farm so long as he and his family could continue to live there. The peasant owner would turn a blind eye to whatever we were doing, and we would let him get on with his coffee farming. It was a perfect arrangement and provided us with an ideal rural base. We set up camp there and began to activate the Margaritan supply line. We contacted numerous other peasants in the vicinity and persuaded them to work with us, without telling them exactly what we were up to.

By the time we were established on our rented coffee farm in the hills, we were doing something different. Instead of us living from the peasants – which is what guerrilla fighters do – the peasants lived from us. We fed them and gave them employment such as building fences and digging ditches and looking after our chickens and goats.

As a group, we began to grow both in the countryside and in the town. We grew and waited, always looking for a reason to intervene in the area. In Porto La Cruz, the sense of regionalism was very strong, to the point where most of the people of Porto La Cruz were xenophobic. The shops were all owned by Arabs, the food shops were owned by Italians and the market stalls were in the hands of the Portuguese. The locals all blamed the government for this state of affairs. The xenophobia was the only real discontent that could be used as a focal point to create resistance. But championing xenophobia was not something we were destined to do or that we felt comfortable about joining. And yet we were there and we were organised and we were ready and standing by to intervene on a given issue; so we had to do something.

I saw that for many of the coastal people, the only form of income was from fishing; and that the fishermen of the east were some of the most barbarously exploited people in Venezuela. I don't know how it is now, but back then in 1968, the fishermen fished in groups. Within each group there was a sentinel whose job it was to climb onto a high rock and survey the sea. The sentinel then signalled to the waiting fishermen exactly where the fish were. Those sentinels were extraordinary: they were never wrong. They not only pinpointed the shoals, but they also said in which direction they were swimming.

The fishermen camped (or squatted) on the beaches between, for example, Colonada and Arepito. They would wait there sometimes for days. When the sentinel signalled to them, the fishermen took to the sea in their canoes. In all weathers, they caught the fish and brought them back to the beaches where the middlemen took over. These middlemen had refrigerated lorries and they paid low prices for the catch of the day. When there was a lot of fish, the middlemen dropped the prices. The fishermen worked extremely long hours fishing in hazardous waters and then earned barely enough to subsist on, while the middlemen got rich. The Portuguese were the owners of the fish markets; they also got rich. We saw that we could work with the fishermen in a far-reaching way; and that is what we began to do.

We had our base camp on the coffee farm which was up a hill some twelve hours away from the town and we had an army. We had a network of supporters in the outlying villages and in the town of Porto La Cruz, and we had an effective supply line continued from Margarita. We also had a network of supporters scattered all over the country, some of whom had moved to Porto La Cruz to join us. The latter category included my sister, Marina, Chilo (who later became my partner), Miguel Nuñez, Luisito and Luis Fernando, to name but a few. Then, taking another leaf out of Fidel's book, I had written hundreds of letters (in code) to the four corners of the country to distant group leaders such as Rodolfo Hernandez Miliani, Lupe, and Jaime Terán. I told them a little of what we were doing and asked them for their solidarity and, if need be, their support.

One day, I was in town with Elías, who had to go to Caracas to make some contacts there. When we were first in Porto La Cruz, we used to keep Elías hidden away. But Elías himself had a theory that the best way to hide was out in the open. He claimed that his supreme confidence and lack of any suspicious behaviour made him invisible to the authorities and potential spies alike. After the fiasco of our forced marches and our three-week trek into the mountains, Elías began to take over a lot of the effective control of our group. He had been told to lie low, but he began to do as he pleased and to move around freely. We drank a cold beer together at one of the brothels and then he set off, while I got my things together and made my way back to the base camp. Among other things, I had mail for some of the men, including a letter for Albertico from his adoptive parents in Paris. It was always a small miracle when any post actually got through. This was not so much because of censorship as the tremendous inefficiency at the sorting office. Sometimes you had as much chance of mailing a postcard to Mars as you did of getting one from France or Italy.

I made the journey in high spirits because, at last, things were beginning to go well. When I reached the foot of the hill where our coffee farm was, I had my first contact with the army. There were soldiers everywhere; I could not get back to the base camp and was forced to take cover halfway.

Our base camp was attacked and our group had its first armed combat. Six of our men were there that day, including Sol Ortega and el Francés, plus the three campesinos. After a few hours, I doubled back into town and tried to find out what had happened. I had heard firing and several explosions and I had seen a thick column of black smoke rising from what had once been our farm. It wasn't possible to move on the first day, so all I got were rumours. Nothing of what I heard was good. It seemed that our entire unit had been wiped out. All six of our men were dead. The farmhouse had been razed. The three peasants had been summarily shot. Apparently, it had been a major intervention, but nobody could tell me how many casualties or deaths there had been on the other side.

On the second day, I was sneaking around the town looking for news when I saw the nephew of the coffee farmer waiting for a bus. He saw me and ran away. He was about fifteen and a lot nimbler than me, so I lost him, but I found out where he was staying. He was with a cousin on a smallholding out of town. I got one of our group to drop me there. The house was long and low, with nothing around except for a very small church. I hid in the church waiting and watching to see who came and went. It was lucky I did, because about fifteen minutes after I got there, an army truck full of soldiers drew up. I hid myself and waited some more. The coffee farmer and his two sons (who until then I had believed dead) were dragged away by the soldiers but there was no sign of the nephew. The military truck drove off and I waited some more.

The church was disused, and empty apart from a couple of worm-eaten pews and a very large, very gaudy statue of Saint Anthony. I remembered from my youth that Saint Anthony was the patron saint of lost things. I thought it ironic – since I had lost just about everything, including six of my comrades – that I should be hiding that day behind his effigy.

The sun set and the small church filled with bats. After about another hour, in which the bats shat all over me in tiny acid squirts, the coffee farmer's nephew appeared on the road, heading home. He was a decent boy and I felt sorry for him. He was about to learn that his whole family had been arrested and his life was pretty well ruined. He passed within a few metres of where I was hiding and I broke my cover and called out to him. He stopped whistling and looked very scared.

I asked him, 'What happened at the farm?'

He shrugged and mumbled, 'Nothing.'

When I told him that the National Guard had just taken his uncle and cousins away, he stared at me for a few seconds and turned very pale, and then his knees sort of collapsed under him. We sat on the parched grass and he told me what he knew, but he hadn't been present at the coffee farm when it was attacked.

By chance, only one of his cousins had been on the farm that day and he had managed to escape. The rest of the family, that is, his uncle and younger cousin, had been in town. Since the attack, he had spoken to neighbours and he knew for a fact that the family farm had been completely destroyed. Every shed had been razed, the coffee crop had been burnt and the house was a heap of ashes. He could not confirm what had happened to our group. All he knew for certain was that Albertico had been killed – shot, apparently, in the first few minutes.

'And the others? What happened to the others? Did anyone see their bodies?'

The boy couldn't tell me any more. In his turn, he asked me

about his uncle and his cousins. 'Where have they taken them?
What will happen to them?'

I couldn't tell him for sure, but I imagined they would, as we
were speaking, be having the shit beaten out of them at some military post, and if they were very, very lucky, after a couple of
months, the soldiers would let them go.

As it turned out, the peasant coffee farmer and his two sons
were not lucky at all because they paid for their involvement with
us with very many years in prison. Even without that knowledge
at the time, I felt bad about what we were doing and why. We had
gone there to help the peasants and we had ended up destroying
a good man's farm and life and that of his two entirely innocent
sons.

It was a time for feeling bad. We heard that Sol and el Francés
and the others had all died with Albertico. I felt bad about el
Francés (who wasn't a soldier at all – he was a novelist and literary critic; he wasn't even Venezuelan). And I felt bad about the
others in our group. I even managed to remember all the good
things about Sol Ortega and to mourn him. But I felt worst of all
about Albertico – he of the big mouth and the boastful ways who
was so charming that an elderly French couple had wanted to
adopt him. After the attack, I destroyed the letters I had been
carrying so joyfully back to camp. Albertico's had been written
by the nuclear physicist's wife. It had ended with fond maternal
advice about how to look after himself. The last sentence but one
had been an injunction as though to any careless young boy
playing tropical tourist from his mother. It had said: 'Albert,
dear boy, stay away from any puddles or pools of stagnant water:
the tropics are dangerous and full of Bilharzia. I shall not sleep
until you write and tell me that you will never swim in sweet
water pools.' And the last sentence read, 'Tell your teacher to
look after you and to send you back safely to your second home
where your "maman" and "papa" are waiting for you with affection always.'

Somewhere in Paris, an elderly woman would never sleep well
again and a one-legged physicist was in mourning. As they had so
rightly said, Albertico was still a child. He was looking forward to

celebrating his eighteenth birthday. And now he would never swim in sweet water again.

I had been his teacher, his mentor, but I had not looked after him. By chance, when he first joined us in Porto La Cruz, he had arrived full of alarmist stories about bilharzia because he had sat next to a tropical doctor on the ferry crossing. One of the first things Albertico had asked me was, '*profe*, is it true that if you go swimming here there are worms that climb up your dick and eat your liver?'

Then I had told him about bilharziasis, or schistosomiasis: 'The bilharzia worms live in the sweet water here. Adult schistosome worms are about 1cm long and hang out in the veins that carry blood from the intestine to the liver. The worms live in pairs, the male holding and protecting the female inside his ventral groove. Once paired, the two remain in constant copulation. The female lays hundreds of eggs each day, which the infected human loses in their piss or shit. In the end, the build-up of eggs enlarges your liver and causes kidney malfunction.'

'*Profe*, are you telling me that these worms fuck non-stop?'

'Correct.'

'For life?'

'Yup! They copulate non-stop for the rest of their lives and by so doing they have infected over 300 million people with bilharzia.'

'Jesus, *profe*! What do you think they did as a species in a previous reincarnation to get that kind of genetic prize?'

The black marks against me are not the ones daubed there by the press. The real black marks are for the coffee farmer rotting in jail with his two teenage sons, and Albertico – a boy who should not have died.

CHAPTER LI

The survivors of our group stayed down in Porto La Cruz, with everyone who was at risk hidden safely away in one or other of the brothels. It was ensconced in a whorehouse that my affair with Chilo blossomed into something more substantial. Our passion was one of the few positive elements at that time. With our base camp destroyed and one third of our original unit dead, our morale was at its lowest yet. Elías returned and took over the command and absolutely refused to be beaten. I didn't want to give up, but I didn't want us to go on as we had been. I managed to win him over to my point of view and we convened a meeting of as many of our supporters nationwide as could come.

In that meeting, I proposed a giant change in our plan. If you remember, I was never in favour of our being in the east. I was against repeating or trying to repeat an action which had continuously failed: the rural guerrilla in Venezuela had failed to catch on. It did not have the popular support it needed to justify its existence. In nearly ten years it had not made a significant improvement in the country. No demands had been met. No abuses had been stopped or even curbed. In short, as a movement it was all over the place.

Our own experience – of training in Cuba for nearly two years and equipping our unit and then landing in the east as an expeditionary force only to march up and down the countryside like four idiots in a comic show – had underlined the futility of our dreams for a rural Guerrilla. There had been one battle in which not a single soldier was hurt, but Albertico was dead, and Sol Ortega, el Francés and three other members of our unit were missing, presumed dead. After many months, our only positive rural achievement was that we employed a couple of dozen peasants on the coffee farm. Weighed against that now was the total destruction of that farm and the imprisonment of our host and his two young sons. I explained how we would certainly have had a greater impact had we gone directly to the Andes.

Then I told them, 'But from having lived with and talked to the peasants and also talked to the people – not the wealthy middle class, and not the landowners, and not the intellectuals, but the real people here in this area – the last thing they want is violence. Their lives are already violent. Every day of their lives is a battle to survive!'

And I was just going to explain why we needed to totally change our plan, when I noticed Sol Ortega's brother arriving late at the back of the room. He came forward to speak. He said, 'I have heard from Sol. After Albertico was shot, he and the others managed to get away.'

The minute he said it, the meeting burst into a spontaneous cheer and then fragmented into total disorder. It took me several minutes to regain control. Once I had everyone's attention again, I said, 'Comrades, we have an army, and we have a network of support, and, thanks to our island friends, we have a brilliant supply line, but I am certain that we should not abuse the power and strength we now have in order to force this area into an armed conflict. On our side, Albertico is dead and we are all ready to die. But the question is: why? And what for? *And who for?* I believe that to continue the armed struggle as a classic rural guerrilla unit would be self-indulgence.'

There was a fair bit of murmuring and dissent in the audience, but I was determined to have my say, so I raised my voice and talked over it.

'It would be a fulfilment of our revolutionary zeal without any roots or reference to the people we claim we are liberating.'

I didn't care how inconsistent it looked. I didn't care how stupid it seemed to propose such a major volte face. My fight had become a battle to convince my comrades that we were wrong. We were on the brink of taking the step that warps.

In Cuba in 1966, I was convinced that the Guerrilla was the only way to right the wrongs of Venezuela. Then I began to doubt the efficacy of guerrilla warfare for my country. The test, however, was in the oven. *Maybe* it would work. Within days of our arrival in the east, it was blindingly apparent that it would not.

During my months in the east, I came across villages that had been occupied by other guerrilla groups in the past, and I found a deep-rooted loathing for everything and everyone connected in any way to the Guerrilla. From the heart of our cities, we, the revolutionaries, developed a rural dream. Our goal to take to the hills and fight became a rural nightmare. The people did not want a revolution; they wanted to be left in peace. I multiplied the handful of traumatised settlements across the whole region, and I realised the terrible danger of unleashing such a negative force.

We decided to do something positive instead: to rob a bank.

I was not what you might call an upstanding citizen because I was happy to turn blatantly criminal and plan the robbery, but I did not want us to become bandits or to go around robbing banks (in the plural). My idea was to establish a working capital – a large lump sum – with which to help a particular project and a particularly exploited sector of the community.

Once again, chance was my friend: because out of all the revolutionaries in Latin America at that time who were wondering how to rob an international bank, I was the one who knew exactly how to do it, thanks to my stint on the management of the French-Italian Bank in Caracas.

With this decision, our group leapt from any kind of Marxist philosophy to a fundamental principle of socialism – the greatest good for the greatest number of people. The sector we could most effectively help was the fishermen's. If we set up a cooperative and bought the refrigerated lorries (each of which cost a small fortune – hence the bank robbery) we could work with the fishermen and empower them to help themselves. Part of my education and training had been in the heart of capitalism, so I understood what sound business principles were. We needed a working capital, but we had to make that capital reproduce itself. I saw that we could make our capital (from the proposed bank robbery) grow by taking a profit share in the fishery cooperative and thereby fund a regional newspaper. ('Yes! You Chinese torturers: a newspaper!') As the Beijing junta had so sneeringly noted, in Venezuela we had a tendency to equate revolution with the press. And I planned to take it further: to eventually start a magazine which could explain our point of view, as opposed to that of both communism and capitalism.

The bank we chose to rob was the Royal Bank of Canada. One of the reasons was the certainty that we would find over a million dollars in used notes in its safe. Another important reason was that it was a major international bank and could thus sustain the blow we were about to inflict on it without harming any of the local small fry who might have their life savings in it. The robbery was my chance to apply all my logic, method and meticulous preparation. It was my plan and my call and, as a piece of ingenious planning, it was a masterpiece. Of course, it was also the brainchild of Elías, and without his genius it would not have worked. For once, I was the thinker, and I was at my best, while he was the man of action – which was exactly what he did best.

By then, we were a small group of eighteen men that had extended to a further forty key people (men and women), with a further band of approximately another hundred, and a much looser affiliation with a couple of hundred more.

No matter how secret things are kept, they tend to leak. At the point when a major bank robbery was a theoretical possibility, it had been spoken of around too many of the second circle of our group to be safe. Once it became work in progress, it was limited to a mere handful of us, but the problem remained that some of the others already knew too much. Partly to camouflage our real target, and partly to raise seed money to develop the plan for that target, there was a trial run on a bank elsewhere.

This first assault, against the Banco Nacional de Descuentos Universitarios, was small, clean and well executed. After the hold-up had been successful, all the talk and gossip, conjecture and spilt beans clustered around it. With a team of only five men, we planned a major robbery on the Royal Bank of Canada. The heist we pulled off there was the most important bank robbery in Venezuela and, up until then, the biggest in Latin America. OK, we stole the money from the tills, but all bank robbers had done that before; what changed with our robbery was that we took everything. We took absolutely every cent that was in that bank.

When you rob a bank, the cashiers and the manager always tell you that they can't open the safe because of not having the combination and because of the time lock. Up until then, robbers always timed their assaults to get the maximum amount of cash from the tills. Well, we did that *and we cleaned out the safe*. Ours was an armed robbery, but it was incredibly well prepared and we were well informed (loyalty has its price, like everything else). So when a gun was pointed at the manager's head, he sang the missing bits of our puzzle and we pulled out a total of 2,600,000 Bolivars from his vaults.

It was the first time anyone in Venezuela – no matter how big or violent a robbery was – had stolen over one million Bolivars. You have to ignore the current superinflation in Venezuela when you see these figures. I am talking about the days when we really had petrol dollars to spend and the Bolivar was a currency worth exchanging. Nowadays, you'd have to take a convoy of trucks with you to rob a bank and remove enough to make it all worthwhile. Back then, though, 2,600,000 Bolivars was a tremendous haul. It was so big it was a scandal; and we stole it without anyone getting hurt – no one was so much as slapped in there, and none of our men was injured or left behind. It was, quite simply, a model robbery and a perfect operation. And the follow-up – thanks, as I have said, to my insider knowledge of international bank transactions – was executed in the same manner. The working capital was safely deposited offshore, minus certain immediate needs which we voted very democratically could ethically be met from the kitty. In our HQ in a Porto La Cruz brothel, we held our first truly triumphant meeting.

We decided unanimously that el Francés should have the price of his ticket back to France. And we decided on the immediate purchase of the refrigerated lorries for the fishing cooperative. We all voted to purchase some new arms. Most of our arsenal had been destroyed in the razing of the coffee farm. I particularly wanted to start a magazine, but nobody else except for el Francés, who was of course a writer, wanted to do that, so it fell by the wayside.

Via our supply line from Margarita, we built up a stash of hand-guns – which were mostly Colt 45s and some Garand rifles, an M16 and an M6 SAR. Elías insisted on a new supply of pineapple grenades, which were, I think, the only misspent money out of the entire sum.

The government response to the Royal Bank robbery was draconian. Nothing pointed back to us, yet people saw that it was an intelligent assault and without any proof at all they leapt to the conclusion that Elías and I were behind it. It was obviously the joint work of a strategist and a military commander and we were the only such duo. Some people said that I was the mainspring and others said it was Elías, but they all assumed it was our handiwork. The police began to arrest and torture, threaten and bribe; and within a week of our meeting, we were all betrayed and the government knew the names of all the people involved. Our entire organisation was forced to scatter and everyone who was anyone within it had to go underground. A handful of us withdrew to the Andes and hid on the hacienda of Jaime Terán, high in the hills of Tempé. There, in the heart of the state of Trujillo, we held another meeting.

That second meeting was a little less triumphant. We agreed unanimously that the armed struggle was over in Venezuela. A new party had been founded by Teodoro Petkoff: the MAS (the movement towards socialism). Everyone was joining it and everyone was legalised. It was our sort of movement, but we were the odd ones out. We were still attractive to some factions of the Left, but we were wanted men. We were bank robbers and any association with us was a hindrance to the MAS; our solidarity began to be uncomfortable to them. They were legal and non-violent, while we were illegal, armed bank robbers.

It would not be possible to operate as a group within Venezuela in any capacity in the immediate future; our money was good but our presence was bad for our fishermen friends. The more we scattered across the face of the earth, the better. Within a month of the Royal Bank of Canada job, there was an exodus.

From the Andes, we began to send members of the group out of the country using the nearby Colombian frontier as an exit point. El Negro Manolito and Elías went to the old safe house in Bologna, from where they joined el Francés in Paris. Sol went to Canada. And Jaime and I went to Italy to rendezvous with Elías, touch base and get our bearings, and then, shortly afterwards, we moved to London. Everyone else in our network was captured, tortured and imprisoned, or forced to flee. Alas, Chilo was among those arrested.

For most of us, it was not just an exodus from Venezuela, it was an exodus from life. We had little choice: the government was out to get us; I was wanted 'dead or alive', while Elías was 'wanted dead'. What had we actually done? What had I, personally, done that warranted waiving the law, dismissing justice and offering a reward to whoever could kill me first?

Don't get me wrong: I am not saying that I was an innocent victim. I was not; but not one soldier, policeman or government official had been hurt or killed as a result of our movement and our efforts in Venezuela after our return from Cuba. Not one civilian had been killed or wounded. The casualties were, quite simply, one man down on our side: Albertico, who died at the camp; and the owner of the coffee farm and his two teenage sons who were rotting in prison. These were things that weighed on my conscience, but which did not in any way merit the kind of measures taken against Sol, Elías, myself, el Negro, el Francés, Chilo and the others of our group. In London, for instance, the CIA was actively following us. The CIA didn't usually go hands-on with Venezuela or Venezuelans. They limited themselves mostly to teaching their torture methods to our interrogators and counter–insurgency courses to our soldiers. After that, they tended to leave us to it because the prevailing myth was that there was no real Leftist risk, no real Guerrilla, no real insurgents, and therefore no real danger of altering the status quo in oil-rich Venezuela. Thus our country would continue to be a nodding puppet to its US master. But back then, with many of those who could say otherwise in prison, others on the run, and others just entering the parliamentary system and thus, in the name of progress, needing to forget, the Guerrilla was either denied or criminalised.

It was standard practice that once a revolutionary or criminal was out of the country, he could do what he liked so long as he didn't return. The world was full of exiled Venezuelans who got on with their parallel lives until such time as they were officially either amnestied or forgiven. This was not to be our case. We were hounded abroad. Our police turned to Interpol and our National Security turned to the CIA.

Instead of my wanting to 'save my people', I had to save my skin. For the next year, our one goal was to stay alive.

Despite all our precautions, the CIA and Interpol had us firmly in their sights for a lot of the time we spent in Milan, London, Oxford and Stockholm, from the end of 1969 until 1972. This begs the question: why didn't they either kill us or have us killed? I see now that the Venezuelan authorities wanted us dead, but to the US government we were more useful and interesting alive. They wanted to see who we talked to, wrote to and met. The CIA knew that something was going on because they had (among other things) intercepted letters that we had exchanged with the Cubans.

Before the Royal Bank of Canada robbery, we had a fairly large popular following, but we had lost any intellectual support we may have had. Communism and communist thought still completely dominated the world of left-wing politics. Our complete rejection of that alienated us from almost all our previous allies and also almost all our friends. Our popular following consisted of people who saw how we worked, and saw that we were serious and that we were seriously trying to change something for the better. No matter how big our dreams had been before we disembarked in the east, we now knew that we could be effective on a small scale in a local issue. And since it looked as though not only could we not return to Venezuela then, but we could never return, we were looking for a surrogate home.

At the end of 1969, we had travelled, we had arms, we had money, and we had absolutely nothing to do.

After the Royal Bank of Canada robbery, the newspapers in Venezuela began what has become a lifelong smear campaign aimed, in particular, at yours truly. I truly became seen as the enemy of the people. I had been listed as such from the age of fifteen, but it had been an empty title until 1969. After that, and to the present day, almost every bank robbery and every criminal act in Venezuela has had my name attached to it like a maker's label.

For the record, after the Royal Bank, my personal involvement and the involvement of our group in bank robberies was over. No one believes this, but we were not involved in any subsequent bank robberies whatsoever, either in Venezuela or abroad.

Anyone with a modicum of information on the subject will attempt to contradict me here, yet I repeat: it was so. You just have to trust me. I am setting the record straight, both where it flatters and where it maligns me. I know that there are hundreds of pages of reportage and taped 'confessions' in the DISIP and SN (the Venezuelan secret and military police) and the CIA files about my participation in other bank robberies, but they are false.

The fact is that I was involved in two robberies only. Admittedly, one of them was the biggest and most sensational robbery in Latin America; so I am not saying that I am *not* a bank robber – far from it: I am. But I am not a serial one.

Why then does my name come up in connection to so many other cases? Well, I see three reasons for this. First, the Royal Bank was an affront both to the Venezuelan and to foreign authorities (the target was, after all, a Canadian bank). The assault was a scoop and an unpardonable insult. Second, because (rather like the Great Train Robbery in England) it was such an affront to the authorities, the persecution that followed it gathered invention like a snowball on a ski slope. And remember, the story was coming out of Latin America – home to magic realism, and the sanctuary of gross exaggeration.

And last but not least, my name was bound to come up over and over again in leftist, communist, revolutionary and criminal circles, quite simply because it was the one name everybody under torture eventually must speak. It is physically impossible not to. Names are asked for and names must be given. Put yourself in the victim's shoes: you want the pain to stop. It won't stop until you give the name of who was behind whatever it is you are being tortured for; you either don't know the name or you want to protect the real person. The pain is unbearable; then you make an informed guess. You say 'Oswaldo Barreto', and it stops. The more times it happens, the more robberies get clocked up to my account, until my tally looks like Casanova's bedpost.

The authorities' files can contain as many documents as they like 'proving' my guilt in dozens if not hundreds of other robberies. They are wrong. I did the Royal Bank of Canada. That was mine. And I did it well.

Part 7

CHAPTER LII

By the time I reached Bologna, in December 1969, I was thirty-five years old. I see people of that age now and they seem young to me. But when I lay down for the first time on my narrow iron bed in San Petronio Vecchio, I felt as though I had lived and wasted a dozen lives and I was exhausted. I wasn't old, but I was by far the oldest in our group.

While almost everyone else had abandoned our cause, Jaime was a surprise new addition. Logistically, he had helped in the past, but never enough to imagine he would join me in exile. Jaime was not only my cousin – distantly, through the Briceños – but we were at school together, both in Mendoza Tría, and then, albeit briefly, in Valera. When the shit hit the fan, it was Jaime who saved us.

For twenty-four years I had followed my dream. In Bologna, I was forced to admit that I had manoeuvred myself into a dead end. I had failed miserably, and I was miserable about it. From saving my people as a nation, I now had the lesser task of saving my people as a group. There were three of us – Elías, Jaime and me – in a foreign country with nothing to do and a lot of people on our tail. Since I was the strategist and the polyglot, and also the honorary European, it was up to me to keep us safe, keep us sane and, eventually, to get us out of there. The one thing we had left, our last shred of integrity, was our loyalty to each other. Like three schoolboys, we swore solemnly that come what may, we would stick together and we would not return to Venezuela until all three of us could safely do so. If that meant spending our entire life in exile, then we would always – to the death – have each other.

Our first month in Bologna was an extraordinary mixture of lethargy and frenzied activity. Elías, in particular, alternated his long bouts of sleep with great bursts of energy. He picked up new interests every time he went out. He joined a flying club and a photography group. He met a Santo Domingan couple and decided that we should all leave immediately for Santo Domingo. He was like a clockwork soldier who had been overwound. When he was 'active' he didn't sleep, he read and studied, trying to cram the formal education he had never had into night study in our freezing attic apartment.

Jaime, on the other hand, was in shock. He had been deeply traumatised by an experience in prison and he knew that he would be unable to withstand another bout of the same. As we escaped from Venezuela, we had so nearly been captured so many times that his nerves were frayed. On arrival in Italy, he took to his bed and took a self-imposed sleep cure for several weeks, surfacing only to eat like a victim of the encephalitic sleeping sickness epidemic that had swept through Caracas in the 1930s.

By the time we did the Royal Bank job, I was involved with Chilo. Wanting to distance her from the robbery, we had temporarily separated. After the assault, when we were betrayed and everything started to go pear-shaped, she was in Caracas while I was in the Andes. As my known girlfriend, she was one of the first people to be arrested. When I escaped to Italy, I knew that she was still in prison; and I knew what our police did to people in prison. It didn't matter that she was a woman: they didn't care. Every time I tried to think of a way forward and out of our stagnant position, my mind kept reminding me: They are hurting her. And every day that we and other members of the group, who were scattered across the globe, continued to live free, I knew that Chilo, who could have spilt all the beans – who knew, for instance, where we were hiding – hadn't done so.

Back in Porto La Cruz, I had lived with Chilo because I was in love with her. In the aftermath of the Royal Bank affair, to that love was added an intense admiration and a debt of gratitude so great that, eventually, I would turn to putty in her hands and be unable to keep any balance in our relationship. However, that unbalance was still in the future. In Bologna, I pined and grieved for Chilo; I could not contemplate any future that left her behind. She was our fallen soldier. Unlike Albertico, who had died in action, Chilo had been left behind. I could not go back and save her, but I had to pull as many strings as I could to help her. Since just about every string I had had been cut in the past eight weeks, my sense of failure and frustration was enormous.

Try as they might, the Venezuelan government could find no connection at all between Chilo and the Royal Bank. Quite simply: there was none. We had chosen to separate previously for that very reason. She was not an accomplice; she had been my lover. Even in Venezuela, it is not criminal to share a bed.

Day by day, the three of us in the Italian safe house sank further and further into doom and gloom. Even Elías found it hard to stay optimistic. News of the persecution, arrest and harassment of everyone connected to us in any way made us decide to move on and distance ourselves from our Bolognese saviours.

It was a time of serious political upheaval in Italy. The Red Brigade was in its heyday; the Italian police were persecuting the Left and routinely torturing prisoners. Italy was a police state under tight surveillance. Our protectors had plenty of problems of their own without having to shoulder the extra burden of harbouring three Latin American bank robbers on the run. We discussed this with our hosts, who generously refused to agree with us; but despite their open offer to stay for as long as we needed, we decided to go somewhere completely new while the heat died down. Our choice was London.

Up until then, none of us had any connection whatsoever to England, but Jaime, with his noble Labastida heritage, was a tremendous anglophile. He wasn't up to much after we left Venezuela – away from his hacienda, like a fish out of water, he hardly breathed – but when it came to discussing where to go, he was pretty adamant that England was the place. Since we were living off Jaime's private income, we had to bow, to some extent, to his choice. Elías and I were not entirely reluctant; we both saw the sense of going somewhere where we were completely unknown, where the police force was renowned for its gentleness, and where we could all learn English. No matter what we did in the future or where we went, knowledge of English, that universal language, was bound to be of help.

On arrival, we went to a tourist housing agency and were rented a house 'a stone's throw' from the centre of London. We had to rent somewhere because hotels had the added risk of our false passports letting us down. I didn't know south London before or the then insalubrious areas of Balham and Clapham, but after taking a six-month lease on a terraced slum house on Abbeville Road, in Clapham South, I certainly got to know it. Our place had one of those English leases whereby you rent a house and somehow find that you have also rented a lodger. Our 'desirable residence' came complete with a mysterious Pakistani, who seemed to live exclusively off turmeric, rice and marmalade – which he cooked in *our* kitchen twice a day. Try as we might, we were unable to get this Pakistani to speak to or acknowledge us. He limited any contact to cowed stares while he cooked. Jaime, whose natural bent was to farm sugar, had a prodigiously sweet tooth and suffered serious mood swings if he didn't have a constant supply of strawberry jam and orange marmalade on tap. Our Pakistani lodger consistently raided Jaime's stock of marmalade.

From plotting the fate of nations and regions, we sank to plotting how to hide and, later, how to spike our stock of orange marmalade. The other notable thing about our inherited lodger was that he had a hacking cough, which shook the thin suburban walls and played havoc with my already grave insomnia. Later, it would also play havoc with my lungs.

Approximately one month after we moved to London, Chilo was released from jail and she flew to London to join us. Yet far from being a group of four warriors, we were four warring factions locked in petty battles and arguments over the most trivial things. Our military strategy and criminal activities were confined to gradually shoplifting the contents of the bookshelves of an international bookshop beside the river Thames into our drab suburban sitting room. I used my time to read and study. In roundabout

ways, I tried to stay in contact with my non-Venezuelan friends
and comrades from the past, resuming links with Salvador Allende
in Santiago del Chile, and with various Cuban and Algerian colleagues, even though, officially, in Cuba I was never forgiven for
having 'abandoned' Fidel and disobeying his orders.

The time we spent in London was a strange grey interlude. We
were doing nothing, our failure weighed heavily on us. All the
news that came from home was bad.

It felt very strange to live in a country which pre-empted any
discussion on the subject of politics by classing it as 'boring'. Such
was the political apathy there that despite having universal fran-
chise, less than half the voting population of Britain could be
bothered to vote and even then (so I was told) if it rained on election day, a further slice of the population of 'glorious' England
stayed away from the polls. *If* it rained? After we arrived it rained
every single day!

No matter where I had travelled before, no matter how exotic
or foreign a culture I came to, there was always a way in. In
London, I felt that I was not just in a foreign country, I was in
another world and it was impenetrable. I think the challenge of
finding some fissure through which to get in kept me going. As a
sociologist, I had my work cut out trying to fathom what on earth
the hippies and the businessmen, the immigrants and the locals,
the snobs and the workers, the hooligans and the drunks, the Irish
and the IRA, the communists and the socialists, Labour and
Conservative, the Liberals and the trades unionists and the neo-
Nazis were about. There were so many groups and they were so
weird to my eye that it made Venezuela seem quite tame by comparison.

There was an almost unshakeable status quo. Even the communists were (and always had been) a tiny minority of fanatics
who had very little popular support because if there is one thing
England excels in, it is tolerance. The English are known abroad
for their hypocrisy. Englishmen speak with a forked tongue, which
I notice on the home turf is called 'being diplomatic' or 'being
tactful'. Whatever the disadvantages of this approach may be, the
advantage historically seems to be a tolerance of even the most
outlandish elements of society. That is not say that such elements

are accepted, but by being *tolerated*, there is never a chance for grievances to build up steam and explode as they tend to do in Latin America. This hypocrisy/diplomacy, or 'the art of compromise', levels everything out, providing safety valves all along the way making everything rather bland and innocuous. No one can say 'England is like this' or 'like that', because everything has a mercurial quality, including the language. When I started to learn English, I was struck by the bizarre nature of its grammar. Take a rule like: 'i' before 'e' except after 'c', except when it isn't. Nothing can ever be quite right but neither can it ever be quite wrong. There is always room for a compromise.

So everything glided along in a vacuous, nebulous form until *BOOM!*, an IRA bomb would explode somewhere in the city. Bombs and bomb scares didn't happen once or twice, they were a regular feature of London life. It was another kind of violence altogether! I was supposed to be an expert in violence, and yet I was a million miles away from even beginning to understand the ethics of terrorist groups or of terrorism per se. Ethics doesn't seem like the most appropriate word – I wanted to know what on earth made such people tick – apart, that is, from an activated bomb. And then the civilian response was, to me, incomprehensible. If a firecracker, let alone a whacking great bomb, went off in the centre of Caracas or Valera, there would be pandemonium! In London, bombs exploded and within ten minutes Londoners were 'getting on with their lives' as though nothing had happened. Before I went there, I used to think all the stuff I'd heard about keeping a stiff upper lip and staying calm under fire was a myth, but I saw it for myself and I saw that it was a gift, or maybe an art. For months and months I could not make sense of that society and my inability to find its wavelength and tune in really bothered me.

It was early March and the wind had just blown a premature attempt at spring off the one stunted laburnum tree on our road and the few straggling plants in the row of neglected front gardens along our street. There had been biblical rains which had kept even Elías confined to quarters for nearly a week, but on that particular day the weather was just grey and blustery. Jaime

hadn't been out of the house for several weeks and between siestas he had taken to pacing up and down our cramped landing like
a caged panther. From his habitual day bed (a hideous brown sofa
with broken springs, where he lay and read, lay and slept, or lay
and stared at the yellowing ceiling), he announced, 'I'm going
out!'

It wasn't much of an announcement but it was out of character
for him because he didn't go out. Elías and I looked up from our
respective studies as he grabbed his corduroy jacket and leapt
down the stairs and out of the front door, slamming it behind him.

'What the hell do you think has bitten him?' I asked.

Elías shrugged. 'Obviously, a woman. Perhaps he's got a date.'

'How can he have a date if he never moves from that sofa?'

Elías shrugged and turned back to his aviation manual. He was
preparing to take the written part of his pilot's licence around that
time.

As it turned out, Elías was right: Jaime had what he called 'a
date with destiny'. His intuition told him to go and stand in the
street, so he did, on the corner of Abbeville Road where it meets
the South Circular. Within ten minutes, he literally bumped into
a girl (I wish it had been a woman, as Elías had suggested, but it
was a schoolgirl) and he fell head over heels in love.

Within half an hour, he had stalked her back to her home and
forced himself into her mother's kitchen. Within two hours, he had
given her almost everything he owned outside of Venezuela.
Within twenty-four hours, he had brought her into our safe house,
told her all our names including our known codenames and his
real one, had told her where he came from and what his background was, and, last but not least, he had asked her to marry him!

Subsequently, this story has come to be considered as the ultimate romance. At the time, Jaime also saw it as such and would
brook no opposition to his chosen bride, but Elías, Chilo and I
were horrified by the idiotic way in which he had completely
blown our cover and probably our lives. The defeatism that Sol
had accused me of in the east crept into my heart and I decided
to leave my fate in the lap of the gods. If I was to be killed or
arrested as a result of Jaime's indiscretion, then so be it! I had
reached a point when I was so tired I hardly had the energy to get

out of bed, let alone to run away. Elías, on the other hand, packed his bag and promptly left for Stockholm.

'Why Stockholm?' I asked him.

He shrugged and said, 'Why not?'

Gradually, it became clear that Veta, Jaime's sixteen-year-old target, was not going to shop us to the police, but, much to my dismay and Jaime's delight, she was taking the marriage-to-a-stranger thing at face value and preparing to move in with us on a permanent basis.

I really thought that I had given up praying, but as I lay and sweated through the long winter nights that were punctuated only by the sound of the Pakistani's coughing and the besotted whispering of Jaime and his child-bride-to be, I prayed for her to go away, get lost or drop dead because I loathed her. What, I asked myself, did they have to whisper about? Jaime didn't speak a word of English, and his airhead fiancée couldn't speak a word of Spanish. The Andean *caudillo* had proposed with the help of a dictionary. Veta spoke French, and I spoke French, but the prospective bridegroom didn't. So, to add insult to injury, I was constantly being asked to translate their nonsense. I say 'nonsense' because that is exactly what it was.

Veta called herself a 'poet' and a 'writer' and carried all the airs and graces of a child prodigy because she had been reading English fiction since she was three. Had she been a contestant in a quiz programme on the eighteenth- and nineteenth-century English novel, she might have shone, but on any other topic she was so ignorant it was alarming. She hadn't read any Spanish, Latin American, Italian, German or Czech writers at all. In fact, if it wasn't English, she hadn't even heard of it. Exasperated by her, but also trying to protect our skins, I did everything I could to get her to leave us all alone. Our dislike was mutual. Having no understanding of the dynamics or history of our group, her maudlin protectiveness of Jaime, as though he were some kind of endangered species, fuelled my dislike further daily. The endangered species in that group were Elías and me!

My fevered thoughts seemed to have given me an actual fever. Each night I lay awake in my room sweating. Where, I wondered, did I go wrong? I was spoilt for choice! There wasn't one point;

there were at least twenty. We tried to find enthusiasm for our life in London, but I, for one, had never found my life so hard. I had never been bored before or tired of life, and sometimes I was both. The highlights of our life were the endless trips we made to the poste restante at the central post office in Trafalgar Square. The arrival of mail was a treat (despite the grim news it inevitably bore) and the lack of mail was unbearable.

Eventually, some good news arrived from Elías on a postcard from Stockholm: he was on his way back. Since all we had was each other, nothing felt right unless we were all together. The fact that very little seemed right when we were together was something I chose to ignore. Our group was more like an unhappy marriage than anything else, but it was the only raft we had in a rough sea, so I clung to it for dear life.

I was used to there never being enough hours in a day, but in London we killed time. When we went out we were often reduced to sheltering from the drizzling rain in the stupidest places. We wandered around electrical showrooms and department stores. Once we even had our lungs X-rayed in a mobile medical unit just so that we could tell ourselves we had done something that day. Jaime killed time by watching television endlessly. It was the most annoying thing about him. He insisted on keeping the electric shadows flickering in the corner of the sitting room even when he was sleeping, so there was a constant black-and-white monologue of gloom. The news was particularly depressing: the West German ambassador to Guatemala had been kidnapped and murdered only days after another diplomat had been kidnapped in Argentina and the two cases between them were heaping disrepute onto Latin America. Suddenly, every London shopkeeper and bus conductor was an expert on Latin American politics. And I could see Veta looking at me, wondering if I was part of their group, as though Guatemala City was a suburb of Caracas; I was of the Left and *therefore* to blame. I already felt so full of blame for my own failures that it upset me disproportionately when she said stuff like that. I knew that it was irrational, but it became a habit to blame Veta, the intruder, for all the daily minor wrongs: everything English became her fault.

I was at such a low ebb I didn't like to credit her with anything good at all, so I refused to acknowledge it at the time, but, actually, thanks to her mother, Joanna (who I thought was worth about ten of the prissy and insipid daughter), I finally found a way into what England and the English society were about. As the weather brightened, Joanna guided us all to such delights as the botanical gardens at Kew, the maritime museum in Greenwich, river trips along the Thames, the local library, Guy the gorilla at London Zoo, a Polish delicatessen that sold decent food, and afternoon tea at the Ritz, to name but a few.

Veta was one of those people who didn't insist on anything. She hardly spoke, and when she did, she didn't really have an opinion. She couldn't even order a cup of tea without consulting with her paramour or her mother. Yet she was somehow able to be vapid and pig-headed at the same time. For us as a group, her absolutely worst trait was her insistence on wearing the most ridiculous fancy dress at all times. No matter how much I or Elías or Chilo remonstrated with her, she refused to dress normally. When I say fancy dress, I mean full-scale theatrical costumes, Edwardian gowns, hats the size of chess tables, elbow-length gloves and God knows what else. I always thought she looked grotesque, but under normal circumstances would I care what a teenager did or didn't choose to wear? The point was: those were not normal circumstances. We were on the run. We were in hiding for our lives and Veta was like a walking billboard saying, 'Look at us, why don't you? Look! Over here!'

CHAPTER LIII

The *Nine o'Clock News* was on the TV and for once, something hopeful was afoot. A new peace plan for the Middle East was being announced to try to end the 'war of attrition' along the Suez Canal. The US secretary of state was speaking, but because my English was so shitty, I couldn't make out most of what he was saying. I was straining so hard to follow it that I scarcely noticed there was a knock at the door. Chilo went to answer it. Outside, framed by the night, there were two uniformed policemen on the doorstep, asking for me by my assumed name. They pushed past her and came in. The house was a narrow terraced affair with a staircase that led straight into the sitting room. The policemen were up the stairs before I had time to move. Elías, who was like a cat in that he could always sense danger, had dived into the bathroom, locked it and climbed out of the first-floor window and away. Jaime had got halfway to his bedroom and got caught at the door.

I was on the saggy old sofa. I looked up at the policemen who were towering over me and I thought: Now they will shoot me. Then I remembered that English policemen don't carry guns – or they didn't in 1970. Then I thought: I wish they would shoot me – I am so tired! They asked me very gravely if I was so and so (the assumed name I was using then). I couldn't be bothered to say no, so I said yes.

They said, 'Would you please come with us now, sir?'

I stood up. I saw Jaime looking at me, and I saw Chilo. They were both afraid for me. I was not afraid for myself. I was too tired. In a way, it was a relief for it to be over. The policemen took me away in their big black car. Through the window, standing near the street corner, I saw Elías hiding in the shadows, watching as the police car drove into the night accompanied by the sound of its own siren.

What followed was the best time that I spent in England. It turned out that the police had come for me because the X-ray taken at the mobile medical unit showed that I had serious TB. It is against the law in England to wander around with an infectious disease, so they came and got me and sectioned me to a sanatorium outside Oxford.

The exhaustion, fevers, headaches, night sweats and aching limbs were not, as I had thought, the side effects of my having screwed up my life – they were the symptoms of tuberculosis. From one day to the next, my life changed again. In the Oxford clinic, I was tucked up and cosseted, nursed and rested by the most caring nurses I have ever met.

I spent an idyllic summer reading and writing there. Once a fortnight, the others came to visit me. The nurses and the other inmates taught me English and I regained the strength and the will to live. In the early autumn I was released as an out-patient and the rest of my group (plus Veta) moved to Oxford so that we could stay together. We rented an apartment in the Cotswold Lodge Hotel and everything began to look a little brighter.

While I had been in the TB clinic, Jaime had moved in with Veta and her mother and had gone ahead with plans for a wedding and the two of them were planning quite openly to go to Venezuela and farm Jaime's ancestral hacienda. Elías had been to Sweden and (don't ask me how) come back with a brand-new Mercedes, and Chilo had begun to tire of our relationship while waiting for me.

Meanwhile, my brother José had finished his geology degree at the Lomonosov University in Moscow and, after an absence of seven years, was going home. He travelled back via England and came to see me. Since Venezuela was the one country I could probably never visit again, we spent some time together. José and Veta became very close friends. He persuaded me to bury the hatchet with her; that instead of constantly bewailing her ignorance I take her education in hand. Being a teacher again had a therapeutic effect on me and I hope that it had a worthwhile effect on her.

Soon after José left, I became more homesick than I had ever been. I was no longer exhausted or terminally depressed, I just yearned for my family and my home. I missed my brothers and sisters, my mother and father and my cousins and comrades and friends. I missed the places I knew, the villages and towns I had grown up in. When José left, it truly sank in that I would probably never see them or him again. I remembered my mother's prophetic question and her fear on receipt of my first letter from a bank: 'What is it about, Oswaldo? Do you have anything to do with banks?'

Upon leaving the TB hospital I had decided, if I wasn't going to see again any of the people and places that I missed and loved then I would, at least, try my utmost to make the rest of my life worth while.

After the initial honeymoon period when each of the group was glad to see me out of hospital and to be reunited, the domestic atmosphere deteriorated rapidly into endless little gripes and rows. Jaime and Veta formalised their curious relationship in which both seemed happy to share a mute bubble unconnected to anything other than a shared intuition that their destinies were linked. The child-bride was (I thought suspiciously) closer to Elías than to her husband. She and Elías were the closest in age (her seventeen to his twenty-six) and they shared an innate joie de vivre. I watched these parallel relationships and was ashamed to find myself jealous of both. Meanwhile, Chilo and I were locked onto a stormy graph of falling out and making up and absolutely nothing about our existence seemed to make much sense.

Since our exodus from Venezuela, our group had been living on the bounty of Jaime's Andean hacienda and his private means. When, from one day to the next, this arrangement dried up because his family stopped sending any payments to him, we decided that it was time to head back to Bologna and the safe house there that was still ours for the taking.

Between making that decision to move and actually leaving, I experienced a little labastida myself. I had been sitting in our private living room at the Cotswold Lodge Hotel all day, listening to everyone bickering and complaining. I had been working on a critical essay on Jean-Paul Sartre's *Nausea* in the hospital and I was trying to finish it off, but with the racket everyone was making I couldn't hear myself think. At about 5 p.m., I had to go out and post a letter and I decided to go for a stroll along the Banbury Road to clear my head. There was so much traffic that I headed into town instead and then, without really knowing why, I went to the railway station, caught the first train from Oxford to London and made my way back to Heidelberg.

I hadn't told anyone I was going (that was the labastida: I hadn't known myself that I would). All I had were the clothes I was standing up in, one of my false passports and about fifty pounds. I didn't call back to the group for several days, which made them assume that, like Mehdi Ben Barka in Paris, I had been abducted and probably killed. We had a very strict procedure about keeping in touch and what to do in the case of danger. We found it nearly impossible to decide what we would eat for dinner on a daily basis and could argue for hours about that, but we were all trained to stay in close contact twenty-four hours a day. When I disappeared, I knew they would be worried. In a funny way, I wanted them to be. I wanted them to stop bickering and to remember why we were there and who we were and what we were supposed to be doing. By disappearing, I cleared my head and jolted theirs into a semblance of camaraderie again.

As soon as I got back, we left for Italy. When I say 'we', I mean Jaime, Elías, Veta and me, but not Chilo. The stress of exile had demolished our love affair and we went our separate ways.

(Though much later – following the cyclical pattern of many of my relationships – we got back together for a while in Latin America. Out of that reunion our daughter, Laura, was born.)

Our time of stagnation lasted for two and a half years: from December 1969 until November 1972. It was one of the worst periods of my life. When I was in Salamanca, I had had the excuse of extreme youth. And each time I have been in prison, I made use of my time. Never before or afterwards have I tried to kill it. But in London and Italy, that was exactly what I did. Sporadically, I made half-hearted attempts to study, but my mind was dull. After I recovered from the TB, I began to regain my strength and energy, but both were fragile and crumbled at the least set-back. I was someone going nowhere despite my almost constant travelling.

Looking back, I wonder why I kept returning to Italy, given that there was nothing for me there. I think it was because I had conditioned myself to find hope there; and in my near hopeless predicament, I could not let that go.

Italy was my mother bear. Every bear cub is dependent on its mother for at least three years and its learning process is long and complex. At the least hint of danger, baby bear is taught to climb up a particular tree and to wait there. Eventually, mother bear will come and rescue her young. As the cub gets older, mother bear leaves him up the tree for longer and longer periods; but always – without fail – she comes back.

Then, one day, when the cub is about three years old and fully grown, without any prior warning, the mother leaves her still-dependent son up the rescue tree and she never comes back. Instead, she moves on to have her next baby bear.

Meanwhile, up the tree, the young bear is waiting. He waits for days and days because he *knows* that he will be rescued and he is trained to stay no matter what. Fear, anxiety, thirst and hunger drive him wild, and yet such is his trust that he stays up that tree. Only when the young bear has to choose between death and disobeying his mother, will he climb down. He staggers down half-dead from hunger and thirst. He is out of his mind with anger at the betrayal. That anger is his drive to survive. Love and trust are dead. It is time to move on.

For over a decade Italy had been my place of comfort and delight. It had fed me when I was hungry and saved me when I was lost. Italy had equipped and sheltered our group. It was my rescue tree. When things went wrong, I scurried up it to wait. Italy had always solved our problems; if I waited there long enough, surely it would now.

*

We left London and arrived in Italy at a difficult moment for our Italian friends. There was nowhere to stay and the police net was tightening around them. They would sort us out soon, they said, but meanwhile all they had for us was a tiny storeroom in a Milanese tenement on the Naviglio Grande. All four of us squatted there. We slept together on a mattress on the floor of our one squalid room. I, of course, couldn't sleep; so I lay there listening to the others breathing. I could see stars through the skylight, but that was all I could see. It was too sordid and tense for the four of us to live crammed into that attic, so Elías and I went to Paris.

By that time, we had very little money. We had deposited the haul from the Royal Bank robbery in such a way that we could neither touch nor spend it. Whatever anyone else might say, I was not a common thief – I was a revolutionary. Having placed a little mini-halo on my head, it drops sideways immediately when I add that, in Italy, we lived almost entirely by shoplifting. Because we had no money and therefore nothing to eat, we shoplifted food, books and Mont Blanc pens. (Why the pens? Probably because both Jaime and I were Labastidas.) I have always been a useless shoplifter because doing it makes me incredibly nervous. The minute I stretch out my hand to steal, I feel as though my mother and Guillermo my brother-in-law are watching me together with the shopkeeper and anyone else in the shop. In Italy, I used to plan my grocery raids with almost as much precision as I used on the Royal Bank.

Despite not having cash, what we did have was a stack of dateless return train tickets from Milan to Paris. One of our supporters worked for the Italian state railway in a ticket booth and had stolen and then donated them to us. This meant that we could travel backwards and forwards across the Alps at will. At first it seemed like a tremendous luxury, but soon it began to pall. Things were not getting any better in Venezuela and we were not becoming any more welcome in Paris. I made even my friends uneasy just by being there. So each time we set off to France, we returned after only a day or two to the discomfort, tedium and frustration of our Italian rescue tree.

At one point, Elías and I went to Stockholm and worked in a

beer factory loading crates. It was supposed to make us feel better, but the strain nearly killed me and I chucked it in after two months and once again scuttled back to Italy. Veta and Jaime had moved into the safe house in Bologna. It had not been possible to use it before because some other needy revolutionary was being hidden there. When he moved out, they moved in. With the money I had earned in Sweden, we were able to lead a reasonably normal life despite our underlying clandestinity. To my surprise, I found myself making friends with Veta. I also found I was able to study as I always had before. Maybe it was just sheer relief not to be lifting beer crates any more, but I began to live my life again instead of just passing through it like a shadow.

Around that time, I began to correspond with various friends in the new Chilean government – including the new president, Salvador Allende, who had been a personal friend since my time at the Sorbonne. Allende's Unidad Popular coalition party was in power and running into serious problems. Maybe, I thought, I could be of help. Not only was there a socialist president in Latin America, but there was a socialist president who happened to be my friend. Since we were now in a position to buy our groceries rather than steal them, I focused my shoplifting activities entirely on stealing books for an in-depth study of Chile. Having something to do that might possibly serve a purpose was so refreshing that I got involved in a torrid love affair with a married woman and another with a demanding but enchanting Bolognese hippie.

Elías had made it quite clear that he would rather shoot himself through the foot than live with a group of clinically depressed couch potatoes. But he was also lonely and homesick and since we, the group, were his surrogate home, he negotiated his return.

That summer of 1972 was the high peak of our Italian graph. It did not take long for the dips to follow. Within six weeks of Elías's return we lost our apartment. A friend of a friend of a friend of our Italian landlord's was arrested and began to sing like a canary. As a direct result, people were being arrested all over Reggio Emilia. Our host gave us less than one hour to pack up and leave for the sake of both his and our safety. The only other city we knew well was Milan, so we went back there and lost ourselves in its grey labyrinth. Without a base, we once again ran out of money and lived almost entirely from Elías's shoplifting. 'Almost' because I did what I could to help, but Jaime was too much of a grand señor, and Veta was too much of a prig, to get involved.

Elías and I prepared ourselves to be of service to Allende and his government. Meanwhile, like saboteurs of our dream, Veta and Jaime egged each other on preparing themselves to play lord and lady of the manor on Jaime's ancestral plantation. They tried to keep this as a secret agenda, but how many secrets can you keep when four people share 20 square metres?

I didn't argue with them or try too much to dissuade them for the simple reason that if Jaime returned to Venezuela he would either be shot or, more likely, thrown in jail; and he knew it. He lived in hope of a letter of pardon. Day by day, like Gabriel García Márquez's colonel, Jaime made a pilgrimage to the poste restante. I hoped that it wouldn't come, but I knew that come what may, in his heart Jaime was no longer a part of our group. The 'all for one and one for all' had evaporated; as had both of my steamy Italian affairs.

Now look at the irony of what happened next. Elías was Venezuela's most brilliant military commander. In all his years of guerrilla combat, he was never outwitted by his adversaries. He was famous in the whole of Latin America. Some people knew of him as Elías, in Cuba they know him as Eliazar, and others know him as Baltasar, which was his actual name. But no one knew the secret of his timing. In Venezuela, there were seminars on counter-insurgency tactics which specifically studied what lay behind Elías's movements, but no one could find a pattern or work it out.

One of the remarkable things about Elías was that he had never been caught. And I mean never. He had never been arrested or pulled in for questioning. He had never been in prison or in one of our unofficial concentration camps. He was, quite simply, an unknown quantity to the authorities. Interpol was looking for him, but they didn't even have his fingerprints. They hardly had a photo and they didn't know his distinguishing marks or what dental work he had had done. He was pretty much unidentifiable and famous for being elusive. Yet, in Milan, he was caught shoplifting in the Standa supermarket.

Day by day, for months, he had been doing our 'shopping' there. It had become so bare-faced that we made lists of the most complicated ingredients and he would steal them for us. For some months, we had been able to eat like kings; since cooking alleviated some of the peripheral tedium, we turned it into a competition, taking it in turns to make fabulous meals.

The Italian police thought that they were arresting a serial shoplifter and they placed a team of plain-clothes carabinieri in the food hall to do it. But Elías knew that if he was arrested, he was a dead man: so he fought for his life. The ten arresting officers had to beat the shit out of him right there between the aisles of food. By the time they carried him to the police station, his face was an unrecognisable pulp.

The passport he was carrying that day was Peruvian. When the Peruvian embassy people were called in, they could not positively identify his swollen, smashed-up face, but they got quite excited at the thought that they had maybe found a Peruvian rebel they had been looking for since 1967. Following that line of enquiry, one of Italy's most notorious interrogators was called in to torture Elías's identity out of him.

Meanwhile, the rest of us destroyed everything that could be construed as incriminating and asked the Milanese Left to hide us while we waited for what we were sure would be the news of Elías's death. The local custom was to push prisoners out of top-floor windows and then tell the press that they had committed suicide. We spent three horrible days of waiting.

Then, miraculously, the Peruvian suspect the police thought Elías was, was captured in Germany *while* Elías was under interrogation in Milan. With nothing to charge Elías with except shoplifting, and following their national policy of not burdening their already overcrowded jails with foreign riff-raff, he was deported. They took him in chains under armed escort to the frontier. Our friends tipped us off which train he would be on. By chance, it was the night train to Paris, the slow train that we had travelled on so many times together in the past year.

We watched discreetly from across the station concourse as he was dragged along the platform. He couldn't walk. His face was grotesque. People's stares reflected more horror than pity: humans shouldn't look like that, and if they did, they should cover their heads with a sack like the Elephant Man. There were plain-clothes police and some foreign agents there, also waiting discreetly. We got someone to approach our battered commander and brush past him and tell him the name of the city where we would next meet. We had a procedure for almost every city in Europe; all we needed was to each know which one it would be. The chosen city was Strasbourg. He was beaten, but he wasn't broken, because he whispered back 'Geronimo!' That was his battle cry.

The next day, I left Italy for Strasbourg and effectively climbed down my rescue tree. After Strasbourg, Elías and I returned to London.

While all around me England slumped into recession and depression, while unemployment rocketed and the 'Troubles' in Ireland escalated in the aftermath of what was called Bloody Sunday to spill over the Irish Sea like viral fear, I was in love. A new element came into my life in Mariana. Never had I found it so true that to love someone deeply gives you strength. Way back in Valera, Nene had tried to explain to me that deep down what really mattered was to find and live a grand amour. I had tried it with Vida but failed by only putting 50 per cent of the equation in place. In love, it takes two to tango. With Mariana, I found the complete sum, and, with enormous relief and gratitude, I re-found myself.

We lived like a couple of lovebirds in Chelsea (where Mariana had a small flat) and I came to see that everything was try-able – if not do-able – and that with sufficient determination it was just a matter of time until I found the chance to try. I grew stronger by the day and sometimes I felt so happy that I walked on air.

Venezuelan style, our small flat became a pied-à-terre for numerous visiting Latinos. In fact, there were almost human traffic jams at times, what with up to ten people sleeping barrack-style on our floor and besieging the one (rather luxurious) bathroom. At the end of 1972, Jaime and Veta eventually returned to London from Italy. Within a matter of weeks of their arrival, Jaime finally received the letter he had been waiting for: he was officially pardoned by the Venezuelan government and thus at liberty to go home. The two of them sailed to Venezuela in the summer of 1973. The rest of us (Elías, Mariana Otero and I) lived on in London and Paris, preparing to set sail to Santiago del Chile.

As someone who had studied military strategy, I was as intrigued as everyone else as to what made Elías choose the seemingly inspired sites and targets of his assault. How did he know where to attack and so constantly surprise the army? I asked him one day and he shrugged and smiled.

'Ice.'

'What do you mean?' I asked him.

'Ice: ice is the secret of my success.'

I didn't know what he was talking about.

'It's quite simple, Otto,' he said. 'I was fighting in Venezuela and Venezuela has a temperature of around 30 degrees centigrade. So it's hot. You get your men together, and they are hot. You fight a battle and you win and then they are really hot. The one thing they want is a cold beer. By that time, the one thing that they would die for is an ice-cold beer. If you give it to them, they stay. If you don't, after a couple of battles they lose interest. I never attacked further than a stone's throw away from ice. That was my criteria.'

CHAPTER LIV

When I arrived in Santiago del Chile in March 1973, the country was on its knees economically and the Chilean extreme right, the CIA and the US government were actively conspiring to bring down Salvador Allende's democratic socialist government.

Despite 44 per cent of the votes in the congressional elections, by the time I moved to Chile with Mariana and Elías, it was crystal clear that the socialist government would be ousted by a military coup d'état. The putsch was coming, it was just a matter of when. Even before Allende took office, the abduction and assassination of Rene Schneider, the commander-in-chief of the army, had made it apparent that the opposition was out for war. Schneider was a right winger who had steadfastly opposed staging a military coup to prevent Allende from taking power and he'd insisted that the constitutional process be followed. The Yankees couldn't let such an old-fashioned fuddy-duddy stand in their way, so they ordered that the 'obstacle' be 'removed'. Schneider's assassination was supposed to rally the Right around the national flag; when it didn't work as a ploy, the CIA and their masters were furious. They had set their hearts on not letting a 'Red bastard' in. And it was disappointing back in the White House because they had all worked so hard!

Allende, as leader of the Unidad Popular coalition party, was the first democratically elected Marxist president in Latin America. Openly opposed to Soviet-style communism and an outspoken critic of capitalism, his greatest crime in the eyes of the US when he came to power was his respect for the Chilean constitution.

The US had done its damndest to keep Allende out of power on three previous occasions. By 1964, the CIA was using a dirty-tricks campaign, which cost them US $3,000,000. In 1970, when the immensely charismatic medical doctor Salvador Allende won the elections despite a US-funded and guided scare campaign, the United States of America was up in arms. Henry Kissinger's take on the democratic result was: 'I don't see why we need to stand and watch a country go communist because of the irresponsibility of its own people.' Nixon's orders were to 'make the economy scream', and scream it did. It yelled and groaned, wept and bled; but still the Chilean majority wanted to keep Allende.

The US ambassador avowed: 'Not a nut or bolt [will] be allowed to reach Chile under Allende. Once Allende comes to power we shall do all within our power to condemn Chile and all Chileans to utmost deprivation and poverty.' Well, the nuts and bolts didn't get through, and his ambassadorial wish about the deprivation and poverty came true. By March 1973, there were drastic shortages of just about everything. Santiago, the huge, sprawling capital, was a place of endless queues, empty shops and complaints. A US-funded truck-driver's strike had virtually crippled the country. Petrol and spare parts were in such short supply that all forms of transport had become a luxury.

The US determined to overthrow Allende, despite their having no vital national interests in Chile. The threat of a 'good example' of a democratically elected socialist who continued to honour the constitution was more than the Yankees could bear.

Allende was a stubborn, gentle, erudite man whose respect for his country and its constitution was slavish. He knew that the fabric of his government was being torn apart by the CIA, and that the smear campaigns and the propaganda war were just a piss in the ocean compared to his US-trained army, which was largely disloyal to him. But he so believed in the freedom of speech and in peace, patria and liberty that he did nothing to curb his enemies, and meanwhile his enemies infiltrated every element of

Chilean society right up to the high echelons of Allende's own government.

There had been a great deal of humming and hawing about our going to Chile. Apart from any political reasons, I was excited about returning to Latin America, and about living in the birth-place of Pablo Neruda and Huidobro. Neruda had almost become part of my genetic luggage. Besides which, to me, as an exile half-formed in Europe while still being Latin American, there was something alluring about a city like Santiago, which has one cultural foot firmly planted in each continent. Well, that was how I felt, but I soon saw that socially Chileans tended to look down their noses at us Venezuelans. They called us 'tropicales' – a derogatory term which blanketed everything Latin and north of the equator. That is not to say that there were not friends to be made – there were – it was just that a certain prejudice first had to be overcome.

Politically, my situation there was ambiguous. I was wanted but not wanted. I had been called, but not called. I was there to help with some government-level matters, but, officially, I was not there. It was all very complex and paradoxical and made me understand all the more the ambivalence of Neruda's lines:

I don't love her anymore, it is certain,
But maybe I love her ...

Back in Valera when I first read them, I had thought they were entirely about a linguistic love thing. In Santiago del Chile, I realised that those lines also identified dithering as a national characteristic.

Allende was a close friend, we shared many views and ideas, but if I was to be of any help to him, he had to *not* be my friend while I was in Santiago. I had to pretend that I didn't know him. Because whatever I/we as a group might have to do there was something that he needed but didn't want (a loyal SAS-type bodyguard to spearhead armed resistance to the inevitable right-wing attack), and, more importantly, that he *absolutely could not be any part of* (because our presence went against his liberal mandate. Only at the very end of his service to his people did he see that the level of foul play lined up against him meant that he too might have to play dirty to save the justice and fair play he so believed in). Besides my personal friendship with Salvador Allende, I had very close friends in his government, but again, I was there because we were needed (maybe, but maybe not), but officially I was not there. So seeing something and not seeing it; wanting but not wanting; being incapable of a quick decision – these were to be key points during my next nine months.

Upon arrival, we booked into a fairly nice hotel and took our bearings. Strictly unofficially, I made contact with the Chilean socialist party. There were a group of socialist political parties that were supported by the government. Of these, the MAPU was significant. It was split into two branches, the Left and the Right. It was important to both Elías and me that we be part of an existing local group, but it wasn't easy to get our foot in any of their doors. Eventually, we were accepted by the Right (but always socialist) branch of MAPU and with their blessing we dedicated ourselves to organising, and later training, that party so that they could resist the inevitable coup.

It was no small task: the MAPU was destitute! They were so unprepared, we didn't know whether to laugh or cry. For instance, they didn't have a single walkie-talkie – not one! They had no communications maps at all. We, Elías and I, made them communications maps. We made their charts, and we tried to discuss basic strategic principles with them. The latter was really difficult because they didn't even know what basic strategic principles were. I tell you, they were all over the place! They were grateful for the help we gave them and they said that they would call us as a group to train a small, effective, paramilitary unit specifically to protect Allende and his government in the event of an unconstitutional attack (which would almost certainly be a CIA-backed putsch).

Well, they said they would call us, but they didn't call. We hung around Santiago and we tried to feel useful as we watched the country descending even further into economic chaos, but after the first few weeks we weren't actually doing anything. We went for day trips to the beach and we ate some great lobsters and we made friends with a number of people, including some Colombians and Argentinians who were all as amazed as we were that nobody was doing anything to protect that vulnerable democracy.

Mariana and I enjoyed a sort of honeymoon with Santiago as our holiday destination; and then we left. We had gone there to help, not to be on holiday. All of us found it depressing to see so clearly what was coming and to be so powerless to prevent it. However, it was not our country and we had no right to do anything unless we were specifically asked to do so.

At the beginning of June, having waited and waited in vain, we moved on to Peru. I had friends and former colleagues there and Lima had been our chosen bolt-hole destination since before we left London. So we rented an apartment and I settled in Lima with Mariana, but Elías insisted on turning right round and heading back to Santiago.

Within the week, he called and said, 'There is something: a lot of something!'

Mariana and I flew straight back to Chile to join him. Sure enough, there had been an attempted coup. They had already named it the Stañazo: the false coup. It hadn't involved the whole army, just one man with a tank testing the waters; but it had scared the MAPU into finally realising that a battle was on its way and heading straight for them all like a guided missile.

Like vultures drawn to a dying cow, the international press was there, gathering and pecking while waiting for the animal to die. The neo-fascist *Patria y Libertad* wasn't waiting. They went right ahead and tore strips off the hide while the fallen cow lay and writhed. Even with the green light they had given us to get started with training a commando group, the MAPU delegates were like almost everyone else in Santiago, staring with big, trusting cow eyes. Supporters from all over the world were going down to Chile to lend their moral support to Allende and his government, but sometimes it looked and felt as though we had all gathered early for the president's funeral. In dribs and drabs, among those coming down were members of our group from Porto La Cruz: Chilo and Julieta, a man called el Cocido, Elías's brother Fedo, and several more. Regis Debray, the French journalist and writer who had been such a close friend in Havana, was also there, undeterred in his revolutionary fervour despite his gruelling experiences in Bolivia with el Che and his own subsequent imprisonment.

Elías, his brother and I were the directors of the group, which numbered in all about twenty people experienced in the armed struggle. There were four Colombians, two Argentinians (including the wonderful el Chango), one Brazilian and a handful of Chileans, but the biggest faction consisted of Venezuelans.

Everything that happened in Santiago during my stay, from July 1973, should be viewed against the backdrop of a countdown. Everyone knows the date 11 September now and can say it is a knell unto mine ear. For Latin Americans, though, there was already another black 11 September, long before the attack on the twin towers in New York. It was on 11 September 1973 that the US-backed coup in Chile caused the deaths of thousands of civilians. 1,102 people 'disappeared' as a result of it. A further 2,095 people died under torture or by extrajudicial execution. Those are the cases that have been officially recognised by the Chilean state. That roll call includes the president elect, Salvador Allende Gossens, who lived his last months like an anti-Mafia judge in Sicily: knowing that he would be killed and wondering when.

The Chilean coup is like an exercise in good and evil. Despite the smear campaigns at the time and the vicious anti-Allende propaganda, with hindsight few people and few politicians do not credit Allende with being a good man, some would say a saintly man. The worst that can be said of him is that he was naive in his belief that good would prevail over evil; that he was short-sighted; and, maybe, that he suffered from his national blight of indecision. None of the above warranted the extreme and inhumane measures taken against either his government or his people.

Within ten days of training our group it became apparent that the people of Chile and their leaders were not going to fight to save their democracy: they were not going to resist. They knew something bad was coming their way and they knew that they didn't want it to happen, but they were all waiting like sitting ducks to be squashed by it.

As a group, we rented a quite big apartment on the Calle Marín, near the Plaza Italia and the centre of town. And as a group, we gathered every day at the house of the Argentinian, el Chango, who had a leather-goods shop near by. Behind this shop he had a garage and workshop because he was also a mechanic. During our training, we had a little sideline in stolen cars, which generated much-needed funds for the various requirements of both our group and the MAPU in general. Stealing a car in Santiago at that time was no easy matter. The shortage of petrol and spare parts was so dire that there was virtually no public transport and people clung to their wheels for dear life. In Venezuela stealing cars is the easiest thing in the world. Even when you hijack one with the driver in it, you just point your gun and tell the driver to get out and he says, 'OK. No sweat!' and throws you the keys. Not in Santiago del Chile! They argue and fight, they challenge you and cling to the steering wheel and refuse to let go. If you don't punch the driver out, you'd be there all week. Because of this, we didn't exactly have a roaring trade in stolen cars. Instead, there was an unsteady trickle, and our Argentinian host took them into his workshop and overnight, as though by magic, he transformed them into a completely different-looking vehicle.

By early August we were trained and ready to intervene and standing by only for a green light from the MAPU. The economic situation was terrible – far worse than anything that has happened in Venezuela in the past decade. Inflation was ridiculously high: $1 equalled 2,200 Escudos, a worker's weekly wages. The people who had money were mostly from the extreme Right (because they had those 10 million CIA dollars to spend).

Half the country was near starvation, but there were still some pretty fabulous restaurants in the city. Of these, El Oriente in the Plaza Italia was probably the best. You could eat your fill on the finest seafoods for a dollar and a half in that restaurant. Having come from abroad, we had dollars. In Chile then, having dollars made you rich. We gravitated to El Oriente.

The mortal enemies of the government were in the extreme right-wing organisation called Patria y Libertad. This group had been legalised thanks to Allende's policy of turning the other cheek; and its central committee also gathered daily at El Oriente. In our first weeks of training, we were as blinkered as the next man in Santiago, so we didn't know that El Oriente was a fascist meeting place.

One day when I was waiting there for Elías, I had to go to the bathroom. As I was going in, another guy was coming out. I should say that at the time in Chile there was a phobia against Cubans. They hated them. Your average Chilean couldn't tell the difference between a Cuban and a Venezuelan – we were all 'tropicales'. The Right was convinced that all the tropicales were preparing to fight them. When this guy (who was a big, strong bull of a man called Irribotes) saw me, he touched my trouser fly and said in a camp voice, 'What is needed to get these little tiny figs?'

I lifted his hand off my fly, pressed it against my dick and pushed it away again; then in my most haughty voice I said, 'Listen, you great big faggot! You need this dick! And I am not what you think I am. I am a horse dealer; and I am here to buy Arras horses and Chilean Criollos, which is something we have done in Venezuela for longer than you can remember. And how dare you speak to me like that!'

He changed his tune and became apologetic and tried to shake my hand.

But I said, 'I don't shake hands with idiots!'

Whereupon he almost fell over backwards trying to explain that he'd thought I was some sort of leftist. The guy had recognised me for exactly what I was, but when I said that I was a horse dealer, he fell for it. He must have seen me several times across El Oriente's dining room – we ate there twice a day sometimes. Suddenly in his eyes, Mariana (who was genuinely rich) and we two vagabonds were super-rich: we had to be if we were buying thoroughbreds. I knew a bit about that because Mariana's father owned racehorses and he really did buy Arras.

I sat down and waited for Elías. When he arrived I told him what had happened and he looked across the room at Irribotes, the touchy-feely guy, and sort of flared his nostrils in a way he had that made him look very aristocratic. The next thing we knew, my neo-fascist would-be friend had sent across a bottle of champagne with his compliments and he came over to apologise formally.

Elías spoke to him very politely but a little distantly, and then, at a certain point, he turned on his charm. Whoa! Within three days, we were so close to Irribotes that he gushed out information. We passed ourselves off as noblemen and that drove him wild: he was the biggest snob I have ever met.

Elías, Mariana and I seemed to have all the credentials he desired: he was an armchair anglophile and we had just come from London. He had travelled a little bit and he knew the names of places in Rome and Paris, but we knew them all. It soon became clear that he wanted to become a part of what he imagined was our jet-set circle. He started sharing everything he had in the hope that we would reciprocate. He particularly wanted to be invited to our stud farm in Venezuela (and, of course, we invited him!).

In return, Irribotes – who was a high-ranking member of Patria y Libertad – gave us exact information on his organisation. He gave us the name of every official, where they lived, where they worked; the make and numberplate of every car; when they were going to plant a bomb, when they were going to collect money; whom they were going to attack: we had it all!

With such information, in one day, or at most two, it would be possible to paralyse the extreme Right's entire terrorist network by hitting their hit men and their bombers. We took all this information back to the MAPU and asked them to give us the green light to act on it and take out Patria y Libertad's terrorist squads.

I told them, 'All we need are some military uniforms.'

Their chairman looked at me as though I was out of my mind for making such an impossible request, and he said, 'Oh, no! We can't do that! It would be a provocation!'

I pointed out that the situation was past that. I explained that we were now at that point when you are mid-flight and the hostess says, 'Brace! Brace!' The plane was nose-diving into the sea. What we were suggesting was the equivalent of having a life-vest.

'For the love of God! Give us a green light! This is the chance in a million!'

During the next days and weeks, no green light came. We continued to meet our erstwhile informer and he kept us updated on heaps of classified information; all of which we relayed to the MAPU, and none of which they acted upon.

Irribotes was not just a snob, he was a social climber par excellence. Whereas at first he had been happy to fantasise about the Ritz and the Via Veneto and our luxurious stud farm in the east of Venezuela, he quickly came to want to hear about society balls and banquets, fund-raising galas and titles of nobility. In order to keep pumping him for information, I supplied him with all that and more.

Our safe house in Bologna had shared a landing with two old ladies whose primary interest was collecting court circulars and royal gossip. These old ladies were very amiable and very lonely, so to be nice to them, I had sat through terribly boring hours listening to what Princess Caroline of Monaco was doing and what Princess Margaret and Lord Snowdon, and Lady this and the Duke of that, were up to. Back in Bologna, I used to find it fatuous, but in Santiago del Chile, it was the best currency I had ever had. I dropped names and titles and social gossip from all the royal houses of Europe and our delighted informer lapped them up and then squeezed himself dry.

To our immense frustration, as far as I know none of Irribotes' secrets was ever acted upon. Because it became daily more apparent that a military coup was imminent, towards the end of August I took some precautions of my own. I suggested to Mariana that while we were training, she go out and rent an apartment for us. As Miguel Otero Silva's daughter, she had credit cards and plenty of money, and she was used to renting apartments when she travelled, so I knew she would be able to find one. We were all still living in the apartment on Calle Marín, near El Oriente, but since we were quite a big group, we had attracted some attention and in the event of any trouble we would have been easily found.

Mariana gave me the key to the new apartment, which was on the San Bara estate on the seventeenth floor of a tower block. It was so close to our existing house (less than 200 metres away) that the two buildings were in sight of each other from the upper floors. We didn't tell anyone else about the new apartment and, that way, there was a safe house in the wings if we needed it.

August became September and still there was no green light from the MAPU to strike Patria y Libertad. The city was full of talk and fear among the foreigners, but the Chileans of the Left were strangely complacent and those on the Right were suspiciously calm. Within our group, there was talk of a trip to the beach at Antofagasta, which Chilo and several of the others were keen to see. There was a lot of discussion about whether to go over the week-end or not and eventually it was decided to leave on a Monday or Tuesday to avoid the crowds and then stay over for two nights.

On the Friday before the weekend in question (which was 7 September), one of the MAPU came and said that two of our group were finally needed for something.

He explained, 'We want two of you to pretend to be lawyers because there is a functionary in the Rancagua penitentiary who wants to give us some arms and he wants two arms experts to pass themselves off as foreign lawyers to get into the prison.'

I told him we could do that without any problem; and he told me we had an appointment at Rancagua for the Monday – 10 September.

I remember that Mariana went out and bought me a lawyerly jacket because I didn't have one. On the Monday morning I set off for the penitentiary with el Cocido. Rancagua was an hour away from Santiago by train and less than 100 kilometres.

When we arrived, the first guy we had to meet said, 'OK, I'll talk to my man. You two stay close by in one of the bars – the entire vicinity of the prison is full of prostitutes so take your pick!'

El Cocido and I went for a little drink and, sure enough, the bars were crawling with girls. Ever since Paris I had been wary of prostitutes, but the ones in Porto La Cruz were so nice that I had sort of recovered from my phobia, and I was just chatting up a green-eyed girl with parchment skin, a mop of brown curls and a really attractive smile, and we had just decided that if we were quick we could finish our conversation in her room, which was right over the bar, when our contact turned up again and said, 'My man is waiting for you now.'

His man turned out to be the prison governor, no less. I was glad of my new jacket because el Cocido and I were supposed to be eminent professors of Law from the University of Salamanca, and I'm not sure that a whacking great erection really fitted my disguise. As the one of us who had actually been to Salamanca, I had to do most of the talking.

In Chile, there was a special body to supervise the prisons. It wasn't the police and it wasn't the army – it was an autonomous body of prison guards. Thus all the prison governors were civilians, and this particular governor was a member of the MAPU. He came forward to greet us.

'Ah! So you are the doctors we were waiting for!'

I said, 'Yes, we wish to see how your prison system works.'

The governor turned to a colonel who was in the room with him and he said, 'Please bring our guests some coffee.'

As prison governor he outranked the colonel and could order him about. As soon as the colonel left the room, the governor hissed, 'It's now that you have to do it! Right now! The putsch is any day. Do you understand? There is no time to lose. Do it now! OK. When the colonel comes back, the one thing you have to ask is, "Why are the guards armed? Is that usual?" – OK?'

A few minutes later, we set off for a tour of the penitentiary and I asked why the guards were armed, as I had been told to do. The governor looked very interested and explained, 'Actually, only four of them are carrying guns, the rest are unarmed because we don't really use the arms, but we have them. In fact, we have a little arsenal for eventual emergencies; would you care to see it?'

We acted as though it was rather an imposition to have to trawl around the arsenal as well, but that out of politeness we would take a look.

There were 150 arms in one small room. All the arms were virgin, pristine weapons. There were Israeli machine guns and over a hundred automatic rifles. As we were leaving the prison, we were alone again and the governor told us, 'You have to come with a truck and hold us up and you have to accuse us of being counter-revolutionary. Lock us all up, overpower the guards – as you can see – only four of them are armed. Then get the arsenal!'

El Cocido and I travelled back to Santiago together with our first contact guy. He hardly spoke except, as we approached our destination, he said, 'We'll have to call a meeting by the end of this week. There is no time to lose; we only have about a week to get those arms.'

I asked him, 'Are you crazy? We have to go back right away!

We have to go back tomorrow. There is *no* time. Didn't you hear the governor say to do it now?'

He wouldn't listen. He said, 'There is a protocol to observe, you know. We will have to call a meeting, and then another meeting and then we can vote on it.'

I insisted that we didn't need a meeting. What we needed were a couple of uniforms and a couple of cars. He got quite shirty and told me, 'We are not hotheads!'

Hotheads? Their worst enemy couldn't accuse them of being that!

We went straight back to the MAPU HQ and I repeated what the governor had said and that in order to act we needed the uniforms and the cars. MAPU had control of a car pool but they wouldn't give any of them to us without one week of protocol. We argued and in the end they refused to help us to get the prison arsenal despite, as I pointed out to them, having sent us there in the first place.

'We can't rush into things. We can't be seen to be part of anything that could be construed as a provocation. We —'

I pleaded with them. 'Look around you! Patria y Libertad are planting bombs and shooting your people down in their houses! They have crippled this country. It is way past the stage of "construing provocation". They will break you – can't you see that if you don't defend yourselves now they will tear you and your people apart limb from limb. This is a CIA operation. This is ...'

It felt like talking to a brick wall. They were so stubborn that they refused to acknowledge how bad things were. Two can play stubborn, so I kept trying until they said, 'Oh, do what you like! Do what you think best so long as you sort yourselves out; and if you fuck up, then leave us out of it.'

I think they were covering themselves: 'Do it, but don't do it. Go but don't go.'

It was clear that some of the delegates agreed with me that a putsch was imminent, yet they were incapable of being decisive or making a move. I had known some of them for years. Most of them were good people, but their sole strategy was to hope that good would prevail. As el Cocido and I left them, the socialist delegates were ready to go home. They came out of their office

and lined up against the wall of their building to say goodbye. At
that moment, a plane flew overhead and they all looked up with
their mouths open the way ducks do when they stand and catch
rain drops in their throats. It looked a bit ludicrous, but it wasn't
funny. It wasn't rain they would catch, it was a hurricane. I
remember thinking that they shouldn't voluntarily stand like that
against a wall. Depending on how things went, they were making
it all too easy for an eventual firing squad. As I walked along the
cobbled street, with its graffiti and hopeful posters about free milk
for school children and being patient with queues, I felt sad and
angry and very frustrated. What were they waiting for, and when
did patience become resignation?

CHAPTER LV

One of our friends, Anna Maria Giovanni, was the niece of a military guy. Through her uncle, some of our group had managed to establish a social contact with a few military types. Chilo even had a sort of flirtation with one of them, which had been going on for weeks. Thus the two women were able to procure the two uniforms. This just left the problem of how to get hold of the cars. I managed to rent a Citroën – actually, it was a Citroneta – in my name (which is to say, in the name I was using at that time). Our plan was to carry out the raid the following morning: 11 September.

It was agreed that phase one would be to hijack a second car and a lorry en route to Rancagua. The consecutive phases of the raid were all worked out by 8 p.m. and there was nothing more we could do until the morning. As a group, we went to eat at the Casa Juancho, a good restaurant in the centre of Santiago. Chilo was there and el Cocido, el Cocido's wife, Elías, el Chango (the Argentinian), a couple of the Colombians, Elías's brother Fedo, and myself. By chance, Mariana wasn't with us that evening. The adrenaline was flowing because it was the eve of an assault and we all felt the excitement of going active after two months of doing virtually sod all. Halfway through the meal, the nervous tension erupted over some petty discussion at the far end of our table. It turned into a heated argument and threatened to become a fight. I had been trying to recruit one of the Colombians into the world of Paul Celan ('No one kneads us again out of earth and clay / No one incants our dust'), so I had missed what the row was about. Being Venezuelans, once the passion was out of its cage, no one kept their voices down. To avoid attracting unwanted attention, el Cocido broke up the dinner party and volunteered to take his wife away. For this, he needed to use the rented car. I gave him the keys to the Citroneta and reminded him that we were scheduled to leave from outside our house at dawn.

He said, 'No problem: I'll be there to pick you up.'

After he left, the atmosphere was still sour so we all split up and went home to get an early night. Elías, Julieta (his girlfriend for the past year) and Co. went back to the Calle Marín. I went back to my secret apartment on the San Bara high-rise estate.

I asked Chilo to come with me so that the concierge didn't get suspicious at a single foreign guy going into the building alone. I had told the building administrator that I was a functionary of UNESCO and that my wife would be arriving that day. To maintain this cover I needed to take my 'wife' to the apartment that night. I would then leave her there while I left at the crack of dawn to carry out the prison assault without arousing undue suspicion. The country was so split between the Left and the Right that little things became extra-important because everyone was spying on each other. I knew from experience that the details and the back story were as vital as the job itself. Leaving early was, in itself, a suspicious act, which I needed to make appear normal.

We had to leave early to hijack the second car and the truck we needed for the raid. We knew that almost the most difficult part would be getting that transport. Since carjacking was more of a noisy charade than a discreet hit and run in Santiago you had to choose the time and place carefully, or the next thing you knew you could have a lynch mob of angry spectators on your back.

Nothing was easy about that raid. Even getting Chilo to come with me to my new apartment was difficult. Since we had split up in London in 1971, Chilo and I had not been 'together' in any way, but she was an active member of our group. Since I was one of the two directors, she was under my command and had to do what I said. But since we were ex-lovers, this was a bit more complicated. I needed her to come and cover for me at the new apartment to give a semblance of normality when I entered the building. Chilo, on the hand, had been planning a jaunt to Antofagasta for several weeks, together with a sub-group of our group. There was a particularly nice beach there and some of the best lobster and seafood in the world. Antofagasta also had salt flats and a unique landscape which were a big tourist attraction. While our activities in Santiago had stagnated, the trip to the seaside had grown as a project whose D-Day, by chance, was the same as mine. The beach-goers' plan was to leave at midnight of that same night (10 September) and drive there while the roads were cool and empty.

Chilo really wanted to go to Antofagasta and she didn't see why Mariana, who was living with me as my common-law wife anyway, didn't pose as my wife. I told her Mariana wasn't available that evening and thus I needed her to stand in for twenty-four hours. After a big discussion about how, when and why go to the beach at Antofagasta, I finally convinced her that I was not bullshitting, I was not trying to get back into her knickers, and I really did need her to come with me.

That night, 10 September 1973, I went to bed and woke up at about 6 a.m. I felt ill – it was nothing specific, but I felt an enormous malaise. While I shaved, I looked out of the window at the seemingly deserted city and at our other house on the Calle Marín, where I imagined the others would also be dressing or shaving in preparation for the raid.

I left the building dressed smartly as I imagined a UNESCO functionary might. I took my briefcase (which actually contained my Browning pistol – the same one I had smuggled from Havana to Prague, to Italy and London, and which was as constant a travelling companion as the cassette tapes I carried of J.S. Bach's *St Matthew Passion* and the battered paperback of Paul Celan's *Mohn und Gedächtnis*) and played the part as I walked past the already alert concierge on my way to find Elías.

As I stepped onto the street, a car screeched towards me. Some guys and a girl were literally half out of the window screaming, 'It's the coup d'état! It's happened. The army has taken over.'

I stepped back into the doorway of my building, A second car raced by, followed by an army truck. Very calmly, I walked back into the building, exchanged a puzzled shrug with the concierge, who was hurrying out to see what was going on, and I took the lift upstairs.

I woke up Chilo and said, 'That trip to Antofagasta will have to wait until at least next year.'

She didn't get what I meant, but I turned on the radio and then it was clear. The Chilean army had staged a coup. Unlike their liberal opponents, the army was super-organised and extremely well prepared.

From early in the morning of that Tuesday 11 September, announcements were made over the radio with orders to the people of Chile. They called these orders 'bands' and they numbered them. Band number 1 was that the army had taken control and the country was now in a state of emergency and under military rule. Band number 3, I recall, was that President Allende had until 10 a.m. that day to surrender. If he did not, then at 10.15 the presidential palace would be bombed.

As Band number 3 was announced, Chilo and I looked at each other as though to say, Yeah! A good bluff! As if they are really going to do that – in 1973 in Santiago in a city full of international tourists they are going to bomb the eighteenth-century presidential palace at La Moneda with everyone in it!

Very cautiously, I ventured back out on the street to find Elías. He was in our other house less than five minutes away, but the streets were filling with military cars and trucks and, to say the least, I felt uneasy.

I had been reading about, talking about and hearing about coups d'état for decades, but I had never been at the core of one before. I had never actually seen one happening. It was eerie.

I found Elías waiting for me. With my Browning, we had exactly two pistols for our entire group; and el Cocido had not turned up with my car. In fact, el Cocido seemed to have disappeared. Meanwhile, the radio announcements kept coming thick and fast.

At 10.15, they bombarded the presidential palace. We heard it in shock and then heard the radio announcement, which was followed by band number 5: 'All foreigners have to present themselves to the relevant local authorities on pain of death.'

Interspersed with the bands there were propaganda bulletins about how Chile had been saved and the constitution had been protected by loyal patriots.

'All Chileans who harbour foreigners in their house have to denounce those foreigners to the relative competent authority on pain of death.'

The key words were 'death' and 'foreigners'. And this was a foreign strike, a US-backed strike hell-bent on destroying any witnesses or troublemakers. Xenophobia reigned and all foreigners were marked and weeded out. What was happening was ruthless in the way that the Nazis had been ruthless.

Our shock tried to turn to action but was choked in the process. We had to make a move. We hurried to our rendezvous at el Chango's leather-goods shop, cursing el Cocido en route and praying that he would, at least, meet us there. There were supposed to be fourteen of our group going on the prison raid. It was hard-going getting through the city because a lot of the streets were blocked and people were panicking. When we got to the leather shop, there was no sign of el Cocido or my car. Only two of the Colombians were there. The others had all disappeared into thin air. Even the Chileans had failed to show. We waited for a while, but it became clear that no one else was coming – not even el Chango, whose shop it was.

This made me very sad. The pavement was full of dust from the newly bombed presidential palace. The air itself was thick with plaster. That day of 11 September was almost certainly the last day when we could make any kind of offensive move, and also the last day when we would be able to shore up our defences. It was war; and it was clear that the enemy would give no quarter. Through dithering, we had lost our chance to either neutralise or pre-empt the putschists; but we still had a chance – one chance – to do something for Chile. From the way everyone talked in revolutionary circles, particularly when in exile in Europe, you would imagine they were all raring to go, dying to get the chance to act. Yet, when that time came, when the action happened, when catastrophe struck and a full-scale war was starting, I kept asking myself: Who are we? Who sent us? And where did we come from?

Back in Valera, when I was fifteen years old, those were the questions I had posed to the usurpers of power in Venezuela. They were questions that had metamorphosed into arrow tips, which had pursued me for much of my life. Sometimes, the arrows changed course and I had to ask the same questions of myself. When at last I had a group and when at last that group was needed and wanted and able to perform a significant task – we were no more than motes of dust settling on the city's cobblestones. The malaise I felt increased as it became clear that before the day was done those cobblestones would run with blood.

'The Lord broke the bread, / the bread broke the Lord.'

Notwithstanding the desertion of our men, Elías, his brother, the Colombians and I set off to find out what we could about what was happening. We discovered that there were military roadblocks encircling the city, all flights in and out of Santiago were cancelled so there was nowhere to go, and without el Cocido and my phantom hired car we couldn't even get around the town. I was separated from Mariana and deeply concerned as to where she was. Was she safely hiding somewhere? Had she been caught? Was she dead or alive? The football stadium was filling up with prisoners: was she among them? The international phone lines were down so I couldn't even contact her family in Caracas to alert them. Her family were powerful people; they knew she was in Chile and they must, by now, have heard there was a coup. I hoped that they were already pulling strings because I had rarely felt as powerless to protect her as I did that day in Santiago.

The sinister bands kept being announced over the radio and by loud-hailers in the streets. Each one seemed even more draconian than the last. A curfew was announced for 4 p.m. and anyone who did not have a safe conduct would be shot. That particular band caught us out because we were still on the street and a long walk away from home. Fedo had some kind of military pass which was a safe conduct for himself and his escort – Fedo had every kind of document and ID you could imagine; it was his speciality – so we got past a few soldiers and made it back to my high-rise apartment by 5 p.m. to hide. The few of us who had made the rendezvous at el Chango's leather shop knew the new address and it became our safe house during the first days of the coup. Mariana knew the address because she had rented it in the first place, but, to my dismay, she wasn't there when we returned. We scuttled into it like rats in a hole and then we got caught out by another band.

The latest one said that anyone who went out after 6 p.m. without a particular kind of new safe conduct would be shot. This band was effective until further notice.

We stayed in my apartment for the whole of Tuesday night and the whole of Wednesday. From our seventeenth-floor window, we watched what looked and sounded like the city of Santiago being destroyed. The quantity and the quality of the gunfire were such that it was hard to imagine anything could be left intact outside. You get to recognise the different types of gunfire and you can more or less tell what sort of weapon is being fired. When you hear upwards from the blast of a .50 machine gun, then you are hearing cannon fire. The noise for thirty-six hours was deafening.

As though that were not enough, our domestic situation was critical. Julieta, who was part of our group, had given birth to a son by Elías only a few months before. She and the baby were with us in my apartment and we didn't have a single drop of milk for that child. So the noise outside was compounded by the desperate screams of a hungry baby inside. When we locked ourselves into my apartment, we were completely unprepared for a siege. We had nothing — absolutely nothing to eat. We didn't even have sugar, so we couldn't even make up a placebo bottle of sweetened water to keep the baby quiet. Having never used the new apartment before the night of 10 September, our cupboards were completely empty. This meant that all the adults there were famished, but then it served us right for not having been prepared. But having no milk for the baby was terrible. On top of everything else, the cries were killing us.

And each new scream hammered home what a disgrace it was that a group such as ours could have been caught so unprepared in our domestic arrangements. By midnight, it was so unbearable that I went and found the concierge and explained that my sister-in-law had been trapped by the curfew with no milk. Remember, in Santiago, outside of the dollar restaurants and the CIA-paid fascists, there were terrible food shortages, so begging for milk was a much bigger thing than it would have been elsewhere. The concierge gave us a little bit of milk and we managed to feed and quieten the baby for an hour. Then the hungry, angry screaming started again and there was absolutely nothing we could do. We were a flat full of illegal foreigners in an extreme right-wing military dictatorship that was threatening to kill all its foreigners, including the legal ones. We weren't tourists caught in a coup: we were left-wing revolutionaries with known records, false IDs and bounties on our heads; and we didn't have a snowball's chance in hell of getting round the fact that we were hiding illegally in our apartment. To keep the hungry baby in was torture, but to have tried to go out would have been certain death.

The next day, having heard the baby's distress, some of the neighbours took pity on us and helped us by donating milk and even some food for us adults.

The bands kept being announced, the bombardment of the city continued, the gunfire kept going without pause and the day dragged on and on. Every little pause and all the interstices of relative quiet were filled with fear. Our group was far from complete. Even among the Venezuelans, Mariana was missing and el Cocido had disappeared.

On Wednesday evening, 12 September, we saw a group of people being taken to their execution. They were pushed at gunpoint out of our line of vision, round the corner of a street, and then we heard the rapid bang bang bang of their firing squad. It wasn't a few shots, it was a barrage of fire. And all the time, for hour after hour, there was the background 'aha ha ha, aha ha ha' of machine-gun fire reverberating through the city. It peaked and subsided as the bombardment ceased and restarted, but the underlying 'aha ha ha, aha ha ha' never stopped.

CHAPTER LVI

On Thursday the thirteenth, the army lifted the general curfew and we ventured out into what we thought would be the ruins of the city. To our immense surprise, there wasn't a hole anywhere, or any shattered glass. From the amount of gunfire and cannon fire we had heard, we expected almost every façade to have been pockmarked by bullets and vast numbers of windows to have been smashed. This was not the case. There was no sign in the streets of what had happened: it just looked like the same old Santiago, and not at all like somewhere in the grip of a ruthless military coup. Thus it was clear that most of the shots, the cannonade and the almost non-stop machine-gun fire of the previous thirty-six hours had been a show to terrorise the civilian population. The army must have been firing off hundreds and thousands of rounds of blanks to keep up a simulacrum of attack and destruction. As a scare tactic it was 100 per cent successful: the populace was terrified.

Given the scale and thoroughness of the coup, Elías and I knew that we would have to try to return to our old house on the Calle Marín and go over it much more thoroughly than we already had, destroying any incriminating evidence no matter how tenuously it linked to us. En route, we bumped into a couple of our Patria y Libertad friends, who were so alarmed that they insisted we let them hide us lest we be executed out of hand with 'the riff-raff'.

'They are shooting first and asking questions later. They will kill you. Literally, any minute now, they will find you and shoot you – they are shooting foreigners like stray dogs.'

It was kind of those die-hard fascists to offer to protect us but we had to cover our tracks to protect, in particular, the Chilean socialists who had helped us. The Patria y Libertad guys were so insistent that they even followed us for a bit, hissing and whispering in fear for our lives, 'You don't understand! They are looking for you, they know about you because the guy you rented the car from has denounced you and it is only a matter of time before they track down your address. You have to let us help you.'

Of course, they had no idea who we were or that we had been playing them like violins. But as men to men, it was touching that they were prepared to stick out their necks for a couple of foreigners when the bands had made doing so a capital offence.

We told them that we had to find Mariana and they left us to see if they could discover her fate, while we sneaked back into our old house on the other end of El Parador.

We worked quickly and efficiently and were out of there again within the half-hour. We knew that our fascist friends were right about it being a burnt location. Since the authorities now knew about my hired car, it wouldn't take them long to get to my new flat, so we made plans to move on to a safer hiding place.

We spent one last night at my seventeenth-floor hideaway (with some provisions) and on the following morning (14 September) I sneaked out to try to find el Cocido and my missing – marked – car. El Cocido had a neighbour called Gloria who was like a Valerano in that she didn't miss a trick. I went straight to her and she told me that el Cocido and his wife had fled to the protection of the Venezuelan embassy. It took me a moment to recover from this news, because of all places, under the circumstances, that was like jumping out of the frying pan into the fire. The Chileans were looking for us in a general xenophobic sort of way, but the Venezuelans had been looking for us for years in a dogged Royal Bank sort of way.

We needed to get to the outskirts of town where a Chilean-Venezuelan – or Venezuelan-Chilean – who was a good friend of mine would, I was sure, be prepared to hide us in his house. With the city crawling with soldiers and CIA personnel, the only safe

way to do this was by car. I told Elías that I could see no option
but to go to the embassy myself and ask el Cocido where it was.
People were being arrested everywhere and escorted to the football stadium. There were rumours that thousands of people had
already been rounded up.

Elías was less than enthusiastic about my suggestion, but since
he didn't have any other plan, he shrugged and said, 'Go to the
embassy if you want to, but they'll fuck you.'

Luckily, the embassy was close by and there were no Chilean
guards around it. Later, all the embassies came under siege, but
that had not happened yet. At the embassy, I talked to a contact
of mine called Pascal Hedra, who was on the staff. He knew me
under an assumed identity. He was a nice guy and we had had a
few drinks together over the past few months and some good talks.

He said, 'You have to stay here. The Chileans are going to kill
you. They are going to kill all the foreigners. Come here and we'll
protect you. They are looking for you, and you will be dead
meat if we don't protect you right now.'

It was a generous offer but I didn't want to go to the embassy.

To my great relief, I discovered that Mariana was safe inside
the embassy. Unlike me, she had no priors and was wanted for
nothing in Venezuela, so the embassy was the best place for her
to be. I didn't manage to see either her or el Cocido, because I
didn't want to step into the diplomatic web. I decided instead to
go and pay our landlord, Señor Amparo, the rent that was due.
It looked as though his house was full of police so I walked
around the block a bit and waited until they left. When I gave
him the money, I could see he was touched. He volunteered that
our old house was now a trap and the police were waiting for us
to return there. Then he said, 'I have your Citroneta in my
garage.'

I pretended to be furious with him but actually I was overjoyed.
'You what? That's my car! I paid for it and I want it!'

'The car is trouble. I'm going to dump it,' he told me.

'No you are not!' I told him. 'It's mine and I'm taking it now!'

He took some persuading, but in the end he showed me where
it was and gave me the keys.

It was still well inside the curfew when Elías and I drove to the house of my Chilean-Venezuelan friend Dr Pozo and his German wife. Meanwhile, Julieta and the baby and a couple of the other Venezuelans sought asylum at the Venezuelan embassy.

We stayed with the Pozos for the rest of 14 September and all of the fifteenth and sixteenth listening to savage bands over the doctor's radio. The army continued to threaten to kill all foreigners who had not registered with the local authorities and all Chileans who harboured them. The news from the city was all bad. Day by day, the state violence was escalating. Day by day, foreigners and Chileans alike were being murdered for situations far more innocent than ours and the Pozos'. With a dragnet and house-to-house searches, it was only a matter of time before they found us and shot both us and our hosts.

Meanwhile, back in Venezuela, our president, Rafael Caldera, had proffered an olive branch to any Venezuelans trapped in Chile. He had given his personal guarantee that any of his co-nationals who had problems back home would not be repatriated to Venezuela if they sought asylum at the Venezuelan embassy. Its doors were open and all Venezuelan nationals were being urged to seek asylum there immediately.

Given this guarantee, Elías and I decided to go to the embassy for help. I know the exact day that we did that: 18 September, because it was my birthday. I was thirty-nine years old. On arrival, I received a phone call from Mariana and shortly afterwards we were reunited.

There were loads of us in that embassy, and over the next few days and weeks many more Venezuelans (and non-Venezuelans) came to seek asylum. Soon after that, the Chilean army put a cordon of guards around the diplomatic compound so that it became virtually impossible to get in.

Mariana was on the passenger list for the very first plane that would be allowed to repatriate stranded Venezuelans. Despite her assurances of continued love for me, I imagined that once she was back home safely, her parents would find it hard to let their beloved daughter out of their sight again. Since I couldn't return, we would be forcibly separated. Mariana was a free spirit, but all our spirits had been severely shaken by the ferocity of the coup.

I was horrified by what I had witnessed and so sickened by the brutality that I wanted nothing more to do with revolutions. I was a qualified banker who had robbed a bank. I was a university professor who had been struck off the academic register, and I was a French lawyer who didn't live in France and who had never practised law.

For reasons too convoluted to go into now, the famous capital from our Royal Bank robbery had, in its turn, been the victim of robbery in the guise of a major fraud. When your ill-gotten gains are stolen, there is no legal redress. We had used the last of a sub-fund of the Royal Bank job to finance our Chilean enterprise. That account was as empty as my own prospects. I had exactly $786 in cash in my wallet and that was it.

To begin with, the atmosphere inside the embassy was exceptional. Having all survived a near-death experience, we were bonded by our shared trauma and the euphoria of our escape. For the businessmen among us and the reactionaries, and the spoilt shoppers who had been caught mid-shopping trip as they took advantage of the spending power of dollars, their visit to Santiago had been a devastating eye-opener. Intermittently, there were pockets of panic as individuals feared that in the new Chilean world of sanctioned terror and lawless excesses, the diplomatic immunity of our embassy compound would not hold and we would all be slaughtered. But on the whole, the panic was reserved for those who had Chilean family outside, who were prey to the dictatorial bands and the army's kangaroo courts and random murders.

The issuing of the bands was relentless. We had got to band number 54 or 55 when I recognised one of the poor buggers who was being hunted 'dead or alive'. The radio was on day and night inside the embassy. Even the most blasé airheads were glued to the news. The barrage of neo-fascist propaganda was terribly monotonous. It was a non-stop deluge of aggression and hate, which after a few days you sort of put on a back burner inside your head. I was talking to a woman whose son was married to a girl from Antofagasta, trying to make her feel a little easier about the fact that she had not heard from them since before the coup, explaining that not hearing in these troubled times was not necessarily sinister, when the radio announcer said, 'The Señor So and So is wanted dead or alive. He was the governor of the Prison at Rancagua.'

This band was repeated so frequently that it was obvious that the prison governor had done something really big. I found out through the embassy staff that he was, as far as anyone knew, the only Chilean to resist the coup. It turned out that taking advantage of the confusion of 11 September, he had taken a machine gun and killed all the prison personnel, after which he had escaped with the machine gun and was on the run. Subsequently, I have often thought about that prison governor: there was nothing about him that made him immediately identifiable as a hero. He was courageous, without a doubt, to have asked the MAPU (his party) to smuggle two arms experts into the penitentiary to examine his arsenal; and he took a great risk in urging us to steal them from him. But to go from that to making a solitary stand when the rest of the country went like lambs to the slaughter was a remarkable feat. He must have known that alone he didn't stand a chance – but he didn't care. He went down making his valiant statement. His story spread through the diplomatic compound and every time the band for his head was reannounced there were cheers of support and admiration for him. When his bands stopped, we all knew he had been either killed or captured. We hoped, for his sake, that it was the former, because the latter could only mean a slower and more terrible death for him.

The ambassador, Tovar, was a pillar of strength and also a nice man. I was able to have a few snatches of conversation with him as one of his numerous guests. I knew that ambassadors could issue passports without going through all the normal channels and, in the dire situation we were in, I knew that he was issuing a few to save lives where he could. So I took the opportunity of cornering him and asking him, 'Do you think you could give me a new passport? Mine is in terrible shape and I really need a new one.'

He told me he was pretty busy but to show him my document and if he thought I needed it he would see if he could find the time to do something about it. I took my ragged (false) passport out of my pocket and held it out to him. He didn't even take it. He just looked and whistled, 'Jesus! That is a mess!'

The adventures of my passport were concurrent to my own but followed a separate track and are too long to relate. Enough to say it was falling apart and would have been a liability even had it been truly mine. As was, it was doubly risky. I had a couple of reserve documents which were fine for outposts of the Third World but would not bear scrutiny by anyone who had a modicum of knowledge. The Braille on one of them looked as though it had been pricked by a clumsy child with an unsteady hand and a darning needle – well, it probably had, since it had only cost a couple of hundred dollars and had been bought via a very dodgy middleman.

A couple of days later, Ambassador Tovar called me into his office and filled out a new legal passport for me. Entirely on impulse, when he said, 'Tell me your full name' – I did.

'Oswaldo Antonio Barreto Miliani.'

He raised one eyebrow, acknowledging both the discrepancy with the assumed name I used, and his decision, under the difficult circumstances, not to enquire any further other than to ask me to repeat it to make sure. I walked out of his office as myself: for the first time in ten years I was me again. I had my name back, all four of my names as they had been decided on by my father, Felipito, and my lineage. Having my name back made me feel that, all appearances to the contrary, I did have a future. I just didn't know what that would be.

CHAPTER LVII

A social anthropologist could have had a ball inside that embassy in Santiago del Chile. While the reign of terror entrenched itself outside the massive gates, inside the refugees quickly forgot that we had all just escaped death by the skin of our teeth and began to concentrate on petty losses and the real or imagined slights that arise when too many disparate people are crammed together for too long. There were feuds and factions, gossip and conjecture, love affairs and potential divorces, and a growing impatience to get out. From having been saved by the Venezuelan government, waves of resentment against that government's slowness in airlifting everyone out began to dominate almost every conversation. As a topic, it took over from trying to guess what was going on in the city and arguing as to whether President Allende had committed suicide as the dictatorship claimed, or whether he had been assassinated by the army as almost everybody imagined.

The embassy staff were incredibly patient with their recalcitrant guests and resisted what must have been a constant temptation to respond to the ungracious complaints by showing them the door.

Eventually, the first plane arrived and Chilo, Julieta, Mariana and a number of other Venezuelan refugees flew back to Caracas in it. Chilo was promptly arrested on arrival but then released after a few weeks. The newspapers had a field day with her, but there wasn't anything the law could throw at her except that we had once been lovers.

Another one of our group had also flown back on that first flight as a sort of test run to see what would happen. The scapegoat faced much lesser charges than any of us and he volunteered to fly home.

President Rafael Caldera had implemented what came to be known as 'the Pacification' in Venezuela. He did this by issuing a general amnesty to everyone involved in the armed struggle. Thus all the ex-guerrilla fighters were given a clean slate and a legal status. It was under this general amnesty that Jaime had been able to return to his hacienda, and almost all my ex-comrades had been able to either return from exile or surface from their hiding places within Venezuela. Regardless of what anyone had done during the years of the Guerrilla, they were free under President Caldera's ruling to take up a normal life and put the past behind them. This amnesty applied to absolutely everyone – except me and Elías.

From abroad, despite having moles in the government, we couldn't tell whether the amnesty applied to the Royal Bank robbery or not. To find out, the case had to go through a court hearing and have a preliminary ruling by a judge: which is exactly what happened when our guinea pig comrade flew back from Chile. Over the ensuing years, I have heard a lot of gossip about this test run, so I want to stress that our comrade was not coerced in any way to get on that plane. He was as free as any of us to have been flown elsewhere if he so chose.

He was arrested on arrival, but on a technicality so it was not possible to charge him with anything whatsoever to do with the Royal Bank robbery. The judge ruled that since the charge had previously been brought by the DISIP (the secret police), the case itself fell under the amnesty and could not be allowed in court.

It is all a bit complex, but the long and the short of it is that neither Elías nor I could ever be charged with having robbed the Royal Bank of Canada. Despite that – or probably because of it – it was still not safe for me to return to Venezuela. We couldn't be charged with our crime, but Elías and I were still 'most wanted'.

Forget what the papers have said and forget the slander (if you can) and look at the cold facts. I have never even killed a chicken! If you think about it, in my case, being 'most wanted' makes no sense – because, really, the *only* thing I had done was that robbery. I mean, as a fighter, I had fought in the street (the way most boys do), but other than that I had never really fought. As to killing anyone – well, I hadn't. The Venezuelan authorities had me down as some kind of depraved monster, so the fact that I could not be legally prosecuted was no safeguard at all at that time, but rather an invitation to make me 'disappear'. There was only one person more 'wanted' and hated by the authorities than me, and that was Elías. As a guerrilla commander his hands were bloodied, but no more than many others' and never arbitrarily.

I don't want to dwell unduly on the injustice of our ongoing wantedness. What I am trying to explain is that, as the mortal enemies of the DISIP, there was no way the two of us could have safely flown home from Chile. After many weeks, our doctor friend arranged for a small private plane to fly us to Mexico City. Six of us went – we were all Venezuelans and we had all been cooped up in the embassy under the protection of Ambassador Tovar.

To my immense relief, Mariana flew down to spend some time with me in Mexico. I had missed her more than I can say. As the weeks went by, I began to fear that she would give up on our tortured relationship in the face of what must have been enormous opposition. Yet, since her return, she had not only overcome her parents' disapproval, but she had also managed to enlist them into helping me return with some degree of safety to Venezuela sometime soon. I think that their preliminary enquiries about this option met with such a barrage of negative responses that they saw for themselves the injustice of my particular case and thus did not need their daughter to lobby them further. With Mariana's father, Miguel Otero Silva, and her mother, Maria Teresa, and their influence, I knew that I had more chance of success in any eventual appeal than with anyone else except the president himself.

All this might seem to contradict the long explanations that came before it, but in the meantime I had set my heart on going home to Venezuela. I was prepared to wait without losing hope but I had to see an actual chance of achieving such a miracle, and I didn't want to wait until I was an old man.

With the Otero Silvas behind my case, there was such a chance, albeit a slim one; but it was there. I cannot stress enough the immense power of Mariana's family. Miguel Otero Silva was not only our greatest living writer, he was also a tycoon. And when it came to lobbying through the press, he didn't just have access to it: he owned our country's biggest newspaper.

Mariana stayed with me in Mexico for a few heady weeks that were, I think, as near as we ever came to having a honeymoon. We moved around quite a lot, no longer out of necessity and for safety's sake, but out of sheer pleasure and for luxury's sake. I loved handing my brand-new passport in at reception. It was a real passport with my real name.

When Mariana returned to Caracas, I found Mexico City sad without her. We had rented an apartment in Lima the previous June and it still had several months to go on its year's lease. I packed up my few belongings, my books and my Bach tapes and a small bag of clothes, which were all that I owned in the world, and I set off for Peru.

Mariana wrote to me regularly (but, I felt, never quite enough) and told me that it would take many months more to sort out my problem. If my case could come to court, I would be OK, she thought, because some sort of deal was being negotiated at the highest level. The problem was keeping me alive for long enough to get me to that court. The logistics were pretty complicated and she warned me that it might take her parents as much as a year to get everything in place for my return.

In all, I have wasted so much time in my life and had so much of my time wasted that I see time as the most precious thing I own. Perhaps I should say 'that I could own' because maybe it doesn't sound so valuable when set against my three T-shirts, my best shirt, spare socks, pants and change of trousers, my handful of music tapes, a battered copy of Rilke and my treasured copy of Paul Celan with its pages stuck down with grime and jam.

I wasn't really doing anything in Lima. I didn't have anything to do. I tried to study but my brain refused to focus. There was a big, colonial-style fan in my bedroom which clunked round and round day and night and seemed to whisper: *Loser. Loser. Loser.*

I had friends in the Canary Islands who had invited me to go and stay with them and I felt I might be able to focus on my writing there. I wanted to write a book on the cocaine industry in Bolivia. One day, I would research this in situ, but Che and Regis's Bolivian fiasco was still too recent for that to be yet. I believed that if I could unwind even a little, I could, at least, begin to structure that book. To unwind, I felt that I needed to spend some time with friends. The atrocities I had heard about and witnessed in Chile had shaken my faith – not in the Church (like Salamanca) or in the Party (like Prague) or in the Revolution (like Cuba) or in being a revolutionary (like the east of Venezuela) – but in man. Our inhumanity as a race dismayed me. I began to make the obvious analogies between the SS and the Chilean Right and the whole cruel loop was depressing.

It wasn't doing me any good to be sitting alone and brooding about why we torture each other. What I needed to do was to think deeply again. Well, actually, what I needed to do was to think. I fancied that some sea air would help with this. At the end of the voyage, there would be Tenerife and my friends. There was a Peruvian ship that sailed this course and stopped en route at Panama City and Curaçao, and La Guaira. As a passenger, I would be entitled to go ashore in each port. I could stroll around and see the sights and eat ice creams on a day pass, or tourist card issued by the purser.

The more I thought of this, the more it appealed to me to sneak into Venezuela like that for an afternoon and to stroll around La Guaira with Mariana and find somewhere to make love and hold her in my aching arms. When we were done, I would scuttle back up the gangplank and sail on to Tenerife. By the time I returned, her family would have made it safe for me to be arrested and stand trial. In a court of law, in Venezuela, under the general amnesty – I might just walk out of that courtroom a free man.

I spent so many days fantasising about this plan and arranging my brief shore meeting with Mariana that by the time I went to buy my ticket, the ship had just left Lima and was under way for Panama. I had bought several Peruvian souvenirs as presents for my Canary Island friends and a beautiful Potosi silver necklace for Mariana and my little bag (with the three T-shirts and the Rilke etc.) was packed. In fact, I had everything I needed minus the boat. Not wishing to give up my jaunt, I chased the ship by air and managed to catch it up and embark in Panama.

The Caribbean was so calm and the ship so stable that I was hardly seasick. Watching the flying fish leap over the surface reminded me of what seemed like a lifetime ago when I had watched them fly over the beaten pewter of the sea as our smuggler's boat made the crossing from Port of Spain to Margarita on the eve of our departure as an expeditionary force. I had been transfixed then by the flying fish and imagined that I saw coded warnings in their phosphorescent wings. Admittedly, on both occasions I was tanked up on cheap rum, but even so, there was something strange and almost choreographed about those fish. My mother was a great one for omens. Had she seen what I was seeing in the formation of flying fish wings, she would have turned back in Curaçao. But I was on holiday and I had suspended thought for the duration. When I wasn't talking to the crew, I spent most of my time sunbathing by the pool on deck because I had decided to tan myself nearly black for when I reached Venezuela. Nothing makes as big a change to one's looks as a change of colour.

CHAPTER LVIII

We docked in Curaçao and I went ashore with my tourist card and did some sightseeing and ate some chicken curry rotis in a little bar by the sea front. And I drank some cold beers and a couple of shots of Curaçao rum with a fisherman who wanted to open a diving school but couldn't get the money to buy the equipment and blamed the Dutch government for keeping him down. Then I went on board again and caught the last of the sun beside the swimming pool. It was the perfect way to catch up with some sleep. I had the excited chatter of returning passengers in my ears and the stench of chlorine in my nostrils as I drifted in and out of a slightly drunken tropical siesta.

As the ship left Curaçao, I heard my name being called over the speaker system. I was being asked to present myself to the captain's cabin. After ten years of always pretending to be someone else, it felt sweet to hear my name ring in my ears, and for some minutes I incorporated its announcement into my dream until I realised that there was a tone of urgency in the insistence and it was a summons not a lullaby.

I went to the captain's cabin and knocked on his door. The captain was sitting next to another officer. They both stood up as I came in. The officer stepped forward and gave me his hand. He introduced himself by name and rank and said that he was with the Peruvian police force.

'Señor Barreto, we see that you have a permit to go ashore in La Guaira.'

I nodded.

'We wish to inform you that there is a warrant out to arrest you the moment you set foot in Venezuela. We know this because from Curaçao we were flown across to Aruba to check the day permits with the Venezuelan authorities and they jumped on yours. It is your right, as a passenger on this ship, not to go ashore. While you are aboard, you are on Peruvian soil and we will protect you.'

I remember thinking Fuck!, because I hadn't known about the mini-flight to Aruba to check the cards. No one had checked them in Curaçao. I took only a few seconds to decide and then I said, 'Thank you, but I will go ashore as planned.'

The captain jumped up and grabbed my shoulder. 'Don't do it, Señor Barreto! From what I have heard, there is something nasty afoot. Stay on board and we will not let one of those bastards up the gangplank. Stay with us!'

I told him that I appreciated his offer, but that I would, nonetheless, go ashore. Both men begged me to reconsider and offered to do whatever it took to help me. The one thing I let them do for me was to inform the Otero Silvas that I was 'coming home' so that my arrival would be as widely publicised as possible. The more people that saw me disembark and being arrested, the less chance there was that I would subsequently 'disappear'.

Word of my forthcoming arrest spread like wildfire around the crew. Between then and our arrival at La Guaira I was inundated by requests from this or that sailor not to give myself up. There was much discussion about why I would be arrested and much conjecture about what would happen to me, but I had made up my mind.

Ironically, I have never known such solidarity as I found aboard that Peruvian ship. The entire crew was on my side and ready to fight for my freedom. It was all I could do to get down the gangplank, such was the volume and intensity of the emotional farewells of the captain, the purser, the Peruvian police officer, the kitchen staff and the crew. Even some of the passengers had been brought into the fray and they too were urging me not to go.

Thus, far from sneaking into Venezuela as originally planned, I disembarked to a crowd of reporters and television crews and a cordon of policemen and soldiers.

Mariana came on board first and we spent a few minutes talking and holding each other. She explained that it was all happening too soon and that there was no guarantee that her father's legal plan to protect me would work. I explained that chance had offered me this opportunity to be done with the police once and for all, and come what may, I was going to take it.

When the time came, there was yet another round of goodbyes and pleas from the crew. They saw me as a condemned man walking into the jaws of death. I explained that it was my choice, out of my own free will, to go towards the waiting policemen. I knew I had more than half a deal. I had more than half a chance, and those odds were higher than the odds had been for most of my life. I was relatively calm, but the crew was panicked. At the last moment, as the arresting officers stepped up to the very edge of the gangplank, the Peruvian crew decided to save me. One of them grabbed my arm and the others formed a human chain to try to physically prevent me from setting foot on shore. I dropped my suitcase and tried to hold myself steady on the railings, but they were too strong.

Meanwhile, the Venezuelan police officers had also panicked, and they began to follow me as I was dragged back towards the deck amid terms of maritime endearment and solidarity. One of the arresting officers grabbed my other arm and I became like a piece of meat being torn between two rival prides of lions.

It took several minutes, and the virtual dislocation of my shoulders, before I could be taken away by the Venezuelan authorities. The whole charade was shown on TV the next day. That was how my mother saw her prodigal son returning – as the trophy in a tug of war. She was angry that I had not warned her of my return. I don't think she ever really believed that I hadn't known of it myself until the last minute. On the newsreels she saw the crowd that was there for me and she felt cheated by not being invited.

'You invited all your other friends to meet you, but you didn't invite me.'

Friends? Mariana was there with about ten key people to witness

my arrest. All the other 'friends' my mother was referring to were
DISIP or police or CIA or army snitches. My real friends, my
closest and dearest, were not there.

During and after my arrest, the atmosphere was not pleasant.
Carlos Andrez Perez had just begun his term as president of
Venezuela, so all the police were Adecos. I had left the country at
the beginning of Rafael Caldera's term and all my problems had
been with the COPEI police (who had been after me for the
Royal Bank). All these things are relative: Caldera's police had
been bad enough, but they were never as bad as the police force
before that – the Adeco police, who in 1974 were newly back in
power.

The violence of my arrest was mitigated, for me, by a funny
incident that occurred shortly afterwards. One of the policemen
was searching through the contents of my suitcase, grabbing stuff
and throwing it on the floor. He chucked a little bottle I had
bought in Lima onto the ground, where it smashed. The Peruvian
Indians make these bottles as souvenirs for tourists. Inside it had
been the figurine of a man floating in a liquid antibiotic, and it was
one of a pair I had bought as presents for my friends in the
Canary Islands. When the bottle smashed and the little man inside
rolled onto the floor, I said, 'It's just as well you didn't break the
other one!'

The offending policeman stared at the human figurine in horror
and then he jumped back as though stung. He turned to me,
transfixed with fear, and said, 'Oh my God! Are they voodoo? Will
something happen to me now? What have I done?'

I was their prisoner and they were roughing me up and I was
afraid. But they had all heard so much about me, and they were so
afraid of me, that they thought I had supernatural powers. I found
it so funny when that policeman nearly shat himself that a little of
the nastiness of my first few days was erased.

I was held in the prison of Catia la Mar, one of the roughest jails
in Venezuela, with one of the highest ratio of inmate killings, I
believe, of any jail in Latin America. As a sort of punishment, I was
kept in almost complete isolation. Little did my jailers know it, but
for a scholar (and coward) like me this was a tremendous luxury.

Mariana's family made absolutely sure that there was a huge amount of publicity around my case and that key people in high places knew exactly where I was at all times. I fulfilled my side of the bargain by managing to stay alive to stand trial. Soon, at the highest level, there was an agreement that I would, eventually, walk free.

I was Mariana Otero's chosen partner; both she and her parents were powerful people. But my notoriety was such that there was no way I could have stepped ashore and walked free. We had to go through the motions of a trial, but I knew from the week after I was arrested that if I could survive a few months in jail and avoid disappearing, or getting shot while 'trying to escape', or 'committing suicide', I would be pardoned and could walk out of the prison gates of Catia la Mar a free man.

Sure enough, and much to the disgust of my many enemies, I was acquitted at my trial. And as though I did not have enough enemies beyond my family circle, one of my sisters had become my implacable enemy over my anti-communist stance. I was free but despised.

During that period, my insomnia peaked. I had recurring nightmares of my Chinese sojourn; in my troubled dreams I kept finding myself before the panel of Beijing petty officials as my life's failures were aired. 'Beware of what you wish for, Comwade Oswado! You wasted your time studying Kafka's decadent *Metamorphosis* and you wanted to go home. Now you are back in Caracas and you have become a bicho. Insects must be crushed, Comwade Oswado! Here in the People's Republic of China, we have eriminated hundreds of mirrions of flies, their families, tribes and sub-tribes.'

There is little more irritating in life than when your enemies are right. I was worse than a bicho, worse than the Chinese flies: I wasn't even capable of flight, I was a crawling species. At least bichos have a life. They work and contribute to their insect society and they don't spiral down into neurasthenia, insomnia and anxiety when their path is blocked. They keep going against all the odds, which, eventually, was what I did too.

I linked up with an old friend from Prague, Dario Lanzini, and together we went to live in a little cottage in Caracas. I managed to get a publishing contract to translate a work on Jean-Paul Sartre and thus became solvent again. I thought I had got such a great deal with that translation because I negotiated an exorbitant fee, way above the normal rates, for my work. Not so! The book was infested with footnotes. The distinguished author and his references and cross-references were so labyrinthine that their erudition reduced mine to slaving for a pittance. Instead of breezing through the translation as planned, I had to withdraw to Bobures and spend five times as long as I had estimated on it.

Bobures is the former port on Lake Maracaibo where as a child en route to Valera from San Cristobal de Torondoy I was first introduced to twentieth-century technology. Where it was once a bustling mini-metropolis, by 1974 it had become a sleepy ghost town inhabited by the descendants of runaway slaves who lived a life of almost total indolence. Children walked the dirt track to neighbouring Caja Seca to bring back blocks of ice in plastic buckets, and a couple of entrepreneurs stole sugar cane from the surrounding plantations to distil into rot-gut rum.

The old town had been largely reclaimed by the jungle and the new town, built under the dictatorship of Perez Jimenez, had been frozen, as if by a spell, on the fall of that dictatorship. All building work had stopped and the place had been left with hundreds of houses in neat tarmac streets lying empty on the edge of the shore. Most of the locals lived in two- or three-roomed mud huts with no sanitation, and no kitchen other than the three hearthstones on a dirt floor and a few twigs beloved of Venezuelan peasants. In twenty-one years, no one had wanted to move into the new housing estate or do anything other than loll in the evening sun on the disproportionately large new pier.

It was a wonderful retreat and it put an end to the foul mood I had worked myself into. As a translator, I completed my task. As a sociologist, I researched the vestigial West African elements among the drowsy hidden villagers. And as a tourist, I waited twice daily for the elderly, blind Alminda Rosa to walk the beach with her basket of home-made empanadas, which were what I lived on. She is the woman I remember most from this period. Alminda Rosa was seventy if she was a day, but as coquettish as a seventeen-year-old. With her I had a tremendous, though unconsummated, flirtation.

When I returned to Caracas, I had decided never again to dedicate myself to politics, and in particular to detach myself from the politics of the Left. If a revolutionary does not believe in imposing his beliefs then he is not a revolutionary. I was no longer one; though I continued to care deeply about the fate of my political friends

Foremost among these was Elías. I travelled to Guadeloupe to meet him, and then to Trinidad to set up a network to bring the people from that group back to Venezuela. Elías wasn't exactly legal, but we procured some identity papers for him and got him back home.

Mariana and I settled down to a friendship, rather than love; Chilo and I had a child but not really a relationship. Our daughter, Laura, was born and I, inadequately but with all my heart, was a father again. Through our child we found the closeness and calm that had always eluded us when lust formed part of the equation.

After that I became involved in an incredibly stormy relationship with a young Haitian woman, Michelle. My third child, Melissa, was born to a fanfare of her parents' flaming rows. I met Michelle in 1975 when I was newly arrived from Chile, so I can say when our relationship started, but I cannot say how long it lasted because it was different from one day to the next from the day it began.

Then, almost simultaneously with my becoming a father for the third time in Venezuela, my first child, my son Ramín, surfaced from the depths of Persia and came to visit me in Venezuela. He was a young man with a fine education, a love of chess and a yearning to know about the silenced side of his heritage.

From having been a solitary and selfish outcast, I became the father of three with all the joys, responsibilities and worries of a family man. Although I continued to live alone, I would never again be a bachelor.

Then one day a friend of mine had called me to say that the deacon of humanities at the University of Caracas had decided to transform the faculty of arts into a school of art on condition that the new school be guided by Joaquín Gonzalez and myself; did I accept? Had I been spoilt for choice at the time – which I was not – the offer would still have been one that truly interested me.

So, together with the great Argentinian art and literary critic (of sad memory) Marta Traba, and Joaquín, we founded the new school under the name of the Institute Romulo Gallegos. It was a school of plastic arts, cinema, theatre and cultural promotion (the latter being my speciality). Later, music was added to the curriculum.

We worked for a year preparing the project and thanks to it I began to regain a foothold as an academic and a scholar. When the shit had hit the fan after the Royal Bank robbery, I had been struck off the register as a professor. Thanks to my position at the Romulo Gallegos I was reinstated as a professor. After that, I was not only co-directing the new art school, I was also eligible again to teach at any university in the world. It was like the sun shining onto my life again after years of gloom.

My next foothold was reached during that time courtesy of an article published by the distinguished husband of one of my colleagues. I wrote a response to his essay which shot it full of holes. There was then a very public literary debate. Thanks to it, I achieved a position in literary criticism circles – the Venezuelan literary establishment applauded my attack and moved aside to make a little space for me to join them. I had always wanted to be a writer and a literary critic – suddenly, I was one. I decided to press my advantage and go deeper into that field.

CHAPTER LIX

At the exact time that I began to explore literature from my vantage point as a director of the Institute Romolo Gallegos, Elías began to explore other things completely. It was from that moment that Elías's group took its step into the underworld and began its descent into darkness. Metaphorically, Elías was my Eurydice and I was his Orpheus. I descended into Hell to bring him back. I managed to persuade him to follow me into the light; but like Orpheus, in our homeward journey I could not look back, and like Orpheus, if I did so I would lose my love for ever.

When you come from a society that, broadly speaking, equates a love of books with a penchant for homosexuality, as a scholar you cannot win. From my early boyhood I had been dubbed a queer. Way back in Valera, when Nene took an interest in me, the town gossips assumed that interest to be sexual – why else would the patrician prince take an interest in a no-go runt like me? Later, all through my revolutionary years, the 'real men', the warriors, dubbed me a queer for my continued interest in books and ideas. Later still, a few of the intense friendships I have or have had with other men have been interpreted as sexual. Of these, the most notable was my friendship with Elías. In a macho world where loyalty is prized but betrayal is the order of the day, true loyalty is hard to comprehend. And the fact that a man can love another man without there being any sexual attraction present is deemed impossible. Yet, in that way – in the way of greater love where a man will lay down his life for a friend – I loved Elías.

I knew when I set out to bring Elías back that I had to walk straight into Hades and straight out again with him in tow. I knew that it would be incredibly dangerous both for me to linger there for any time at all and for him to stay there any longer. Whatever pleas he came up with and whatever sweet tunes he played on his lyre (which, of course, in Venezuela was our little four-stringed guitar), my chosen path was elsewhere and I could not be in his underworld.

However, my attempted salvation of Elías was yet something else to add to my long list of failures. For some years he was a lost man; something about what he was and what he could have been and what he became broke my heart.

He paid dearly for the things he did, as you will see. But I also paid dearly for our friendship. The longest time that I have spent in jail and the worst abuses committed against my mind and body as a detainee were as a direct result of my lasting friendship with Elías. My stubborn obstinacy enabled me to keep going as a would-be guerrilla for many years. And my stubborn obstinacy had enabled me to rebuild my life several times from a heap of rubble and dust. In the two decades from 1974 to 1994, that same pigheadedness enabled me to continue along my path as a scholar despite the harassments and arrests that became the story of my life.

I loved Elías, but I would be lying if I did not add that I loved him a little less, for instance, while undergoing water torture to encourage me to remember details of his plans that I could not have betrayed had I wanted to because I never knew them. And sometimes, as my secrets were being beaten and singed out of me (when there were things about Elías and his shenanigans that I *did* know), I was tempted not to take my greater love to its ultimate conclusion.

I would have laid down my life for Elías the man, but not for his wild capers. Even as the wires and prods plagued my flesh I knew that if I admitted to knowledge of any of his plans or told of any details as yet unknown to the police, I would incriminate

myself as much as the friend who had dragged me down with
him.

When I was in prison I used my solitary confinement to ponder
life. When, eventually, I was allowed books, pen and paper, I used
my time to study and write. When I was released from solitary
into the shark pool of the 'common criminals', I used my gift as a
teacher to set up shop among the rapists and murderers teaching
what I could to men whose thirsty minds had never received a
drop of water. Thus, in jail, I regained my title as *el profe* and not
only survived the rough environment but made friends, and set a
few, at least, of my fellow inmates onto a different, better path.

When I was not in jail, I turned my intensified insomnia to
good use and studied during my sleepless nights with the intensity
I used to have as a young man at the Sorbonne.

Meanwhile, my children grew into men and women, trailed by
one last son in the final lasting relationship I have. This sometime partner, Eglée, is a librarian. Neither she nor I know who or
what we are in relation to each other – in that, we dither straight
out of Neruda: tumbling in and out of love and lust. Eglée was
my student in 1975 but we only started to go out eight years
later. That is important to me: I have never dated women who
were my students or women who were in any way under my
command. When Eglée finished her doctorate in Brazil was when
we began our cyclical love. Our son, Iván Darío, was born on 26
February 1994.

Some years before his birth, something happened which once
again turned my whole life upside down. It would revive every
fear I had ever had and it would entail yet another struggle with
the Grim Reaper. At the time it occurred, I was a professor of
sociology at the University of Caracas. I had just come back from
a sabbatical year in Bolivia, during which I wrote a book on the
drug trade and its effect on the country and on Latin America in
general (a subject I felt had become notorious without being adequately or intelligently analysed). Despite the guerrilla war the
authorities had continued to conduct against me, trying to sabotage my every endeavour, I had attained a certain eminence in
academic circles within South and Central America, and to a

lesser degree in Europe (where my writings on Sartre had brought me some critical acclaim in France).

I had travelled regularly to France – usually to Paris – to lecture, speak and consult on various matters. The most notable of these was for the appeal of Pierre Goldman, who as el Francés had been the companion of my guerrilla days. When the trumped-up murder charge he was in prison for came to the Court of Appeal, I dusted off my French law degree and became one of his defence team. The scandal of the legal injustice and the anti-Semitism of his case when he was first sentenced had earned him the name of the Modern Dreyfus. I was there more as his friend than his helper, yet I sat among some of the finest lawyers in the world, who rallied to defend him, and we – they – got him off.

The French Right and the anti-Semitic faction vowed they would kill Pierre Goldman for his left-wing views and the dishonour they claimed the publicity around his appeal trial had brought to France.

Time went by and nothing came of the threats. Pierre married a woman from Guadeloupe and together they lived in Paris. In 1979, quite by chance, I was visiting the Goldmans when Pierre's wife went into labour and was admitted to a private maternity clinic. On the night that his first and only son was born, Pierre talked at length about his conviction that the French Right was still intent on assassinating him. It was 1979 and he was an acclaimed French intellectual living in Paris, so such a hypothesis seemed not only extremely unlikely but a little absurd. Rather than have an argument about it, we drank to his baby and he reached for his African drums.

That night, in celebration of his son, Pierre played until the small hours. The following day, on the steps of the maternity clinic, in broad daylight, he was gunned down and killed by a neo-fascist group called L'Honneur de la Police.

Ten thousand people attended his funeral in a procession led by Jean-Paul Sartre. I was one of the many, and one of the ones who spoke over his grave.

One by one, my friends and family were dying. Teodoro Petkoff's political party, the MAS (Movement towards Socialism), was doing well at the polls. My brother José had been a delegate and ardent campaigner for it. In 1977, José had died pointlessly from the injuries he got in a car crash, when a tyre on his jeep had exploded on the motorway. I say 'pointlessly' because with better medical attention he could have lived. At the last minute, it was Rusián Schmitter (the Slayer of the Plains) who beat the pervading lethargy and managed to get a small plane to land in the hospital's forecourt with a top surgeon on board and everything needed to medivac my brother to a decent clinic in Caracas. But alas, José (like our mutual friend, el Che) was asthmatic, and he died on the trolley on the way to the plane for lack of a tracheotomy that could have been (but wasn't) performed at any time during the previous forty-eight hours.

After José's death, Rusián and I became close friends, until he too died some years later.

One by one, the bright lights that were my brothers and sisters have been blown out. Of the ten Barreto brothers and sisters, there are now only five of us left.

And then there was Elías – 'one of Nature's gentlemen', as a very fine elderly English gentleman once commented on Elías's impeccable manners and natural grace when we lived in Oxford. And so he was, but he was one of Nature's gentlemen who had descended into a dubious world in which his addiction to action sometimes clouded his ethics. Elías continued to be the most wanted man in Venezuela. His actions were often independent of any popular support other than the kind of support given to a bandit king.

On 7 September 1992, Elías was betrayed by one of his own gang and gunned down in an ambush at Maracaibo airport on his way to steal a private plane. Such was the size of his execution squad that I am told there was very little left of his body to identify. It was, I suppose, inevitable that he would die a violent death. Yet it is also a reflection of the violent and in many ways unjust society we inhabit in Latin America that when a criminal is caught he is splattered over the tarmac in a hundred pieces instead of being put under arrest and tried in a court of law.

If I haven't made my lament over the lack of global justice clear by now, I never will, since it was what drove me to live my life as

I have. It was what drove an Argentinian medical student to live
and die as he did. It was what has spurred innumerable men and
women (some of whom have stepped in and out of this story) to
sacrifice their lives for the greater good. In my case, I didn't
achieve much good – I spent a long time getting nowhere.

Not so long ago, I was in a supermarket in Caracas in the fruit
section. On the other side of the heaped fruit, I saw someone I
knew and my heart leapt as towards a friend. I knew I knew him
well but I couldn't immediately place him. He was holding a
mango and squeezing it to test its ripeness. I smiled across the fruit
and waved. The man looked back at me, puzzled. I wanted him to
smile back and acknowledge me, but there was a blank moment
instead. And then he recognised me and he looked to either side
of him quickly, dropped the fruit and hurried away in confusion.
    Then I remembered who he was and how I knew him. I felt
sick and a little dizzy. (I have a heart condition now and dizzy
spells are fairly common.) He was my inquisitor. He had broken
my flesh day after day on more than one occasion. Between those
cruel sessions, he had returned and gently tried to befriend me in
the traditional carrot-and-stick method used by policemen and soldiers all over the world.
    Such is the bond that grows between a torturer and his victim
that a kind word and any gesture of approval become as welcome
as a lover's touch. I had never known such a concrete example of
where love and hatred blur into one. For two days after I went
home, I sat in my apartment and felt like a broken old man. I
asked myself what kind of pitiful wreck I had become to have
sought comfort from the recognition of the despicable (and sadis-
tic) bastard who had been my torturer.
    According to *The Art of War*, there are six types of ill-fated
army: running off, lax, sinking, crumbling, chaotic and routed.
Alas, I knew them all. I didn't need anyone or anything else to rub
it in: I was a loser. I had got so that I could live with the idea, but
not when it involved grinning like a monkey to a piece of shit like
that. How could I have come so far only to ask the same questions.
Who was I? Who sent me? And where did I come from?

*

In 1990, shortly after that incident, my whole life was turned upside down again by another new start. I was invited by the French Ministry of Defence to form part of their national think tank on strategy. I was to move to Paris as a VIP guest of the French government and to begin immediately to brainstorm with the eminent group selected to advise the government on strategy.

I at once called my old friend, the writer and journalist Regis Debray. He was one of the few people able to see how truly funny it was after my previous existence(s) in France to be returning with such pomp and ceremony.

Very much in keeping with the random nature of the rest of my life, it then took a new turn for reasons beyond my direct control. In 1991, within months of my meteoric promotion in Paris, the malign tumour in my throat had ended my brief government career.

After my cancer cure, I wanted to lock myself away and be somewhere in the countryside where I could study and have access to a major library and not need to speak to anyone (because of my reaction to the chemotherapy). Regis Debray arranged for me to lock myself away in a Jesuit Cultural Centre, where I devoured almost everything ever written about narcotics. The most significant of these is the famous North American archive the 'Drug File'.

The months of solitude and study with the Jesuits restored me. It gave me the time I needed to recover from the shock of having had inside me the thing that I most feared. After I had recovered sufficiently to travel, I spent the summer in Italy with old friends in a tiny village outside the ancient walled town of Città di Castello. And then I went home. Well, I returned to Venezuela, because I wanted to go home, but 'home' to me would have to be in the Andes. As I grow older, I realise that I would like to end my days there. That would be my choice.

Despite what the papers say about the vast sums of money I have stashed away from a life of crime, I have nothing but my books and clothes and a few knick-knacks gathered on my travels. Some years ago, when I was back in Valera, Jaime Terán asked me why I didn't get myself a little cottage somewhere up near Mendoza Fría. I pointed out to him that such things are pipe

dreams to a man in my financial position. Rich people never
understand about not having money. When I told him that I could
not afford to buy a house, however small, or even a peasant's
shack, and that I neither owned nor could afford to buy a plot of
land to build one on, he said, 'Really?'

Six weeks later, the deeds to a piece of land on his ancestral
hacienda arrived by registered mail.

I cannot tell you what a comfort that piece of land is to me.
Over the years, I have built a little cottage there, and I know that
soon I will be able to go to that last safe house and write and think
as I have always yearned to do.

When I eventually move back to the Andes, my luggage will be
my books and notes, my thoughts and some conclusions, of which
the following pot pourri of thoughts on revolutions is, perhaps, the
most relevant.

I continue to be interested in revolutions and to care about
them to the point of passion, but in a different way now. From
when I was a kid until I was about forty years old, I believed in
love as a kind of madness which mutually excluded other loves.
And I also believed that an intellectual who concerned himself
with the emancipation of his fellow men (which is what a revolutionary is) was obliged to convince others – in particular, the
dispossessed – of what they had to do to emancipate themselves.

After the age of forty, I began to change to the point where I
am now. I believe that every human being is free to love as many
people as he chooses. More than that, I believe that 'love' does not
exist in the singular, but as 'loves' in the plural. I find that the
same applies to revolution. Nobody has the right to force anybody
to emancipate him or herself. Emancipation, per se, does not exist:
only *emancipations*. Revolution is only justifiable when a lot of
people concur in the realization of the necessary change and not
when they follow an illuminate: be he a man or a party.

For some years I have been writing a book entitled 'All Against
the Leader'. It is my testament and it falls into the school of
thought of Étienne de la Boétie, the French thinker who inspired
Montaigne.

My other books are not only unfinished but have been so for

years. When and if I finish them, they must speak for themselves and be judged on their own merits and not my recommendation. One is a study of Latin America as a continent in relation to other continents. And the other, which I need to revise, or rather tidy up, is my 600-page study on Bolivia and its drug trade. The latter is the fruit of the ten-year-long study I made on Bolivia as an example of the dismantling of the Spanish empire and the emergence of a Latin American nation.

Twenty years ago, I received a research scholarship to compare what had been written about Bolivia so far and the country's reality. It was an extraordinary journey across the entire country in which I realised that very little had been written about its singular characteristics, in particular, the Altiplano. Even in the broadest terms, Bolivia is unique. Every civilisation in the history of mankind has been based on grain (such as wheat, rice or maize). Only Bolivia had a grainless empire and staked its survival instead on the potato lyophilised into what looked and felt like little dried stones. When these were soaked, they once again became edible; the Aymaran Indians were able to store them for over a hundred years.

I came across this Aymaran ingenuity quite by chance in the early 1970s when I was eating some instant mashed potatoes in a café in Oxford and asked the 'chef' how they were made. He explained the heat-freeze principle of lyophilisation and mentioned that the Bolivian Indians had been doing it for several thousand years. I was hooked.

The first book I wrote on Bolivia is deposited in the Department of Investigations of the CELARG in Caracas. The second one I wrote in France.

And I will, I hope, find the key to the poetry of Paul Celan and his exploration of the German paradox. Celan goes further than all the poets before him to take his poetry beyond reality transformed into metaphors. Paul Celan wrote for whoever was capable of digging deep enough in his verse to find his hidden messages. And just as Celan claimed to have received such a key sent by the persecuted Russian poet Osip Mandelstam, so I (a nobody) am searching the whole time for the messages Celan has sent to me. It is the most serious and almost mystical game I have ever known.

In the meantime, I have reached the end: not of my life, but of this narrative. The doing will continue at a cerebral level; and I intend to continue to piss my enemies off by staying alive for as many more decades as I can. It is unlikely that that will happen, but then look at how unlikely most of the things that have happened to me were!

José Martí believed that 'the best way of telling is doing'. For over half a century, that was what I tried to do. Now, with a string of failures under my belt, my last shot at doing is in the telling. At best it will serve some purpose to others. As I have said, the fact is that things just happened, and I really don't know if that is my particular fate, or if it is that of twentieth-century man in general. At worst, though it pleases no one else, this memoir will delight my enemies. And last but not least, I have told most of my secrets, and keeping secrets is like swallowing stones.

No one kneads us again out of earth and clay
no one incants our dust.
No one

Blessed art thou, No One.
In thy sight would
we bloom.
In thy
spite.*

---

* Fragment of Paul Celan's 'Psalm'.

Also by Lisa St Aubin de Terán

KEEPERS OF THE HOUSE

'Exceptional first novel, richly evocative and cunningly crafted'
Observer

Since the eighteenth century, the eccentric and flamboyant Beltrán
family have ruled their desolate Andean valley, but the dynasty is
now almost extinct.

Lydia Sinclair, seventeen and scarcely out of school when she fell
in love with Don Diego Beltrán, leaves England for her new
husband's vast and decaying estate – Hacienda La Bebella. As her
husband becomes more withdrawn, she takes refuge in unearthing
his ancestors' tragic history. Benito, the family's oldest retainer, tells
Lydia that fate has brought her there to chronicle their decline and
recounts tales of splendour and romance, violence and suffering.
From these she weaves a rich gothic tapestry.

'A haunting and unforgettable work of art' Paul Bailey

THE HACIENDA

'Lisa St Aubin de Terán writes with extraordinary vividness and clarity... She faces reality with a courage and skill that left me not knowing which to admire more: her gift as a writer or that she had the guts to carve out a place for herself in such an unforgiving world' *Independent*

'Powerfully engrossing' *Observer*

At the age of seventeen Lisa St Aubin de Terán followed her new husband, South American aristocrat and bank robber Don Jaime Terán, to his *hacienda*, deep in the Venezuelan Andes. Once there, Jaime virtually abandoned his new bride to fend for herself. With only two pedigree beagles, a pet vulture and one peasant girl for company, Lisa St Aubin de Terán became *la Doña* – and lived for seven years among *la gente*, an illiterate, feudal people who she says 'have been the greatest influence on my life and work'.

MEMORY MAPS

'Sensual, impressionistic prose that recreates vividly her experiences' *The Times*

'I am a wanderer: one with a hoarder's love of houses and things . . . I am tracing here a memory map of all the places that have stayed with me and, since this is also a map of all the voyages of discovery, this is also the story of the getting to those places'

In *Memory Maps* Lisa St Aubin de Terán charts a life spent in all corners of the world, from Wimbledon to the Venezuelan Andes, from the Caribbean to Ghana, and confesses to wanderlust and fate being her chief guides. An itinerant lifestyle creates an unpredictable personal life though, and *Memory Maps* is the extraordinarily vivid record of a life lived without boundaries.

'Its power leaves you awed and grateful and eager to flick to the start and, with trembling fingers, begin again' *Scotsman*

'An extraordinary woman . . . if you encountered her as a character in a novel, you'd want to read on' *Express*

SOUTHPAW

Antonio Mezzanotte in Umbria, the blind man who gathers village gossip in his one good hand, La Rusa who runs her Rainbow brothel in the Andes; Eladio 'the mad man' who searches with his mute son for the eagle they stubbornly believe will restore them to health; Otto, the political prisoner called Proff who shares his cell with a killer; tiny Silvio the poet on Buona Vita Street; Nunzia, the family cook whose heart is chopped like parsley on marble when love comes her way.

In many senses, these are the dispossessed – prostitutes, peasants, shopkeepers, mothers among others – the 'southpaws'. The title reflects the awkward, unexpected elements of these people; each a survivor, each a fighter in his or her own way and each both dogged and shaped by their different approach to life within the narrow parameters of the rules of the ring. Their excellence is shown as much in their ability to receive blows as to administer them – as in boxing.

This collection is laced with Lisa St Aubin de Terán's intimate knowledge and love for the people of Venezuela and Italy – the countries she has called home.

You can order other Virago titles through our website: *www.virago.co.uk* or by using the order form below

☐	Keepers of the House	Lisa St Aubin de Terán	£7.99
☐	The Hacienda	Lisa St Aubin de Terán	£8.99
☐	Memory Maps	Lisa St Aubin de Terán	£7.99
☐	Southpaw	Lisa St Aubin de Terán	£6.99
☐	The Virago Book of Wanderlust and Dreams	Lisa St Aubin de Terán	£7.99

The prices shown above are correct at time of going to press. However, the publishers reserve the right to increase prices on covers from those previously advertised, without further notice.

Virago

Please allow for postage and packing: **Free UK delivery.**
Europe: add 25% of retail price; Rest of World: 45% of retail price.

To order any of the above or any other Virago titles, please call our credit card orderline or fill in this coupon and send/fax it to:

Virago, PO Box 121, Kettering, Northants NN14 4ZQ
Fax: 01832 733076   Tel: 01832 737526
Email: aspenhouse@FSBDial.co.uk

☐ I enclose a UK bank cheque made payable to Virago for £ . . . .
☐ Please charge £ . . . . . . to my Visa/Access/Mastercard/Eurocard

Expiry Date ☐☐☐☐   Switch Issue No. ☐☐

NAME (BLOCK LETTERS please) . . . .

ADDRESS . . . .

. . . .

. . . .

Postcode . . . . Telephone . . . .

Signature . . . .

Please allow 28 days for delivery within the UK. Offer subject to price and availability.

Please do not send any further mailings from companies carefully selected by Virago ☐